"Did you . . . did you want to come in?"

He shook his head. "It's late. I just wanted to make sure everything was all right."

A bit of relief mingled with disappointment at his refusal. "It is, thank you. And your hand?"

He held it up and smiled. "Won't scar. You're a good nurse."

God he was cute. And sweet. His continual check-ins with her were beginning to get to her. She was used to cops knocking on her door, but never to ask if she was all right. Never to deliver her soup, or firewood, or . . . a friendly smile.

She was so alone here. Lonely. Tucker was becoming an invaluable friend, even if she hadn't spent too much time with him.

It was a fragile thing, this friendship. One that was going to shatter if he ever found out what had really brought her here.

SILENT NIGHT

C.J. KYLE

AVON

An Imprint of HarperCollinsPublishers

This is a work of fiction. Names, characters, places, and incidents are products of the author's imagination or are used fictitiously and are not to be construed as real. Any resemblance to actual events, locales, organizations, or persons, living or dead, is entirely coincidental.

AVON BOOKS
An Imprint of HarperCollins*Publishers*
195 Broadway
New York, New York 10007

Copyright © 2014 by Heather Waters and Laura Barone
ISBN 978-0-06-207967-1
www.avonromance.com

First Avon Books mass market printing: November 2014

Avon Trademark Reg. U.S. Pat. Off. and in Other Countries, Marca Registrada, Hecho en U.S.A.
HarperCollins® is a registered trademark of HarperCollins Publishers.

Printed in the U.S.A.

10 9 8 7 6 5 4 3 2 1

To Kyle and Carmine

Acknowledgments

To Jay Beeler, for all the brainstorming help. Any mistakes are mine and do not reflect poorly on your brilliance.

To Lauren Burke, for being my beta reader and helping to keep the story moving.

To Catherine and Kym, for all your research help. Again, any mistakes are mine and do not reflect poorly on your brilliance.

To the Knoxville PD and the local detectives for answering all of my questions. Thank you for your dedication and service. And once again, any mistakes are mine and do not reflect poorly on their brilliance.

To the local priest who never ducked my calls, even when I asked the same questions more than once.

To Roberta Brown. Steadfast agent with loyalty and heart to spare.

Prologue

Sunday

HE DUCKED BEHIND the brick walls of Levi High's gymnasium and pulled a pack of Newports from his dusty denim coat. He hated opening day festivities when tourists took over Christmas, Tennessee, like the privileged bitches they were. Family vacations? What a joke. He lit the cigarette, inhaled, and let the minty coolness coat his throat before exhaling onto the bare fingertips hanging out of his fingerless gloves.

Pressing one foot to the wall, he leaned against it and cupped the cigarette in his hand as a small family rushed past toward the parade. A mother, a father, a kid in a stroller . . . and the only perk of tourist season: a teenage daughter. She gave a slight smile as they passed him. He played it cool. Didn't smile back. Gave her a suave nod instead.

Screw the vendors selling chestnuts. He'd rather have *that* in his mouth any day. Sweet tits. Nice little ass.

Yeah, keep dreaming, schmuck.

As he watched the girl disappear, he flicked his cigarette into the bushes and cleaned dirt from under his pinky with the pocketknife he'd stolen from his dad's nightstand. What did she taste like? Shit. What did *any* girl taste like? At this rate, he was going to die a virgin. He was fifteen and hadn't even had a girlfriend. Not unless he counted Susan Parker from fifth grade. The girls in this town were all goody two-shoes, anyway. Living in the Bible Belt sucked.

Loudspeakers crackled to life overhead and "O Little Town of Bethlehem" rang out, making him groan. He kicked off the wall, pulled his hood over his ears, and headed down Main Street. He dug an Altoid from his back pocket, popping it into his mouth in case he ran into anyone who might blab to his father and earn him another ass kicking. His ribs still hurt like hell from the shit storm his mother had caused that morning. So he'd forgotten to wash his cereal bowl. Did that mean he deserved to get the hell kicked out of him?

They were all assholes.

He passed St. Catherine's Church and sneered at the Catholics who left Mass smiling and happy. What did they know about God? What did any of them know? The Presbyterians, the Baptists, the Catholics? They were all so fucked in the head, so damned brainwashed, it was pathetic. They didn't even acknowledge that their beloved Christmas was actually a pagan holiday in the first place, celebrated by the very people they shunned since the beginning of time. He'd learned that in the only place that brought him any pleasure—the Christmas Public Library, where he headed now.

As he marched up the steps to the glass doors, he stopped and cursed. It was closed for festivities.

He tried the door anyway. Locked.

Leaning against the stair rail, he watched as the Ferris wheel sparked to life and the green and red Christmas lights wrapped around the lampposts on every corner flickered on. Opening night had started. In a matter of minutes, the street would be lined with people gawking over corny floats, fire trucks, and Mayor Levi dressed as Santa for the first parade of the season.

He leaped over the rail and headed to the alleyway behind the library. He'd just lit another Newport when he realized he wasn't alone. A figure dressed in black appeared, and he tensed. It wouldn't be the first time he'd been jumped in an alley. But as light fell over the man's face, he exhaled and tossed his cigarette into the snow.

"What are you doing here?"

"Same as you," the man said.

What was the guy's name? He couldn't remember. Didn't care enough to ask, either.

The man pulled a pack of cigarettes from inside his coat and held them out. "Want one?"

Was this a trap? "I'm cool."

The man sat on the back steps of the library and held a cigarette in his fingers. He never lit up, though.

"Your family still go to New Baptist Church off Noelle Road?"

"Yeah." This lame ass better not try and sell him on the benefits of being a Catholic versus a Baptist. He was neither, and he planned to keep it that way.

"Still make you go?"

How did this guy know that he'd *ever* gone to church with his family? He hadn't been in over a year, and he was pretty sure this guy was relatively new in town.

"I don't want to be rude or anything, man, but I'm not into the church stuff, so . . ."

"Fine, fine. Not here to convert you or anything. Just wanted to sneak a smoke." The man smiled. "Go on home. I didn't mean to keep you."

He tried to smile back, but was pretty sure what came out was a smirk. He headed to the other side of the building, away from the man and back toward Main Street. It wasn't until he was well past the Dumpsters that he'd realized he'd been fiddling with his pocketknife the whole time he'd talked to the guy.

"Perverted creep," he whispered.

"Not very Christian of you." The voice was directly behind his ear, and as he turned, he found the man looming over him, something long and shiny in his hands.

The object was around his throat in a flash, and he was shoved to his knees before he could register the panic building in his chest.

"What the fuck . . . are you doing?" He gripped the steel band at his throat with one hand while the other fumbled in his pocket for his dad's knife.

He could see the man's lips moving but couldn't hear the words through the pounding of his heart in his ears.

With shaking fingers, he managed to slip the knife open, and plunged the small blade into the prick's thigh. The son of a bitch let out a grunt but didn't flinch or ease the grip on the wire.

Abandoning the useless weapon, he clawed at his neck, trying desperately to get his fingers beneath the wire as it sliced into his thin skin and cut off his air. His muscles became slack. The already dim alley began to fade. No longer able to support his own weight, he fell to his side.

The hold on his neck eased and he pulled in great gulps of icy air, trying to blink through tears blinding his semiconscious state. His stomach convulsed and he spewed his dinner all over the bastard's feet. As the man stepped back, he pulled himself up, turning and running before the man could grab him again.

He didn't make it three feet before something cold and hard pierced his left thigh. He stumbled, made it one more step before his legs gave out. He tried to break his fall with his hands but his face smashed against the brick wall. As he landed in the dirty snow, the weight of his body drove the blade deeper into his thigh, stopped only by the blinding pain of steel ricocheting off bone.

Taking a second to search the darkness for his attacker, he grabbed the long wooden handle protruding from his thigh and tried to remove it. The pain was too intense. He was shaking too badly. He was crying like a pussy, and all he could think of was that he should have stayed home with his drunk mother.

"You fucking psycho!" Turning onto his belly, he pulled himself along the snow-covered gravel. Something pressed into his back, stopping his sorry attempt to escape. The blade was ripped from his left leg. Pain gagged him, made him scream, but his pleas were drowned out by the festive cheers and applause of the Christmas in Christmas Festival. A swoosh rang in his ears as the weapon sang through the air to slash into his right leg.

The Ferris wheel creaked nearby, fireworks popped overhead, and laughter, squeals, and distant, muffled carols played over the loudspeaker. It all provided a sickening contrast to the horrors happening behind the library. The blade sliced through his frayed jacket and splayed open the flesh beneath, carving into his back as easily as if he'd been made of butter.

He wanted to run, but his body was too racked with

pain to obey. He was so scared. An added humiliation of warmth spread through the crotch of his jeans. He thought of all the gods he'd read about, prayed to each and every one of them as he gripped a loose brick, rolled, and tried to find the monster.

He should never have looked back. If he hadn't, he might have been spared the terrifying sight of metal shoving its way between his ribs. The metal sliced through tendons and muscle before banging against bone.

"Please." He choked as he rolled to his stomach. "Wh-what did I do?"

Hot breath fanned his ears. The stench of onions gagged him. "Thou shalt not worship false gods. You deny His graces, refusing to accept the blessings He gives you daily. It is because of Him that you have lived this long."

Blessings? God had forgotten about him long ago. Certainly wasn't thinking of him right now. He'd prayed for the beatings to end. Had prayed for someone to see what was happening to him and stop it. The cops had been useless. The courts too slow to do anything but piss his dad off even more. How did he make the lunatic understand? He hadn't forsaken God. God had forsaken him!

"Your sins can no longer go unpunished."

A cry tore from the deepest part of his soul as something sharp snatched at his neck, yanking his skull toward the heels of his boots. The loud crack of his spine breaking was followed by the peaceful numbness he'd been searching for. The tender flesh covering his trachea shredded, ripped, dripped blood onto the snow beneath him, but he no longer cared.

"Death hurts far less than dying. Embrace it."

Yes. Embrace it. It wasn't so bad really. No one could hurt him again. All he had to do was press his cheek to the snow and it would all be over . . .

"May God save your soul." Hot breath cocooned his ear. "And should He find your sinning soul black, may the devil feast upon it, instead."

Blood bubbled from his mouth as the world dimmed a little more.

He could have sworn he saw God. No. Not God. It was a girl with a long blond braid and a plethora of freckles on her nose and cheeks. Susan Parker. It felt like the last genuine smile he'd ever received from anyone had come from her. Remembering it brought him an odd cloak of comfort.

Susan.

He felt himself smile as he finally remembered.

She'd tasted like cherry ChapStick.

Chapter 1

CHIEF TUCKER AMBROSE unzipped his jacket and pushed his radio back into its holster. Despite the snow flurries screwing up his crime scene, anger prevented him from being the least bit cold. He squatted by the garish red stains and ran his gaze along the dots splattering the nearby brick exterior of the Christmas Public Library. Because of the snowfall, it was impossible to see which direction this gory mess had begun or ended. Hell, it was impossible to tell much of anything. And worse, what the snow didn't cover now, the water would wash away once it melted.

It looked like something had been slaughtered, but there was no sign of anything wounded . . .

It reminded him of things he'd seen on the job in Chicago. Scenes that had driven him to give up the city life seven years ago for small-town living. And for seven years, he had. Stolen bicycles were the bane of his existence here. Not bloody crime scenes.

Bloody, *bodiless* scenes.

It had to be a prank.

"Make sure you get Mrs. Perry's statement," he muttered, even though he knew it would be a waste of paper. The only useful thing the old librarian had done tonight was call in the scene. She'd seen nothing, heard nothing, and remembered nothing out of the ordinary. Just the bloody mess she'd found when she'd taken out the last of the night's trash. "The woman can remember the time and date Lisa checked out *Moby Dick* in the seventh grade, but can't remember what time the last person left the library tonight."

He watched his lieutenant, Andy Bowen, carefully push a trash can away from the exit door with the toe of his boot, and upon finding nothing, turn the beam of his flashlight toward the two circular windows overhead. Tucker returned to the bloody snow and swiped the tip of his glove through some of the red. It was still tacky. Not that old. He frowned. An animal maybe? It wasn't uncommon for tourist kids, bored with their serene family vacation, to find creative ways to entertain themselves.

Tucker had been patrolling the parallel street during the parade. Had stood at the end of this alleyway just a short time ago. How close had he come to catching the pranksters in the act?

He strode to the Dumpster the library shared with the antique shop next door and carefully lifted the lid with his gloved thumb. He didn't see anything out of the ordinary, but he'd have someone comb the contents anyway.

Andy moved to the far corner of the alley, his flashlight beam the only thing marking his location. They worked at separate ends of the scene for nearly an hour until they were sure they'd gone over every inch. Tucker sighed and threw his tools into the trunk of his cruiser.

They didn't have CSI detail in Christmas to do his job for him, and he wanted to send this blood off to the lab to find out if it was human.

It damned well better not be human.

Not that he wanted to find some wounded animal somewhere, but the other possibility was worse. This was a quiet town, one where no one but him locked their doors because they had no reason to. Tourists and townies seemed to understand that, once they crossed into the town's borders, even fistfights weren't tolerated.

He glanced at his watch. It was almost midnight. He and Andy had been on duty for nearly eighteen hours, at work before dawn setting up crowd control for that night's parade. If they continued to push themselves, they'd end up missing something that could be important. Better to get fresh eyes here for now.

"Call Jim and Darren," he said to Andy. "They've had most of the night off and can finish up here. Make sure they comb the Dumpster, see if they spot anything we might have overlooked. Think I took all the photos we need, and for Christ's sake, remind them to rope the area off this time, will you?"

Andy scowled. "If they even know where to find the tape."

The last time Sergeant Jim Franks had been in charge of roping something off, it had been an open manhole and a twelve-year-old kid had ended up riding his skateboard right into it. They were lucky the parents hadn't sued the entire town. Mayor Levi had been dogging Tucker's ass about such safety matters since.

Nice, normal problems.

"Just make sure they have the tape before they get here." He removed his hat and set it on the car's hood as he rubbed the back of his neck, chafing his skin with his rough gloves. "I'll wait for them to get here and you can call it a night. I'll see you in the morning."

"Doubt they're asleep yet," Andy said. "Shouldn't take more than thirty for one of them to get here. You go on home. I don't mind waiting. This is probably nothing more than a firecracker up a cat's ass or something, anyway."

"Only if the whole damned thing exploded." And no guts to be seen. No matted animal fur. No little furry body. Tucker sighed. "Make sure the blood is sent in."

He grabbed his hat off the hood of the car and dropped it back on his head. "Gotta love tourist season in Christmas."

Tuesday

MIRANDA HARLEY PULLED the large black Range Rover into Peggy Jo's Café parking lot and let it idle as she worked the stiff muscles in her neck, shoulders, and back. She'd driven more than five hours to this little town, and she was exhausted, her bones sounding like a box of Rice Krispies with every movement. She had to meet her new landlord, and then, hopefully, she'd be on her way to a warm, soft bed.

A woman passed in front of the lot, adjusting the droopy garland hanging over the diner's welcome sign. Quaint town. Nothing at all like Dayton.

Miranda's stomach growled. She hadn't eaten since breakfast. She double-checked the cash in her wallet. Barely enough to get her through a few weeks. Good thing the cottage was cheap when rented on a weekly basis. Killing the engine, she grabbed her duffel from the passenger seat and exited the Rover.

"Try the beef stew! No one does it like we do!" the garland woman shouted, offering a wave.

Miranda gave a nod of thanks and pushed open the heavy doors. She glanced around the dinner crowd, looking for anyone who appeared to be waiting for her.

A woman with high, nearly bouffant hair greeted her. "Have a seat. Anywhere you'd like."

Miranda smiled. "I'm supposed to be meeting some-one here. A, um, Taylor? Trevor?" She fished in her purse for his information while she talked. "He owns the Nativity Cottages near the river?"

"You mean Tucker?"

She stopped fishing. "Yes, that's it. Is he here?"

"No, but I'll make sure he finds you when he shows up."

Miranda thanked her and chose a booth near the door. She'd barely scooted in when the bouffant woman tossed a menu onto the table.

"Specials are on the board." She pointed to the chalk-board with the neon script detailing the nightly deals. "Be back in a moment to take your order. Anything to drink in the meantime?"

Miranda wanted wine. Desperately. But she was driv-ing. "Water. With lemon please."

She glanced over the menu, settled on the stew, and closed her eyes. A gust of cold from outside pulled her lids open again, and she found herself watching a tall man built like a quarterback stepping through the tinkling doors. Miranda swallowed, hating her-self for even noticing how appealing he was. But who could blame her? She'd been so consumed with other things lately . . . getting laid had fallen so far down on her to-do list that she couldn't even find it anymore. A man like that could spark even the deadest libido back to life.

The waitress led him to Miranda and grinned. "Here he is."

The man smiled down at her. "Miranda, right?"

He eyed her, and she squirmed a little. The term *landlord* had conjured an image of an old man with glasses. This guy certainly didn't fill that bill.

"Yeah, hi." She thrust out her hand awkwardly and shivered as his warm one engulfed her fingers. It took her a moment longer than it should have to let go. "Tucker?"

"That's me. Mind if I sit? I have some paperwork for you to fill out and then we can get you settled in."

"Sure. I was about to order something. I hope you don't mind if I eat while we talk. It was a long drive."

"Not at all. I could do with something myself." He handed her a small stack of papers. "Have a look over those while I decide what I'm in the mood for and I can answer any questions you have."

Occasionally, his gaze met hers over his menu and she looked away, embarrassed that her sixteen months of celibacy were catching up to her. She hadn't come to this town for romance or sex. God, she needed her life back. Needed to get laid. Needed to be anywhere but here.

She leaned back as Bouffant slid a glass of water in front of her. Miranda glanced up to see the name badge that proclaimed her *the* Peggy Jo.

"What's it going to be?"

"I'll have the beef stew."

Her new landlord flashed a grin that revealed two perfect dimples. Of course he had dimples. No Superman was created without them. "Coffee. Meat loaf. And your amazing cornbread."

When Peggy Jo walked away, he turned those dimples toward Miranda. "The stew is great, but she tends to run out during dinner rush. Figured I'd leave some for you tourists to sample."

She turned her attention to the papers in front of her and pulled a pen from her purse. "This is for weekly rentals, right? I'm not sure how long I'll need the place and want to make sure I can renew without someone else's reservation knocking me out of a place to sleep."

"I block off the cabins a week in advance. If you think it might be longer, let me know before checkout on Sunday. The sooner the better each week." He leaned back and Peggy Jo slid a coffee in front of him.

Miranda watched him, her pen hovering over the agreement. "I'm surprised you don't have a line of renters. I saw the property on my way in. It's nice."

And a landlord like Tucker would draw women from all over for a nice stay in town. She wondered how many he looked at the way he was looking at her right now. Eyes slightly shielded by heavy lids and long, dark lashes. Sleepy-looking with a hint of no-nonsense.

"I do. But out of the five cottages, I try to keep two freed up for the week-by-week renters like you."

She smiled. "Are you always this accommodating?"

"I try." He flashed those dimples again. "So, what brings you to Christmas?"

She sipped her water. Why she was here mattered only to her right now. "Why does anybody come here? Christmas in Christmas. Quaint."

"Yes. Families usually. Did you come to get away from yours?"

Miranda squeezed the wedge of lemon into her water and studied him. He had a friendly smile that caused little lines to crinkle around his eyes. Despite the warmth in those eyes, she had no desire to open up and spill her story to him. "Don't have much left."

Just her brother. And she certainly couldn't spend the holiday with him.

She could all but see the gears turning in Tucker's head as he tried to figure her out. His gaze dropped to her ringless left hand. She glanced at his, in turn, and found it as naked as her own.

Why did that make her smile?

Peggy Jo set their meals in front of them and pointed her pen at Tucker. "Let me know when you want dessert. Just pulled an apple cobbler from the oven."

"Best cobbler in three counties," Tucker said, digging into his meat loaf.

Miranda was content to watch him eat. She'd been around all walks of life and had learned to tell a lot about a person by the way he ate. The poor families she'd worked with in South America had scarfed down their food, their bowls held close to their chests for fear of someone taking them away. Busy people tended to share the same mannerisms, barely breathing between bites so they could suck down some nourishment before the next work-related emergency struck.

But it was kids she liked to watch the most. Their sheer enjoyment over something as simple as macaroni and cheese always brought a smile to her face. They were the ones she tried to emulate with each and every meal, never forgetting to take pleasure in a hot bite of something rich and creamy. Especially now, when she had to pick and choose which meals she could afford to eat.

Tucker was none of these types, though. He sat straight, one hand beneath the table, the other holding his fork lightly. Impeccable manners. Good upbringing. He reached for his coffee, and her gaze dropped to the Rolex on his wrist.

"Aren't you going to eat?"

As if on cue, her stomach grumbled. Tucker laughed. The richness of the sound washed over her. She shivered, her empty stomach quivering for something more than food.

"Go on, dig in."

She took a spoonful and moaned with delight. The garland lady had been right. Miranda had never tasted anything so rich and flavorful in her life. She'd existed on fast food and gas station junk for months. In contrast to that, this was like eating at a four-star restaurant.

She looked up to find Tucker watching her. His lids were at half-mast again. His Adam's apple bobbed as he worked to swallow his meat loaf. "Sorry, it's just really good," she said around another spoonful.

"No need to apologize." He slid the plate of cornbread closer to her. "Wait until you try that. Better than cake."

He wasn't wrong. Miranda swallowed the moist, sweet bread and chased it with a gulp of water to keep herself from finishing it off. They were halfway through their meal when his cell phone rang. He set his fork on the edge of his plate and sipped his coffee.

She eyed the lit-up phone at the edge of the table. "Aren't you going to get that?"

"Everyone's entitled to an uninterrupted meal now and then. Including me." The chirping silenced and he dug back into his food.

As Miranda finished filling out the agreement, Peggy Jo returned with two bowls of hot cobbler with a large dollop of cream on top and coffee. "Hope you saved room."

She hadn't, but she took a little bite, licking the cream

from her spoon. She caught him staring and quickly tucked her tongue back where it belonged.

When was the last time someone had looked at her like that? She sighed. This guy was a charmer. Trouble with a capital T.

"Here you go." She slid the paperwork across the table. "Think that's everything. First week's rent up front, right?"

He glanced over it and rose to dig a set of keys from his pocket and set them on the table. "Yeah. Plus a hundred-dollar deposit if you have pets."

"I don't."

He pushed the keys toward her. "Then these are yours. Cottage C, the one you requested." He picked up his fork and poked at his cobbler. "Why'd you want that one anyway? It's usually the last rented out. Most people prefer the river view."

She tucked the keys into her purse and retrieved the check she'd already made out. "I can see rivers anywhere. I'd rather have a view of the town."

"Well, it was a pleasure, Miranda." His deep voice sent another shiver down her spine. It had lowered an octave, as though he was purposely trying to make himself sound sexier. "My place is two over from yours. The main house. Can't miss it. Don't tell Peggy Jo, but I make a pretty mean stew myself if you want to share another mea—"

"Hey, Chief!"

In unison, they turned toward the shout. Peggy Jo leaned against the counter, her hand covering the mouthpiece of the phone.

"Yeah?"

"Lisa needs you to call her back. Says it's important."

"Thanks." He mumbled an apology as he pulled his cell phone from his pocket.

Miranda swallowed, all the warmth he'd given her before now chilled solid again. "Ch-Chief?"

He stared at the phone as he pushed buttons. "Yeah. Small police department, but it's mine."

"I thought you were in realty."

She struggled to wrap her brain around this new development. She didn't like police. At all. Her Superman had just turned into Lex Luthor.

"When I bought the property, it came with the cottages. Might as well earn some extra on the side, right? Excuse me, I have to make this call. You know your way to the place?"

She nodded, unable to say more.

He lifted the phone to his ear. "It's Tuck. What's the emergency?"

Miranda toyed with her cobbler, trying to give him as much privacy as the booth allowed. Maybe she should try one more time to find an empty room somewhere else.

She sighed. She'd already done that search weeks ago before settling on the cottage. She'd have to sleep in her car or in another nearby town. If she hadn't just filled out the agreement, either option would be more pleasant, but she had no choice. She couldn't afford to lose that down payment.

She was stuck with the badge as her landlord.

"Send Andy . . ." he was saying. "How long ago? I'm on my way. No need. I remember where it is." He disconnected. "Peggy Jo, can I get a to-go box for my cobbler? Duty calls."

"Sure thing, Chief."

"Is everything all right?" Miranda asked.

"Yeah it's probably nothing, but I still need to check it out." He pulled a card from his pocket and jotted a number on the back. "That's my cell number. You can catch me at my office most days. If you need anything . . . like company for another meal, give me a call. I don't usually have to eat and run like this."

"It's fine." She took the card and slipped it into her purse. No way in hell was she calling that number unless her plumbing became an issue.

The *cottage's* plumbing. Not hers.

Peggy Jo appeared with Tucker's to-go box and two checks. Before Miranda could protest, he paid both bills and rushed into the snow flurries outside.

Both women turned to watch Tucker disappear inside a large white truck. "You're one lucky lady."

Miranda shifted her gaze to Peggy Jo. "What makes you say that?"

"The chief doesn't smile like that at all the pretty tourists. Or buy them dinner. And he *never* shares his cornbread. Must mean he likes you."

When she was alone again, Miranda pulled Tucker's card from her purse. She couldn't afford to let anything get in the way of why she was here. Not even two extremely charming dimples.

With a sigh, she left the card on the table and slid out of the booth, slipping her duffel bag over her shoulder as she went. She unlocked the Rover's driver door and was about to climb inside. As she glanced over her shoulder, the table she'd shared with Tucker was in clear view.

"You are a damned fool," she cursed herself, rushing back inside to snatch the card off the table before the busboy could toss it in the trash.

A damned fool indeed.

Chapter 2

THE CABIN WAS just what Miranda had expected. It was set up much like a motel room with the living area taking the majority of the space, a small kitchenette and dining area, and a decent-sized bathroom attached to the bedroom. A little Christmas tree set up in front of the window fit the red and green holiday decor. The best part was that the cabin was perched on a slight hill, allowing her an unobstructed view of the town in the distance.

Mascara wand in hand, Miranda paused her post-shower ministrations to peer out the small bedroom window at St. Catherine's. From here, she could barely see the big brick walls punctuated with stained glass windows, the ornate door and grand steps leading to it. Under the evening sky, it looked just like most of the other Catholic churches she'd seen in her lifetime, just a tad smaller and with fewer people entering and exiting.

Of course, she was in the Bible Belt now. Likely the Baptist churches were a lot busier than the quiet St. Catherine's, but other than a lone groundskeeper shoveling snow off the walkway, there was very little activity around the building itself.

No one really seemed to pay it much mind, either, as they strode past with their families toward the evening's festivities at the Town Square. After her dinner at Peggy Jo's, she'd driven the streets to get the layout and noticed the gridlike patterns of the roads here. Everything led back to the Town Square, where City Hall sat center stage, bordered by a busy park complete with snow hills for sledding, and edged all the way around by wrought-iron gates sparkling with green garlands.

It was all very quaint indeed, but given her reason for being here, that quaintness had become downright chilling.

She returned to applying her makeup. As she carefully traced her eyes with liner, she sneered at the black hair spilling around her face. It didn't look natural at all. But she'd dyed her red hair on the slight chance she'd be recognized.

She touched up her lips with a combination of ChapStick and lip gloss to protect against the cold. The beef stew and cornbread she'd enjoyed only a short time ago now sat in her belly like bricks. She popped a couple antacids in an attempt to settle her stomach.

Flipping open her suitcase, she pulled out a clean ivory sweater and slid it over her jeans. The matching knit hat was a little too large for her small head, but it would help keep her ears warm. She slid her soggy Converse on over two pairs of socks, grabbed her parka and purse, and headed out into the cold. If she procrastinated any longer, she'd lose the courage to go at all.

Because almost everything she needed was within walking distance, she'd parked the Range Rover in a garage a couple of blocks over and covered it to conceal her Ohio plates. Better to save her funds for lodging and food and maybe a pair of shoes that didn't soak in water like a sponge, rather than waste it on gas.

She frowned at her feet, carefully choosing her path down the gravel trail entwined around the cottages and leading to a paved drive near the main house. Tucker's house. *Chief* Tucker.

Frowning, she wrapped her coat tighter around her body. His house was small for a man who owned a Rolex. It was a single-story ranch style that somewhat resembled a log cabin—painted a shade darker than the tan cottages surrounding it. There were no lights on inside that she could see, and she assumed he was still dealing with whoever had called him away from their dinner.

Not that it mattered. She couldn't afford to spend any more thought on him and his badge.

With a sigh, she opened the gates at the front of the property and stepped onto the sidewalk that would take her to Main Street. She walked, head down to protect against the cold, until she was at the street corner directly across from St. Catherine's.

The groundskeeper she'd seen earlier had disappeared, and all the proof of the work he'd done on clearing the walkway and sidewalks with him. Already a fine layer of white dusted the concrete. Checking for traffic, or, rather, for horse-drawn carriages as that seemed to be the travel method of choice around here, Miranda jogged across the street and up the wide steps into St. Catherine's.

She stopped in the vestibule and made a mental map of her surroundings. Discreet gold plaques marked the way toward the reconciliation chapel and church offices down the right wing. To the left, a children's chapel and a nursery. The emptiness was eerie, but she wasn't sure this place ever filled enough to make her not feel like she stood out.

She stepped into the nave, stopping by the baptismal pool. She didn't dip her fingers into the holy water or cross herself. This had not been her faith in a very long time. The muted light accentuated the red sanctuary lamp and the tier of remembrance candles. The way the firelight danced across the stained glass windows did nothing to calm her tingling nerves.

Scanning the chapel, she saw no movement near the altar. All the pews were vacant. And if the confessional near the far wall was in use, there was no light to guide the lost. She stepped back into the aisle. This time, however, she did bow her head to the crucifix mounted behind the altar and offered a quick prayer for safety and guidance.

Returning to the vestibule, she collected several pamphlets and scanned them. Times of Mass and confession, prayer requests and upcoming events. She stuffed them in her pockets and made her way down the right hallway, stopping to glance into the confessional chapel. Finding it empty as well, she moved to the end of the hall.

This was the day she'd been dreading. The first possible face-to-face contact with him. But she had to know. Had to see for herself that he was really here. Chasing a ghost on the Internet was one thing. Standing in his vicinity was quite another.

But she had to do it.

Miranda gripped the doorknob firmly with one hand, her other hand feeling around the contents of her purse to make sure the camera was still there. The hard, circular metal of the lens brushed her fingers and she exhaled with relief. The tremble in her fingers rattled the knob and created an echo loud enough to drown out her racing heart. Tightening her grip, she twisted to the left. Just as she was sure it was locked, the knob turned to the right and the door was yanked open.

She would have bolted if her feet and brain had been capable of communicating with each other.

"Can I help you?" Cloaked in shadows, the figure towered over her, making her feel small and vulnerable. She took a defensive step backward and placed her hand on her throat.

"Can I help you?" The voice asked again.

"Father?"

The shadow shifted, stepped into the hallway. The recessed lights shone down upon him, haloing his blond head. "I'm sorry, Father Anatole has left for the evening. Is there something I can help you with?"

She exhaled and realized her knees were trembling. She braced herself against the wall and smiled up at the groundskeeper.

"I—I just wanted to introduce myself." Thinking on her feet wasn't her forte, but this excuse came easily. "I'm new and considering coming to Mass, but I'd like to meet the priest first."

Two men dressed in black clerical suits exited another office down the hall and headed the opposite way. Their footsteps slapped against the stone floor as the groundskeeper motioned for her to follow him back toward the vestibule.

It was really hard to concentrate with all the fear screaming in her head. She'd thought she'd just run smack into Anatole. Now that she knew she was safe, she still couldn't quell the wave of nausea quivering in her gut.

"He should be in by sunrise." He jutted his chin toward the disappearing men. "You could meet with one of our deacons if you'd like."

"No thanks." She followed him outside, the cold air giving her some sense of clarity as it blasted her in the face. Anatole wasn't here. Which meant his office was empty.

Did she dare go through with it now that she'd run into this man? God, she was still trembling.

"Thank you for your time, Mr. . . . ."

"Simon Capistrano. Groundskeeper." He smiled. "I'm around three or four days a week if you need anything. I'm new here myself, but I'm getting the hang of things."

Miranda forced herself to return his smile and started down the steps. "Maybe I'll see you at Mass sometime."

She hastily made her way across the street, not looking back until the weight of his stare dropped from her back. When she finally did, he was gone.

Well, that didn't go as planned.

She was itching to get into that office, but Groundskeeper Simon might put two and two together and rat her out if Anatole reported a break-in. She'd been trying to open his office door when Simon had caught her, after all.

Shit.

Was it worth the risk?

She chewed her lip, pondering.

Definitely worth the risk. But not tonight. She'd give it a few days and hope that Simon forgot about meeting her.

Chapter 3

AN HOUR OR so after his pleasant dinner meeting with his new tenant, Tucker was worn out. Lisa's call hadn't been for a stolen bicycle or anything so easily dismissed. Fifteen-year-old Ricky Schneider had been missing for two days. Tucker had been called out to the Schneider house several times for domestic abuse—had locked up the father no fewer than three times in the seven years since he'd taken this job, and wasn't the least bit surprised that Stan and Tanya Schneider had been too involved with their booze to notice their son Ricky's disappearance any sooner.

After he'd responded to the call, Tucker had left them to give their statement to Lieutenant Bowen downstairs among their empty bottles and full ashtrays, while he ventured upstairs, where yellow nicotine covered each wall he'd passed like a coat of paint. The thick shag carpet looked like something left over from the seventies, coated in cat hair and the stench of dried urine.

When he reached Ricky's room he sneezed and shut the door behind him, noticing that in the boy's room, the air was easier to breathe than in any other area of the small townhouse.

He pulled the camera from his bag and began snapping pictures. Given the kid's home life, this was probably a runaway situation. With parents like those two buffoons downstairs, Tucker couldn't blame Ricky for wanting to get away.

He slid the photo Tanya had given him from beneath his arm and studied it. Good-looking kid if he ignored the horrendous piercings jutting out of Ricky's nose and eyebrows—but they were better than the bruises and blood that had decorated the kid's face the last time Tuck had seen him. In the photo, he was wearing a black, grungy T-shirt and torn jeans. Denim jacket that looked about two sizes too small.

He searched the nightstand and dresser for any phone numbers or friends' names, but couldn't find a single one. There was no computer to search, no phone left behind. Not even a yearbook. If this kid had friends, he hadn't brought any evidence of them into this house.

Tucker looked at the photo again and remembered his last run-in with Ricky. He'd been jumped three months or so ago by a group of preppy teens with too much time on their hands. The grandfather had reported it. Tucker had met with him. Nice enough man who'd died just after Halloween. Maybe his death had sparked Ricky's decision to leave.

Or maybe . . . His mind flashed to the bloody scene behind the library and his gut twisted.

He made another note to look into the report on the beating. He'd pay a visit to the kids who'd done it. See if they knew anything or if there was any chance it had happened again and Ricky was out there somewhere, hurt and unable to get help.

Teens. The biggest pain in this town's ass.

He closed the nightstand drawer and dropped to his knees to look beneath the bed. There was nothing there except a box full of metal band posters and a journal. While nothing was written in the journal, there were sketches. The kid had talent. It looked as though he'd drawn at least two dozen sketches of various gods of mythology. Dragons. Ancient symbols.

Judging by the content of the artwork, Tucker was ready to guess that Ricky Schneider had no use for the religious aspects of this town. Tucker didn't know much about witchcraft or the Wiccan religion, but he knew pentagrams when he saw them. He also wasn't closed-minded enough to believe that pentagrams themselves meant anything bad or evil-intended. They were just stars, used in many religious and scientific drawings. But they were hidden in a box under the bed for a reason.

If Ricky had run away and there was a chance he'd return, Tucker didn't want to cause him any more life suckage by calling his parents' attention to the box. He took snapshots of each page, put the journal back in the box, and slid the box as far back beneath the bed as possible. Retrieving an evidence bag from his pocket, he slid a hairbrush inside before venturing down the hall to the bathroom. There, he bagged the lone tooth-brush laying on the counter and another comb, then closed the door behind him and headed back downstairs where Lieutenant Bowen was finishing taking the parents' statements.

Tanya Schneider sat sloppily at the small kitchen table, puffing on a cigarette, her eyes glazed from the half-empty bottle of tequila in front of her. Her partially opened housedress gave him an unwanted eyeful of sagging, leathery cleavage freckled with age spots. Her husband stood by the fridge, looking way more pissed than worried about his son's fate.

Tucker held up one of his bags for verification. "This Ricky's toothbrush?"

Tanya nodded.

"I think we have everything we need here," Bowen said, closing his notebook. "You're sure he doesn't have any social media accounts?"

Stan sneered. "What's he going to use them on? Kid doesn't have a phone, and the last computer we had in the house broke about five years ago."

Tanya sighed. "He could have made one at that damned library, Stan."

"The library?" Tucker asked. "He go there a lot?"

She nodded, inhaled, blew a ring of smoke so thick she had to squint through it to see him. "Every damned day. I don't care though. Kept him out of trouble for the most part."

Tucker pulled his phone from his pocket and did a quick search on both Facebook and Twitter. There was a ton of Ricky Schneiders on there. He'd have to go through them one by one to see if any belonged to their kid.

To Bowen, he said, "Have someone go check out the library computers. See if we can find a social media account, something that might give us an idea of who his friends are or where he might have gone."

"The kid don't have any friends." Stan jerked open the refrigerator, rummaged around for a minute, opening the crispers before taking a beer from the shelf and slamming the door.

There was no food on the shelves.

Tucker turned back to Andy, who looked at the parents and shook his head. Tucker could read the disgust in the lieutenant's eyes. Having come from a broken home, Andy took situations like this a little personally.

"And you're sure he hasn't called home or any of his friends?"

"Why would he call us? Kid hasn't had much use for us since he was in diapers." Tanya Schneider gripped her cigarette between her teeth and poured a double shot of tequila into her glass. The woman was well beyond being shitfaced. "And we told you, he don't have friends. Little punk ran off. Stan says he'll come home when he gets hungry enough."

As she brushed her hair behind her ear, he noticed a knot circled with a black ring on her cheek. "How'd you get that bruise?"

She gingerly touched her face, glancing at her husband. "I tripped on thin ice."

I'm sure you did. Eggshells and thin ice. This house felt made of the things. Once again, his mind flashed back to the blood in the alley. If it did belong to Ricky, there was a possibility it had everything to do with Stan Schneider.

The last time he'd had Stan before the judge, the judge had warned Stan that if he saw him in his courtroom again, Stan would do substantial jail time, along with losing his parental rights. Maybe Stan Schneider had taken care of Ricky to make sure that didn't happen.

And maybe you shouldn't jump to conclusions.

Tuck took several deep breaths to calm the anger churning his gut. Until he knew otherwise, he'd stick to the assumption that Ricky had simply had enough and ran away.

"Do you have any family? Someone Ricky might have gone to?"

Someone you can go to if I haul your prick-ass husband to jail?

"Of course we have people, but they would've called Stan the minute Ricky showed up on their doorsteps."

He handed her one of his cards. "If you hear anything, or need anything, please call."

Tucker closed the notebook and stuffed it in his pocket as he tossed his equipment bag over his shoulder. "We'll notify you if we find anything. If Ricky calls or comes home, please let us know right away.

He said the words more out of habit than anything else. He was rooting for the kid to have found a safe place with a distant relative—somewhere far away from the hell that had been his home.

Wednesday

MIRANDA ENTERED THE police department and took a minute to let the warmth from the overhead vent thaw her. She still couldn't believe she'd convinced herself to come here. Tucker seemed like a nice enough guy, but he was law enforcement. She couldn't forget that.

But then, she wasn't here for a date or anything. He was her landlord. There would be times, like now, when she couldn't avoid him. If she hadn't woken up this morning certain that she had icicles hanging off her toes, she wouldn't be here now.

As long as she was careful not to fall for his dimples and kind eyes—and kept her reasons for being here to herself—everything would be just fine.

"Can I help you?"

Miranda smiled at the woman sitting behind the oval

counter that separated the reception area from the offices behind her. She had to be five or six years younger than Miranda, but lines of fatigue and frustration marred her forehead, making it impossible to guess her true age.

"Lisa, did you get the reports back from the hospitals yet?"

The receptionist held up her hand for Miranda to wait a moment and spun in her chair, facing the voice that bellowed from the back of the office. "Called every hospital from here to Knoxville, and spoke to most of the GPs and pediatricians as well. If any of them saw Ricky lately, then he never used his real name. Nothing at child protection, either."

Tucker entered the waiting area, and Miranda's entire body came alive. She'd begun to wonder if she'd imagined how attractive he was. She hadn't.

He tossed a file on the desk in front of Lisa while Miranda pulled herself together. "Since you have a rapport with Mrs. Perry, why don't you head over there and interview her for me. If he used the computers, see if she kept a log so we can determine exactly what he did while he was there. Did he meet up with anyone? Express interest in going anyplace in particular? That sort of thing."

"Shannon's due shortly. Want me to go now or wait on her?"

"I'll hold down the fort until she gets in. Just get back as soon as you can. And if you bring me something useful, dinner for you and the kids is on me."

Lisa stuffed her notepad in her purse, grabbed her jacket from the back of her chair, and rushed past Miranda as if worried Tucker might change his mind. The stress lines had completely disappeared from the short blonde, erased by the excitement of her new assignment.

"Well hello there." Tucker said, noticing Miranda for the first time. His smile was warm and inviting. The twinkle in his eyes suggested he was glad to see her.

She offered a tiny wave. "If this is a bad time, I can come back later."

"No need." He came around the desk. "First night in the cottage okay?"

"The heat doesn't seem to be working and your instructions didn't say where to find extra firewood."

Was it the man or the badge pinned to his chest that made her hands sweat and her heart race? "I should have called or left a note on your door—"

"Not at all." He glanced at his watch. "I was about to grab some lunch. Have a meal with me, then we can head over there so I can give the furnace a quick look."

"Thanks, but there's no hurry. I just wanted to let you kn—"

"You wouldn't make a guy eat alone, would you?" He flashed those dimples and her resolve melted. "There's a hot dog stand across the street. Not a big deal."

"I—"

"Just sit tight, all right? I won't be but a minute."

Even though the intelligent half of her brain screamed at her to slink away when he disappeared back down the hall, she sat and kept her ass firmly planted in the hard plastic chair.

Why? What the hell was wrong with her?

He was so different than Detective Langley had been. She could see that right off. Tucker was friendly and had a ready smile. But did that make him different enough that he might believe her if she spilled her guts?

Another receptionist swept in, this one about nineteen or twenty with long dark hair and no-nonsense black-framed glasses. She gave Miranda a curious look as she took her seat behind the desk and threw a graffitied backpack on the floor.

"You waitin' on someone?" she asked Miranda, popping open the lid to a steaming cup of coffee and taking a tentative sip.

"Chief Ambrose. It's okay. He knows."

The girl grunted and turned her attention to the computer screen, and Miranda slid her phone from her pocket. She pulled up Safari and typed in "Father Peter Anatole." She'd run this search a million times already, but every day, she typed it in anyway, hoping for something new. Still, the most recent search page led her here, to Christmas, with an article from the *Christmas Chronicle* proclaiming him the new priest at St. Catherine's.

"Ready?"

He was wearing his Stetson again. She kind of liked it. She gathered her belongings and followed him outside, zipping up her parka as she went.

"Mind if we stop by the *Chronicle* on our way back to the cottage so I can drop off a photo for them to run?"

"No problem."

As they walked, she was well aware of her inability to make small talk, and she felt bad that he had to fill in the awkward gaps alone.

"Sure a hot dog is okay? Can't guarantee I have time to sit down for a meal and check out your cottage, too, but—"

"A hot dog sounds great." For once, she actually *wasn't* hungry. They grabbed a couple hot dogs and cider from the nearest vendor and ate in silence as they walked back toward the cottages.

Her footsteps faltered when she noticed they were

across the street from St. Catherine's. Tucker walked a few steps ahead before realizing she was no longer with him. When he gave her a curious glance, she thought as quickly as she could and dug her camera from her duffel.

"Sorry. I have a thing for historic buildings. Mind if I take a look?"

He checked his watch. "Your heat might have to wait another couple hours."

She contemplated telling him to go on without her, but the thought of having the chief of police at her side should she run into Anatole was too irresistible. "I don't mind."

Standing this close to him on the street corner, she could smell the faint hint of his aftershave. She liked it. She also liked the way he was looking at her now, like he was trying to figure her out. And not in the I-know-you're-up-to-something way she'd become accustomed to in Dayton.

"We don't have a lot of historical buildings," he said. "The town's less than a hundred years old. The oldest thing around is the First Baptist Church, but it's been abandoned since they opened New Baptist more than a decade ago. If you're looking for historic, St. Catherine's doesn't exactly fit the bill, either. It can't be more than fifty years old."

She forced a smile. "All Catholic churches feel a bit historic to me. If it's a problem, I can go alone."

Please don't make me go alone.

He held up his hands. "No, not a problem. We can go. The new priest isn't exactly friendly, but it's usually pretty vacant this time of day."

Miranda swallowed and tried to summon a look of excitement rather than pure trepidation. "Thank you."

She could tell by the look he gave her that it wasn't his idea of fun. He glanced at his watch again. "I just need to go in here first."

She looked behind her and saw that the *Chronicle* was only a couple feet away. "No problem."

The small shopping center of businesses was quaintly decorated for the season. Miniature snowmen lined the walkways beneath the awnings, and every window had some sort of holiday garishness staring back at her. Tucker pushed open the last door on the right. Two women sat inside the otherwise empty office space, both so focused on their jobs that they didn't notice Tucker and Miranda walk in.

Leaving Miranda at the door, Tucker interrupted, passed them a few photos, and returned to her, earning her very curious looks from the women in the cubicles.

The last people Miranda wanted to meet were reporters. She ducked outside before he could try to introduce them. Tucker followed.

"So? St. Catherine's?" he asked.

She smiled. God, he was adorable. Those stupid dimples were going to do her in if she wasn't on guard at all times. "Yeah."

When they stopped at a crosswalk, Miranda turned in a full circle. She'd thought it was her late evening drive through town that had caused her to miss it, but she hadn't seen a single fast-food joint anywhere.

"What are you looking for?"

"Mickey D's?"

Tucker gave her one of his dimpled grins. "You'll have to drive over to the next town, about fifteen miles away, for that. Christmas isn't big on franchises. We have the Marriott over by the station because they agreed to design the hotel to fit the theme of the town.

Besides, people who come here . . . they seem to prefer mom-and-pop joints. Places like Peggy Jo's that offer from-scratch kinds of foods."

He guided her around a puddle. When they reached the other side of the street, he didn't drop his hand from the small of her back. She didn't move away.

Miranda stopped at the bottom of St. Catherine's stairs. Knowing that the priest would likely be inside made her rethink her decision to come by here. But this was why she'd come. To find Anatole. To see for herself that he was actually here, and if he was, to find *anything* that might prove she was right about him.

Even if it did leave her palms sweaty and her knees weak.

"Something wrong?"

"Nope." She took a deep breath and pulled out her camera. She snapped a few blurry pictures of windows she didn't give two shits about, her gaze wandering from the viewfinder to search the premises for any sign of Anatole.

She shifted the camera angle and captured a shot of Tucker before joining him on the steps.

"Sorry I can't give you any history on this church." Tucker opened the heavy doors and guided her into the vestibule. She pretended to take a couple more pictures, moving around the entrance hall, her gaze hunting, searching.

"It's pretty," she said, feeling as though she'd be expected to say something. And it wasn't a lie. The few seconds she'd spent in here last night hadn't been long enough for her to appreciate the architecture.

"I agree."

Miranda glanced at him and knew by the way he looked at her that he wasn't talking about the church.

As he studied her face, she suddenly felt on display, and vulnerable and . . . Her belly flopped. She was in a church. That last feeling was highly inappropriate.

Near the corner of the church stood a man dressed in a black frock, surrounded by a couple of deacons. Though she couldn't see his face, she knew, even from the back of his head, that it was Anatole.

She quickly lifted the camera and snapped a shot, willing him to turn around long enough to capture his face, and yet praying that somehow, he wouldn't see her in turn. He'd thought he'd left all of Dayton behind. Well, he hadn't left *her* behind. She was going to find proof, damn it. No matter what it cost her.

"Hey, miss? You still want to meet the father?"

Miranda's finger finally remembered how to stop snapping that damned button, but the rest of her forgot how to move. Behind Tucker, Simon, the groundskeeper, was waving her over, smiling like a loon.

As Simon walked closer, she waved him off. "No, really. He looks busy. Some other tim—"

"Nonsense." With a nod of greeting to Tucker, Simon called out to Father Anatole, and Miranda's guts turned to water.

God save me from helpful people.

Ignoring the questioning look Tucker shot her, she tried to think of a way to get herself out of this situation. But it was too late. Father Anatole, leaning heavily on the cane in his left hand, was limping straight for her.

Chapter 4

As Father Anatole strode forward, his arm outstretched in preparation to shake Miranda's hand, her insides boiled with such a ferocious anger, she thought she might very well erupt from it.

She barely listened as Simon made the introductions, re-vomiting her spiel about wanting to meet the priest before attending Mass. As she talked, she avoided eye contact, terrified of the slight chance Anatole might recognize her.

"Thank you for introducing us, Simon," she finished, finally forcing herself to look Anatole directly in the face. "It's nice to have met you, Father."

The words came out, chased by a little river of acid that tasted a lot like syrupy throw-up. She looked to Tucker. "Ready?"

"Have we . . . have we met before, Ms. . . . ."

Panic seized her. "No. We haven't."

The priest's eyes narrowed, but not with venom. It was more of a look of curiosity. The same sort Tucker kept casting her way. "You look very familiar to me."

"I get that a lot."

Taking Tucker's elbow, she waved a fake, shaky fare-well at the priest and the confused-looking groundskee-per, before hurrying down the steps toward the crosswalk.

Way to play it cool, dumb ass.

"What was all that about?"

Ignoring Tucker's question, she dropped his arm and darted across the empty street. He'd either keep up, or he wouldn't. Either way, she was getting the hell away from the church and that evil prick of a priest.

He kept up, taking her elbow this time, and making her turn around. From here, she was still visible to Ana-tole and his little group. She was shaking. And sweat-ing. She unzipped her parka, letting the icy air burrow its way through her knit sweater.

"Hey. You okay? Miranda . . . I think you're hyper-ventilating."

She felt herself being lifted, but her brain was too thick to register much else. Everything was spinning. Sucking in one breath took all her concentration. Then she was being placed on something hard. A bench? Warm hands cupped her cheeks, then pressed her head down, stretching out her spine as those hands pushed her face between her knees.

"Breathe in as deeply as you can. Slowly. Miranda? Can you hear me?"

Yes, she could hear him. Barely. Blood rushed to her brain and muffled every other sound in the world. Tucker's big hand rubbed her back, her shoulders, her hair.

What was she doing here? Why did she think she could do any of this? She was a nurse, for God's sake, and she couldn't even tell when she was hyperventilating!

She took in a big gulp of air and her brain cleared.

Just a bit. Slowly, she sat up. "I—I'm okay. Thanks. I'm
. . . I'll be fine."

"Ready to tell me what that was all about?"

Would he still find her attractive if she yacked all over
his uniform? Probably not. She inhaled again. Looked
around. Couldn't see Anatole anywhere. Her body cooled
a degree or two and her insides stopped squirming.

"I, um . . . I don't really like priests," she said. It
wasn't a complete lie. Ever since Anatole had turned
her world upside down, she'd had about as much faith
in men of the cloth as she did men in uniform.

"Then why'd you want to meet him?" Tucker placed
the back of his hand to her forehead. Seemingly satisfied
that she wasn't going to burst into flames, he dropped it
and set it on her knee instead. She liked it there.

She had no lie at the ready this time. She chose to
pretend she hadn't heard the question. "I think I need
a nap."

And a stiff drink.

The look on his face told her he knew he'd just been
purposely brushed off, but he was gentleman enough
not to call her out on it.

TUCKER PULLED HIS cruiser in front of his house that
night and cut the engine. His back ached from sitting
in front of the computer for the majority of the afternoon, searching every Ricky Schneider account on
every social network he could think of. For nothing.
He hadn't found one single hint that their Ricky might
have used any of them.

Bowen was still pulling up the library's archives,
however. Maybe the Internet history from those computers would be a little more helpful. Mrs. Perry certainly hadn't been. Lisa's talk with her had been a bust.

The kid came in, used the computers, read some books. That was all she'd had to offer.

He'd bought Lisa's dinner anyway.

He sighed and gathered the brown paper bag from the passenger seat before stepping out into the snow. It crunched beneath his boots as he passed his own front door and the tempting heat waiting inside, his gaze focused on Miranda's door two cottages away.

The slight hike up the hill to her door felt like a trek up a mountain at this hour, but he kept the bag close to his chest, protecting the heat within. Once he'd knocked, he leaned against the porch railing and took a weary breath.

She opened the door, stared up at him with those big brown eyes that he was beginning to find devastatingly charming . . . and mysterious. This woman had secrets, and he found himself drawn to figuring them out.

Wanted to meet Father Anatole . . . but didn't like priests. What the hell was that all about?

"It's almost eleven," she said by way of greeting.

He thrust the bag toward her. "Soup. In case you're still not feeling well. It's Peggy Jo's chicken noodle. Pretty good."

As she took the bag, her lips stretched into a smile. "I thought you might have come to fix my heat and show me where the firewood is. This might be even better."

Shit. He'd forgotten all about his landlord responsibilities. Ricky's disappearance was consuming most of his brain right now. "I'm sorry. I can take a look at it now so you don't have to sleep in the cold."

She glanced over her shoulder inside the cottage, then swung the door open wider. "Come on in. You sure you're not too tired?"

"I won't get any sleep knowing you're in here hovering under the threat of hypothermia. Shouldn't take long." He stepped inside, raised an eyebrow at the fire crackling in the hearth. At least he hadn't wakened her. "Looks like you have enough firewood to get you through the night, anyway. I'll make sure I drop more off on your porch in the morning before work, but for future reference, there's an unlocked shed behind my house full of it if you need more. I have some EZ gel starters if you'd like some, too."

"That's okay. I know my way around building a fire." She set the paper bag on the small kitchen table and pulled out the Styrofoam bowl filled with soup. "Want some?"

He shook his head. "I'm just going to check your heater and get out of your way. Just wanted to make sure you were all right. You scared me this afternoon."

Her smile turned bashful and he found it utterly appealing. "You're sweet. I'm fine, though. Really. Please, don't worry about the heat tonight. I can sleep in here in front of the fire and you can come by tomorrow to see what you can do. You look exhausted."

The concern in her voice, and the way she watched him like he'd pass out on his feet any second, chased some of the fatigue from his muscles. He couldn't remember the last time someone had been worried about him. He hadn't realized he'd missed it . . . or how much he enjoyed that spark of energy such concern created in him.

"You sure you don't want some?" She held out the Styrofoam bowl. "Or I could make some coffee. Sorry, but I don't have anything stronger."

"Sit. Enjoy your dinner." He opened the breaker panel, then flipped the switch off, then on again. The whoosh of the heat kicking on filled the small cabin.

He held his hand to the vent. "Looks like that did the trick."

Her smile eased the last of his fatigue from his bones. "Thanks."

"You're welcome. I'll come by tomorrow and figure out why the breaker tripped. If I forget, please come over and remind me. You can share my heat and a bottle of wine."

He hadn't meant that in a sexual way, but the way her spoon stopped halfway to her mouth and her gaze slowly trailed over him, he knew how she'd taken it. What would she do if he closed the two feet between them and . . .

All his blood flowed south.

He flipped the panel closed. A piece of sharp metal caught his hand, slicing into his palm. He cursed.

"Let me see." She placed her bowl on the table and moved to his side.

"It's fine. Just a little cut." It burned like hell but he wasn't about to tell her that.

"Come on." Her hands gripped his and shifted toward the light. "Oh, that's nasty." She pulled him to the sink and stuck his hand under cold water. "Keep it under the water, I'll be right back."

Before he could protest, she disappeared down the hallway. She returned holding the biggest first aid kit he'd ever seen. When she turned off the tap and wrapped his hand in a soft kitchen towel, he smiled down at her. "Accident prone?"

She glanced at him with a frown. "Excuse me?"

He nodded at the box on the edge of the counter. He kept a small kit in each cabin's bathroom, but it held only the necessities. Hers looked like it might hold half a hospital pharmacy.

"Oh." She laughed, releasing his hand long enough to flip open the lid on the large box. "Occupational hazard."

"Doctor?"

"Nurse," she corrected. "My last post was in Bolivia. Before that was Haiti. You get used to being overprepared for anything."

He watched as she dried his hand and examined the cut. "Looks clean, but keep an eye out for infection." She placed a dollop of ointment on the cut, then a square of gauze before wrapping it securely. Miranda handed him several packages of gauze and the tube of cream. "Clean it a couple times a day, but don't use that for more than forty-eight hours. If it gets red or puffy, see your doctor."

"Yes, ma'am." He tucked the items into his pocket and took an uninvited seat at the table. She grabbed a cup and spoon from the sink, poured half her soup into it, and passed it to him before sitting down. "So what made you become a nurse?"

"I wanted to help people." She shrugged, concentrating on her soup for several spoonfuls before continuing. "Taking care of people, making a difference in their lives, giving them a little hope when they have none, means something important."

He nodded, completely understanding. Miranda's reasons for joining the medical profession weren't that different from his reasons for being a cop. He hadn't been able to help his sister, but he could potentially help someone else's. He'd given up his way of life, his family, everything he knew for the chance to give hope to those who didn't have any.

Blue-collar work. His father hadn't been happy about that at all.

"Corny, huh?"

Tuck looked up from his soup. "Not at all. In fact, we have a lot in common. Those reasons are exactly why I joined the police academy."

Miranda tucked a strand of hair behind her ear. The smile on her face warmed the room better than the newly repaired heater. He found himself watching her eat. It wasn't until she tried to smother a yawn behind her hand that he realized how long they'd been sitting at the table.

"I didn't intend to hang out half the night." He placed his mug in the sink. "Thanks for the doctoring."

"Sorry," she said around another yawn. "Thanks for fixing the heater and for the soup."

"My pleasure."

"Night." She shut the door, and he stood staring at it for a long moment, trying to gather the nerve to knock again and ask her to dinner. The click of the deadbolt locking stilled his hand. Frustrated that he was so rusty with women, he bent his head against the cold and walked back to his place. He opened the door, then glanced back toward Miranda's cottage. The curtain ruffled, falling back into place. He smiled.

There was more to Miranda than a pretty face and he really wanted to get to know every aspect of her.

Chapter 5

Thursday

Miranda curled in the recliner in front of her living room window and stared out the frosty window at St. Catherine's. She didn't know how the people of this town dealt with Christmas year-round. For most people, herself included, it wasn't an easy time to survive when it came only once a year. Three hundred and sixty-five days of ho-ho-hos and sleigh bells would turn her suicidal.

She clutched her backpack, slipping her hand inside the outer pocket to check for the ninth time to make sure the cameras were still inside. She'd gone over her plan at least a dozen times, had made two practice runs by Anatole's home. The minute the Mass bells rang . . .

She prayed like hell this break-in attempt would go unnoticed. If she got caught, the priest would know that she was on to him. What that would mean to her safety . . . She shuddered, not even wanting to think about what Anatole might do to her.

As the mantel clock's hand ticked slowly, she thumbed through the newspaper she hadn't had time to read that morning. There was no mention of Tucker's missing teen. Highlights of the festival dominated the front page of the thin *Christmas Chronicle*. The remaining three pages were filled with upcoming parties, an engagement announcement, and a call for volunteers to help out with a local Baptist church's food bank.

Small-town life at its finest . . .

By the time the clock read five-fifteen, she'd zipped her parka to her chin and was well past ready to get this over with. With a glance toward Tucker's house, and seeing no cars in the drive or lights on inside, she took a deep, shaky breath and opened the iron gates separating his property from the rest of the town.

She couldn't blow this chance. She needed to see what Anatole was up to. Maybe find evidence that would finally land him behind bars. She knew from the church pamphlet she'd swiped that Mass ran for about an hour on Thursdays, starting at five-thirty. That meant she had about forty minutes to get to his house, get in, place her cameras, and get out again without being discovered.

Piece of cake.

People meandered the streets enjoying the ongoing festival. Their laughter blended with the piped-in Christmas carols. She tucked her head against the wind and headed to the parking garage, trying not to focus on anything other than tonight's mission.

She kicked the snow from her shoes before climbing inside the Range Rover, cranked the heat, and wiggled her fingers in front of the vents. Why did her legs feel like rubber? She could totally do this. No one should be there . . . she was pretty certain Anatole lived alone. Get in, get out, drive away.

She could definitely do this.

Refusing to acknowledge her shaking hands, she opened the console and pulled out a black beanie. She shoved it on and crammed her hair inside it before checking her reflection in the rearview. If anyone glimpsed her from behind, she'd look more like a teenage boy than a fully grown woman. For once, she was happy about her petite frame and bulky jacket.

She slid her gloves on, put the SUV in drive, and exhaled as she pulled onto Main. It was a five-minute drive to Anatole's. As she hit the red light just past St. Catherine's, the Mass bells chimed over the town and Miranda's entire body broke into uncontrollable trembles.

"I can do this, I can do this, I can do this."

The DJ on the radio laughed, his timing a perfect mockery of her mantra as he rattled off a jolly ad for a snowball war to be held next week. She turned off the radio, too rattled to take any more noise in her already overcrowded head.

As she approached Anatole's little house, she slowed, drove past his driveway, squinting to make sure there was no sign of vehicles or movement inside. The house sat on a wide lot, and there weren't any neighboring houses. As long as she stuck to her plan, she was pretty sure she could remain unseen.

At least, that was her prayer for the evening.

She parked behind the gas station a quarter mile down the road, got out, and glanced through the window of the small building. An elderly man was watching television and hadn't even noticed her arrival. Good. And in a town like this, she doubted they'd have security cameras running at all times.

The SUV sat on the back side, near the Dumpster and the bathrooms, out of view of the window. So unless he emptied the trash, he shouldn't even know she'd ever been there. And if he did, hopefully he'd just assume she was in the women's room and think nothing of it.

She checked the bag she'd brought with her. A screwdriver, flashlight, a small crowbar she'd found behind the seat of the SUV, the cameras, and her cell phone. All the things a girl needed to get inside somewhere she shouldn't be.

Easing the bag's strap over her head and tugging her hat farther down over her ears, she slid down the embankment and followed the road from the safety of the trees back to Anatole's. It took a minute to gather her courage before she could make herself dash across the open road.

When she was safely ensconced in the woods around Anatole's, she rested her head against the rough bark and pulled in huge gulps of icy air.

I can't do this.

Yes, the hell you can!

Anatole's house stood just beyond a scattering of trees. A yellow porch light cut through the shadows, lighting up the grounds just enough to keep her from breaking an ankle, but the rest of the house was dark and quiet. If she approached from the rear, she shouldn't be visible at all from the road.

All she had to do was get off her ass and get it over with.

She sprinted up the driveway and around the back, stopping near a toolshed on the far right corner of the house to dig the flashlight from her bag. She checked the back door and windows. They were all locked.

With a more determined stride, she continued to work her way around to the left side of the house, saving the front as a last resort. About halfway down the length of the building she spotted a window open just a crack. It was smaller than the others, and would probably dump her in a sink or tub, but at least it was open. Retrieving the screwdriver, she pried out the screen. Thankfully the window slid open without a groan of protest. Needing a boost, she carefully moved the battered trash bin beneath the sill. She pulled herself up and stuck her head inside. As she feared, her entrance was over the kitchen sink, but there was no sign or sound of anyone inside.

She aimed the beam of light at the small, spotless sink and pristine counters. At least the man washed up after himself. There was nothing to knock over or break on her way in. There was also no way she'd fit through the opening with her thick parka on. Removing it, she shoved it through first, then hoisted herself onto the sill. Spider-Man she wasn't, but she managed to make it inside without putting herself in the sink or breaking her neck when her foot slipped on her jacket and she landed on the floor.

"Real graceful," she mumbled, snatching her jacket out of the sink and moving into the living room. The room was small but neat, everything in its place. A ceramic nativity scene lined the mantel, and a Charlie Brown–style Christmas tree stood on a round table. There was no television or even a radio. A large Bible sat on a glass coffee table. She gave it a quick flip-through before returning to the mantel.

Taking one of the cameras from her bag, she positioned it carefully in the manger. She pulled out her cell phone, started the monitoring program, and checked the view. After adjusting it twice before she was satisfied that she had the best location, she moved down the hall to the single bedroom.

Like the main room, there were no frills. She checked the closet, but found nothing out of the ordinary. Clothes perfectly organized by function and color, a large plastic container holding what looked like summer attire. At the bottom, a flawless line of shiny shoes and a tiny box that shot her adrenaline into high gear for a moment before she discovered it contained nothing more than a collection of laminated baseball cards.

The nightstand held nothing of interest, either, nor did the narrow space under the bed.

She quickly positioned the second camera by the window, just above the curtain rod where it couldn't be seen, and checked the feed before returning back down the hall toward the bathroom.

It was freshly cleaned and, other than a shelf of extra toiletries on the wall and a bottle of Tylenol in the medicine cabinet, there was nothing. Back in the hall, she pushed open the last door and found herself in a home office, and smiled. He was far more likely to hide something here than at his church office.

Making sure to memorize where everything was so she could put it all back where she found it, she emptied each desk drawer, glancing through files of past or future sermons and church-related agendas. Nothing personal, and certainly nothing incriminating.

She sighed, positioned and checked the third camera, carefully tucked against the wall atop a massive crucifix facing the desk, and rubbed her eyes.

Defeat was a lead weight in her gut as she searched the rest of the little house. Other than his baseball cards, there was nothing personal. Anyone at all could have lived here.

Making her way back to the kitchen, she bypassed the window. No way was she leaving the same way she'd come in. She closed it, making certain to leave it open a crack like she'd found it. She'd have to replace the screen when she got back outside, but other than that, she couldn't see any evidence that she'd been here.

And three of her cameras were in place.

At least she'd done that much right.

She struggled briefly with the deadbolt on the back door. Staying in the shadows, she stumbled to the front of the house. Checking to make sure she was still alone, she found a slot in the porch's awning and placed the last camera there, making certain it had a clear view of the drive and the front door.

After a quick check to verify its position, she started back to the rear of the house so she could replace the screen she'd removed. The sound of a car's engine startled her, forcing her back into the shadows. She broke into a full-body sweat and her brain lost all communication with her body. Her feet were rooted to the ground, her gaze on the driveway as she hugged the side of the house and peered around the corner.

Get the hell out of here!

Switching off the flashlight, she searched her surroundings for a better place to hide, but before she could find one, headlights cut through the darkness. She tried to make herself as small as possible and watched as Father Anatole climbed out of the car and strode toward the house. The moment the door closed behind him, she bolted into the trees and back toward the main road, not stopping until she was back at the gas station and safely locked in the SUV.

Friday

Two days had passed since Tucker had last seen Miranda, and she was all he could think about. He'd checked in on her again last night, but she hadn't been home. He'd fixed her heater anyway and had left a note telling her she was still welcome to come by for the wine he'd promised, but she'd never showed. And today, he'd been too busy looking for the Schneider kid to try again. Didn't mean he didn't want to.

"Chief?"

Tucker sighed and forced his attention back to his lieutenant. "Yeah, sorry. I heard you. A kid with no social media accounts in this day and age . . . maybe he created one under a different name?"

Andy Bowen collapsed onto the chair across from Tucker's desk and tossed his hat on the empty seat beside him. "He could have created a hundred under different names. But without the names, how can we look?"

"And the library computer search?"

"Pretty much anything that could be Googled, was Googled. I did find some pagan pages in the history, but there's no real way to tell who pulled them up. Mrs. Perry isn't all that up to date on her technology. There's no log-in or codes required. It's a veritable free-for-all."

Tucker flipped open Ricky Schneider's file and looked at the picture of the kid again. The *Chronicle* had posted it that morning, and flyers had been hung on nearly every window on Main Street. But there had been no more calls about Ricky since Wednesday. The last one he'd received had been a cold lead, the wrong kid. The article in the paper had sparked nothing.

Sad that a kid so young could go missing and the only people who noticed were his pathetic parents.

"Doc Sam called this morning and confirmed the blood behind the library didn't belong to an animal," he said. "She's going to run the brush and toothbrush you took from his house, see if there's any DNA on there that matches it."

Andy's eyes widened. "You really think the kid was killed?"

Tucker shrugged. "No way to know at this point. Still praying it's a runaway case, but have to cover all our bases."

He rubbed his forehead, a massive headache forming between his eyes. He'd already checked every bus station and airport in a hundred-mile radius. If Ricky had run away, he hadn't left a paper trail that Tucker had been able to find yet.

Tucker felt like he was chasing a ghost.

Chapter 6

MIRANDA STEPPED ONTO her porch to collect the day's issue of the *Chronicle* and found yet another stack of fresh firewood waiting for her beneath the window. She smiled, collected the bundle, and returned inside to drop the logs with the five she still had left from yesterday. Tucker was stealthy. She hadn't heard her porch steps creak once.

Still smiling, she dropped back into the chair she'd been occupying all day and opened the newspaper she'd forgotten to snag that morning. Her eyes needed a break from the strain of staring at her laptop all day. Her stomach rumbled. She hadn't even thought to eat since noon and now it was a little past eight.

Her gaze drifted down to the newspaper. The same teen boy's face that had graced the front page for the past couple of days stared back at her. The same photo Tucker had dropped off for them to print. The same face looking at her wherever she went from flyers posted all over town. There was no big story to accompany the picture. Just a large block of text asking: "Have you seen me?" followed by the kid's name, age, and last known whereabouts.

Poor kid. And his poor family.

Miranda closed the paper and leaned back in her chair. She should call it a night. She'd been watching the camera monitors on her computer since yesterday, and other than watching Anatole eat, sleep, and come and go, she'd yet to see one interesting thing inside his house. She had to get her cameras into St. Catherine's. Had to watch him where he spent most of his time.

But how the hell was she supposed to get in there unseen? His house had been nicely secluded. But the church? Right smack in the center of Main Street. It wasn't going to be easy.

She jiggled her mouse to stop the screensaver on her laptop just as a knock pounded on her door. She jumped up, slamming the lid closed, her heart stuttering at the unexpected sound.

Wrapping her robe tighter around the pajamas she hadn't changed out of all day, she peered out the window to find Tucker standing on her porch, hat in hand, his badge glinting at her beneath the lamplight. He saw her and she gave a slight wave of her fingers before making her way to the door and opening it.

"Hi," she said, suddenly very aware of how desperately she needed a shower and that she hadn't run a brush through her hair since that morning. The mess of black was now piled loosely on top of her head in a sloppy bun, stray bits sticking out in every direction as she caught a glimpse of herself in the door's glass.

He opened the screen, the squeak jolting in the otherwise peaceful night. The faint sound of carols playing from Town Square carried into her cottage, reminding her how close it was till Christmas Day, and how close she was to spending it alone. Again.

"Just wanted to make sure you were all right. Haven't seen you in a while."

"Thank you. I've been catching up on some reading." *And spying.*

He nodded. "And the heater's still working?"

He'd been by to fix it when she'd been breaking and entering. She hadn't thought to thank him yet. And in all honesty, she wasn't sure she wanted to. She wasn't keen on the thought of him being in the cabin without her. She had things—especially now—that she certainly didn't want him to stumble upon. "Sorry I haven't stopped by to thank you. It's running fine."

Small talk. She hated it so much.

"Did you . . . did you want to come in?"

He shook his head. "It's late. I just wanted to make sure everything was all right."

A bit of relief mingled with disappointment at his refusal. "It is, thank you. And your hand?"

He held it up and smiled. "Won't scar. You're a good nurse."

God, he was cute. And sweet. His continual check-ins with her were beginning to get to her. She was used to cops knocking on her door, but never to ask if she was all right. Never to deliver her soup, or firewood, or . . . a friendly smile.

She was so alone here. Lonely. Tucker was becoming an invaluable friend, even if she hadn't spent too much time with him.

It was a fragile thing, this friendship. One that was going to shatter if he ever found out what had really brought her here.

"Listen," she heard herself say. "Tomorrow's Saturday. If you don't have to go in early, you could stop by? I have some eggs and bacon . . . I make a mean omelet. If you want to, I mean. It's okay if you don't."

She was rambling like a buffoon. Why hadn't her college offered a class in social interaction along with proper bedside manner?

"Sorry. Just wanted . . . didn't mean to put you on the spot . . . you know, forget about it. I'm sure you have—"

"Are you always this nervous when you invite someone to breakfast?"

"Yeah. No. I mean I don't—"

His rich laughter shut her up. She was making an ass of herself trying to do something nice to thank him for the meals, heater repair, and daily firewood delivery.

"I really wish I could take you up on your offer but I have an early shift. Rain check?"

"Yeah, sure. Anytime."

"Good night, then."

He was halfway back to his house before she closed the door and returned to her computer. She studied the screen, trying to focus on the grainy images and not on the rejection burning in her belly or the sadness it evoked. Tucker had a life. She couldn't expect him to spend all his free time with her. He had to work. She shouldn't take it personally.

But as loneliness settled around her, she took it very personally. Cursing, she stood and plucked the small Christmas tree from the table by the window and shoved it in the closet. She didn't need any more reminders of just how alone she truly was.

THIS TIME, WHEN Tucker walked back to his house, he didn't turn to see if Miranda was watching him. If she was, it would be enough to make him change his mind about her breakfast invitation.

Unlocking the door, he made his way down the hall to the shower. He did want to have breakfast with her, so why had he turned her down?

He flipped on the shower and leaned against the counter. His reflection mocked him. "You're a damned idiot."

That he was. He scrubbed his hand over his face. Having an early shift wasn't reason enough to reject Miranda. He had to eat regardless. It could have been with her.

But she was a tenant. A very temporary, week-by-week tenant. Getting any more mixed up with her wasn't smart.

Yet he'd asked her for dinner.

He wasn't stupid. There was a very juvenile part of him that had wanted her to feel the same rejection she'd slapped him with.

As he stripped off his clothes, he could have sworn he heard his reflection laugh at him, and with good reason. That kind of attitude certainly wasn't going to get him laid.

Chapter 7

Sunday

"I've been by the church and talked to Father Anatole," Michael Levi said, loosening his tie as he settled on the bed, shoes and all. "He's going to submit my request to the diocese, but it's not going to be an easy process."

"Do we have to go through all this? Can't we just get married in another church?" Jennifer settled beside him and rested her hand on his chest.

It had been a beer kind of day. He popped the top off the bottle he'd grabbed on his way in. Actually, it had been a whiskey kind of day, but he was fresh out. And he was sick of having the same conversation with Jennifer over and over. He loved her till death and beyond, but sometimes he wished she'd just let things be. Would understand him just a little more, the way Bethany had.

He sighed. "Because despite everything I've done in my life, I'm still Catholic. I can't enter into another marriage until the first has been annulled. It doesn't matter what church the service takes place in."

She was Catholic as well, but had never really practiced the religion so she couldn't fully grasp the rules and processes of their church. Her parents had divorced, something she constantly threw in his face. But her parents hadn't stepped foot in a church since her christening, and her mother hadn't been bound by guilt as he was. Breaking a sacrament was nothing to her.

But for him . . . it still meant something.

He swallowed a quarter of the bottle before turning his attention to Jennifer's crown of blond hair resting below his throat. Hopefully, all of this would be resolved soon and they'd finally be able to move toward a real future together—even though they'd been together for several years already.

"Have you told them yet?"

Michael looked at her reflection in the glass but didn't answer. Of course he hadn't told them. He didn't intend to until all the paperwork was finalized and the process was under way. Then maybe they'd see Jennifer as his future and not just his mistress.

Ignoring her question, he grabbed his jacket and dropped a kiss on Jennifer's forehead. "I'm going to take a drive. Clear my head before I head to the main house. See you Tuesday night?"

She nodded, looking absolutely pitiful. Leaving her was getting harder and harder, but in order to keep his family—especially his grandmother—from sniffing around, he had to carefully divide his time between the hotel and Levi estate. When he knew his grandmother, Ethel, was going to be around a lot, he stayed there. When she was busy, which was blessedly often, he came back to Jennifer, feeling more and more guilty with each new departure.

"I really would love to meet them," Jennifer whispered. "I hate feeling like a dirty secret."

"I know. I'm sorry." And he truly was. His mother would probably accept Jennifer the way she did everything else, with impeccable manners, a smile, and a lot of Southern hospitality. His dad would be reserved, watchful, wondering what all this might do to his career—and the career he still hoped Michael would step into.

Ethel, however, was going to be the hardest to win over. She was already talking about him moving into *her* home, and resuming his life with his wife and daughter. They didn't, *couldn't*, know yet that he was involved with someone, that he'd brought her here, and he wanted to keep it that way for a little while longer.

"Tuesday." He kissed away her pout. "I'll take you to a nice dinner. Just you and me."

She didn't look the least bit appeased when he left her and rode the elevator from the presidential suite to the lobby. As he waited for the valet to bring his car around, Michael pulled out his cell phone and dialed Bethany's number again. Like the three dozen times before, he got her answering machine. "Bethany, it's Michael. I know I'm the last person you ever want to talk to again, but I really need to see you. Please, call me back."

He tipped the valet and slid into his pristine, white Audi R8. He fastened his seat belt and pulled out of the hotel's parking lot. He still had an hour or so to kill before he would be expected at his grandmother's dinner table, so he didn't have a destination in mind and found himself driving aimlessly toward the waters of the Duvet River, his childhood stomping grounds.

Years of swinging on old tires and rope swings, fishing and skinny-dipping as he got older, led him there like a magnet. How long had he fantasized about getting away from backwards Christmas? Away from the aspirations of his family, running the small town since its inception? And now, all he could think about was returning here. Where his memories were the happiest and people respected him. Not just because of his bloodline, but because he mattered. Smiles went a lot further here than hundred-dollar bills stretched in Los Angeles.

He drove over the wooden bridge that connected the river to the old hermit Walt's place and cut the engine when the tires hit the snow-banked sands of the shore. He saw headlights behind him, but they turned in the opposite direction, leaving him alone. Make-out point. Another fond memory. Of course, back then, it used to be *on* Walt's place. But by the time Michael had reached make-out age, Old Walt had become too ornery to mess with and his friends had moved to the other side of the river.

He thought of Bethany. She'd loved this place. Bonfires during summer and beer guzzling with their friends. She'd been a good wife. Too good. The mundaneness of their Cleaver-like marriage had been too much for him. Had put too much on his shoulders. Earn all the money while she took care of the house. The potential kids she couldn't stop talking about. It had been nothing to her because she hadn't minded him living off his parents' money one bit.

He tried Bethany one more time, and when she didn't answer, tossed the cell phone into the passenger seat where it promptly slid onto the floor. Ignoring it, he climbed out of the car and moved to the water's edge. Careful of the ice accumulating on the mud, he sat on a pitted railroad tie and looked at the cluster of trees still standing tall and strong against the countless harsh winters they'd faced. Bethany had called it a giant fairy ring, had thought it was magical. He still remembered the night they'd discovered that magic for the first time.

Everything had changed in that moment. There'd been no going back. His entire future, dismantled and put back together that night with pieces created out of hormonal teenage mistakes. But at least they had Charlotte. He wouldn't have changed that outcome for anything in the world. Ten years old, and the apple of her daddy's eye.

A family of raccoons shuffled out of the woods to the empty fire pit, scavenging for food. He zipped his coat and tucked his hands in his pockets. He sat until the cold and snow drove him back to his car. Before he could close the door behind him, something gripped his arm. He was yanked from the seat like he weighed nothing at all, thrown into icy mud and left there, dazed.

"What the hell?" He pushed up onto his hands, but something—a boot?—connected with his ribs. The force of the blow rolled him to his side. "What are you doing?"

Michael struggled to his feet, ready to beat the living shit out of the bastard.

He swung, but before his fist could find its target, the hooded man ducked. When he straightened, his left hand curving overhead, the hood moved just enough to give Michael a glimpse of a long beard. It was askew. A fake? He tried to see the man's eyes, but something silver glinted in the moonlight seconds before a pipe crashed into his arm, then his leg.

Michael cried out and fell to his knees, gripping his

injured arm close to his stomach. "Take the car! Take it! It's yours!"

The pipe smashed into the side of his head, and as his brain clouded, he heard the distinct crack of his jaw breaking. Pain rolled through him. His stomach pitched violently and he spewed blood and vomit onto the ground. He tried to find his feet but the figure pressed his boot against Michael's head, digging his broken jaw into the mud.

"Whoever divorces his wife and marries another commits adultery against her." The pressure on his head was replaced by the sting of something cold around his neck. "Divorce will make your wife an adulteress. It would be kinder to make her a widow. She has done no wrong and should not have to pay for your crimes against her. What God has joined together, let no man put asunder."

His broken jaw and the wire cutting into his throat prevented him from answering. He gurgled, choked on his own blood. He clawed at the mud, trying to find a weapon. Something sliced into his good arm. The thwack of the blade cutting into him rang out in the still night.

Michael's cry of pain and outrage was nothing more than a moan. He curled into a ball, trying to make himself as small as possible as the blade sliced into his legs, his back.

The faces of his loved ones danced before his eyes. Bethany and Jennifer . . . and Charlotte. Sweet, sweet Charlotte. The women he'd loved most in his life and had let down so gravely.

His bellow was nothing more than a gurgle as he wished he could make amends for all the wrongs he'd done. In the distance, a coyote howled, a dog joined in on Michael's attempt to wail in agony, turning it into a chorus.

"Pray the good Lord has mercy on your soul, for your death will finally bring peace and a chance at happiness to a tormented soul."

The man's fist gripped Michael's hair, pulling his head back toward his ankles and snapping his spine. The wire cut off his air. Michael was going to die. As the world began to fade and spots danced before his eyes, Michael's gaze found the circle of trees. The giant fairy ring. In the center stood his sweet Charlotte. Her bright smile and shy wave brought him peace as he exhaled his last breath.

Chapter 8

FROM HER LAPTOP, Miranda watched the grainy image of Father Anatole climbing into his sedan and pulling slowly out of his driveway. She checked the clock over the kitchen sink and took a deep breath. For two and a half days, she'd watched his dull routine. Wake up at five, some brief exercises on the floor by his bed—push-ups, sit-ups, a few poses of what might have been middle-aged-man yoga. A quick breakfast, always the same thing. Boiled egg, blender drink, and what looked like oatmeal. Shower. By six-fifteen, he was out the door, not to return home again until evening, where the routine was just as mundane.

It was just past eight in the evening, and he hadn't yet come home. It was what she was hoping for. He was usually home by seven, but tonight, the town was scheduled to have a full fireworks display at the park in Town Square. The church might finally be empty . . .

She'd have to hurry. The church was close enough that she could be back before the fireworks were over if she was quick about it.

Twenty-five minutes later, she was standing at the side of St. Catherine's, wet snow and icy wind pelting her stinging cheeks. She'd scoped out the chapel, found it empty, but had also found Anatole's office locked. She was no lock picker. Cursing her luck, she'd headed back outside and now stared at the window in front of her. She'd counted twice to make sure it was the right one. If she was wrong, she'd have wasted precious time.

She had no choice but to go for it. There was no telling when she'd get another opportunity like this. Looking around, she blinked against the blowing snow, making certain there was no one around. Finding no one, she stood on her tiptoes and tested the window. It was unlocked.

Thankfully, the sill wasn't that high off the ground. She hoisted herself onto the ledge and shimmied forward. Just before her hands reached the floor, someone grabbed her calves and yanked her out of the window.

TUCKER WALKED HIS patrol of Main Street as the fireworks display lit up the sky. As he passed each family and spectator, he handed out a flyer with Ricky's picture on it, his old training putting a pit of despair in his stomach. Forty-eight hours. That was the window of hope for finding a missing person. Ricky Schneider had been missing for a week now. And today, he'd found out that the blood in the alley was a match to Ricky's DNA. He'd spent a good portion of his afternoon at the Schneider house, explaining the new development. Tanya had surprised him with an outburst of tears he hadn't thought her capable of.

Stan hadn't said a word.

Tucker had every intention of bringing the asshole in for questioning but was pretty damned certain the bastard wouldn't cooperate one bit unless Tucker showed up with a warrant for his arrest.

And since he had nothing to base a warrant on . . .

What a fucking mess.

All hopes of Ricky being a runaway had disintegrated. All Tucker could hope for now was that he was hurt and unable to get help.

But there'd been so much damned blood.

"Merry Christmas," he said to a passing couple. "Please take this and call the number at the bottom if you see this boy."

He passed them a flyer and watched with disgust as they smiled, walked on, and promptly threw the paper in the trash without so much as glancing at it.

No one ever thought *they'd* be the one to see a missing person. To have information. That was why those forty-eight hours were rarely successful. People just didn't bother with things that didn't concern them personally.

His phone buzzed. It was dispatch. Frowning, he answered. "Shannon?"

"No, it's Lisa. Shannon went home sick. Sorry, Chief, tried to radio but you didn't respond so I had to call your private line."

Tucker cursed. He'd left his radio in the car to charge while he patrolled. "No problem. What is it?"

"Got a call from St. Catherine's. Apparently there was an attempted break-in. Father Anatole asked that we send someone right away, but I didn't know who you wanted to pull off their post to take the call."

Tucker felt his frown deepen. "I'll take it. You said attempted?"

"The priest caught the culprit in the act so you might want to hurry. Said he's got things handled till you come but he's not exactly spry."

"On my way. Will radio in when I get there."

"Ten four."

The call went dead and Tucker put the phone back in his pocket, already heading toward the cruiser he'd left parked in front of City Hall.

This night just kept getting longer.

So much for keeping her cover.

It had been twenty minutes since Father Anatole had caught Miranda Winnie-the-Pooh-ing it through his office window. She'd been stupid to think she could successfully break in, and the little cameras in her bag were making her twitch. Hopefully, the police wouldn't check her bag when they arrived or she'd have a lot of explaining to do. But she'd been caught trying to break and enter. She was probably screwed.

And she'd only made it halfway through the window.

If she could just get Anatole and his minions to find a distraction, she still had a shot at placing the cameras. But how the hell was she supposed to do that? Anatole hadn't taken his eyes off her since he'd escorted her into his office and told her to sit while he called the police.

Her guts were a knot of nervous threads. Frayed threads. Really, really *old* frayed threads. Every time Father Anatole's pacing by the window brought him closer to her seat, she tensed, and every time she told herself that he didn't scare the piss out of her, her insides gave another little tremor to remind her that she was a liar.

His three deacons stood at the office door, should she try to escape, and talked among themselves. Distracted a bit. But not Father Anatole. He was watching her like a hawk. As though running was even an option. Her legs would never obey *that* command. She was pretty sure she'd just melt into one of the cracks in the scuffed plank flooring, one big boneless pool of terror.

She looked at the cracks. Might not be such a bad getaway . . .

What a wasted, disastrous night this had turned in to. And on top of it all, she was probably going to end up spending the night in jail.

Father Anatole stopped pacing to study her better. "You're sure we haven't met before?"

It was the third time he'd asked her that since pulling her out of the window. "I told you, we met the other day."

"Yes, and there was something familiar about you then, too." He fingered his salt-and-pepper goatee, the glint in his eye letting her know he wasn't buying one word. "You still haven't told me why you felt compelled to break into the church."

Since yanking her out of his window, he'd asked her that repeatedly as well. She still didn't know what to tell him. Why hadn't she come up with a story before coming here?

Because your brain doesn't have room for anything else anymore. Father Anatole has taken up each and every cell . . .

"I checked out of my room, and turns out I can't leave town yet," she lied. "All the motels are booked and I just needed a place to sleep until a room opens up."

Another of the deacons moved to her side. "They *are* booked, Father. My sister and her brood were forced to stay with me." A circumstance he obviously disdained, given the look of constipation those words evoked on his face.

Anatole still didn't look like he bought her story, but now that the deacon had backed her up, he didn't seem as eager to call her a liar anymore. She said a silent prayer of thanks for that small blessing. She needed to get the heck out of here and regroup, figure out her next move. It was going to be a lot harder to maneuver around Anatole now that she'd put herself on his radar.

A car door slammed outside, saving her from another awkward lie, and Anatole rushed back to the window, followed by his deacons. As they watched through the glass, she fumbled in her bag, clutched a camera between her fingers, and quickly cupped it.

She stood, feigning interest in what was happening outside, and gingerly reached up and pushed the small camera between two books on the top shelf behind her. Her heart pounding, she elbowed her way between the men to shake off any traces of guilt that might be cloaking her.

A man stepped around the front of a squad car. Her body sent a jolt of awareness long before her eyes could detect who the newcomer was. This was just getting better and better. It was Tucker.

Of course it was Tucker. Her luck wouldn't have it any other way.

Regardless, he was a welcome sight. At this point, jail was a much safer place than here with Father Anatole. She glanced at the camera again. It was noticeable, but small enough that it shouldn't draw immediate attention. She hoped.

Tucker disappeared from view, and a few seconds later, she could hear his footsteps coming down the hall. She braced herself, swallowed the bile of indigestion building in her throat, and sat back down in her chair, her gaze nervously dancing around the doorway. He didn't look at all happy when he appeared.

He didn't seem to notice her as he stepped into the

room, the deacons partially blocking her from his line of sight. He shook Anatole's hand. "Father."

"Chief." Father Anatole rubbed the deep lines between his eyebrows.

The deacons moved aside and Tucker finally noticed her, his head jerking in surprise. "Miranda?"

She offered a little wave of her fingers. "Hi."

He looked back at the priest. "This is who you caught climbing through your window?"

"Long story," she muttered, silently pleading with him to get her the hell out of here. She braced herself for more questions, and more lies. She despised liars and hated that she'd become one, but she didn't know whom she could trust.

Tucker removed his hat and turned on her. "All right. Start explaining."

Mr. Friendly Deacon repeated the story she'd told them. "She didn't know we kept the chapel doors unlocked."

"She was breaking into my office, which I do keep locked, however," Anatole added.

"So she broke in through your window?"

Anatole's gaze narrowed. "I sometimes crack it open for fresh air. I must not have locked it back."

Tucker's glare sent a heat wave over her. She was about to find out if melting through the cracks in the church floor would get her out of this mess. "Looking for a bed, huh?"

"I—um—"

He opened his mouth, closed it again, and faced the priest. "Do you want to press charges?" he asked, saving her from an explanation she couldn't possibly give in front of the people she'd lied to.

"I don't see why that would be necessary. If she was

looking for a place to sleep, then there really was no harm done," Friendly Deacon said.

Father Anatole narrowed his gaze. "No need to penalize anyone for looking for a place to stay. Nothing was taken, and she didn't break the window she was crawling into. If all she really needs is a bed, maybe you could simply help her locate one."

"Pretty sure that won't be a problem," Tucker drawled, shooting her a Lucy-you-have-some-'splaining-to-do look. But since he didn't seem on the brink of giving her away, she stood and moved a bit closer to him.

His hand clamped around her elbow like a vise. The tingling jolts of awareness were quickly chased away by his cold, hard stare.

"Let's go." He motioned toward the door, stopping to look back at the priest as he shoved his hat back on his head. "I'll have someone stop by tomorrow to get a statement so it's on record."

Father Anatole waved him away. "No need. I'd rather just drop the matter altogether."

Tucker muttered an insincere thank-you and ushered Miranda down the hall and outside. She followed him as fast as her nearly frozen legs would allow.

Why had she ever thought she could do this alone?

Tucker swung open the squad car's back door and helped her in. Her gaze settled on the steel mesh barrier separating her from the front of the vehicle. He might not be arresting her, but she certainly felt like a criminal.

"So." He slid behind the wheel and started the car. He tossed his hat onto the passenger seat and ran his fingers through thick, black hair. "Why were you really sneaking into the church at this hour?"

She glanced out the back window and found Anatole watching her from his office. A shiver snaked down her spine and she spun back around. Tucker was watching her through the rearview mirror, his scowl revealing fine lines on his forehead that hadn't been there the last time she'd seen him.

She blinked against the massive headache creeping from the back of her skull to behind her eyes. "I screwed up. Can't we just leave it as a colossal case of bad judgment?"

"I want answers, damn it, and I want them now. You were intent on taking his picture the other day, then nearly keeled over after you got away from him. Now he's catching you breaking and entering. What are you really doing in my town, Miranda?"

"I didn't technically break in. They caught me before I got more than my shoulders in the window." She held his gaze in the mirror. He didn't show the slightest hint of amusement over her smart-assery. He was rightfully pissed off at her and she didn't have anything to tell him that he was going to readily believe. "Is this the part where I ask for a lawyer?"

"You're not under arrest. Yet."

She shrugged, exhausted and frustrated that all her planning had come to nothing so far. That she was the one sitting in the back of a squad car while Father Anatole was still free.

Soon, she was going to prove the truth. That Father Anatole wasn't a God-fearing man of the cloth.

He was a goddamned murderer, a serial killer, and she was the only one in this town who knew it.

Chapter 9

"YOUR NAME REALLY even Miranda?" Tucker blasted the cruiser's heat and directed his gaze to the rearview at the lady who, a few days ago, had been the first woman to catch his eye in months. Now she was a potential criminal in his town—whether Father Anatole pressed charges or not. She'd still been breaking and entering.

"Yes." She met his gaze in the mirror, and he quickly turned his concentration to driving through the haze of white sticking to the windshield before being flicked away by the wipers. The cycle continued over and over again, nearly hypnotizing as the squeak of the rubber blades shaved the snow from glass.

He could hear her scooting around on the vinyl seats and risked another glance. She pressed her head to the window and closed her eyes. He pulled into his drive, jumped out and opened the gate, then got back in. She still had her eyes closed as he drove around his house toward her cottage.

He was tired, and his gaze strayed again to the rearview. Her mouth slightly parted and her breath fogged the window. She was just as hypnotizing as the snow, but at least looking at her was waking up his body.

"Pretend to sleep all you want, Miranda. You're not leaving this car until I have answers."

She said nothing.

It was almost a blessing when Lisa's voice crackled through the radio and shattered the silence. "You there, Chief?"

He pressed the button on the mic clipped near his shoulder. "I'm here."

"I know it's late, but I need you up at Old Walt's place on North River Road."

"He die or something?" Wouldn't be a surprise. The crotchety old man was older than God. Tucker glanced at the radio clock. It was just after midnight and all he wanted to do was climb into bed and get a little shut-eye. But when a department consisted of a total of five uniforms during off-season and a mere twenty this time of year, late nights weren't unusual.

"Since he made the call, I doubt it. But someone did. Said there's a body on his property."

Tucker let that settle over him for a moment. "Hiker?"

They didn't get a lot of hikers this time of year, but he supposed it was possible someone had gotten too friendly with the Great Smoky Mountains wildlife.

"Don't think so. Walt made it sound a bit more ominous than that."

His mind flickered to the bloody scene behind the library, to Ricky Schneider. His stomach clenched. Was it possible he'd finally found the missing kid?

"He sounded pretty freaked out, Chief," Lisa's voice said. "I've already called Andy. He'll be meeting you there."

"What exactly did Walt say?"

"Just that there was a body on his property. Said it looked like some kind of religious ritual or something."

Miranda gave a soft "No . . ." from the backseat. He glanced at her, saw her mouth agape, her body rigid.

He pressed the mic again. "ETA ten minutes max. Let Andy know."

"Roger that."

Tucker turned to look at Miranda. Her teeth worked over her thumbnail as she stared blankly back at him. "You all right?"

"Does this . . ." He could hear her swallow before she cleared her throat. "Does this sort of thing happen often here?"

"We get our share of hiking accidents."

"In this weather? That woman . . . she said it was religious. "

"It's Christmastime in a town called Christmas, Miranda. There's religion everywhere."

As Miranda tried to open the locked door, the door handle popped. He climbed out and opened it for her. "This isn't over," he said, helping her from the car. "Tomorrow, you will tell me who you are and what you're really doing here."

Miranda looked up at him, her face pale and her lips quivering. She pulled out of his grasp and stepped back, allowing him room to climb back into the car.

"I mean it," he said. "Don't even think about disappearing."

She gave a faint nod as he climbed back into the squad car and headed toward North River Road and Walt's place.

THE MINUTE TUCKER pulled out of the drive, Miranda bolted back down the drive toward the side streets and the garage where the Rover was parked. "North River Road, North River Road," she chanted, forgoing the elevator and taking the stairs two at a time.

She threw the tarp off the Rover, unlocked it, and shoved the tarp inside before jumping behind the wheel. She quickly punched the street name into her GPS. Thankfully, the system found the road and mapped directions. Slamming the door, she squealed out of the garage. Her heart was thudding, drowning out the sounds outside her closed window.

A body. Religion. It was all she could do to stay focused on the snowy road and not plow into any of the shiny lampposts flickering green and red as the electronic voice told her to take a left turn at the next light.

Her mind played over all the photos she'd collected. Three men, each killed on a Sunday, every one of them posed in a religious setting. It couldn't be happening again. Anatole had gotten away with murder. He'd fled Ohio a free man. He had no reason to start killing again.

"In a quarter mile, turn right on North River Road," the voice told her from the dash.

She replayed the conversation she'd overheard. Had Lisa mentioned whether the body was male or female? She couldn't remember. White-knuckling the steering wheel, she turned onto North River Road, her knees rubber as she tapped the brakes and tried to get her bearings. Which way from here? She took a left. Found a dead end. Backtracked. At the end of the other side of the road, she saw the faint red hue of taillights bouncing away from her.

She chased after them.

Chapter 10

THE DUVET RIVER appeared through the black trees, and the cruiser bounced along the rutted track Old Walt called a driveway. Tucker pulled to a stop behind the squad car already parked beside a rickety toolshed where Walt's watchdog furiously barked at Bowen.

Tucker popped the trunk, grabbed his duffel bag, and worked his way through the snowdrifts to where his lieutenant stood with Walt, trying to calm the hound.

" 'Bout time you got here." The pipe clamped between Walt's yellowed teeth bobbed as he spoke. He was an old man who looked closer to ancient, with the personality of the Grinch's first cousin. Gray hair hung over his eyes and bags of skin drooped from his chin like the jowls of his old dog. "Called that dispatch of yours three times and it still took over an hour for anyone to get here."

"Twenty minutes," Andy corrected with a nod of greeting in Tucker's direction.

Walt glared at the lieutenant. "If you had gotten your

ass up here the first time I called, you might have seen whoever put that body on my lake."

"Let's get to it," Tucker muttered, too tired to deal with the ornery old shit.

Andy pulled his flashlight from the hook on his belt and let Walt lead the way a short distance down a little-used path. When the river came into view, he stopped and trained the beam on a clearing in the snow, protected from the weather by a canopy of trees that acted as a natural roof. Tucker's gaze followed the light until it stopped at the thickest clump of trees.

A body lay slumped against the base of the largest oak and Tucker was immediately transported to his past in Chicago. Every day, a new body, a new broken family.

Anger boiled in him that he was facing the same thing here, in Christmas. Whether foul play was involved, he could tell from the placement of the body that he wasn't dealing with a natural death. The best he could hope for was a suicide, because otherwise, he was likely dealing with murder. Possibly Ricky's murder.

As they made their way closer, Walt stayed back. "Ain't going near it again. Still can't get that stink off me."

"You touched it?" Tucker snapped. He pulled a box of gloves from his duffel bag and handed a pair to Bowen before sliding a pair on himself.

Walt yanked the pipe from his mouth and thrust it at him. "Not like I was expecting a corpse right here by Trapper's favorite pissing spot, now was I? Didn't see the blood. Tried to shake him awake."

Tucker sighed. So much for an unmolested crime scene. He pulled his camera from the duffel, stuffed a few plastic evidence bags into his pockets, and began snapping photos of everything in the vicinity.

Footprints, most likely Walt's, zigzagged around the

trees and stopped beside the body before retreating back the way they'd come. Paw prints circled the scene far enough away that it looked as though even the old guard dog hadn't wanted to get too close.

Tucker knelt beside the body. Andy squatted across from him. The body was clothed in a silky shirt, buttoned to his chin, an awkwardly knotted tie, and a suit. Every piece of his clothing white. Blood soaked the collar at his throat and dark hair hung over his eyes. His head had fallen forward, hiding his face from Bowen's light, and in his hands Tucker saw what had made Walt mention religion. A huge crucifix, easily six inches long, lay clasped between his hands against the man's stomach, and a Bible lay closed on his lap.

Not suicide.

Tucker's gut twisted. But it also wasn't Ricky. He let that thought exhale in a puff of relief.

He picked up a leaf. The splash of red spotting it was tacky, not exactly fresh, but it wasn't old enough to have dried, either. Andy gently eased the man's head back, revealing a massive cut around the neck and a very obviously broken jaw.

"Don't touch him!" Tucker snapped.

Hands in the air, Andy backed away apologetically. "Christ above." All the color drained from his face. "That's Michael Levi. The mayor's son."

Fuck a duck. "You sure?"

"Yeah. He looks exactly the same as he did in high school. Haven't seen him in years. He used to come to St. Catherine's every Sunday with his family. Jesus." Andy looked uneasy, and possibly ill. "We don't really get murders here, Tucker. I'm sure you noticed that. Maybe we oughta bring in the TBI?"

Tucker shook his head. One scene wasn't going to interest the Tennessee Bureau of Investigation. "It's all right. I've done this before." More times than he cared to count . . . even if he'd been out of the game for seven years and felt rusty as hell. "Call Doc Sam. Get her down here ASAP so she can send the body to Knoxville for an autopsy."

Tucker took pictures of the Bible and crucifix but wouldn't take them as evidence until the doc had a chance to see the scene as is. He stood and studied the surroundings again. How the hell had someone gotten up here, placed the man's body against the trees, and gotten out again without leaving so much as a single footprint on the dirt-packed ground surrounding the body?

Michael Levi wasn't a small man by any means. Easily over six feet tall. Whoever had done this had either been really strong, or would have had to use something to carry the body.

Tucker looked to Walt. "How 'bout you tell me what went down here tonight?"

Walt chewed thoughtfully on his pipe for several seconds. "I let Trapper out to piss about thirty minutes ago and he started raising one hell of a ruckus 'round his pissing tree. Figured he'd caught whiff of a damned tourist who couldn't read all them no trespassing signs I put out. Grabbed my shotgun and came out to find this."

"And Trapper didn't alert you that anyone had been here earlier? No idea when the body was put here?"

"Dog's hearing's worse than mine. Nose can't be beat, but his ears . . . nah, I didn't hear nothing." Walt tapped the hound's head. "Last time I was out here was before supper and wasn't nobody here then, that's for sure."

"What time was supper?"

" 'Round six or so."

"Did you see footprints? Drag marks? Anything else left behind by whoever was here?"

Walt spit. "Look around, Chief. Anything that mighta been here's already been washed off by tonight's snow."

Tucker held tight to his frustration. "I realize that. But there might have been when you found—"

Something rustled in the trees behind them. Tucker lifted his light, shone it on the deep recesses of the copse, directly onto Miranda's pale face.

Her eyes grew wide, and he could see her preparing to run. But as he stood to go after her, she surprised him by not running away from the scene, but directly toward it.

"Son of a bitch!" Turning, he raced toward her, catching her when she stopped at the tree line. He grabbed her arm and yanked her to his chest. "What the hell are you doing?"

"I'm sorry, I had to—it's—I needed to see for myself." She was staring at the body, trembling, ghostly pale. Her words were whispered, and when he spun her to face him, he saw tears in her eyes. "Oh God, no. I think I'm going to be sick."

He hustled her back toward the path before she could contaminate his crime scene. He held her hair, but turned his back to her, trying to save a bit of her dignity as she deposited the contents of her stomach into the pristine snow.

"Who the hell is she?" Andy stopped beside them.

Tucker ignored him. Miranda wiped her mouth as she turned to face him, tears glistening in her eyes and rushing down her cheeks.

Tucker gave her a slight shake. "What the hell are you doing here, Miranda?"

He tried to read her, but her face gave no explanation for her outburst. Her teeth chattered so loudly that he couldn't make out her mumbled words. He guided her to the cruiser and popped the trunk, pulled out his spare coat, and slid it over her parka.

"Go home, Andy. No sense in both of us waiting here."

"Who is she, boss? Want me to take her in?"

"Nah. She's my problem for now." He fished inside Miranda's coat and came up empty. "Where are your keys, Miranda?"

"C-car."

"And where'd you park the car?"

She didn't answer. Tucker swore. "She drives a black Range Rover. Find it. Make sure it gets taken back to my place. She's one of my renters."

Andy looked confused, one eye narrowed, the other brow raised. "You're letting her stay?"

"Just do it." His patience worn thin, Tucker popped open the back door of his cruiser and none too gently placed Miranda inside.

He glanced over his shoulder. "You too, Walt. Get on home. Take Trapper with you. I'll make sure your property is violated as little as possible."

The old man spit again and glowered. "I don't want no reporters sticking their noses 'round here tomorrow, either. You keep this under your belt or there'll be a lot of journalists with pencils crammed up their asses."

"Not smart to make threats around an officer of the law. Go on now."

Walt grumbled his way back toward his house, and Tucker looked down at Miranda. She wouldn't look him in the eye.

"Did you know that man, Miranda?"

"No."

"So you just reacted that way because you saw a dead body?"

"Yes. No. I need a minute to think!"

To hell with that. "Think about what? You followed me to a crime scene and nearly contaminated the shit out of it. The time for games and stories is long past, Miranda. Why the hell are you really in my town?"

Her wide eyes searched his face, and Tucker stood still, watching her, waiting her out. "If you'll take me to the cottage, I can show you something you might want to see."

Show him something? "Are you trying to fuck with my head, woman? Show me what?"

She glanced toward the body, invisible now beneath the shadows of trees and night. "Did he have a burn on his face? Between his eyes?"

Other than the broken jaw and sliced throat, he hadn't yet had time to detail anything about the victim's face. "Why would you think he did?"

"Just look. If he does, then I'll know I'm right."

"Right about what?"

"I need to know." She held his gaze. "Please."

Tucker clenched his teeth. "Move your legs."

She looked as though she wouldn't obey, then slowly swung her legs inside the car. He slammed the door with more force than necessary.

He left her there and returned to the body. The packed dirt beneath the trees was now becoming muddy from the light layer of blowing snow. He knelt and rested his elbows on his knees, his gut churning as he imagined the forthcoming conversation he was going to have with the mayor. Telling someone his son had been murdered was something he'd hoped he'd never have to do again. That he was going to be the Reaper's messenger tonight and leave a family bereft was giving him an ulcer.

He would be breaking every damned rule in the book if he touched the body, but he suspected Miranda knew something about all this, and if playing her little game was going to make her speak up, he'd play. For a little while.

The white suit jacket pooled around Michael like a silky blanket, soiled with mud and blood and a few bits of pine straw. Gently, Tucker pushed the hair from the pale face, revealing wide green eyes frozen open. He shone the beam of his light over him.

At first, the only things he saw were the man's blue-tinged skin and those eyes. He held his arm above his head, changing the position of the light so he wouldn't have to touch anything more than the strands of hair his fingers had brushed.

And there it was, burned into the center of the man's forehead. The sign of the cross.

What the hell was going on in his town?

Chapter 11

FROM THE BACKSEAT of the police cruiser, Miranda could hear Tucker talking on his radio even before she could see him step from the darkness onto the dirt road. But she couldn't make out what he was saying. Had he seen the burn? Would he even tell her if he had? She hated putting her trust in someone she barely knew, someone in a line of work that had let her down more times than she cared to count.

But what choice did she have? This was *his* town. She didn't have any connections here. And after what she'd just seen, keeping to herself was no longer an option. The only way she could get the details she needed was to trust Tucker with the information she'd been gathering since her return to the States.

And hope like hell that he'd be different.

Detective Langley, the lead detective in Dayton, had listened to her suspicions for all of ten seconds. Once he'd confirmed that the priest had been out of town when one of the murders had occurred, Miranda had been chastised for wasting the department's time and money, before being dismissed. It hadn't mattered that she'd talked to parishioners in the neighboring towns who'd confirmed that there were several hours unaccounted for. Hours that would have allowed Father Anatole to murder and pose the bodies. The detective had talked to the same people and many more.

But he'd had his man—one that would certainly make him look better to the city than arresting a man in cloth would have. So now an innocent man was sitting in prison. And then Father Anatole had disappeared. And she'd tracked him here. And now . . . it was happening again.

Tucker opened the rear door and peered down at her. "Want to explain how you knew about that burn?"

"Take me to the cottage," she said. "I'll tell you everything."

"How 'bout you just tell me now, or would you prefer to wait until after I've booked your ass for obstruction?"

Anger lined his eyes and forehead, and she could tell that whatever he'd seen had disturbed him a good deal. She understood how he felt. She'd seen only photos of such scenes and still had nightmares consistently.

"I can't prove to you that my story is true unless you take me to the cottage," she said.

Fatigue shadowed the small, hollow curve above his sharp cheekbones. "You better be damned sure whatever you have to show and tell is worth me leaving my crime scene in someone else's hands."

She swallowed, thinking of her pitiful stack of clippings that might now become her saving grace. "It could save lives."

He pressed the button on his mic. "Bowen?" he said, releasing a sigh that suggested she'd pressed his last button of patience. "Turn around."

Miranda pulled her key from her inside jacket pocket, unlocked the door, and stepped inside her cottage. Tucker took off his hat and tossed it on the small table in the breakfast nook. It looked as though he was wearing every minute that had passed since his bedtime on his face and shoulders.

"All right. Make this good."

Her battered backpack sat on the floor of the narrow hall's closet. She grabbed it, dumped the contents on the sofa, and retrieved from the messy pile a worn accordion file folder that looked ready to fall apart. Praying she wasn't making a huge mistake, she handed it to him and made her way to the kitchenette for caffeine to keep them both awake and alert while she spilled her guts.

While he pulled the contents out one by one, she tapped her fingers on the counter. The moment the percolating coffeepot stopped, she snatched the two cups out of the draining board, filled them, and took a seat by Tucker in the nook, passing him his drink.

He took a sip and looked up from the newspaper clippings. "What do the Rosary Killings in Ohio have to do with my town?"

"The Rosary Killer struck on three consecutive Sundays. Each murder held a religious aspect." She fiddled with the chipped edges of the table, her heart racing now that she had both coffee and Tucker's attention in hand. How much did she tell him?

She sighed. Best to start at the beginning.

"Almost two years ago," she began, "a man was killed in Dayton—"

"Where you're from?"

She shook her head. "I came here from Ohio, but I'm from California . . ." She carefully laid out three photographs, each portraying a brutally murdered man, the mark of the cross burned into each of their foreheads, a crucifix clutched in their hands, a long rosary chain placed somewhere on their bodies, and a Bible somewhere near or on them. Other than that, there weren't many similarities. But the one glimpse of the Bible she'd seen at the river . . . she'd known in her soul that it was linked to Anatole. "That man at the river . . . he's part of this. Number four. Look. Recognize anything?"

She pointed to the Bibles in the photos and the crucifix held in the victims' hands. "Just like at the river, isn't it?"

His face paled just a bit, and she knew he was seeing in these clippings another version of the horror he'd seen tonight. What the photos didn't show, but she was sure that man's autopsy report would, were the throats that had been garroted so deeply that only a fraction of the men's spines had kept their heads on their shoulders. Or the gashes on their arms and legs that had kept them too weak to fight. Or the broken spine that had kept them from escaping. All things Miranda was certain he'd discover about this victim.

"After seeing that man . . . I don't think he's going to be the last murder you see, Tucker. This started in Dayton, and the same man who killed these men there has come here."

His gaze remained on the clipping. "This have anything to do with why Father Anatole caught you trying to get into his office?"

"Yeah, but I didn't know . . . Never mind. Just look." Her palms were sweating and she was pretty sure she was about fifteen seconds away from a stroke. She saw the same look of skepticism in his eyes that she'd seen in Detective Langley's. He'd chosen not to believe her half-cocked story—as he'd called it. Was Tucker going to come to the same decision and dismiss her proof? How many more men would die before someone took her seriously?

"The one at Walt's place? You knew he'd be burned."

"I saw the Bible. It's too coincidental that you'd have a killing here, with a freaking Bible . . . if . . . if you found the burn on his head . . . Tucker, please believe me. The cross burned on that man's head was a tainted version of a blessing. A sign that holy water would have scorched him because he was uncleansed of sin. All of these victims had the same mark. He's creating his own perverted version of the Catholic sacraments."

His almost-black eyes narrowed and watched her until she squirmed in her seat. "Let's say this isn't all bullshi—"

"It's not—"

"You're talking about a serial killer. You're saying his MO revolves around the Catholic sacraments . . . which he began in Dayton according to all these." He flicked the clippings as though they were worth nothing more than discarded candy wrappers.

"He did." Keeping the disdain out of her voice was virtually impossible. Tucker was proving to be no different than Detective Langley; looking at her like she was crazy.

"And you just assumed he'd start all over again in a new town?"

She swallowed and her dry throat burned. It was as though all the liquid in her throat had traveled to her eyes. They itched with the need to cry, because in all honesty, his question poked a very sensitive spot with her.

"No," she whispered. Had she anticipated any such thing, she would've come far more prepared. But she'd assumed he wouldn't risk being caught now that someone else had been convicted for his crimes. That was three months ago. Throughout the entire trial and investigation, the killings had stopped. If Anatole hadn't planned to stop killing, why had he waited three months since the verdict to begin again? "I came here to see if . . . I don't know. Maybe he would slip up, get comfortable . . . give me something to take back to Dayton as proof. I never . . . I never suspected he'd start again. At least not someplace as small as this where it's harder to hide."

"Just going on a whim here, but I'm guessing you're talking about Anatole. That's why all the pictures? The B and E? The man walks with a cane and you think he's capable of this?"

"You make him sound like a crippled old man. He's not. He's a very healthy man in his late fifties, and he's strong."

And she'd seen with her own two eyes that he was religious about working out every morning.

"Okay, but he still depends on a cane. That's going to hinder his movements."

"You'd be surprised. He was Bobby's—the convicted man's—priest in Dayton. They were friends. They worked out together. Please don't believe for a minute that he's feeble." She removed her jacket and wished like hell that she could turn the air on. No matter what the temperature outside was, she was beginning to sweat. "When I heard the lady on your radio mention religion and dead body in the same sentence, my gut knew. I had to see. But until that moment, no. I didn't assume he was killing again."

"You're basically telling me you think I have a serial killer in my town," he said. "One who kills men."

"I know it's strange, but it's not unheard of." She gestured to the clippings. "Obviously, since all these were men, too."

As she sat back down, he held up the last article she'd clipped. The one of Bobby being carted off back to jail after the verdict had been read. Handcuffed, head down.

"Look, I appreciate that you believe everything you're telling me," Tucker said, cooler, if possible, than he'd been before. "But all you're giving me to go on is a priest who lived where the murders occurred and is now in my town when we get our first murder in decades. The same could be said about you, showing up in town just before a man is killed."

"We both know you don't suspect me, Tucker. You saw what was done to that man and I'm not strong enough to do *that*."

She could tell by the look on his face that she was right. He'd very likely already tried her in his head and found her incapable. She was counting on that, anyway. Getting herself locked up wasn't going to do anyone any good. Especially Bobby.

"For someone who didn't suspect anything, you sure were ready to show me all this."

The overhead light dimmed and cast him in a shadow that made him look like someone out of the Old West. Stubble lined his sharp cheekbones as they sucked in when he sipped his coffee, and she was having a hard time thinking straight beneath those damnable eyes of his. They were so piercing, she felt exposed, emotionally stripped, and extremely vulnerable. She decided it was best to be as honest as possible without giving too much away.

"I knew there was a slight chance I'd have to explain what I was doing."

"Did you lie about being a nurse? You really a reporter or something?"

Let him think what he would, as long as he listened. His assumption might just be her salvation, as long as she didn't outright lie about it.

"Bobby was a lawyer who was in the wrong place at the wrong time, but it wasn't a coincidence," she said, skating right over his question. "Someone made sure he was seen in those places and turned him in when the cops got too close to the truth."

"Which is?"

"Someone with a *calling from God* who he feels will be better served cleansing the Earth of the wicked than helping save their souls through something as simple as confession and prayer."

He drummed his thumbs on the table and stared at a photo of Father Anatole standing outside the courthouse beside Bobby. "So, Father Anatole. Was he ever suspected?"

Miranda took a sip of her cooling coffee and shrugged. "Only because I demanded they listen to me. But he was off their radar almost before I'd finished talking to the department."

She tried to read his face for signs that he might be even the least bit inclined to believe her. She saw only exhaustion. Terrified that he'd lose interest in her story before she'd had a chance to explain everything, she handed him one photo at a time.

She set out stacks of clippings and photos. "Baptism. Confession. Holy Communion." She swallowed. "Those three were completed in Dayton. Confirmation. Marriage. Anointing the sick. Holy orders. Those were left undone."

"Where do you see that? I see nothing here that specifies any sacraments being recreated."

"The Dayton police found something that led them to believe that's what was happening. I wasn't privy to those files. All I know is that this murder looks a lot like those. If you want the facts, you'll have to get them from the police files."

She took a deep breath before continuing. "After what I saw tonight, I'm terrified he's going to finish re-creating them right here in your town, with *your* people. If he is, more men will die. The Rosary Killer struck on Sundays. The man by the lake was killed tonight . . . on a Sunday. You have the chance to stop him before he frames someone else and disappears. Again."

She held her breath as he pulled the last stack of clippings toward him and slid one from the bottom. "Nothing you have proves this Bobby Harley guy isn't guilty of all charges."

"Isn't that dead man in the woods proof enough?" She searched her mind for anything that might erase the look of doubt on his face.

"It could be a copycat."

"It's not." She glared at him, fatigue making her temper and patience short.

After what seemed an eternity, he shut his eyes and sighed. "I'll have to contact the department in Dayton, but nothing here proves that Father Anatole is anything more than a grumpy man who came here from Dayton, just as you did." His dark eyes fluttered open and nailed her with a glare that sent a shiver of apprehension up her spine.

"I know you have no reason to believe me. I'm not a cop, and you don't know me from Adam. I get that. But please, please keep an open mind," she said. "If I'm right, but you ignore me, more men could die here in your town. Are you willing to risk that?"

Chapter 12

THE POLICE DEPARTMENT'S break room was warm
enough to allow Tucker to remove his jacket as he sipped
his coffee and tried to figure out what to do about the
woman in his office. He could have left her at the cottage, had her come in later when they were functioning
on at least a couple hours' sleep. Instead, he'd insisted
she accompany him so he could make a copy of her
files for his records. Granted, he hadn't actually insisted
anything. But when she'd refused to let him take her
files, she'd volunteered.

His gaze shifted across the hall to his window. Miranda sat board straight, the worn file folder on her lap,
her hands folded over the top as if he might rush in
there and take it from her. She had nothing to worry
about. He'd already called Dayton. Detective Langley
hadn't been in, but Tucker had been assured his call
would be returned as soon as possible and that files
would be forwarded with Langley's consent.

Until Tucker heard differently, he would work off
the assumption that some psychopath had likely read

about the Rosary Murders and had made the mistake of trying to recreate the crimes here, in Tucker's town.

Big, big mistake.

However, Miranda's question gnawed at his gut. Was he willing to risk another death just to save himself the pains of the possibility of an active serial killer in his town? He only had one scene and one victim. That was hardly the makings of anything serial . . .

He thought about Ricky Schneider and his stomach twisted. No. Ricky was a kid. This guy worked with adult men.

But if it was a copycat, there was no rule saying he couldn't have screwed up his first re-creation with someone easier to kill than a heavy adult male.

The Rosary Killer struck on three consecutive Sundays . . .

Miranda's words played in his mind. Ricky Schneider had disappeared on a Sunday.

Tucker refused to think about that possibility. Michael Levi had been left where he'd be easily and quickly found. There was no reason to jump to conclusions until Tucker had a reason to connect the two cases. Until then, Ricky remained a runaway. At least on paper. In his mind, he wasn't so sure.

Lisa reached around him and grabbed a mug off the shelf above the tiny sink and filled it with fresh coffee. Even though she should have clocked out at midnight, she was still around, determined as always not to leave until Tucker did. Despite her young age of, what? Twenty-five? Twenty-six? She was as professional as they came, a single mom hell-bent on joining the force herself one day—something Tucker was constantly trying to talk her out of.

Taking a couple packets of sugar from the bowls

beside the coffeemaker, she pointed to the hall. "Who's that?"

"Anatole's B and E."

Andy strode into the break room and gently nudged Lisa out of his path to the coffee. Like Tucker, the lieutenant looked like he hadn't slept in a week. He poured a cup and leaned against the counter before yawning wide enough to catch a hippo.

Tucker felt for him. "Body on its way to Knoxville?"

Andy nodded. "And I gathered all the samples from the scene you asked for. We found a car on the other side of the river. Had it towed in for forensics, but on first glance it looked clean. Made sure the entire half acre is taped off and took more pictures of anything I thought you'd want on the chance it could be the primary crime scene. Some of the stones around the fire pit looked disturbed so I bagged 'em. Saw something on them that might have been blood but couldn't really tell." He yawned again. "Knoxville will e-mail a copy of all the photos and notes from the autopsy when they're done, too. Doc won't be able to tell us anything until the DNA results come back from the state lab and she can tell if any of it belongs to our perp, but she asked for a rush on them."

"Thanks," he muttered. "You did good. Now go home. Get some sleep. And Andy?"

"Yeah?"

"Thanks for taking over the scene."

Andy nodded toward Miranda. "She tell you anything useful?"

"Maybe." *Maybe not.*

"Think she has anything to do with this?"

"That little thing?" Lisa laughed. "Is that what you brought her in for? She's like five-foot-two and small enough to break in half with a strong cup of coffee. Besides, women like guns and poison. The pictures I saw . . . It would take one hell of a monstrous woman to do that."

"Can't rule anything out." Andy took off his hat and used it to wave farewell. "I'm out. See you in the morning."

Lisa dumped out her coffee and rinsed the cup. "That go for me, too? I'm beat."

Tucker nodded. "Thanks for staying. Hope your sitter didn't mind."

"She'll be happy for the extra money."

"I'll talk to Shannon, see if she can hold your seat till you come in in the morning."

The early morning dispatcher wouldn't have a problem picking up a couple of extra hours to help Lisa out. That's the way they were here. A small family. Watching each other's backs. The whole town worked that way. It was only one reason he had difficulty thinking of Father Anatole as a possible murderer. The priest might be the new, cranky old uncle to their family, but he was part of it now just the same.

It was also the reason another ulcer was eating its way through Tucker's stomach. The town was going to riot when they found out one of their own had been killed. He trusted Andy and Walt to keep the news from leaking, but in a town like this, there were ears everywhere. He'd be lucky if he had a day before he'd have to prepare a statement for the local paper.

He waited for Lisa and Andy to disappear before forcing his body to move in the direction of the office. When he stopped in the doorway, Miranda looked up at him, her dark eyes glazed and watery.

"You're free to go. But not far—"

"Trust me. I won't be leaving until that bastard is behind bars." She stood and draped her purse across her body, holding the files close to her chest. "Good night, Tucker."

"You need a ride back?"

"No offense, but I think I'd prefer a walk."

As she passed Shannon at the reception desk, Tucker's gaze drifted south to the tired swagger of her derrière. He was exhausted. That was the only explanation for where his mind was beginning to wander now. Hell, he didn't even know if she'd ever really been interested in him. For all he knew, she'd used him for his badge.

He slid behind the wheel of the cruiser, watching her. Her parka hood covered her head, and the farther away she got, the smaller and more fragile she appeared. He felt all kinds of wrong taking pleasure in the way her body moved as she jogged. She was definitely trouble, with her sad eyes and Snow White visage.

Dark hair, pale skin, rosy lips and cheeks. Trouble indeed.

He'd met a lot of young reporters over the years chasing their breakout story and they'd all shared one thing—excitement. In Miranda, however, that telltale hunger seemed to be hidden behind a sheen of desperation—*if* it existed at all. Maybe she really was a nurse. If so, then what would she gain from trying to nail Anatole?

He was so tired his brain wasn't finding answers to any of his questions. There was still so much work to do, but it would wait. Right now someone could walk up to him and confess to crucifying Jesus and he'd likely tell them they were free to go if it meant he was, too. The cold crept inside the car, forcing him to crank up the heat. He pulled out of the parking lot and turned south toward his bed, slowing only once when he passed Miranda to ask again if she wanted a ride. She waved him off and kept walking.

His body might be a few hours past exhausted, but he couldn't shut off Miranda's voice in his head detailing each of the murders and her certainty that Father Anatole was the man responsible. A lead lump sat in his stomach at the realization that he had a family in his town who had no idea their son had been killed just hours ago.

The image of Michael Levi's body slumped against the tree churned that lead lump in his gut. He checked the clock. It was nearly midnight. No matter how tired he was, he wasn't going to be able to sleep. Not with Michael's face clogging every damned brain cell he owned.

Passing his property, he continued toward the outskirts of town. Andy had said that Michael had once attended St. Catherine's with his family. There might be a way to question the priest without coming right out and accusing him of anything.

Just before he reached the town limit sign, he turned onto Anatole's drive and followed it a short distance through the trees to the tiny house the parish provided for the priest. A soft light shone from the front porch and flickered yellow against the pristine snow piling up around the weathered guardrail. Tucker killed the engine and stepped out.

Before he could make it the short distance to the porch, the door opened and Father Anatole greeted him. "A little late for a visit, Chief Ambrose. Everything all right?"

Tucker took off his hat out of respect, even though his ears and scalp immediately felt the sting of cold. "A man was killed tonight and Lieutenant Bowen thinks he might be a member of your congregation. His family is, anyway. I thought you might go with me to notify them."

The priest crossed himself. "That's horrible. Who was it?"

"Michael Levi."

The priest frowned. "Related to Mayor Levi?"

Tucker nodded. "His son."

Father Anatole's face fell. He stepped aside, allowing Tucker to enter, and closed the door behind him. "Of course. I'd be happy to accompany you. Just give me a moment to dress."

Tucker dusted some snow off the shoulder of his coat and followed the priest into the small kitchen. He watched Anatole disappear down the hall, leaning heavily on his cane, the limp even more pronounced tonight, and tried to picture him brutally murdering a man. The image just wouldn't come.

Not that Father Anatole was old. But he was a man of God. There was something too pure in that to accuse without damned good cause *and* proof. Of course, Tucker still planned to ask him what he knew about the murders in Dayton, but that would wait until Tucker had read every word of the files being sent to him.

He took a moment to look over the photos hanging on the fridge. Most people hung pictures of loved ones, but Tucker couldn't see a single one that didn't spotlight the priest. They were of Father Anatole and his deacons, Father Anatole preaching at the pulpit, Father Anatole baptizing a child. The good father seemed to like looking at himself a good deal.

"All right then, we can go."

The father had dressed in record time. Bible in hand,

he led the way back through the house, pausing to grab his keys from the hook by the door before stepping outside. He shivered, pulling his coat closed at the throat.

"Winter here is difficult to manage when you're not used to it," Tucker said. "But after living in Chicago all my life, it's not so bad, really. Where are you from, again?"

Father Anatole looked at him from over his shoulder. "Ohio. Gets a bit cold there, too, but we didn't get tourists this time of year like Christmas does. I don't understand the willingness to come and spend the season here, if I'm honest." He carefully made his way down the snow-covered porch steps. "Why not head to Florida or somewhere else that offers relief from the cold?"

"Guess it takes all kinds," Tucker muttered. "Thank you for coming with me." Tucker waited while the priest climbed into the front seat before making his way to his. "I'm sure the family will appreciate having you there."

"It's the least I can do."

He studied the priest for a moment. He rubbed his Bible, his lips moving in what Tucker guessed was silent prayer. He scanned the cover of the leather-bound Bible, searching for similarities between it and the one found on Michael Levi's body. Both looked like standard-issue Bibles found in churches everywhere. Nothing remarkable.

He sighed and started the engine. Thanks to Miranda, he was looking for suspicious behavior where none existed. Of course the priest would be upset about visiting a family who'd just lost their only child. It would make him a monster if this didn't disturb him.

He didn't try to pull the priest into conversation as he drove up the mountain toward the secluded Levi family estate. The huge mansion, sitting on a peak overlooking the town, had been built by the Levi family not long after Christmas had been founded.

He pressed the call button on a panel centered on the large ornate security gate decorated with lit wreaths and gaudy garlands of gold and green. Within minutes, a tired, slow-moving guard made his way out of a small gatehouse hidden behind a nest of tress. He bent to peer into the car, waving at the priest before turning his gaze to Tucker. "Can I help you, Chief?"

"Hi, Fred. We need to see Mayor Levi."

Fred glanced at his watch. "After midnight?"

"If it could wait, do you really think I'd be here now?"

The guard punched in a code, then turned back to Tucker. "Do you wish to see the whole family?"

"Just the mayor."

"Follow the drive to the left until the end, round behind the main house. I'll let him know you're coming."

"This place is like stepping into another country." Father Anatole glanced at Tucker.

Tucker remained silent. It really did seem more European here than in any other part of Tennessee he'd seen. Huge groves of oaks and elms overhung the long, winding driveway, shielding it from most of the snow. There were three houses on the hundred acres plus the house where Ethel Levi's mayoral son resided with his family. The mayor's was the last and most distant from the main house, and by the time Tucker pulled up to the porch, the front door was opening and the mayor himself was making his way outside, tying the sash of his robe as he walked.

"Chief," he said, the minute Tucker stepped out of the car. "What brings you . . ." His gaze shifted to Father

Anatole. Fear clouded the man's eyes. His voice quivered when he asked, "What's happened?"

"Can we come in?"

"Steven? Is everything okay?"

At the sound of Tilly Levi's voice, Tucker's gut sank. He'd hoped to tell the mayor and allow the man to tell his wife in private. From his experience, Tilly was as nice as they came. Always bringing refreshments to the town meetings, greeting citizens and tourists alike with warm embraces. Things never went well when he had to tell a mother her baby wasn't coming home again—and this was the first time he'd ever had to do so with someone he knew and liked.

She appeared in the doorway, her hands patting at her brown, shoulder-length hair, her fleece robe closed from ankle to neck. She smiled, her gaze welcoming. "Good morning, Tucker, Father Anatole." She swatted her husband's shoulder. "If your meetings get any later we'll forget how to sleep at all. Let them in, honey, it's starting to snow again. Can I offer you gentlemen some coffee? Tea?"

The fact that, unlike her husband, the thought that he was bringing them bad news hadn't yet struck her humbled Tucker. In her world, things like this didn't happen. Christmas was immune, especially the town's leaders. He loathed having to be the one to burst that bubble.

"No, ma'am," Tucker mumbled, then asked again. "Can we . . . sit somewhere?"

"Sure." Tilly smiled again. "I'll just show you to the sitting room and leave you men to it."

"Actually . . ." Now that they were both here, might as well suck it up. Tucker looked plaintively at Steven.

"I think—I think he wants to talk to both of us, Tilly."

Tucker spent the next half hour feeling like the Grim Reaper. By the time he was finished telling the family their son was dead, he felt unclean and guilty as hell that he had no answers for them. Leaving Tilly in the arms of her watery-eyed husband, he grabbed his hat and offered his apologies one more time.

"If you need anything . . . anything at all, please call me or come by." He glanced at Father Anatole, who sat on the other side of Tilly, silently clutching the woman's hand as Steven rubbed her shoulders. "Let's go, Father."

As Tucker and Father Anatole retreated to the door, Tilly's voice followed them. "Father? Can you stay?" Her meek voice carried the hoarseness of tears. Tucker's heart broke a little more, knowing he'd just taken a very strong woman and turned her back into a terrified, grieving child.

"Of course."

Feeling rightfully like a dismissed outcast, Tucker found his way out alone. He felt horrible for the Levis, but at least he hadn't had to contend with Steven's mother, Ethel. That, he was sure, would come all too soon. As would questioning Father Anatole. He was glad he'd brought the priest, however, even if he hadn't figured out a way to subtly question him. If the priest offered any solace to Tilly, the trip by Anatole's house hadn't been wasted.

His cell chirped in his pocket and he answered it as he unlocked the cruiser. "Ambrose."

"This is Detective Langley from Dayton PD. I have a message to call you. Sorry for the late hour but—"

"It's fine, I appreciate the quick response." He started the engine and the heat.

"Why exactly are you asking about the Rosary Killer?"

Tucker sat in the driveway and relayed the details of his crime scene. When he was done, the detective was silent for a long moment before releasing a heavy sigh.

"And you think it's related to the murders here? Not a copycat?"

"I didn't say that. But I have a lady here who does. Just hoping you could fill me in a little on her. Tell me if I should give her any credence."

The sudden burst of laughter on the other end of the line startled him. "'Bout five-foot-two? Red hair? Big brown eyes and nice little tits?"

Tucker frowned. "Not a redhead, no."

"Name's Miranda Harley?"

"Yeah, Miranda—" His chest tightened and a bubble of anger exploded somewhere around his lungs. "What was that last name?"

"Harley."

"As in—"

"Bobby Harley. The Rosary Killer. She's his sister."

Chapter 13

MIRANDA WAS THE Rosary Killer's sister.

As soon as Tucker hung up with Detective Langley, he hit the gas and drove, blinded by anger, to his house. He spent five minutes digging out her rental agreement, crumpled the paper in his hand, and marched to her cottage. He pounded on her door loudly enough to wake the dead, and judging by the frightened look on her face when she answered, she didn't appreciate it one bit.

"What the hell are you do—"

Tucker thrust her rental agreement in her face. "Miranda Hartly? You lied in your agreement?"

Her face paled. "No I—"

"Yes, you did. You're Bobby Harley's goddamned sister. Did you not think that was important information for me to have?"

She took the paper, uncrumpled it, and read, her teeth gnawing on her bottom lip. Then, with a roll of her eyes, she threw the paper back at him. "It says Harley. I never lied about my name. And to be honest, I was surprised you didn't put two and two together when you read about Bobby. That, however, is not my fault."

Tucker pressed his thumbs into his eyes, trying to dig out the painful throb that had taken root there, and then read the name again.

"There's a loop in my L. Maybe it looks like a T and my L an E but they're not. I didn't lie on that agreement, Tucker. I wasn't brave enough."

How could he be so stupid? His gut had insisted she'd been hiding something, but he'd never suspected it was something like this.

"Why didn't you tell me you were his sister?"

But now it all made sense. Of course she wanted to pin these murders on someone else—even if it meant taking down the very priest her brother had leaned on. As long as her brother went free, to hell with everyone else.

Man, he sure knew how to pick 'em.

"Would you have listened to anything I said after that? I didn't expect you to never figure it out. I just needed time for you to hear me out."

It was bad enough she was wasting her own time and efforts. Now she was wasting his, too. The Dayton police, the prosecutor, and a private investigation firm hired by Miranda—not to mention her own files recounting the murders—all zeroed in on Bobby Harley as the killer.

He braced his hands on the porch railing and glared at her. He'd been drawn to her pretty face and big brown, sad eyes, and she'd played him like a fool.

He was too tired for this shit.

"Good night, Miranda," he said, pulling his keys from his pocket. He headed back to his place, felt her watching him as he strode away. But he didn't look back.

He was afraid if he did, his professional walls might be weakened by the pleading look in those damned eyes.

"Women," he muttered, throwing open his door. Despite his better judgment, he cast one glance through his window toward her cottage before pulling a beer from the fridge and downing it. "Nothing but trouble."

Monday morning

MIRANDA WOKE WITH a scream stuck in her throat and her eyes on fire. She broke free of the blankets snaked around her body and leaned against the headboard, hugging her knees to her chest. Last night's drama weighed down her eyelids, and she squeezed them shut against the horrific image of the body in the woods. Except in photos, she'd never actually seen any of them before, and she prayed she'd never see another one.

She fumbled for the bedside clock and blinked at the neon digits. Seven in the morning. She'd barely slept five hours. She rubbed her cheekbones with the sides of her thumbs. They were achy. As was her jaw. She felt like she'd been in a knock-down, drag-out fight, but it was just her painful habit of clenching her jaw in her sleep that caused the uncomfortable stiffness. With a groan, she climbed out of bed and stumbled to the coffeemaker.

As it percolated, she booted up her laptop and waited for the screen to flicker to life. She had to go over every second of Anatole footage from last night—from the house and the church. Maybe she'd find something on that recording that pointed a finger at him, some evidence that he was responsible for what had happened to that man in the woods.

Maybe then, Tucker would finally believe her.

She poured a cup of brew and sat in front of the computer, allowing the rich, aromatic steam to drift up her nose and finish waking her. She clicked a few buttons and while she waited for the recordings to load on her screen, her thoughts turned to Tucker's late night visit.

He'd been so angry, and rightfully so, but she hadn't lied to him. She should have told him who she was, but dealing with Detective Langley had quickly taught her to be careful whom she trusted with all of her truths. Just because she was Bobby's sister, and desperate to free him, didn't mean she'd accuse an innocent man. She wanted the real killer behind bars. And yes, she'd do whatever it took to see that happen.

Would Tucker do any less if it were his brother sitting in prison?

But it wasn't his brother, it was hers, and all he saw was her deceptions. She hated herself for the distrust and fury she'd seen in his eyes. She liked him and had thought of him as a potential friend. But she'd blown any chances of that happening now. She half expected him to show back up on her porch steps, demanding that she leave town before sunset. In his shoes, she would probably feel the same way.

Now he was more likely to think she was a complete liar, even though she'd told him upfront that she was a nurse. It wasn't her fault if he'd thought she'd lied about *that*.

All she had to hold on to now was Bobby's word and an unwavering belief in his innocence. Even if the anger burning in her belly made her want to smack the hell out of him. How could he be so gullible?

Bobby had found the first body while out for his morning run two Decembers ago. It had been too late to help the victim, and all he'd managed to do was get blood on his clothes. Then, the second and third bodies were found in places Bobby had been only hours before. When the police had returned to talk to him after each murder, Bobby had thought they were simply doing their jobs. He'd never suspected that they were slowly building a case against him. Miranda didn't understand how the police could have been watching her brother so closely but never catch him in the act of anything untoward.

On top of that, the killings had stopped once Bobby had become the sole suspect and it looked certain he would be arrested. That fact only made it easier to assume they'd had the right man.

Someone had set him up—found him an easy target after his arrival at that first, fateful scene. Most likely, a criminal he'd helped put away. At least, that was Bobby's explanation.

And Miranda believed him. When their parents had died, she'd just turned nineteen and Bobby seventeen. She'd raised him through his final years of high school, had worked three jobs to get him through law school while she took out loans upon loans to get herself through nursing school. Three Christmases ago, he'd turned twenty-eight and had given her a check wrapped in a box the size of a television, filled out for enough money to pay back every single dime of those loans with a letter thanking her for all she'd sacrificed for him. He'd been fast-tracked through his law firm, winning cases that had moved him up the ladder quickly and had the potential to become the youngest partner in the firm's history. At age twenty-nine, that's exactly what he'd become.

She'd been proud. Satisfied that she'd had a part in that.

That Bobby wasn't a killer. She knew him better than anyone in the world, and there was nothing anyone could say to make her believe that the sweet, loving kid had somehow become a murdering psychopath in the five years she'd been working out of the country.

Whoever was responsible for setting Bobby up had been close enough to have known where he had been just hours before each killing. And they had to have known when he would and would not be able to provide a witness for his alibis.

But all that considered, Miranda believed setting Bobby up had been more about having a scapegoat than any sort of revenge. The murders had been far too personal. Too gory. Too . . . religious. They hadn't been about framing Bobby. They had been about the victims and their killer.

Just like the one she'd glimpsed last night.

She should have known it wasn't over.

She looked down at her full cup of coffee and frowned. It had grown cold, not one sip applied to the cause of fully waking her. She reached for her purse on the chair beside her and pulled out a new pack of antacids. She popped a chalky disk into her mouth and chewed, tasting nothing as she tried to focus on breathing deeply. She had to get a grip on the nonstop anger eating a hole in her stomach or she was going to end up lying uselessly in a hospital bed.

And even if it didn't cost her a visit to the local health clinic, allowing her emotions to get the best of her was what had gotten her busted trying to sneak into the church last night.

With a sigh, she settled in to watch last night's footage of Anatole.

THREE HOURS LATER, Miranda closed the lid of her laptop and stifled a yawn. Of all the footage she'd seen, the only interesting tidbit she'd witnessed was watching Tucker knock on Anatole's door around midnight last night. She'd watched him walk through Anatole's kitchen, leave with the priest, and the priest return home alone again around sunrise.

Where had they gone together? Tucker hadn't mentioned seeing the priest last night. Not that she could judge him for keeping secrets when she'd kept a fair share of her own. Still, it bugged her. Not to mention terrified her. If Tucker confronted or spooked the priest, who was to say that something horrible wouldn't happen to Tucker? Or that Anatole wouldn't disappear to complete his killings someplace where she couldn't find him?

The thought of something happening to Tucker made her ill. She barely knew him, but she knew enough to know she liked him. He was a good man. He'd proven that on several occasions with her already.

Feeling sluggish, she showered and dressed, hoping a hot lunch might make her feel more alive and get her out of her own head for a bit. Glancing at her still damp canvas sneakers, she grabbed an extra pair of socks before stuffing her feet into her shoes. She grimaced, making a mental note to buy thicker socks. Her dwindling funds concerned her, but if her work in third world countries had taught her nothing else, it had taught her to survive on very little.

She double-checked that her phone was charged before shoving it in her purse and grabbing her jacket.

As she made sure her door was locked up tight behind her, she saw the Range Rover one of Tucker's officers had parked on the snowy gravel drive. Tucker's cruiser was nowhere to be seen.

She moved the truck back to the parking garage, making sure it was completely covered beneath the tarp before heading to Town Square on foot, trying to decide where she could get the most substantial meal for the least amount of money.

The weathered but well-kept storefronts displayed their goods in large windows framed in ice crystals and holiday decorations. All painted either pristine white or robin's-egg blue, the houses just visible down connecting streets fit with the town's quaintness, with their wide front porches and festively decorated swings.

Despite the cold wind blowing the snowy powder in every direction, people were shoveling their walks and visiting with their neighbors, trying to be heard over the salt truck humming down the main street. Even though they didn't know her, everyone she passed offered a wave and a "good day" before returning to their tasks. Obviously, news about the murder hadn't yet gotten out. Hopefully, it would stay that way, at least for a little while.

It was sickening to think they were all so unaware. That any of them could be found at any time, their bodies butchered and their families bereft.

The cold bit into her nose and cheeks, and she pulled her hood tighter around her face, her gaze steady on the police department sign just a block away. She wasn't ready to face Tucker again but she had to know what he was going to do with the information she'd given him. Wanted to know where he'd gone with Anatole last night. Maybe after she'd filled her stomach. She was going to have to find a grocery store soon and stock her little kitchen. She couldn't afford to keep eating out.

She didn't see the puddle forming outside the florist's door as she stalked past. The cold water soaked through her Converse and the stinging bite to her toes sped her feet as visions of them turning black with frostbite made her wince.

"Just the person I wanted to see."

At the sound of the familiar baritone, she spun around to find Tucker looming behind her. She had to tilt her neck back to look him in the eye. She stared at his mouth, a little too wide for his face and thin. But the bottom lip . . . She shook herself.

She cleared her throat, uncomfortable that she saw him as anything more than just a badge. "I have to eat. I'll come by when I'm done."

"We have donuts in my office. Let's go."

Her stomach churned with dread. He already knew all her secrets, but somehow she didn't think he was satisfied with that. But at least donuts were free.

"I've already told you everything I know," she muttered, following him toward the police department.

"The hell you have. It's time for details, darling. I have the mayor's dead kid in the morgue and you're going to tell me everything and anything that might help me understand who's doing this."

"I already told you who's doing this—"

He took her elbow and none too gently guided her around another puddle before opening the door and waiting for her to pass. Once they were inside, he waved at the receptionist dispatcher. "Morning, Lisa."

"Morning. You're late."

"Wanted to check on the Levis."

The dispatcher's face softened. "How they holding up?"

He shrugged and ushered Miranda around the desk toward the hall before turning back to Lisa again. "I trust nothing about last night has leaked?" he asked. "There's no crowd outside demanding a lynching yet."

"Not a peep. Not sure how long you're gonna be able to keep the *Chronicle* off the scent though. Helen's already been in to see if there's anything she can write about."

Tucker frowned and led Miranda to his office.

Her stomach was in knots. "Who's Helen?"

"Editor of the *Christmas Chronicle*. Pain in my ass." He closed the door. "Sit."

She stayed where she was, itchy and uncomfortable with being so close to him now that he was looking at her differently. Like a criminal, rather than a woman he'd been obviously attracted to yesterday.

"Sit," he repeated. "I don't bite that hard."

"That's what they said about my neighbor's Rottweiler when I was six. I ended up with twelve stitches on my left thigh."

Taking a deep breath, she slowly slid her arms out of her parka and sat, cradling the bundle of fabric in her lap.

He braced his hands on the arms of her chair and leaned toward her, hovering just inches from her face. "You lied to me, Miss *Harley*."

He was so close, she could feel his breath on the tip of her nose and smell the coffee that wafted with it.

"I showed you that L was not a T. I didn't lie to you—"

"Not about that. It occurred to me this morning that you lied to me about being a reporter."

"No, I didn't. I told you I was a nurse. I just didn't correct your assumption that that was a lie."

"Potato, po-tah-to." To her great relief, he left her to sit behind the large desk.

"I've met enough cops who'd rather do what's easy rather than what's right, and I don't think I owed you any personal information until you proved you weren't like them." She leaned forward, looked him dead in the eye. "Why were you with Anatole this morning?"

He raised a brow and she instantly realized what the hell she'd just done.

"How do you know I was with Anatole? You really are stalking him, aren't you?"

"I . . . feel more comfortable knowing where he is."

"So what? You watch him? Spying through windows?"

She said nothing. Anything she said could be used against her in a court of law. The last thing she needed was to give Tucker another reason to lock her up.

"Are you going to tell me why you were with Anatole?"

He glared. "I had a family to notify of their child's death. A Catholic family. It's part of his job."

"Do you plan to question him? I mean, without proof . . . I don't want anything to happen to you. He's dangerous, Tucker. If you believe nothing else that I tell you, believe that, please. For your own good."

"I *plan* on doing my job, lady. I'm not the sort of guy who'll accuse a man of the cloth based on one stranger's theory. Nor do I give explanations for anything I do on the job or outside of it."

"It's not a theory. I showed you my proof last night."

"You showed me a bunch of clippings from a case that has nothing to do with me. Everybody has a past. Father Anatole's is none of my business. Why are you so damned positive he had anything to do with those murders, anyway?"

"Several reasons, actually."

"Then start talking."

Miranda brushed her hair behind her ears and sighed. "Do you know who Bobby had been the closest with those months before the murders? Father Anatole. Working in the private sector, defending people he believed were guilty and getting them acquitted of their crimes, had started to take their toll on him. He'd needed guidance. A friend."

It should have been *her*. Maybe if she hadn't been so far away Bobby would have turned to her instead of to the priest when his life had started to spin out of control. But how could she have known? She couldn't have predicted his world would soon implode so horrifically.

"When I'd left for South America, Bobby had had a beautiful girlfriend, an expensive home, and his dream job working for a large firm in Dayton."

"So he'd turned to his priest for spiritual and moral guidance."

Miranda nodded. "Father Anatole had asked Bobby to help those less fortunate with free legal advice." His letters had become a little more frequent again . . .

Until they'd abruptly stopped for good.

"Bobby's last letter had stated how happy he was working pro bono for the church shelter. It had doubled his workload, which he hadn't seemed to mind at all, but in hindsight, I'm certain it gave the priest everything he'd needed to set Bobby up for the murders, too. Anatole knew Bobby's whereabouts often enough to follow behind him and dump a body. Always in a place they'd be easily found. Always with plenty of witnesses to identify Bobby because he had been in those places. Just not when the murders had occurred."

He leaned forward, steepling his fingers. "I want to offer you a warning here. Everything you're saying about Father Anatole sounds like it's coming from a desperate sister."

"That's not true. He befriended Bobby. Knew that my brother had been seen and identified. He framed my brother and got away with it. Who is he going to frame this time? That old man because the body was found on his property? Me?"

"So he's from Dayton and knew your brother. If that's enough to prove guilt, then you'd be a prime suspect right along with him. And *he's* not being a pain in my ass."

"I was in South America when those murders happened!"

"You weren't in South America last night."

"No, I wasn't. I was halfway through the father's window if you'll recall."

"You mean the same time he was pulling you out of that window?" Tucker leaned back again and clasped his fingers together. "Are you seeing my dilemma now? If you couldn't have killed that man because you were at the church, how could Father Anatole have done it?"

Chapter 14

"WE DON'T KNOW yet what time that man was killed, Miranda," Tucker said. "That's my point. You can't give me an alibi until I have a time of death. Neither can Father Anatole. I'm sorry that you haven't had a good reason to trust the law, but I'm also not stupid enough to completely ignore all you showed me last night and told me today, any more than I'm stupid enough to simply take your word for all this."

He let his words register with her while he sipped his coffee. Not one bit of makeup on and she was still cute as hell. But the last thing he needed in his life was a five-foot tiny ball of crazy.

"If you do decide to question him, you'll be careful?"

The distrust in her eyes bothered him, and the concern behind the distrust confused him.

He didn't like being punished for other people's crimes. "I appreciate you worrying about me, Miranda. I really do. But believe it or not, I used to deal with cases like this a lot back in Chicago. I'm not an incompetent ass." He sighed and leaned back in his chair. He also didn't have all the resources he'd had in Chicago, which was going to make things a lot harder and a lot slower. "I'll question him because Michael Levi deserves every ounce of my effort to find his killer, and I can't afford to set aside anyone who might be a suspect. Even you, so I hope you don't have plans for leaving town anytime soon."

"I told you I wasn't going anywhere until Anatole's in jail where he belongs."

Unless she had some sort of super power, she would have had a hell of a time moving someone the size of Michael Levi around. However, she had an entire file folder filled with details of past crime scenes. If anyone could pull off a copycat murder, unfortunately, it was Miranda Harley.

"And I hope you understand," she continued, "why I didn't just blurt out that Bobby is my brother. He deserves a champion, too, Tucker. Bobby was just as much a victim of the Rosary Killer as those men were. His life was taken from him, only he was never put out of his misery."

There was no doubt in Tucker's mind that she believed every single word she was saying. He tried to imagine his sister in jail and it sickened him. Worse was picturing her there undeservedly. Miranda loved her brother. There was a fierce loyalty in her defense of him that Tucker admired and respected.

"I'll do what I can. But you're going to have to trust me, all right? No lies. No *omissions*. And for God's sake, no more breaking and entering. Can you promise me that?"

"No more lies. I can promise that."

But not the omissions. Not the breaking and entering. He rolled his neck, popping the tension from his shoulders. "Stay out of trouble, Miranda. That's not a suggestion. Just because I'm willing to listen doesn't mean I won't throw your ass in a cell if it means saving me from headaches I don't have time for. Got it?"

"Got it."

He rolled his eyes at the stubborn set of her jaw. "Let me nose around the Dayton case and see what my gut tells me before you do anything stupid. Will you at least give me that much, or should I just put your name on a cell now?"

Her jaw released and her shoulders relaxed. "I can give you that."

"Then I think we're done here."

She stood, but halfway to the door, she turned to look at him again. "Are you planning on letting the town know what's going on? Maybe post a report telling them to lock their doors? Set a curfew? Anything? It might spook Anatole enough to at least stop him for a while, until he thinks he's safe again."

He sighed. "Not until I know what's going on. Having a town in an uproar can cause a lot more chaos than this department has the manpower to handle. I assume I can trust you to keep quiet?"

Her nod was barely perceptible. Silently dismissing her, he turned his attention to Levi's case file in front of him. When he didn't hear the door open, he looked back up at Miranda. She was staring at the file.

"I'd give anything to have been able to stop that, you know. Even the chance at catching Father Anatole this time isn't worth that man's death. I'm truly sorry."

He believed her.

She opened the door and started to leave again, but swung back around before she could step foot in the hall. "Tucker?"

"Yeah?"

"Nose around quickly, okay? If I'm right, and he's still going in order, this might have been the sacrament of marriage. That leaves confirmation, last rites, and holy orders. You only have six days to prevent another rite from being recreated."

As the door clicked shut behind her, Tucker rubbed his eyes. Six days to prevent another killing when he had no leads and no real suspects—unless he took Miranda at her word and considered Father Anatole. That also meant he'd have to follow his gut about this being a copycat and consider her, too.

He reopened the Levi file and scanned the forensic report sitting on top. Michael Levi's car had come back clean, so no leads there, either. Bowen had been right about the car's location being the primary crime scene. They'd found blood, nearly washed away by snow, close to where the car had been parked. But Tucker was fairly certain that blood belonged to their victim. He could always hope he was dealing with a sloppy killer, but the chances of him being *that* sloppy were slim.

Grabbing a pen, he jotted down the four sacraments Miranda had listed. He wrote Michael's name next to *marriage*. Was Michael planning to get married? If so, why would that alone make him a target for the killer?

He took the paper and moved to stuff it in the file folder only to pull it out again. Next to *confirmation* he wrote the name Ricky, and beside it, a question mark. Tucker thought about the box he'd found under the boy's bed. Would his lack of faith be enough to make him a target? He wasn't a grown man, but confirmation took place at a young age. Was that reason enough for the killer to change his MO? Or was it proof that they really were dealing with a copycat and he'd chosen his first victim to be someone weak, easier to kill? A practice murder?

He called Bowen, instructed him to get a more detailed, formal statement from Ricky's parents regarding where'd they'd been the night Ricky had disappeared, and grabbed his hat in preparation to hit the streets.

A rap on his door stopped him. It cracked open, and the coroner, Samantha Murray, popped her head in. "You on your way out?"

He'd worked with Doc Sam a lot, but never on a case like this. He sincerely hoped she knew her shit. "I was, but it can wait. Tell me you have news for me."

"Drove straight here from Knoxville. I want credit for that, damn it. Tired as hell, but I wanted to fill you in before I caught up on all my missed sleep."

Tucker fell back into his chair, scrambling for pen and paper. "Credit noted. Have a seat."

She dug through the big satchel on her shoulder and passed him a folder. "Keep in mind, I only know what they found in the prelims. Won't know more till the full autopsy report comes in."

"Do you have a time of death for Levi?" He opened the file, scanned the documents as she spoke.

"Going on core temp and rigor, between six and eight."

That was quite a large window to find an alibi for Anatole or anyone else, for that matter.

"Any idea when we'll get an autopsy?"

She raked a hand through her messy blond hair. "It's only been a couple of hours and they're swamped, but they promised to put a rush on it. I'll be there when they do the autopsy, of course, but unfortunately we're still working off their timetable. The chief ME and I are friends, but I can't promise that will move things along any faster. I was lucky to get the information I have."

He reached for his coffee, grimacing as the icy coldness passed his lips. "Any other details you can give me now? Anything you might have made note of at the scene?"

There was always a chance he'd missed something that she'd seen.

"The shirt and pants he was found in were about two sizes too small, while the jacket was way too large. And before you ask, no. There was no sign of any other clothes anywhere. Not so much as a pair of socks. So whoever put him in these must have taken the victim's clothing with him."

He was going to have to go back over the scene at Walt's. Do a grid search there and where Levi's car was found himself to make sure they hadn't missed anything, check all trash cans and Dumpsters in the area for a set of men's clothing. More than likely, it would take questioning the family to find out if anything stood out as missing from Michael's body. A watch, a ring. Something personal like that.

"Hey, don't look so defeated." Sam smiled and eased off the desk. "I do have something that might help you with leads while you're waiting for information."

She dug through her satchel again and pulled out a paper bag, from which she pulled out a smaller, plastic Ziploc containing something silver.

Tucker took it and frowned. "Jewelry?"

Sam snapped on a pair of latex gloves and opened the baggie, spilling its contents into her palm. "It's pretty darned distinctive. Looks like something that could have been handcrafted right here in town. Maybe you'll catch a break."

The piece looked fragile, almost made of thread, the silver was so thin. Tiny black pearls beaded the circle, unworn by worried fingers as they were meant to be. The intricate crucifix sparkled as it caught the overhead light.

"I found it wrapped around his upper right arm, stopping at the bend of the elbow. If you didn't lift his sleeve, you would have missed it."

A rosary. The Rosary Killer.

Tucker felt a little ill. He took the sealed evidence bag from Sam. "We need to get this to the lab. Maybe the killer left some trace evidence when he secured it on Levi. And let me know when you're back from Knoxville with the autopsy results?"

"Sure thing."

Tucker watched her go and took a second to himself before gathering Ricky's file and shoving his hat on his head.

Acid boiled his stomach. He had to find that kid.

Dead or alive.

Chapter 15

TUCKER SPENT MOST of the afternoon at the high school and library. Even though there were a couple of weeks till winter break actually started, a lot of families had already left town, their kids armed with a month's worth of schoolwork. While tourists came here for the holidays, many of the townies did the exact opposite and sought warmer climates, so there weren't as many kids to talk to as Tucker would have liked.

Of the kids who'd remained in town, only a few recognized Ricky from his photo, but other than saying he was just a weird kid, they didn't have anything to offer. His teachers weren't any help, either. They knew Ricky. He was quiet, kept to himself, didn't have friends. They suspected there were problems at home since Ricky missed a lot of school, but none had ever reported it. That fact made him ashamed of his small town for the first time since he'd arrived.

Every minute that passed, he was feeling sicker and sicker about how this case was going to end up. Even if the kid's disappearance had nothing to do with Michael

Levi's, no one lost that amount of blood and just disappeared like that unless foul play was involved.

The kid had been jumped before by his classmates . . . and his father . . . but so far that had been a dead end. Bowen had called in a few minutes ago. Both Mr. and Mrs. Schneider had pretty solid alibis for the night their son disappeared. The owner of the local bar had seen to that when Bowen had called to verify that they'd been there all damned day. The blood in the alley had been too fresh that evening for them to have done anything to the kid before that.

He had nothing to bring Stan Schneider in for now.

How did a kid just disappear?

He drummed his fingers on the school's reception desk, waiting for Principal Plough to finish with his parent conference. The receptionist offered him a flirty smile as she glanced up from her computer.

"Sure I can't get you some coffee, Chief?"

She was a cute brunette with nice eyes, and a couple weeks ago, he might have asked her out for that coffee. Right now, all he cared about was getting some small tip that would point him toward a missing teen. Not to mention, she wasn't Miranda.

"No, thanks." He jutted his chin toward the closed glass door in the corner. "You sure you told him I was here?"

She nodded. "Of course. He won't cut the meeting short, though. He's been waiting for them to have time to come talk about their daughter for weeks. It could be a while, if you wanted to come back later."

The school bell rang and within seconds, the corridor behind him was filled with the sounds of opening classroom doors, teen footsteps clomping to lockers, roughhousing, and laughter. Tucker thumbed through the file under his hand. He was going to wear the damned thing out.

"Do me a favor," he said, still rummaging through the papers. He'd wanted to get Plough's permission before calling in the kids, but the man was taking too damned long. Tucker was going to have to work around the principal. "Can you call . . . here it is . . . can you call three kids up here for me? I'd like to talk to them about something."

"Possibly, but it will be a few minutes. I won't be able to locate them until they're in their next class. About five minutes."

He pulled out the sheet of paper listing the names of the kids who'd jumped Ricky months ago and read them off for her while she scratched them down. He wouldn't be able to officially question them without their parents present, but he might get lucky and see some flash of guilt on the brats' faces when he mentioned Ricky. Or fear when they saw whom they'd been summoned to talk to.

Their reactions might be enough to let him know if he was on the right track.

"Thanks. Is there a quiet place I could meet them in? Library maybe?"

"Vice Principal Carthage is out for the day. You could use her office." She pointed toward another door behind the reception area. "Right through there."

He waved the file at her. "Thank you"—he glanced at the name plaque on the desk—"Sheila."

"Not a problem."

Tucker sat behind the desk and flipped open Ricky's file. He set out the single-page data sheets he'd gathered when Ricky's grandfather had filed the assault charges against the teens. No one, not the school, other students, or the parents he'd spoken to, had labeled the kids bullies. They claimed they were just strong-willed leaders.

He'd thought they were all full of shit.

There was a soft tap before Shelia opened the door. "Chief? Here are two of the boys you asked to see. The third, Mark Welby, has already left for Christmas break."

"Thanks again, Shelia." He stared at the kids until the receptionist closed the door softly behind her. Wanting to keep them on edge, he didn't offer them a seat. Instead, he leaned back, crossed his arms over his chest, and glared.

When they were both squirming and looking at each other, the stockier of the two held out his hands and, with nothing but attitude, demanded, "What?"

Tucker narrowed his eyes. He glanced down at the forms, looking at the names printed beneath the photos. "Why don't you tell me, Caiden?"

"How are we supposed to know why you hauled our asses in here, man?" the one named Derek asked.

"Tell me about your attack on Ricky Schneider."

"Are you for real? You already got us forty hours of community service for that. You can't send us before the judge again for the same thing."

Tucker raised an eyebrow. "Wasn't aware they taught pre-law in high school."

"It's called television, man," Derek snapped. "Also know you can't question us without our parents."

"Not questioning." Tucker motioned to the chairs before the desk. "Just wondering when the last time you saw Ricky was."

"That kid's a freak. Whatever he told you, it's bullshit. We haven't seen him in weeks. Don't talk to him unless someone makes us."

Derek was trying to act like a badass, but Tucker could see the confusion in his eyes. He kept looking at Caiden, wondering what they should say or do next. Without their little ringleader, they were no better than all the other Ricky Schneiders in the halls.

"Honest, Chief Tucker, the last time we saw him was in English two, maybe three weeks ago. He tried to pick a fight, but we didn't say or do anything. You can ask Mr. Davies. He was there the entire time."

"What did he want to fight over?"

"History," Derek said. "Can we go now or do we need to call my dad?"

Derek's dad was a lawyer and Tucker almost told him to make the call. He could haul them and their parents to the station again. But these two buffoons didn't have the initiative to do anything without Welby egging them on. "You can go."

Tucker made a few notes on the boys' files, then headed out behind them. Another dead end.

He strode outside and tossed the files on the passenger seat.

Then he headed straight for St. Catherine's.

Everything in the Schneider house had depicted a Baptist background, not Catholic, and given what he'd found in the boy's room, he was pretty sure Ricky hadn't considered himself either. This should have made Tucker feel better about the implausibility of Ricky falling victim to their killer. Less contact with priests and pastors and whatnot.

But one sacrament wouldn't stop screaming in his head. *Confirmation.*

Outside the church, the groundskeeper was shoveling his usual quota of snow. "Father Anatole in, Simon?"

"Yessir. They all are. Preparing for a meeting of some kind. Want me to let him know you're here?"

"That's all right. I'll find him." Tucker fished the photo from his breast pocket. "You haven't seen this kid around here, have you? His family doesn't attend St. Catherine's, but he's missing and I'm leaving no stone unturned."

Simon squinted down at the photo, his reaction the same as everyone else's he'd showed it to. They'd all already seen the photo plastered all over town, and now barely gave the photo he held out a second look. "I've only been in town a few weeks, but I've run into him a few times at the library. Sorry to hear he's missing."

"When's the last time you saw him?"

Scratching his head, Simon looked heavenward. "Couple weeks maybe? He was reading when I went in to make copies of the Sunday programs."

"Thanks again." Disappointed, Tucker headed up the steps, stomping his boots as he went to shake off the snow. He headed down the corridor of offices and didn't have to knock on Anatole's door. It was open.

The priest sat behind his desk, looking over a stack of papers, a pair of reading glasses perched on the end of his nose. He looked up at Tucker and plucked them off his face.

"Chief, how can I help you?"

Tucker tossed the photo on the desk. "Seen that kid?"

Anatole put his glasses back on and picked up the photo. "In every store window in town. Why? Is he part of my congregation?"

"No. Just covering all my bases." Tucker helped himself to a chair and rubbed the brim of his hat. Times like this made him wish someone else was in charge. "I know this is coming out of left field, but would you mind telling me where you were last night?"

Anatole leaned back, and Tucker knew he was walking a fine line between doing his job and fucking up royally.

"This about the kid? I already told you I don't know him—"

"No, no. We have a situation—sensitive in nature—and I'm just trying to place everyone so I can move forward."

Father Anatole didn't look like he was buying what Tucker was selling and he watched Tucker with dark, narrowed eyes. "I was pulling a young girl from my office window, which you well know."

Tucker nodded. "And before that?"

"Watching the fireworks with my deacons." He leaned forward. "Should I be concerned that you're asking me all of this, Chief?"

"Not at all. Once your deacons confirm you were with them, everything will be fine."

He stood, feeling knee-deep in shit of his own making, and hurried from the office before he gave in to the temptation to ask him about things he wasn't yet ready to ask. All of Miranda's accusations about Anatole were clouding his judgment, and he had a hard time looking at the priest without suspicion.

And maybe that was a good thing. A copycat was still a high possibility, but that didn't mean he could ignore everything she'd told him. It was, perhaps, pride, more than facts, that kept him from believing her outright. He knew that. Too many coincidences between her story and the facts.

But there was no way in hell he was going to accuse a priest outright of murder without substantial proof.

He checked with the deacons, who confirmed that they were, indeed, with Anatole before finding Miranda climbing through the office window. However, when he'd asked if they'd been separated from Anatole at any point during that time, they couldn't quite remember.

Were they trying to protect their beloved priest?

Chapter 16

Tuesday evening

MIRANDA HAD SPENT most of the day in her cottage, mindlessly flipping channels on the television, her computer nestled in her lap as images of Anatole's empty home were displayed on little grainy squares in front of her. The right side of her screen, where footage from Anatole's church office was broadcasting, had been a little more lively, but other than a brief moment of intrigue when Tucker had appeared, nothing exciting had happened there, either.

He hadn't stayed in Anatole's office long, but in those few minutes, she'd wished more than anything that her cameras had supported audio. What were they talking about? Had Tucker broached the topic of the Rosary Murders? Had Tucker at least asked him about the murder here in Christmas?

It was driving her nuts that she hadn't been able to hear, and the images had been too small and distorted for her to read lips.

There weren't enough *I Love Lucy* reruns to distract

her from those questions. She'd reached for her phone at least a dozen times, but never allowed herself to call the station.

Around seven that evening, gravel crunched beneath tires outside her window. Every time another cottage renter had come home today, she'd rushed to look, just as she was doing now, her nose pressed to the window like a puppy's. This time, it was Tucker. And as he climbed out of his cruiser and slumped against it, he looked so tired, she had a wash of pity for him.

He glanced in the direction of her cottage, and as her hope that he'd come talk to her began to bubble, it burst just as quickly when he headed to his own door instead.

Her wave of pity for him washed away and she grabbed her parka, closed the door behind her, and bounded across the lot to his house, decked out in her most worn flannel pajamas. He might be tired, but she wouldn't sleep at all if she didn't speak with him.

He opened the door before she could knock. "Go home, Miranda. I'm not in the mood—"

"Five minutes. Please?"

The way he looked at her now was so different than the way he'd looked at her when they'd first met. The warmth in his eyes had shifted to coldness, and she knew he held her partly responsible for bringing these tragedies to his town. With time, he'd realize none of this was her fault, that Anatole would have struck again whether she was here or not. But for now, she could deal with his stoniness if she had to. After all, she hadn't exactly been forthcoming with her reasons for being in his town, who she was, or much of anything for that matter.

"Tucker," she said. "I'm freezing. Please? One cup of coffee and I'll go."

She certainly wasn't above begging. The wind was biting through her red and black pajama pants, and her fingers were stiff from the cold. She blew on them, waiting, her breath exhaling in a puffy white cloud.

He sighed and swung the door open. "Coffeepot's in the kitchen. I have to shower. Then . . . five minutes. That's all I've got in me."

She hurried to the small kitchen and heard a door close down the hall. As she waited for the water to percolate, she took in her surroundings. Two bedrooms, one bath as far as she could tell. The kitchen, living room, and dining area were all together in one large cube. Everything was either brown, black, or white. Comfortable and humble. Just like their owner.

There were a few pictures spaced on the mantel. They were of him and a couple of girls who shared a family resemblance. Sisters maybe. A few more of him on vacations—fishing, skiing, hiking up a mountain. Happy and smiling.

It took a few minutes for her to warm enough to remove her parka, but eventually she was able to peel it off and lay it on the table. How was she going to ask him what he and Anatole had discussed today without letting him know she'd been watching?

God, if he found out she had cameras on Anatole . . .

What? There'd be no relationship? Was that her worry? Like there was a chance for one now? Whatever had sparked between them when she'd arrived, she'd already destroyed. And it wasn't like she was here for a dating game. If finding the truth meant losing Tucker's friendship . . . so be it.

That thought made her incredibly sad.

She sat beside her parka, her gaze flickering to a

manila corner poking out from the hood of her coat. She fingered it, gently sliding it out from beneath, glanced down the hall to make certain Tucker wouldn't stumble out and catch her. She could hear the water turn on. Heard the swoosh of a curtain closing.

She opened the file.

She'd half expected the missing teen's face to look back at her, but instead, it was a man she didn't recognize. She checked the label on the folder. Michael Levi. Another picture, she knew instantly. It was the man in the woods. She'd never seen his face. Her fingers shook as she lifted the crime scene photos and looked them over.

Everything about them resembled the murders from Dayton.

Anatole, you son of a bitch.

A piece of paper flittered to the floor. She retrieved it, her gaze swinging from reading to the closed bathroom door, her heart pounding and her fingers trembling.

Peter Anatole. At the time of murder, spectator of the fireworks display at Town Square. Verified by deacons. Still no exact time of death to know for certain.

It wasn't an official statement. More like a personal reminder of something to add to the file. But at least she knew now that he *had* asked Anatole where'd he'd been the night the man in the woods had died. That meant he hadn't dismissed her accusations completely.

That was something.

The water cut off. She quickly replaced everything inside the file, slipped it back beneath her coat, and hurriedly searched for cups.

When she turned back to the table, Tucker stood in the doorway dressed in black pajama pants. She couldn't help but stare at his bare chest, knew she was gawking and forced herself to turn away while he tugged a thermal shirt over his head.

She sat down, waiting for him to join her. He didn't. "Why are you here, Miranda?"

Now that she'd already found the answer to her question she didn't know what to say. Why hadn't she just left? Because then he'd see the file and know she'd looked at it. He'd probably come to that conclusion anyway. The steely glare he held on her wasn't one of trust or friendship.

Not anymore.

She blew across her cup and took a tentative sip. "I know you're upset with me, and I really am sorry I didn't tell you who I was when I realized you were the local law enforcement, but you have to look at this from my perspective."

"Really?" He pushed off the wall, finally joining her at the table. "And what might that be?"

She hated that bite of anger in his voice. "What would you do if it were your brother? If he was in jail for a crime you knew in your soul he didn't commit? Ask yourself, if you weren't a cop, what would you do, Tuck, to find what you needed to free him?"

He sipped his coffee and remained silent, but some of the anger disappeared from his eyes. "The thing that bothers me the most is you're not asking how I'd go about catching the killer. Your concern is for your brother. No one else."

"It all goes hand in hand. Find the evidence, catch the real killer. Yes, my main concern is Bobby, but I want to help stop this. I don't want anyone else to die."

His posture relaxed slightly. "You're going about it all wrong."

"How should I go about it then?"

"Legally. By the book. You can't go off half-cocked accusing people and trying to break into their place of business."

Or his home, she added silently, thinking about the cameras recording every movement Anatole might make. "I went to the police. They were no help."

He sighed, stretching out his legs, and closed his eyes. When he opened them again, there was no lingering anger, just sheer exhaustion. "You can't put the faults of others on everyone you meet. You should have been honest. When you hide behind half truths, people aren't inclined to help you, even if they wanted to."

She swallowed, put her cup down, and stood. "I'm being honest now. Can't that be good enough?"

He didn't reply. Taking that as a hint to leave him alone, she slipped on her parka, searching for something to make things right between them. She had nothing.

"All right then. Good night, Tucker."

She was halfway down the porch stairs when he said, "I'm going to give this case every bit of the attention it deserves and find the killer. But I'm not going to let your theories cloud my judgment."

Miranda returned to her cottage feeling defeated. She'd spent the last year neck-deep in assholes, and had forgotten what a genuinely good guy was like. Now that she'd met one, she'd screwed things up royally.

Her chest hurt. Maybe she was having a panic attack. Maybe she was grieving the loss of a potential friendship. Either way, as she locked the door behind her and rekindled the fire in the hearth, she felt horrible.

She glanced at her laptop, still sitting where she'd left it on the sofa, but didn't have the heart to reach for it. She was sick and tired of obsessing over Anatole.

But people were dying again . . . and Bobby was still in jail.

Before Anatole had left Dayton, she'd documented every move he'd made, but she'd never had to look over her shoulder while she'd done it. But since he'd caught her trying to break in to his office . . . anonymity was no longer a luxury she possessed.

Her life had become *his* life, and it was making her crazy.

That thought soured her stomach. She'd give anything to have Bobby here with her. He'd always been better at sneaking undetected into their parents' room in search of Christmas or birthday gifts. Of course, if he was here with her, she wouldn't have a reason to be here at all.

She had to get out of here. Had to get away from the damned computer. Hell, she had to eat. She hadn't had more than a sandwich all day. Her stomach growled and she checked her watch. It was only eight-thirty. The town vendors would still be out. She could at least afford a snack.

She pulled herself to her feet and padded to her bedroom, dressing quickly in jeans, a sweater, and her brittle Converse. Within fifteen minutes she was crossing the street toward Town Square. She passed St. Catherine's and forced herself to give it no more than a cursory glance. As Simon emerged from his shed to chase off a couple of skateboarding boys who'd turned the stair rails into their own amusement park, she made her way to a cart selling roasted chestnuts. She followed the invisible cinnamon nutty cloud to the man dressed in green and red elf garb who was scooping nuts into paper cones.

She was about to step into line when she felt a hand on her shoulder and nearly jumped out of her skin. She spun around and found herself face-to-face with Tucker's dispatcher. Lora? Linda?

"Eddie is sweet as pie, but he's a chronic nose picker," she said, nodding in the direction of the vendor. "Trust me, you don't want his nuts."

Miranda grimaced. "Thanks for the tip."

"Miranda, isn't it?"

When Miranda nodded, the petite blonde introduced herself as Lisa and smiled.

"If you're hungry," Lisa said, "I'm heading to Peggy Jo's for some meat loaf. My ex has the kids tonight and there's no way I'm doing the domestic thing for one."

"I was just going to grab something qui—"

"C'mon. My treat."

Miranda took a step back. "You take every tourist to dinner?"

"Just you." Lisa's blue eyes twinkled and she beamed another blindingly chipper smile in Miranda's direction. "I'm nosy, and you have Tuck's panties in a bunch, so you got me a bit curious."

"I really don't think—"

Miranda's argument was cut off when the woman slipped an arm through hers and began pulling her around a trio of teens trying to cross the street. For such a small woman, Lisa the dispatcher possessed the power of a mule.

In order to stop herself from being dragged, Miranda stumbled to keep up. From her peripheral, she caught sight of Eddie with a finger jammed up his nose and decided a hot meal on someone else's dime didn't sound too bad.

"Okay, okay, I'm coming." She yanked her arm free, not sure if she was annoyed or amused by the situation.

Chapter 17

MAIN STREET WAS crowded with people taking part in the events in the beautiful park surrounding City Hall. Lisa didn't slow until Peggy Jo's flickering café lights appeared behind a carriage passing down the adjoining side street.

"Since you're paying for the meal, you should know there's nothing to talk about," Miranda said. "Not where your chief and I are concerned."

"I don't know all the details yet, but from what little I've been able to pull out of Tuck, I know you won't be packing up to head home anytime soon." Lisa smiled. "Might as well make a friend while you're here." She pulled open the diner door and ushered Miranda inside. "Grab a booth. I need to powder my nose."

She left Miranda feeling slightly dizzy in the crowd of people milling to and from the counter, sloshing beers onto the floor as they went. Elvis Presley sang a muffled version of "Blue Christmas" somewhere near the restrooms where Lisa's golden ponytail disappeared down a small hall. Miranda scanned the crowd in search of an empty table. A khaki Stetson caught her eye. She stepped to the side for a better glimpse, half hopeful the owner was Tucker even though she knew he wasn't likely to venture out again tonight.

It wasn't.

She didn't have time to digest why she was so disappointed by that observation before Lisa returned and had her by the arm again, leading her toward a booth in the back. They were seated and had menus in front of them before they could even remove their jackets. Miranda glanced again at the khaki Stetson's owner, as though maybe his face had changed in the last sixty seconds. She recognized him from the crime scene, but couldn't remember his name.

Lisa reached for a napkin and sprinkled some salt on it. When she caught Miranda watching her, she smiled. "Keeps the napkin from sticking to the sweaty glass." She turned her attention to the man in the Stetson. "Cute, isn't he? That's Lieutenant Andy Bowen. But a word of warning: Doesn't matter the temperature, that man's bed never has a chance to get cold."

He was handsome, in a pretty-boy way. Not her type at all. He gave a nod to Lisa, followed by a questioning look when he spotted Miranda. Lisa waved him over. Miranda inwardly groaned. How was she expected to find her social graces when the lieutenant was watching her like he half expected her to start stealing the silverware?

Feeling like a third wheel, she only partially listened as Lisa introduced them and Lieutenant Andy Whoever slid into the booth beside the dispatcher.

"Yeah," he grumbled. "We've met. Last time I saw you, you were trying to fuck up our crime scene. No, wait, you had just broken into a church."

Lisa cleared her throat. "Bygones, all right? We're all just hungry."

She smiled at Miranda and blessedly pulled the lieutenant into a conversation that had nothing to do with murder, Tucker, or Miranda. Miranda focused on her menu in hopes of keeping from being pulled into their conversation.

The pair talked to each other mostly, thank God, leaving Miranda to order and devour half her meal without feeling the need to respond with more than a grunt or a shake of her head. Whatever curiosity Lisa had about her apparently didn't compare to the obvious torch she was carrying for Andy.

"Will you be leaving town soon?"

Miranda looked up from her plate to find Andy staring at her. He'd taken off his hat, his dark blond hair sticking up in the back making his question sound far more innocent than the glare he was shooting in her direction suggested.

She stopped chewing and swallowed, leaning back against the booth to accept whatever challenge he was throwing at her. "Soon enough."

"Good. We don't get much crime here. Breaking into the church . . . and that stunt you pulled out at the river . . . I think it's better for everyone if you just keep on moving."

"Andy Bowen, you show some manners!" Lisa smacked him across the shoulder. "Your mama wouldn't be the least bit happy, you talking to a lady like that."

"Ladies don't climb ass-end through church windows in the dead of night."

"It wasn't ass-end," Miranda muttered, uncomfortable by the direct animosity but refusing to cow to it.

She'd dealt with enough bureaucratic assholes in her line of work to know that one sign of weakness was like blood in the water to men like them.

He mumbled something incoherent and slid out of the booth, his gaze firmly on Lisa, as though he'd already dismissed Miranda from his company. "See ya tomorrow, Lis."

Intrigued by Lisa's sighs, Miranda followed her gaze to watch Andy swagger from the diner. Her type or not, she had to admit, his backside was definitely sigh worthy. She turned back around. "I take it that's not the ex?" Miranda muttered.

"Andy?" Lisa picked up her fork. "More like the one that got away. And now that I'm single, he's gun-shy." She took a bite of her meat loaf. "Well, that and he's terrified of my kids. My little girl thinks she's in love with him and my son emulates him."

She dragged her fork through mashed potatoes, painting them with ripples of gravy. "Andy's dad wasn't a stick-around kind of guy and he thinks it's genetic or something." She smiled, but her eyes didn't quite light up. "Let's just say he's relationship-phobic."

By the time they finished their dinner, Miranda knew that Lisa was twenty-seven, had lived in Christmas her entire life, and had married her high school sweetheart, only to divorce him seven years later. Her kids were six and three and she'd worked for the police department since graduation. Now she hoped to enroll in the police academy in the spring. She thought of Tucker as her brother and had a major case of the hots for Lieutenant Andy that, to date, hadn't been satisfied, but she wasn't about to call it quits on him yet.

For someone who'd claimed to be curious about Miranda, Lisa had been surprisingly forthcoming with personal information and hadn't asked much at all of her so far. But how long would her luck last?

She checked her watch. It was too early to beg off to go to bed, but maybe there was some other way to make an escape before Lisa realized she still knew as little about her dinner date as she had when they'd sat down.

Miranda wasn't quick enough.

As the waitress cleared their dishes, Lisa leaned across the table and pinned Miranda to the booth with a demanding stare. "Okay, so I let you eat in peace. Now tell me, what's your story? You got a family back in . . ."

Miranda toyed with her water glass, debating whether or not to fill in Lisa's blank. As far as she knew, no one other than Tucker knew who she was or why she was here. The last thing she needed was for word to get back to Father Anatole that the perpetrator of his B and E was from the same place he'd come from. But what did it matter, really? Tucker knew, which meant the rest of the department was going to have access to all her information.

"I have a brother back in Ohio."

"Oh yeah? You guys close?"

"Used to be. I don't get to see him as often as I like right now."

Lisa made a tsking noise. "My family's meddling might drive me to drink, but I can't imagine not seeing them every day. You two have a falling out or something?"

Miranda reached for her water and drank half of it. "Something like that."

It wasn't exactly a lie. Bobby had refused her visits for months. His pride was so damaged, he couldn't even look his big sis in the eye anymore—a fact that tore her to pieces. She still sent him weekly letters, but she didn't know if he even read them.

Lisa let out a long sigh and folded her arms over her chest. "All right, out with it. Why are you in town breaking into churches and making our boss scowl every time we bring you up?"

"Maybe it's because I was caught wiggling ass-end through the church window?"

Lisa chuckled. "Thought it wasn't ass-end?"

Miranda felt herself smile.

"And I'm guessing you're not going to be any more forthcoming with *that* information?"

Exhausted, Miranda released her stress in one long exhale. "I like you. And I appreciate the meal more than you know. But I'm not real talky. I've already given my statement to the chief. I'd rather just leave it at that."

Lisa's grin faltered a bit, but only momentarily. "Well. Can't blame a girl for trying. You want dessert?"

Relieved that Lisa seemed able to take a hint, Miranda shook her head and glanced out the frosted window while Lisa ordered herself a bowl of banana pudding with two spoons.

"It's crazy good," she said when the waitress disappeared, "and they give you enough to feed a family of four, so you might as well share . . ."

Miranda stopped listening. A flash of black against the white snow had captured her attention and she found herself staring at the back of a frock, her heart pounding and her body breaking into a cold sweat as she watched the man carry on a conversation with a young man at the corner crossing light. She could only see the back of his head, but she knew without doubt it was Father Anatole.

Miranda leaned closer to the glass, trying to get a

clear view of the man he was with. But as she pressed her hand to the cold glass, Father Anatole turned and stared right back at her.

She was already heading for the back door as he was stalking toward the diner.

Chapter 18

THE TAPE MARKED off every square foot of Walt's property both on this side of the river and the side where Michael Levi's car had been found. Four-foot-by-four-foot grid patterns, covering six acres of private property in hopes of finding *anything* they might have missed during snowfall. Today was the first day when the sky was dry and the snow wasn't fresh, and Tucker meant to take advantage of every second of it.

Bowen approached him dressed to the waist in bright yellow, waterproof fishermen's waders. The sight of him made Tucker chuckle.

"I look like a giant condom," Bowen growled. "I'm not looking forward to this."

"Sorry, but I need you to lead the others in the river. Don't trust anyone else."

Bowen looked pleased by that, but quickly returned to his normal scowl. "We only got three nets so I'm just taking Franks and Goiter with me."

"Big enough to scrape the bottom?"

"Better be. If that shit gets higher than my hips, I'm not going to be happy."

"All right. Get started. Send the others to me for assignment on your way up."

Tucker watched Andy disappear up the trail toward the men still taping off the last of the area closest to Walt's house. The old man sat in his rocking chair on his porch, puffing on his pipe and obviously pissed off that his territory had now become police domain.

"Bear with us, Walt!" he hollered, following Andy's trail. "We should be out of your hair by sundown."

"Better be!"

"Tucker, wait!"

The feminine voice turned him around and stopped him dead in his tracks. Miranda. What the hell was she doing here? He marched back down the path, his temper boiling as she shut the door to her car and jogged toward him.

"What the—"

"I ran into Lisa at the coffee shop and she said you'd come here to do a grid search of the crime scene. I . . . I want to help, Tucker."

He felt the muscle in his jaw tick and unclenched his teeth. "You're. Not. A. Cop. Why do I feel like I'm constantly reminding you of that?"

She pointed up the hill. "You're short on manpower. I can help."

He didn't want her anywhere near this damned scene. "We already have our teams."

"Then I'll be on yours. Please, Tucker? You told me last night that I was going about my search for the truth all wrong. Well, I'm taking your advice. This is legal. I'm a fresh set of eyes, not to mention I know better than any of those men what happened here."

He studied her for a moment and contemplated tossing her over his shoulder and throwing her back in her car.

"I either look around with you now, or I break the law and do it later. You know I will. There's not as much snow today. It's the best—"

"I know it's the best time for it, damn it. That's why we're here."

Maybe he could send her to the river with Andy. Would serve her right to spend the day wet and cold.

His luck, she'd catch cold and his conscience would have him taking care of her again. No thank you. She'd burned her bridges with him and he wasn't about to build a new one.

"If I'm with you," she continued, "you could keep an eye on me."

"Goddamn it." He stormed away, hoping like hell she wouldn't follow, but of course she did. He led her to his cruiser, opened the trunk, and handed her the ski pants he kept in there. "Put these on. May not be any snow today but the wind chill will knock you on your ass when we hit the shade. And I swear to God, if you so much as stray two inches from my side, your ass will be back in your car faster than you can say your own name. Got it?"

She grinned at him like a fool and, like an equally big fool, he felt his walls soften. Damn her to hell. She wanted to save her brother, which he admired and respected. But damned if she wasn't the biggest pain in his ass.

"Scout's honor."

Like he could believe she'd ever been a Girl Scout. "Let's go. And I mean it, Miranda—"

"Not one toe out of line." She looked up at him from her bent position as she tugged the too-big ski pants over her jeans. She had to roll them three times to keep from tripping on them. "Thank you, Tucker. It means a lot that you're letting me be useful."

"Just don't make me regret it." He waited for her to finish zipping up, then led her to the group of cops still awaiting their assignments. "Here's what we're going to do . . ."

BIG MISTAKE. BIG, big mistake. Miranda was freezing, and four hours into their search, they still hadn't found a single thing that the snow hadn't washed away. She leaned against Tucker's cruiser, cupping the thermos of coffee he'd given her in her cold hands. Her gloves had been worthless, too worn to protect her from the biting wind, and she wouldn't be surprised if her fingers turned black and snapped off before she left.

The sun would go down in another four hours or so, which meant the day ahead was still long. Lunch hadn't helped the grumbles passing between the men, and while she didn't exactly have a fondness for Lieutenant Bowen, she couldn't help but feel sorry for him and his soaked men. They looked utterly dismal as they huddled over the hot bowls of soup Lisa had brought them.

Tucker stepped away from them to join her and she forced a smile. No way in hell was she going to let him know how miserable *she* was. He'd barely said two words to her since they'd started as it was.

"Have I been a good girl so far?"

"Day's not over yet, unless you're giving in."

"Not a chance."

"Was afraid of that." He jutted his chin toward the river. "We'll be starting over there as soon as lunch is over. Don't think that side will take more than an hour or two to comb."

Thank God. She watched Bowen paw through a pile on the ground. "Don't suppose they found anything in those nets? Makes sense that anything helpful might have washed into the river with the snow melt."

"They're digging through their catch now. Everything from shoe laces to trash in there, though. Not holding out much hope of anything obviously belonging to our victim or killer."

At least he was talking to her now. She didn't want him to stop. "You never know. Should I help them?"

"Think you're going to find something obvious that they won't see? Hoping for a rosary or something?"

She gave a one-shouldered shrug. "Again, you never know."

"Pretty sure if they find something so blatantly out of place, they'll let me know. You ready to get started again?"

No. She really just wanted to climb back into Bobby's Range Rover and blast the heat. But if he was up to more, so was she. Tonight, she'd soak in a nice hot bath and sleep for a week. But for now, she was part of the team. Being useful. A new burst of energy filled her.

"Let's go." She set her thermos on the hood of his car and followed him past the men toward a wooden bridge that would lead them to the other side of the river.

"We found the victim's car here," Tucker said, gesturing to the shore. "And bits of blood there." He pointed to a pile of rocks. "But the rest of the area still needs combing. It's only an acre on this side, but I want to walk the road off the property as well. It leads in from a side road connected to town, and was likely our killer's getaway path."

"Looks well worn. This a common spot?"

"Make-out point for teens. I've been told they used to do it on the other side, but Walt put a stop to that. Can't imagine he's any more thrilled having them on this side of the river, either."

"Maybe there were teens here making out that night? Maybe someone saw something? You haven't released the story yet, so it's possible someone would come forward if you did."

"Don't have to release a story for someone to tell me if they saw something like a murder."

"Yeah, but they could have seen a car or something. Maybe they saw Anatole lurking about or—"

"Stop it." The glare he shot her felt like a slap. "Stop using his name like he's been convicted already. I have to remain objective, Miranda. I have to do my job right. I'm not discounting him, but I can't let a killer go free because I become as obsessive as you over one suspect. Can you understand that?"

No, she couldn't. There *was* no one else to suspect. It was Anatole. But she wouldn't push her luck. She needed Tucker to keep letting her help with the case, and today was a small step in that direction.

"All right. If you promise to keep an open mind about Anatole, I'll be a little quieter about him. Deal?"

He was obviously losing his patience. Instead of answering her, he turned his back on her and made his way down the river's shore. She followed in silence, afraid anything else she might say would set them back again.

Whiskey. She was going to have whiskey while she soaked in bubbles and hot water.

She passed the pile of rocks near where he'd said they'd found the victim's car and bent to knock them around a bit, looking for anything that looked like it didn't belong. Something gold flashed atop the thin layer of snow that remained beneath the river rocks.

"Tucker?"

"What?"

"There's something here."

Even though she wore gloves, she was terrified to touch it, terrified anything she did now would contaminate whatever it was. Tucker squatted beside her and used his gloved hand to pluck the gold from the ground. It was a pendant. Scratched up and old. Not gold, as she'd thought, but rusted.

"What does it say?" she asked, shaking more from the possibility of a discovery than from the weather.

"It's worn. Can't read it." He ran his thumb over the emblem covering the small square of metal. "Looks like the word *orphanage* down here at the bottom. Can you see that?"

He held it out so she could see, and indeed, it appeared he was right. As he dropped it into a baggie and sealed it, her hopes soared. Maybe today hadn't been a total waste after all.

"Don't do it, Miranda," Tucker said, grabbing her hand and helping her stand.

"Don't do what?"

"Get that look on your face that tells me you're pinning all your hopes on this. This thing could belong to anyone. Make-out point, remember?"

And just like that, her hope deflated like a pathetic, three-day-old birthday balloon.

Chapter 19

TUCKER STOPPED IN front of his house and killed the engine. His bone-weary sigh echoed through the squad car's cabin. Miranda knew she should excuse herself. She was just as tired, nearly frozen, and covered in muck. However, instead of making a quiet escape, she sat quietly, watching Tucker.

His eyes were closed. Dirt smudged the shadowed stubble along his jaw. The slow, steady rise and fall of his chest made her wonder if he'd fallen asleep. He looked so at peace. The deep grooves on his forehead were gone. As were the lines around his eyes. The ever-present tic that had taken up residence along his jaw since he learned who she was no longer pulsed.

Today had been horrible. She'd been so wet and cold and dirty. Despite that, she'd enjoyed every minute of it because Tucker had allowed her to work by his side. To help with the case, all legal-like. They didn't have any answers, and other than the medallion she'd found, they'd come up empty, but it was something, and she felt damned good about it—even if Tucker kept trying to tamp down on her excitement by reminding her that it might not belong to the killer.

The cold seeped into the interior of the cruiser. She reached out to shake him awake. Before her hand could connect with his shoulder, his head turned and she found herself lost in those soulful eyes.

"What?"

She dropped her hand. "I, um, thought you'd . . . Thanks for letting me help today."

A tiny smile pulled at his lips, disappearing as quickly as it appeared. "Did I have a choice?"

Miranda grinned. "You could have locked me in a cell."

That made him laugh. "Not sure it would have been enough to keep you contained. You do have a habit of screwing up my crime scenes."

"Hey." She held up her hands. "Didn't touch a single thing this time."

"This time," he repeated, but she liked the smile she heard in his voice even if she couldn't see it. "Let's get you inside. I think you look worse than I feel."

"Such flattery won't get you invited in for coffee."

"I think I'm going to hit something a little stronger." When he looked at her again, a deep sadness filled his eyes. "Sometimes I really hate this job."

"If you hate it so much, why did you become a cop?"

"I don't hate being a cop."

"But you said . . ."

"That I hate the job. Days like today when we're looking for evidence remind me why I became a cop in the first place. And with it always comes memories I'd much rather not visit again."

She waited for him to continue. His brow furrowed, the deep grooves returning. She was sorry she'd asked the question now. Sorry to be the reason he was remembering whatever he was remembering.

"Sorry," she muttered. "I shouldn't have pried."

He shrugged. "It's not a secret. My sister Olivia went missing when I was fifteen. It took three days of combing the woods and vacant houses before we found her. Doing the grid search today reminds me of that night. I couldn't do anything to prevent what happened to Olivia, but I knew that I could help others."

"She was . . . Was she de—"

"Dead? Yeah." He squeezed his eyes shut. "My dad buried himself in work, and my mother gave her grief to her pursuit of social climbing. Me and Gloria . . . we were left to deal the best way we could. She got married, had kids. I joined the force."

"Gloria is your sister also?"

He nodded. "Two years younger than me and a hell of a lot stronger. They don't like what I do. A civil servant in the family doesn't compute. Gloria finally accepted it, though."

Miranda's throat went dry and she felt the burn of tears behind her eyes. She'd thought Bobby sitting in prison for a crime he didn't commit was horrible. What Tucker had gone through was a million times worse. At least her brother was still alive, still had a chance at freedom.

She reached across the console and squeezed his hand. "I'm sorry."

When she tried to pull her hand back, he gripped it tighter. His fingers were ice-cold.

She didn't know how long they stayed that way, but when his hand finally moved, it felt a bit warmer.

"So," he said, sounding a bit awkward. "I have whiskey waiting for me."

He stared at her so intently, she thought for a moment

that he might kiss her. When he leaned in, she licked her lips, uncertain whether she wanted to move in to meet him more quickly or run for her life. His hand reached across her belly, and pushed her door open.

No kiss. Disappointment cleared up her confused feelings. She'd wanted him to kiss her. Damn it.

"Good night, Miranda."

Before she could respond, he was out of the car, gathering his gear from the trunk. She stepped into the icy wind. "Hey, Tuck? You would have given anything to save her."

"Yes, I would have."

"Then maybe you can understand why I'm doing this for Bobby. I'd do anything to save him, too."

Thursday morning

TUCKER HANDED THE evidence bag to Andy and watched the lieutenant leave with the same bubble of hope in his eyes that Tucker had seen in Miranda's yesterday. In a few minutes, Andy would be on his way to the Knoxville crime lab to see if they could place the medallion they'd found. Hopefully, in a few days, he'd have something new to look into.

But as he'd told Miranda, anyone could have dropped the pendant. Just because it had been found in the pile of rocks where they'd collected blood samples didn't necessarily mean anything.

The hope remained anyway.

He sat at his desk, sipping his coffee, opened the folder containing the copies he'd made of Miranda's clippings, and dropped them. God, he'd almost kissed her last night. What the hell had he been thinking?

Her desperation to help with the search had really
gotten to him. Her need to help someone she loved . . .
She wasn't a liar by nature. He knew that much. Any
deception she might have taken part in had been done
for what, in her eyes, had been a greater good.

He couldn't completely fault her for that. If Olivia's
killer hadn't been caught and convicted, he might have
done the same thing.

And damn it, he liked Miranda.

A lot.

And what happened if she was right? If Anatole really
was a murderer, he had to know. Political correctness
wouldn't get him very far if he remained tentative about
stepping on the church's toes.

If she wasn't right, and he did accuse Anatole . . .

He was pretty sure he was developing an ulcer.

Opening the file again, he studied Miranda's clippings of the three victims found in Dayton. Different
hair color, similar builds, perhaps, but only in the sense
that none of them was particularly overweight or too
thin. And they were from different walks of life for
sure—a janitor, an IT specialist, and a bank manager.

He pulled out his cell and called Sergeant Franks.
"It's Ambrose. Where are you?"

"Heading back to the station now. Had a tourist with
a flat. Stopped to help. Talked to the local jewelry maker
in town. Says that rosary is from an overstock Web site
and very popular. He sells at least a hundred a week."

"Get with the Levis. See if they remember what Michael was wearing the night he was killed and then head
to the town dump to look for anything that matches
their description."

"I'll keep you posted."

He hung up and dropped the phone back in his pocket as the door opened and Lisa stuck her head in. "Got a minute?" He nodded and she stepped inside holding a large cardboard box. "Think these are the files from Dayton you've been waiting on."

Tucker relieved Lisa of her burden and placed the box in the corner by his desk. When she made no move to leave, he asked, "Everything okay?"

She opened her mouth, closed it again. Her face scrunched in that way he'd come to learn meant she had something to say that she was pretty sure he wasn't going to like.

"Out with it."

She sighed. "Don't be mad, but . . . how much do you know about that Miranda woman you picked up for the B and E?"

He tensed and raised a brow at her. "How much do *you* know?"

"Would be less than nothing if I hadn't taken her to dinner the other ni—"

"You what?" The question exploded from Tucker's throat so loud, Lisa jumped.

"Good Lord, I didn't break any laws. I took the woman to dinner. What the hell is wrong with you?"

He inhaled, hoping to suck in a bit of patience along with the stale, office air. Miranda hadn't mentioned any of this to him yesterday. Not that it was really his business or anything, but . . . he didn't like Lisa nosing around his private life, and he couldn't think of another reason that she'd reach out to someone she knew perfectly well had caused trouble for the department twice.

"Nothing. I just . . . why would you do that?"

"She was in line for Eddie's nuts, that's why. And because I'm curious. Let's face it, Tuck. I haven't seen you frown so much as I have since that girl came to town. I wanted to know why."

If Miranda told Lisa her story before he'd had a chance to feel out every corner of it, he'd have the dispatcher breathing down his neck every damned moment of every damned day. Lisa was a girl's girl, and if she took a liking to Miranda Harley, she was going to fight right alongside her if she thought even half of what Miranda said was true.

Tucker opened his mouth to respond, but she held up a hand to cut him off. "Hear me out before you blow another gasket."

She wasn't going to let this go until she'd said her piece. He shut his mouth.

"I wanted to know why she'd gotten under your skin so quickly. Sadly, that woman is as tight-lipped about her life as you are about her."

"Maybe she doesn't like meddling people, either."

She glared. "I bought her dinner and told her about myself first. Since you like her, I wanted to find out what her story was. If you spend half a minute talking to her, it's obvious she's hiding something. Something we might need to know."

"What makes you think I like her?"

She rolled her eyes.

There were times when Lisa forgot that just because they were like family, it didn't give her the right to pry into his business. Before he could growl out a lecture, she rambled on.

"Funny, but I couldn't find any Miranda Harleys living in Ohio that matched our new tourist. But I did a Google search—I know, not a reliable source—but, look. That's her. She had red hair, but that's her."

Tucker scanned the printed document and accompanying color photo. It was their Miranda, all right. Redheaded and dirty and surrounded by kids in a tropical location. The caption read, *American medical team Dr. Seamus Connor and his nurse, Miranda Harley, traveled all the way from California to administer free vaccinations to this small town in Bolivia.*

Lisa pulled out some more papers. "So I followed links from there until I found her education information. I was able to trace all the way to her senior yearbook at Lowell High School in San Francisco." She held up a black-and-white printout of Miranda slightly turned away from the camera, a bead of pearls around her neck above the scooped collar of her senior portrait gown. "Check out the next one. Look who's standing beside her in the photography club."

She traced her finger along the caption of the group photo.

Bottom left: Jeff Disick, Shane Smalley, Miranda Harley, Robert Harley.

Tucker rubbed his neck, feeling a well of guilt over Lisa's obvious excitement over her discovery. When she found out he already knew, she was going to be the one who blew a gasket.

"Lisa—"

"No, listen. That's not all. I did another search for any Harleys in Ohio since she told me she had a brother there and I found him. It was in all the papers a while back. He's—"

He sighed. Time to come clean. "The Rosary Killer."

"Right and—wait, what?" The pink flush of excitement drained from Lisa's cheeks and her face fell. "You know?"

"Yeah, Miranda told me what he's been accused of, but—"

"Not accused of. *Convicted* of. Big difference. Why—why didn't you say anything?"

"I'm trying to stay open-minded until I review all the evidence. Miranda thinks they convicted the wrong man, but she's a desperate sister and I'm not naïve to that."

"Are you out of your ever-lovin' mind?" Lisa braced herself against the desk to glare at him. "Her brother murdered three men. Three, Tuck. We haven't had a murder in Christmas in . . . in . . . hell, even I don't know when. She comes into town and suddenly we have a dead man. And not just any dead guy, but the mayor's son. Did it occur to you that she could have something to do with it?"

Tucker raised his brows. "You're the one who said she was too small to have killed a man like that."

"That was before I found out who she was." She crossed her arms. "You should've told us."

"And I would have. Just as soon as I had something to share."

"Fine. Share why she's here."

Tucker really didn't want to get into the whys of Miranda Harley right now. However, since Lisa had already uncovered Miranda's history, there wasn't a need to keep the last of the details a secret. "She thinks her brother was framed."

Lisa rolled her eyes. "By someone in our town? Let me guess, she thinks it's someone at the church and that's why she was breaking in."

He didn't bother to answer. It only took a few seconds before Lisa put the pieces together. Her eyes widened and she looked toward the door to make sure it was closed before whispering, "She honestly thinks a priest or one of the deacons had something to do with setting her brother up? Don't tell me you believe her? That's just crazy."

"Father Anatole, to be exact. And I don't know what to believe since I don't know the facts." He gestured to the box she'd brought in. "I'm hoping that whatever's in there will help me out with that."

"Her brother is sitting in jail, tried and convicted of murder. That's all the facts we need."

"And what about Michael Levi? Some of the details about his murder match those of the men killed in Dayton. Don't we owe it to Michael to look at every possibility, even the crazy ones?"

Some of the anger faded from Lisa's eyes. "Since your mind's made up, I guess so." She pointed her finger at him. "But no more keeping me in the dark, Tucker Ambrose. I've never spoken one word of anything that happens in this office to anyone outside it. I deserve more trust than you've shown."

"You're right." He pointed at the box. "Will it make you feel better to help me go through all this?"

She clamped her mouth shut. "Think that's going to get you out of the doghouse, Chief?"

"Hoping." She loved a good mystery. He was counting on this one buying his way back into her good graces.

Her gaze strayed to the big, beckoning box. "I want overtime pay."

"There's no money in the budget for that."

"Well . . . you're buying my dinner, at least."

"I'll order takeout."

She kept her head down but couldn't hide the return

of her excitement. Before she could pull the lid off the box, however, a commotion from the reception area stilled her hand.

"What's that?" She craned her head to try and glimpse out of his office window.

"Oh man," Lisa whispered. "Looks who's finally back in the country. Lucky us."

When Tucker joined her at the window and saw who was causing the ruckus, his shoulders filled with a new source of tension and the throbbing in his temples returned. "How can someone so old look so damned intimidating?"

Lisa didn't answer. She didn't have to. There was no explanation for Ethel Levi's power over other people, and right now, that power was demanding to see Tucker. Her husband had run this town with a steel fist until he died, and now her son was running it under her thumb. A kinder, softer version of his father, but still bound to do Ethel Levi's bidding.

Lisa chuckled.

"What?"

She shook her head. "At least you're out of the doghouse with me," she said, heading for the door. She glanced back at him and grinned. "Can't be pissed at a dog whose tail's tucked between his balls. Unclench, Tuck."

Chapter 20

"TELL THE CHIEF I want to speak to him. Now." Ethel Levi's voice carried down the police department's halls to settle right behind the migraine already gnawing at Tucker's brain.

He dropped into his chair and massaged his temples. The old hen wouldn't care about things like waiting for DNA tests and autopsies. She'd want answers and he had none to give her.

"Mrs. Levi, I'll take you to see him, but you're going to have to calm down first."

"I. Am. Calm." Venom punctuated Ethel's words, and though Tucker couldn't see her, he could imagine her face scrunched up and her eyes narrowing into their normal bow-at-my-feet slits. "Go. Get. The danged. Chief."

Tucker sighed and stuck his head into the hall. "Send her on back, Lisa."

He caught a glimpse of Ethel's smirk as she jammed her clutch under her armpit and stormed in his direction. Lisa offered him a pitying glance, any lingering traces of her satisfaction over his predicament gone. "I'll bring you some coffee, boss."

It would probably be unprofessional to ask her to Irish it up.

Ethel's thin, bony body slid into the chair across from his desk, her ankles politely crossed beneath her chair and her spine ramrod straight. Too vain to ever allow herself to gray, Ethel's continually dyed her hair dark brown. The strands looked as brittle as her bones, and her pencil-drawn eyebrows rose while she waited for him to be seated.

"Since you haven't the guts to come to me, I figured I'd come to you." The words were clipped as though they tasted foul and she couldn't wait to spit them out of her puckered mouth.

"I wasn't aware you'd returned to the States, Mrs. Levi. I assure you I had every intention of talking to you. I know your family is grieving and I'm doing all that I—"

"I don't want your pity." Ethel lifted her chin, and Tucker thought he saw her lower lip quiver for a fraction of a second before she regained her composure. "I want to know what you're doing to get justice for my grandson."

He reached for a bright yellow notepad and pen on the edge of his desk just as Lisa returned with two mugs of coffee. She set one in front of him and the other in front of Ethel before quietly slipping from the room. "I'm happy to answer anything I can for you today, but since you're here . . . I'd like to ask you a few questions as well, if you don't mind."

"If it will help. You should know, however, that I contacted Helen the minute Steven called me. I paid her to keep the circumstances of Michael's death quiet. The

Chronicle won't be interfering until I tell them to, which I'm assuming you don't want any more than I do. The last thing we need is to scare tourists away and bring hardship on the town unless absolutely necessary."

"I appreciate that."

He noticed a tissue balled tightly in her clenched, gloved fist, and a bit of his guard dropped. She might be the meanest biddy in town, but she was also a grandmother mourning her grandchild. People often considered the ones being buried as the victims, but Tucker knew better.

It was the family left behind that felt the most pain. He'd been carrying his own version of that hell since he was fifteen. But Olivia's murderer was behind bars where he belonged. Michael Levi deserved that same sort of justice.

"This can wait," he said. "If you'd like a little more time."

She glared again, her lipsticked mouth turning down and casting a hundred more wrinkles on her seventy-year-old face. "What I'd *like*, Chief Ambrose, is for you to stop chasing tourists' skirts and do your job." She leaned forward, the balled tissue rolling from her hand to sit atop her knee as she gripped the edges of the desk and stared him down. "Oh, it's all over town, how you're traipsing around with some hussy renter of yours instead of focusing all your energy on our Michael. Is that how they did things in Chicago? Is that why Michael was killed? Because you can't do your job?"

Let it slide. She's hurting and old and just downright mean. Let it go.

"How about we stick to the facts, Mrs. Levi, and stop worrying about hearsay? I know your grandson had just returned to Christmas last week, is that right?"

"That's right. He was staying with me most nights."
She closed her eyes and he could see her struggle to keep
her composure. "Other nights, he stayed elsewhere. He
said he needed his own space . . . he didn't leave town
on the best of terms with any of us."

"And why is that?"

She narrowed a glare on him. "Personal family business."

"Ma'am, I understand some things are sensitive, but
right now, every fact can help me find your son's killer."

"You understand, discretion for my family in all
things is vital."

"Of course."

She studied her lap for a moment, contemplating. Finally, she said, "He left his wife and daughter nearly
nine years ago. We didn't approve. Divorce, Chief Ambrose, isn't something our people do."

"So he's divorced?"

She shook her head. "Separated, though I suspect
he intended to file, despite knowing it would kill us. I
heard him on the phone. Talking about the possibility
of having the marriage annulled."

"And his wife? Does she live around here?"

The look she gave him suggested she thought he might
be the biggest moron ever created. "If she did, don't you
think you would have already known she existed?"

He ignored the barb. "Where can I find her?"

"Bethany lives outside Nashville. I haven't seen her in
years, but she allows us to fly Charlotte in twice a year."

"Charlotte?"

"Their daughter." Ethel unclasped her clutch and
pulled out a wallet-sized photo of a smiling blond girl.
"Michael's been fighting for joint custody recently, but

he stayed away for so long . . . he decided disrupting her life wasn't the kindest thing to do."

Tucker wrote down the names and chewed on the information. A scorned wife?

It wasn't impossible. Jim and Darren would be making a trip to Nashville tomorrow.

As he scribbled on his legal pad, Ethel cleared her throat. "You should know, he has a harlot."

"Excuse me?"

This time, when Tucker looked at the old woman, she refused to look him in the eye as she spoke. "A tramp. A hussy. He tried to keep her a secret, didn't know I knew . . . but the people in this town . . . they're loyal to me. Has her holed up in that presidential suite at the Marriott. That's why he wouldn't stay with me every night. I'm certain of it. You should talk to her."

"I will. That's good information, Mrs. Levi. You've been a great help."

Whatever softness Ethel might have been close to revealing was sucked back into her frigid shell. "My grandson wasn't perfect, but he was a Levi and we love . . . loved him. I won't have his reputation dirtied. I want him buried with his dignity intact."

"I understand." Tucker remained silent for several seconds then asked, "Why did Michael choose now to come back?"

"Why does any grown person return to the nest? A chance to start over. I think he really wanted to convince the family to agree to his divorcing Bethany. No doubt to marry that floozy. Why else would he have brought her here?" Ethel worried her gloves in her hands. When she studied Tucker again, the fragility of her actions was gone.

"I'm going to find who did this to your grandson, Mrs. Levi."

"You'd better. And I want his body back as soon as possible so we can give him the proper burial he deserves."

Tucker sighed and made a mental note to call Doc Sam later today. Burying her grandson might make Ethel a tad more patient.

"I'll see what I can do."

He stood and escorted her to the exit, and as she walked away, he saw her as a heartbroken grandmother. Slumped shoulders, brittle bones, shaky legs. With more determination than ever to make sure he missed no detail, he closed the door and picked up his phone. He started to dial and changed his mind, shoving his phone in his pocket. The Marriott wouldn't give him any of the details he needed unless he showed them a badge.

Which he fully intended to do.

Chapter 21

"HEY, TUCKER. WHAT brings you by?"

Tucker removed his hat and greeted the Christmas Marriott Hotel's manager, Daniel Benson. "I have a couple questions about one of your guests that I'm hoping you can help me with."

"Of course. If I can. Come on back." He led Tucker down the hall toward his office and shut the door. "Have a seat and fill me in."

Tucker sat and placed his hat on his knee. "I'm hoping you can tell me for certain whether Michael Levi is . . . or was . . . one of your guests."

Benson's fingers hovered over his keyboard, and some of the color drained from his face. Apparently, this was one of the loyal residents Ethel had mentioned. "It's fine. I've already talked to Mrs. Levi. I just need to know exactly when Michael checked in."

"You'll understand that I'll need to verify that with her?"

"Of course."

Benson stood and headed for the door. "Excuse me for just a moment, please."

He disappeared and Tucker sighed. He couldn't blame the man for wanting to protect his job.

When he returned, the color had returned to his face. "My apologies," he said. "Mrs. Levi said I'm to help you however you need as long as we're discreet."

"Absolutely." Tucker pulled a small notepad from his shirt pocket. "Could you tell me when Michael checked in?"

He sat again and his fingers moved over the keys. "Mr. Levi checked in last Wednesday. He secured the suite through the first of the year."

"Did he check in alone?" Tucker asked, even though he knew the answer. He hoped the manager would provide a name.

Benson turned back to his computer and worked in silence for a few moments before turning the monitor toward Tucker. He turned the monitor so Tucker could see it. "A Jennifer MacNeil checked in with Mr. Levi."

Tucker made note of her name. "Has anyone been hanging around or asking questions about him?"

"No, sir. I assure you, had someone been harassing one of our guests, we would have contacted you immediately."

"What about the last couple of days? Has Ms. Mac-Neil received any guests?"

"We don't keep track of that." His returned the monitor to its original position, and his fingers moved over the keys again. "But I can tell you that the only calls made from the room have been requests for room service or housekeeping. Hmm, since Monday, there have been only two calls for room service—soup on Monday night and tea and toast this morning. There have been no incoming calls at all. Cell phones . . . people don't need our phones much at all anymore, do they?"

"I suppose not." Tucker went over the crime scene in his head, searching for any missing details this man might be able to help fill in. "Did Mr. Levi valet a car?"

"According to the valet records he had the car brought to him Sunday evening about six. There's no indication of when he returned. I will check on that for you."

"No need," Tucker said, knowing it wasn't a mistake in recordkeeping.

The manager folded his hands on the pristine desktop. "May I ask what this is about?"

Ignoring the question, Tucker stood and put his Stetson back on. "What's the room number?"

"Presidential suite. Top floor." He opened the drawer and slid an embossed keycard across the desk. "Here's the key for the elevator. Just return it to the registration desk when you're done."

"Thanks."

The elevator took him nonstop to the fifth floor and opened to a gold-plaqued door.

He knocked.

"Michael?" a voice called from inside. The door was jerked open. "Oh, thank God you're—" Blue eyes ringed in red splotches blinked up at him. "Can I help you?"

"Ma'am, I'm Chief Ambrose with the Christmas Police Department." He showed her his badge, let her take it and study it for a moment before fastening it back onto his belt.

With trembling hands, she gripped the door, her knuckles turning white. "Is this about Michael? Is he all right?"

"May I come in?"

She stepped back, allowing Tucker to enter before

closing the door. The suite was enormous. Hardwood floors glistened in the firelight. To his right was a dining area big enough for eight, and to his left, an office area, and he assumed the master suite stood behind the closed door. Tucker followed her into a large living room lined with a wall of shuttered windows.

Jennifer muted the widescreen television mounted over the mantel. "Please just tell me. Is this about Michael?"

"I'm afraid it is." He gestured for her to sit, afraid her legs would give out if she didn't. She stood still, rubbing her arms, the oversized shirt she wore barely hiding her shaky legs.

"He . . . he's okay, isn't he?"

Whatever happened to Michael, Tucker's gut told him this woman had nothing to do with it. However, she was one of the last people to see him alive. She might be able to give him details Ethel Levi hadn't been privy to.

"Ms. MacNeil, we found Michael. I'm sorry but—"

"No," she whispered. "Don't you dare say it."

She already knew. There was no need to say the words. He braced himself for an outburst. Instead, she simply hugged a pillow to her chest, closed her eyes, and rocked softly for several minutes. When she opened her eyes again, he could see her struggle to hold back her tears. "I knew it. I felt it . . . What—what happened?"

"Ma'am, is there someone I can call for you? Someone who can stay with you for a while?"

"I don't know anyone here." She pulled her knees to her chest and rested her cheek on the pillow. "What happened?" she asked again.

"We're not sure yet, ma'am."

She gripped her shirt closed at her throat, her gaze focused somewhere over his shoulder, then she dropped her face into the pillow and released body-racking, heartbreaking sobs.

Tucker gave her a moment to pull herself together, and when she finally lifted her head to look at him again, her entire face had broken out with the same red splotches he'd noticed around her eyes.

"I know this is difficult, Ms. MacNeil, and if I had the time to do so, I'd tell you this could wait. But I'm afraid it can't. Do you think you can answer some questions now?"

She gave a slight nod, and he could see her throat working to swallow. He made his way into the small kitchen, found a glass, and filled it with water from the refrigerator. He gave it to her, and she swallowed half the glass, splashing the liquid onto her white shirt as she gulped. The minute he left, she'd probably reach for something stronger. But for now, he needed her brain to work properly, so water would have to do.

"Could you tell me when you last saw Michael?"

She set the empty glass on the coffee table and wrapped herself back up in the blanket. "Sunday. He stayed here Saturday night, but h-he was supposed to spend Sunday and Monday at his grandmother's before she left for Italy. It's not been easy for him, trying to balance time with me and with them. There are a lot of personal matters weighing on him."

"The annulment, you mean?"

Her eyes widened in shock that he knew but she quickly regained her composure. "Yes. He was getting counseling at the church for it."

Tucker's ears pricked. "What church?"

"St. Catherine's. He used to go there with his family. He was disappointed that his old priest wasn't there anymore, but the new one was working out all right."

"Father Anatole?"

She nodded.

Miranda's accusations were getting a little harder to ignore with each passing day. Anatole advising the victim had to mean *something*.

"You said he was supposed to return to you after Monday night. And you didn't report him missing when he didn't show up?"

She shook her head. "When he didn't call . . . I wanted to do something. But he hasn't told them about me and I was terrified if I called attention to myself and he was fine, he'd be furious with me."

Tucker sighed. Secrets. Never good. "Has anyone been by to see Michael? Called him?"

"Not that I'm aware of. You'd have to check his cell phone. He has—had it with him." She blew her nose and he could see she was getting ready to cry again. She reached for her glass, saw it was empty, and set it back down. Tucker refilled it for her.

He hated pushing her when it was apparent that she was barely holding it together, but if someone was threatening Michael, or following him, then she would most likely know. "Do you remember anyone he might have met with?"

She stared at the closed drapes, lost in thought for several minutes. With a sigh, she looked back at him. "Other than his family, no. He had an appointment with the priest on Sunday after Mass, and then he came back here . . . to me. Other than that, he didn't mention anyone."

"You didn't go with him? To see his parents?"

She rubbed her eyes. "Michael's family is very tradi-tional. He wanted to wait until the annulment was in process before taking me to meet them."

"Has he met with or spoken to his wife?"

She shook her head. "I know he's tried, but as of Sunday she hadn't accepted or returned his calls."

Sensing she really had nothing else to offer, he stood and placed his card on the coffee table. Maybe the ex-wife would have more to say when Jim and Darren visited her in Nashville tomorrow. "Again, I'm very sorry for your loss, ma'am. If you think of anything else, please give me a call."

She started to close the door, but Tucker thrust his hand out, stopping her. Something she'd said was now simmering in his brain and it didn't make any sense.

"Sorry, Ms. MacNeil, but . . . are you sure he said Father *Anatole* was the priest he'd been talking to? Are you positive it couldn't have been one of his deacons?"

She shook her head. "I'm positive. He would never take something so delicate to a deacon."

"Did you ever meet the father?"

"Yes. He insisted on sitting down with both of us before going any further."

The simmer in his brain was beginning to boil. He didn't have a picture of Anatole, but he pulled out his phone and did a Web search. As he typed, he asked, "Could you describe him for me, please?"

The sigh she gave sounded perturbed, but he kept his gaze on the spinning icon on the phone, waiting for the page to load.

"About six foot? Dark hair with some silver. A beard. Not a full one, but a chin beard I guess you'd call it? He—"

"This him?" Blessedly the page loaded and St. Catherine's Web site came into view, Anatole and his deacons posing on the "Staff" page.

"Yes. In the middle. That's the man I met."

It was definitely Anatole.

"Thank you. Sorry for the bother. You've been a great help, ma'am."

He let her shut the door and stood alone in the hall for a long moment.

"Lying son of a bitch," he whispered.

If Michael Levi had been talking to Father Anatole about his annulment or divorce or whatever . . . why, then, had Anatole pretended not to even know Michael existed when Tucker had taken him to notify the Levis of Michael's death?

Chapter 22

TUCKER PEELED OUT of the hotel parking lot and sped toward St. Catherine's. This one lie . . . it shone a light on everything Miranda had suspected and he'd be a complete ass if he continued to brush her theories off.

He wanted answers.

He pulled the cruiser into St. Catherine's, taking up two parking spaces, and stormed inside. The church was, as usual, virtually empty, and he headed straight for the hall of offices.

Anatole's was locked.

"Shit," he said, then remembered where he was and rolled his eyes at himself.

"Can I help you?"

He whirled around to find a deacon behind him, carrying a stack of books nearly taller than he was, and peering at Tucker from over the top of them.

"Where's Father Anatole?"

"Snowball Wars at the school. I'm the only one still here. Everyone participates but someone has to hold down the fort." He smiled. "Community support and all that. Can I leave him a message?"

Tucker didn't answer. He left the deacon standing there with his tower of books, and headed to Levi High School.

"WHAT'S YOUR FLAVOR?" The young vendor's smile was filled with metal, his braces glinting beneath the midday sun as he shoveled seasoned popcorn into paper bags.

Miranda couldn't help but smile back. After finding that medallion at the grid search, and her talk with Tucker afterward, she felt that things might actually be looking up. She tried not to get her hopes up, as Tucker had instructed, but yeah, that wasn't working. Even after reviewing the recordings of Anatole from her cameras, and not finding him doing anything worth getting excited over, she knew something would come of that medallion. It had to.

"Caramel," she said, her gaze flitting to a set of moss-covered iron gates behind the canopied cart. "What's going on in there?"

"Epic snowball battle at the high school." Braces scooped kernels into a bag. "You still have ten minutes to join a team and help build the arsenal before the fight begins. There are snow forts constructed to the north, south, east, and west. You just have to see who's short a man. Or woman, sorry."

She considered her finally-dry Converse and wrinkled her nose. The idea of deliberately placing them in a blanket of thick snow wasn't appealing at all.

"Or you could just watch. There are usually bleachers set up around the perimeter."

"Maybe next time," she said, paying the kid and

turning to go. She didn't, however, take a single step to leave. Behind the vendor, Father Anatole was ushering a group of middle-school kids through the iron gates of the school. Miranda's stomach lurched and she scanned the street for someplace to hide.

He was going to watch a snowball fight? That image did not fit the one she knew from Dayton. Straight-faced, no-nonsense, pious. The idea of him watching a bunch of children frolic in the snow creeped her out even more.

Blessedly, he disappeared inside the gates without so much as a glance in her direction. She let herself breathe and licked sticky candy coating from her finger.

Maybe she *would* go to the snowball fight. Best to see exactly what the priest was up to. Then she could decide what her next move would be since her clumsy cameras weren't showing her anything useful.

Maybe he was scoping out possibilities for his next victim. She almost tossed her uneaten popcorn in the trash as she made her way toward the bleachers, but reconsidered. Her funds were dwindling and throwing out perfectly good food felt utterly foolish. She was going to have to consider selling Bobby's Range Rover if this went on much longer. At this rate, it would be only a few weeks before she was going to need a cup and a sign offering to work for food.

She hadn't let herself worry about it much until now, when popcorn was the most filling meal she'd had in twenty-four hours. She could support herself nicely doing what she loved. But there was no time for working when Bobby's life was on the line. Even though she was doing all this for him, she couldn't stand the thought of reaching out to him for a handout to fund this escapade of hers.

The bleachers were set up, as promised, beneath a

large awning edged with icicles and dirty run-off. She took a seat at the nearest end of the snowy football field, where she could make a quick escape and still blend in with a large group of spectators. Her gaze surfed the crowd in search of the black frock. She spotted it accompanied by a couple of deacons, limping on a cane across the center of the field between two large, icy walls, a half smile on his goateed face.

Anatole struggled to add his stockpile to those haphazardly placed along the plywood and snow forts. His cane slipped in the snow and he stumbled. Simon the groundskeeper appeared from behind the wall and steadied him. Anatole patted the man's hand before disappearing behind the heaping piles of white fluff.

Jesus, he's actually going to play.

What the hell was this? Where was his scowl? His upturned, I'm-too-pious-for-this-frock nose?

Knowing a murderer was in such close contact with young, impressionable people sickened her. But there was nothing she could do. Everyone wanted proof before they'd even consider that a priest was capable of murdering three men. Four, she corrected, turning away from the scene before she did something stupid and landed in jail, where she'd be no good for anyone. At least if Anatole was throwing snowballs, maybe he'd be too busy to be looking for a next victim.

But she couldn't stomach the thought of watching him any longer. Her popcorn was shriveling back into tiny kernel-sized pebbles in her stomach. She slung her purse over her shoulder and stood, only to find her path blocked by a big, solid body that smelled wonderfully familiar.

"Going somewhere?"

She dropped back to the cold bleacher. "Tucker. Hi."

He sat beside her, blocking her escape, and sighed. "Been one hell of a long day and it's not even half over."

He shifted in order to see around the pompom cap of the spectator in front of them, his leg pressed against hers. She suddenly felt overheated, but she managed to keep from fanning her face.

"Why are you here, anyway?" he asked. "Taking a break from your snooping?"

"Just watching the snowball fight like everyone else in town."

His eyebrows rose in question. "You expect me to believe that you came here to watch a snowball fight? One that Father Anatole just happens to be participating in?"

Instead of answering, she fired off her own question. "If your day's been so long, why are you here instead of out trying to make it shorter?"

He watched her so intently that she was certain he was looking into her head and finding the answers to his questions for himself. "It's my job," he finally answered, turning back to the battlefield.

Something was bothering him. He was tense and stony, though she didn't feel it directed at her this time. That was a nice change. What had happened to sour his disposition so much? Did it have to do with why he was here, watching Anatole, rather than working his investigation? *Was* he working the investigation right now?

She felt him pull away from her side and decided to keep her questions to herself. If Tucker was finally getting over some of his anger toward her, she didn't want to rekindle it.

"Should we make things interesting?" he asked. The playful change in his tone took her by surprise.

"What do you mean?"

"Pick a team. If it wins, dinner's on me. If mine wins—"

"I can't afford to buy you dinner."

"I'll think of something."

"Not sure I'm up for losing a bet when I don't know the stakes."

"Fine. If I win, I'll still take you to dinner, but you have to answer my questions." He leaned closer, his voice barely a whisper. "I want to talk to you about Anatole."

She swallowed. Something *had* happened.

"You don't have to buy me dinner to get me to talk about him."

"Yeah, well. Small town. I'd rather do it in private."

"You can come by and—"

"Will it really kill you to let me take you out? I'm not asking you to marry me."

"Don't snap at me." She sighed. "You said it has been a long day. I'm just trying to make things easi—"

"I could use a break, all right? I have something to do after this fight is over, and then I'm picking you up for dinner. Got it?"

Well, not exactly the nicest way to be asked out. But he wanted to talk about Anatole and she wasn't about to turn that down.

"All right. But what if I win?"

He looked at her from the corner of his eye, his face still turned toward the field. "You get to go through the Rosary Killer's files with me."

A tingle zinged through her veins. He wasn't dismissing her anymore. Something had happened to make him think she was right about Anatole and he wanted her help, her opinion. This was no kindly offer to appease her. He needed her.

"You're on," she said, trying to keep the smile out of her voice.

He grunted, his gaze so focused on Anatole now, she felt a kinship with him. Finally, someone who looked at the priest the way she did. She dug back into her popcorn, her appetite returning as she settled in to watch the fight.

She scanned the crowd of participants, spotting a group of older kids standing around a structure built like Fort Knox. Large snowballs were perfectly stacked in preparation for war. These kids had done this before and certainly looked like winners to her.

Miranda turned back to Tucker. "I want them." She pointed out the kids standing closest to their side of the bleachers.

"Fine. But that gives you the advantage. If I take the younger group, you have to wear something other than jeans if I win."

"Like pajamas? Sweats? Oh, I know, how about a khaki uniform like yours? Do you even *own* other clothes?"

She'd rarely seen him in anything else.

He poked her parka. "Do *you*?"

"Touché."

"I was thinking of something sexier. Maybe show a little leg. Some cleav—"

"Seriously? It's like ten degrees out. Besides, I don't exactly have anything like that packed. Sorry."

"I'll pick you up at eight. Now shush. Game's starting."

Shush? People all around them were cheering and laughing and he wanted her to shush?

How pathetic was she that she was looking forward to a semi-date with Tucker when she was staring straight at a murderer? Very, very pathetic. But she couldn't help it. She wanted to go. And not just for the free meal this time.

Chapter 23

TUCKER WAITED UNTIL Miranda had left and the football field cleared before pulling out his cell phone. Lisa answered with a huff.

"Bad day?"

"Nothing I can't handle." She sighed. "Ex stuff. He wants the kids again this weekend but he just took them last. Not your problem. Sorry. What's up?"

"I need you to pull the phone we found in Michael Levi's car from the evidence locker and print out the recent in and outbound call logs for me."

"I'll leave them on your desk for you." He could hear her moving around and knew she was on her way to do as he'd requested. "Anything else?"

"Actually, yeah." He gave her the details as he made his way down the bleachers. "Can you do that for me?"

"I should tell you this isn't in my job description, but I won't."

He spied Anatole heading for the gates. "Thanks, Lis, gotta run." He disconnected and stuffed the phone back in his pocket as he sped up to catch him on the sidewalk.

"Mind if I walk with you, Father?"

Anatole looked at him, still smiling over his team's victory, which, in turn, had been Tucker's in his bet with Miranda. "Of course. Did you watch today?"

"I did. Congratulations." The last thing he felt like doing was partaking in small talk, but he certainly didn't want to have this conversation in the middle of the road. "I was hoping for a moment of your time."

"I was heading to my office. I'm a bit famished after all of that and my leg"—he tapped his cane on his boot—"is growing a bit stiff."

Tucker wasn't about to be dismissed. "We can talk there."

Anatole scowled. "Very well then."

They strode side by side into the church and down the hall, their footsteps holding a conversation of their own as they echoed down the corridor. Tucker worked to tamp down his anger. The last thing he wanted to do was blow up and lose the chance to catch Anatole off guard with his questions, but he was damned close to doing so.

His time with Miranda had calmed him for a bit, as had the promise of seeing her tonight. But now that he was with the priest, venom over being lied to was once again seeping through his blood.

As soon as Anatole sat behind his desk and opened a brown bag which he'd pulled from a drawer, Tucker started in.

"I was hoping you could answer a question for me, Father Anatole."

The priest unwrapped a sandwich, held out half to

Tucker. Tucker shook his head, and Anatole took an indelicate bite. Once he swallowed, he returned his attention to Tucker. "Let's hope I can answer it for you."

"Why didn't you tell me that you were counseling Michael Levi in the matter of his annulment and new engagement?"

Father Anatole's hand froze midway to his mouth. Tucker inwardly grinned. He'd definitely caught the bastard off guard. Anatole took a sip from a water bottle, taking an excruciatingly long time to swallow.

He's thinking. Trying to cover his damned ass. He knows I've just caught him in a lie.

"No offense," Anatole said finally. "But the priest-penitent privilege prevents me from disclosing anything discussed in confession or because of that confession. It is utterly private and sacred."

Tucker smiled. "But I never asked what you talked about. I never asked anything at all. Yet when I informed you that he'd died, you led me to believe you didn't know him. Certainly claiming to know someone wouldn't break a trust."

He watched as Anatole's Adam's apple bobbed slowly up, then down. Anatole steepled his fingers and studied Tucker for a long moment.

"You caught me unaware that day. I'll admit. You were taking me to see his grieving family, and they didn't know I was seeing their son for these matters. It just felt safer to claim ignorance to avoid their demands to know things that were too private to share. My loyalty, Tucker, isn't to the grieving, though I feel for them greatly. It is to the people who come to me, directly, for help."

It had been years since Tucker had had to properly interrogate someone for a crime like this. He was rusty, but right now, he wanted to take Anatole into the station, shine the light on him, and make him tell the damned truth. And it hadn't been so long that Tucker didn't know a liar when he saw one.

He was definitely looking at one now.

MIRANDA STUMBLED OUT of her second shower of the day, and as she dried off, she checked the time on her phone. She and Tucker had parted ways two hours ago, and he was due to pick her up in forty-five minutes. She dug through her suitcase, frustrated that all she could find were jeans and sweaters, all of which could use a trip to the Laundromat.

So much for a sexy date.

A knock on her door caused her to drop her towel. He was early. Frantically, she gathered the material around her body and padded to the door, cracked it open, and found a young girl smiling on the other side.

"Yes?"

"Ms. Hurley?"

"Yes."

The girl held out a box. "Delivery."

"I didn't order anything."

"A gift. I'll just set it here."

The girl backed away, obviously aware of Miranda's wariness. When she disappeared, Miranda snatched the box and flung it on the kitchen counter, her heart racing. She took a few deep breaths, chastising herself for the mental images consuming her. What? Did she expect to find body parts in there? A bomb?

Anatole didn't know who she was, or where she was staying. It couldn't be from him.

With trepidation, she plucked the little ivory card attached to the ribbon sealing the box closed.

If I can't wear my uniform, neither can you. —T

A bubble of excitement made her fingers tingle. She carefully pulled the item from the box. An ankle-length black dress with a thigh-high slit, long sleeves, and a plunging neckline. Beneath it lay another card.

Wasn't sure of your size. You can't be mad at me if it's wrong. And yes. There's cleavage. Deal with it. I'm still letting you cover your legs. Mostly.

She checked the label. She was a size four. The dress was a size two. At least he'd guessed in the more flattering direction.

Collapsing onto the bed, she took a moment to breathe. He'd bought her a dress. This had suddenly become a real date. What the hell had she gotten herself into?

Chapter 24

TUCKER ARRIVED AT exactly eight o'clock, his palms sweating like an acne-prone high school kid's. How would she react to his gift? Think he was a pompous ass and throw it in his face, or . . .

She opened the door before he could knock, and all the air blew out of his lungs in a long whoosh. Her dark hair was piled loosely on top of her head, her eyes painted with smoky shadow and her lips a vibrant red. The long black dress hugged her body like a second skin, the neckline showing him just enough of her cleavage, and the slit just enough of her thigh to make him instantly aroused.

"Damn."

"It's tight," she said. "Flattered you think I'm a size two, but I had to lie flat on the bed to wiggle into it." She gave a little spin and smiled. "Thank you though. It's lovely."

His gaze trailed down the soft curve of her hips, and he laughed out loud when it reached her feet. Beneath the evening gown, she wore her Converse sneakers.

She stuck out a leg and wiggled her foot at him. "Wait till you see the whole ensemble. With my parka, it's a complete hot mess. Sorry. It's all I've got."

"What size shoe are you?" Still laughing, he pulled out his phone.

"You're not buying me—"

"Hey Lisa?" he said into the phone. "I'm swinging by in about ten minutes. What can you loan me in a size . . ."

He looked questioningly to Miranda.

"Six," she said.

"In a size six shoe? Yeah. Size seven is fine. Thanks, Lisa. I owe you one."

He shoved the phone in his pocket. "Taken care of."

She smiled, and the bashful way she looked at him made his heart race. "You look very nice."

He looked down at his suit and thanked her. He usually reserved the black jacket and tie for funerals and weddings, but he didn't mind admitting that he'd pulled out all the stops for her. He wanted her to see him as more than a badge tonight.

Hell, if he was honest, he was hoping the night would end up in his bed. He'd even bought new underwear.

"Shall we go?"

She frowned, picked up her parka, and slid it on.

"You're the best-looking hot mess I've ever seen." He took her arm, and led her, sneakers and all, to his Raptor.

A quick stop by Lisa's provided Miranda with a pair of strappy black high heels and a cream, waist-length faux fur coat, all of which she was trying to put on in the car. As they headed from Lisa's to the restaurant, she struggled to get out of her Converse and into the heels, and he found himself laughing at the whispered curses flying out of her mouth every time he turned a corner.

Finally, she leaned back, out of breath, and slid her arms into the coat. She refastened her seat belt and looked at him. "Nice weather tonight," she grumbled.

Tucker chuckled. "You really suck at small talk."

"All right then," she huffed. "What would you like to talk about? Should we dive right into Anatole?"

He frowned. "How about we have a nice, relaxing, nonstressful dinner conversation first?"

"Well, we've already determined how badly I suck at small talk, so it's up to you to fill the silence."

Tucker thought over their conversation options. Considering where her brother was, discussing him wasn't an option. Discussing Tucker's family wasn't exactly nonstressful, either.

He sighed. "So, I guess it is nice weather we're having tonight."

Her bark of laughter was warming. He pulled into Reggiano's and parked in the first available spot in the near-packed lot.

"Can't I just wear my Converse? I'm decent on heels, but snow is treacherous enough without adding three inches to the struggle."

"That's what I'm here for. Stay put." He rushed around to her side of the car and offered her his hand. To get her down from his lifted truck, she had to slide down his body. By the time she was on her feet, they were both breathing hard.

He draped his arm loosely around her waist, offering support as they made their way through the snow. They entered the restaurant and he helped her out of her coat. She reached up to adjust the neckline of her dress and he took her hand to stop her.

"You look beautiful," he whispered. "And stop looking around. I chose this place because it's outside town limits and the chances of us running into anyone are slim." He addressed the tuxedoed maître d'. "Reservation for Ambrose."

Without glancing at the book opened on the brass stand before him, the man smiled. "Right this way."

They were led to a small table near the window overlooking a lit, icy pond. The maître d' took Miranda's coat, pulled out her chair, and placed a napkin in her lap. "May I suggest a bottle of wine?"

"Is Marco still storing the '61 Brunello?" Tucker sat across from Miranda, loving the way the backdrop of the snowy night and the candlelight danced across her skin.

"I think he might have a bottle or two left. I'll be right back."

Tucker thanked him and as he reached for his menu, caught Miranda staring at him.

"You're staring."

"Didn't figure you for a wine guy."

He shrugged. "Occasionally." His gaze fell to her throat, then below.

"Now *you're* staring." She looked down at her plunging neckline as though checking to make sure one of her breasts hadn't escaped bondage.

"Stop fidgeting. You are gorgeous."

She smiled and a pink hue lit up her cheeks. "Thank you. I . . . It's been a while since I had a reason to dress up in"—she held up her hands—"something like this."

"It's okay, I'm out of practice myself. But you're doing fine so far."

"Out of practice?" She smirked, as though he'd just given away something he hadn't meant to about himself. "The night we met, you were wearing a Rolex. I know because it looked a lot like my brother's and he's no stranger to the finer things in life. And tonight, you order fancy wine off the top of your head. You said yourself that your mom was a socialite. I'm sure you spent plenty of evenings doing things like this."

"It's been a long time since I had much use for my family's money."

She held his gaze. "But you kept the Rolex, custom-tailored suit, fine wine, and"—she ran her hand down her side—"and the ability to purchase this on a whim."

"I like nice things. What of it?"

Miranda shrugged. "I think it's your way of holding on to them. Maybe just a little."

Tucker wanted to deny her claim, but perhaps, in a tiny way, she was right. "I kept the watch as a way to remind myself that material things aren't important. The money, well, I have it, but I don't obsess over it and certainly don't make it the definition of who and what I am."

"Fair enough." She turned her attention back to the menu, blessedly ending the unpleasant topic.

"How about you?"

She glanced at him from over the menu. "What about me?"

"Get along with your family?"

Her smile was soft and a tiny bit sad. "Yeah. I did."

"Did?"

"My parents died in a car accident just after I started college. It's just me and Bobby now."

"I'm sorry, I didn't mean to bring up pain—"

"It's fine. Not all the memories are great, but not all of them are bad, either." She toyed with her water glass. "What about a significant other? Long-term or no-strings kind of guy?"

He thought over the question for a minute before answering. "I was in a long-term relationship, once."

"What happened?"

"Sonya and I started dating in high school. After graduation, I applied for the academy and enrolled at the University of Chicago—just like we'd talked about hundreds of times. Instead of staying local, she decided to accept a scholarship to a college in Florida. I soon found out that long distance relationships don't work. What about you?"

She laughed softly. "I dated the same guy through high school and most of college. We'd talked about marriage but our careers took us in two completely different directions. We gave it everything we had, trying to make it work, but someone would've had to give up on their dreams and neither one of us wanted that for each other. So we parted on good terms and have remained friends."

He tried to picture her happy and in love with another man and found himself frowning. Not that he hadn't expected her to have a past, and not that he had any hold on her. But the image wasn't pleasant regardless.

He was saved from thinking about it more by the arrival of the wine. When he approved the sample, the sommelier poured their drinks, then discreetly disappeared.

"So, we've talked about the weather, our families, and our exes," she said as she dipped her finger into the wine and ran it around the edge, making it sing. When she stopped and sucked the dark red liquid from her finger, he forgot how to breathe. "Ready to get into why you wanted to talk to me? Gotta admit, it's driving me crazy not knowing."

The waitress appeared and Tucker ordered a sampler appetizer for them to share. Even though the subject of

Anatole tasted bitter on his tongue, he sighed, knowing he wasn't going to get anywhere this evening until the topic had been covered.

"I still don't have proof," he said. "But I'm willing to take you a little more seriously after my day today."

He explained what had happened, watched her brown eyes grow wide as she sipped her wine and could almost feel her excitement from the other side of the table. What was making him queasy was thrilling the hell out of her.

He wasn't sure what to make of that.

"I don't want to say it, but I told you so. He's a liar, Tucker. And more than that, he's a killer. I wouldn't have come all this way if I wasn't sure of that in my bones. I would have stayed in Dayton, still looking for proof there rather than betting all my money on one suspect. And I mean that in the most literal sense. I've given up my life to finding the truth."

"And you'd be okay with the truth if it turned out you were wrong?"

She nodded. "My conscience would be sore for thinking ill about an innocent man, but I'd get over it. The truth is more important to me than anything because that's the only thing that's going to give Bobby his life back." She took another sip of wine. "I want to help you go through those files, Tucker. Please? I know I didn't win the bet, but I promise I can be objective. If anything smells like I'm wrong, I won't force the issue."

"We'll see." It was all he was willing to promise. "For now, just answer a couple of questions for me so we can get back to our evening."

"Okay. Fire away."

"You know the history of the Dayton murders probably better than anyone. Did Anatole have a connection to all the victims? Was he counseling them like Michael? Or did they go to his church? Anything like that?"

"Just one. He presided over the wedding of the second victim. He performed the baptism of his kid, too. But the others, no. That's why I had such a hard time getting Dayton PD to listen to me. Nothing tied Anatole to the others."

"Then you're basing your suspicion of him on his relationship with Bobby? Have you talked to your brother? Does he agree with you?"

A sadness filled her eyes. "He won't see me. He wants me to just forget about him. Like that's possible."

"I'm sorry."

Her smile was faint. "Don't be. He can ignore me all he wants but I'm not giving up on him."

"Obviously. He's lucky to have a sister like you."

He considered his own sister. Had he been as cruel to Gloria when he'd walked away from his family as Bobby had been to Miranda?

He hated that the mood had turned so maudlin. "You know what? We can talk about this tomorrow. Come by my office, we'll talk about letting you go through the Dayton files, all right? For now, let's just enjoy the evening. I don't know about you, but I could damned sure use a break from all this."

A very brief break. Aside from a murderer, he still had a missing kid to find. He had a feeling there would be very little downtime in the near future and he wanted to relish this one.

"I thought you asked me here to talk about the case?"

"I want to spend time with you. Is that so hard for you to accept?"

"Yeah, I guess it is. After all, I have been a bit of a thorn in your side since we met."

"A bit? You've been a major pain in my ass." Tucker refilled her glass. "I can understand what you're doing. Especially after today. But if we do find something substantial that points at Anatole, your illegal bullshit could keep us from getting a conviction."

She saluted him with her wine. "Fair enough."

"So no more secrets? No more screwing with the case outside of how I allow you to assist?"

She studied the tablecloth for a long moment. "There are things that I've—"

The waitress arrived and she clammed up, leaning back so the appetizers could be placed in the center of the table. Tucker plucked a piece of fried mozzarella from the hot plate, popping it into his mouth. Grease poured onto his tongue, scorching the roof of his mouth. It took everything in him to keep his cool and not spit it back out. After a moment, he was able to finish chewing and swallowed.

"Hot," he muttered, throwing back half his glass of water. Her efforts to hide her smile as she put one of everything on her plate saved his pride. A little. "You were saying?"

She paused, midway to bringing a toothpick layered with Caprese salad to her lips. "I don't remember. Must not have been important."

She smiled. Olive oil dripped from the small square of mozzarella sandwiched between the basil leaf and tomato on her toothpick. She licked it away.

As he watched her open her mouth and pluck the cherry red tomato from the toothpick, her lips closing around it as she gave a slight pull, he took a sip of wine and pushed his half-touched glass away.

The waitress appeared again, this time toting a steaming plate of spaghetti and meatballs for Miranda and Tuscan meat loaf for Tucker. Miranda dove in with gusto, manners obviously the last thing on her mind as she slurped her noodles and wolfed down her meatballs.

Watching her was the most entertainment he'd had during a meal in a long time.

She caught him staring and flashed him a crooked grin. "Sorry. Hungry. Want some?"

She thrust her fork toward her spaghetti and splashed the white tablecloth with sauce. She definitely had an appetite.

"I'm good."

Shrugging, she set her fork down, refilled her glass with red wine, and drank. Deeply. By the time she set about eating again, a glassy sheen had coated her eyes.

She rested her chin on her hand and twirled her noodles around her utensils. "Aren't you going to eat?"

He looked down at his meat loaf. It looked great with its chunks of carrots and egg staring up at him from the crisp white plate. Yet it was hard to muster an appetite with so much death on his mind.

"It's hard to eat when someone's staring at you," she said, wiping her mouth and leaning back in her chair.

He smiled. "Just enjoying the show." He pointed at her glass. "You might want to slow down."

She glanced at her glass, then back at him. "I'm not drunk."

"If you say so."

She wrinkled her nose and pulled a noodle from the pile with her fingers. Tilting her head back, she slowly lowered it into her mouth. Tucker lost his ability to produce saliva.

She licked her lips. "You going to just drop me off at

my place? Because I have to tell you, Chief, you're looking at me like your intentions may not be motivated by good deeds."

Focusing every last bit of his attention on his meat loaf, he dug in, an old Rod Stewart song DJing his discomfort. *If you want my body, and you think I'm sexy, come on, sugar, let me know . . .*

"I can call you a cab if I'm making you feel uncomfortable."

She grinned. If he didn't know better, he'd say there was a bit of desire flashing in those dark eyes of hers. A little pout in those full lips. At some point he must have missed, she'd put her flirt on.

Probably just the wine in her, but that didn't make it any less sexy.

"I don't get you, Tucker Ambrose," she said, lifting her wine to her mouth. "When you're not scowling at me, you look at me like you're trying to surmise what kind of undies I'm wearing."

She leaned across the table and grabbed his wine, pouring the contents into her glass. He caught a whiff of her when she moved back. Soapy. "It'll be interesting to see which side of you wins."

It damned well would be.

"Well, in all fairness you seem to have a knack for pushing my buttons. When you're not doing that, you're sexy as hell. I can't be blamed for noticing."

Her smile lit up her eyes and she leaned in to whisper conspiratorially. "For the record, it's a thong. White and cottony, but still a thong."

He groaned and the napkin on his lap raised a fraction.

This woman had no idea what she was doing to him. She'd had a lot of wine, and it was all he could do to remind himself that he was a gentleman. He stuffed cash into the bill folder the waitress had placed on the edge of the table and inched his way out of the booth quietly commanding his southern sniper to stand down.

"Come on, I'll take you home." To her place, not his. Next time he was ordering a vintage bottle of sparkling cider.

She made no effort to stand. Instead, she watched him from beneath her lashes. The smoldering look she directed at him made his dick twitch. He sat back down and placed his napkin back across his lap.

"It's nice to see you out of uniform," she said. "Kind of miss the hat, though. I do like that part. Do you have a black one?"

He barely heard her. He was still picturing that thong she'd mentioned. "What?"

She sighed. "Black hat?"

"Oh. No."

"A shame." She pushed her glass away. "Maybe I *have* had too much. Either that, or you're just very tempting."

"I haven't done anything."

"Men like you don't have to. Your dimples do the job for you." She gave an unladylike snort. "Do you know, the night we met at Peggy Jo's, I actually thought you reminded me of Superman. And come to think of it, I think you might be a rare breed of man who could pull off those tights."

With a sigh, he tried to think of anything but Miranda's inviting innuendos so he could walk out of the restaurant without embarrassing himself. Since she was already trying to stand, he didn't have much time to get all the blood in his body to return to its proper places. She held the edge of the table and leaned over to get her purse, the sexy curve of her ass filling his line of sight.

Tucker rushed to his feet, taking her elbow in hand, and helped her to the coat check.

As she slid on Lisa's faux fur, she swayed against him. "The world's spinning a little bit." She wrapped her arm around his hips.

He somehow managed to get her into his truck without doing something he'd completely regret or that she'd resent him for in the morning.

When he got inside and reached across to buckle her in, she leaned forward and nuzzled his neck. "You smell good."

He jerked back, his head smacking the rearview. He gritted his teeth. "Sit back so I can fasten you in."

When he tried again, her wine-scented breath caressed his neck. He considered turning his head and kissing her, desperate to know how the Brunello would taste on her tongue. He gritted his teeth, not even bothering to attempt to hide the effect she was having on his body. When he'd returned to his seat, he was stiffer than the gearshift.

Miranda noticed, her eyes widening and her cheeks flushing as she stared, unapologetically at his crotch. She smiled and looked away, resting her forehead on the window as Tucker grumbled beneath his breath and carefully maneuvered the Raptor through the icy streets back to Christmas.

He'd never been so happy to arrive at his destination as he was when he pulled in front of her cottage. His hands ached from clamping the steering wheel in his fists, and he was pretty sure he'd chipped a tooth from clenching his jaw so tightly to keep from saying something stupid like, *Mind if I come in and use your body before I head home?* as easily as someone might ask to use a bathroom.

"We're here." He shifted in the seat to look at her. "Miranda?"

She didn't respond. Each deep, breast-raising breath fogged the window slightly. She was sound asleep. Her long hair had come loose from its knot, spilling around her face and accentuating the creamy whiteness of her skin. He lowered his head against the steering wheel and cursed. He could wake her, but he was beginning to think carrying a sleeping Miranda to bed would be far safer for his good intentions than helping a stumbling, flirty Miranda make her own way.

Killing the engine, he made his way to her side and fished in her bag for her key. He lifted her in his arms and carried her up the small porch. When he reached the front door, he had to adjust her weight to work the key, tilting her toward his chest and causing her breasts to press against him.

By the time he kicked the door closed behind them, Miranda's eyes were open. Her gaze was still cloudy, but focused intently on him. Shit.

As quickly as possible, he made his way to the back of the cottage toward her bedroom and laid her on the bed, feet dangling over the edge. He threw her bag on the floor. The sound of her steady breathing promised that she'd fallen asleep again.

After adjusting the heat to take the chill from the room, he returned to the bedroom. His gaze traveled up her legs where the skirt of the dress had wiggled up to her knees, and settled on the sweet curve of breasts nearly tumbling from the deep V of the neckline.

Starting with her feet, he quickly worked the straps of the heels, tucked them under his arm to return to Lisa, and slid the open coat from her arms. No way in hell was he touching the dress. One less thing for him to strip her of—and tempt himself with.

"Come on, let's get you under the covers."

As if in slow motion, she reached out and cupped his face. Her cool fingers quickly warmed against his heated flesh. She traced his lips with her thumb. Tucker held himself perfectly still, watching her.

When her hand fell limply back to her side, he held her against his chest so he could jerk back the covers. As he tried to lay her back on the bed, her arm snaked around his neck.

"Let me go, Miran—"

She pulled his head down, her lips brushing ever so slightly across his. "Mmm," she sighed against his mouth. "I've wanted to do that since I first met you."

"You're drunk and—"

"I told you I'm not drunk." She nipped his lip and he was a goner. He pulled her close and deepened the kiss. The taste of the wine lingering on her breath and lips went straight to his head. He wanted more. He wanted *her*.

But not like this.

When she trailed her hands over his shoulders to the buttons on his shirt, he ended the kiss. "You don't know what you're doing."

He placed her against the pillows and tucked the covers beneath her chin. Hopefully she wouldn't remember this in the morning. If she did, he was pretty sure her pride was going to take a beating. He didn't want to be the cause of that.

He pressed a kiss to her forehead, then did the exact opposite of what he wanted to do.

He left.

Chapter 25

TUCKER GLANCED AT Lisa's coat and shoes, still perched on the corner of his desk the next afternoon, and contemplated moving them to the reception area for her to pick up. The damned coat still smelled like Miranda, and he was having a hard enough time trying to forget about their kiss in order to focus.

He'd made the right decision in leaving her last night. But damned if it hadn't been hard as hell. All night, he'd tossed and turned, contemplated returning to her just to check on her, and knowing he wouldn't leave again if he did.

He was feeling every moment of his restless night now.

Grumbling, he quickly finished his lunch and made one last call to the ME's office in Knoxville, his third in an hour, to make sure they'd call him whenever they finished with Michael Levi's autopsy, no matter the time of day. He'd also asked, albeit fruitlessly, for a rush so the family could hold a funeral.

He'd been laughed at for that one. All they'd been able to tell him for sure was that the blood on the rocks Bowen had bagged was a match to the victim. No hope of finding the killer's DNA on them anymore.

Trying to remain focused, he picked up the report Lisa had left on his desk and scanned Michael's phone records. The incoming calls matched his family's numbers, as did some of the outbound calls. He'd called one number over two dozen times. He checked the report Goiter and Franks had submitted concerning their visit with Levi's estranged wife, Bethany Levi. It was a match.

Setting aside the phone records, he read the interview notes with Bethany. She'd stated that Michael had wanted joint custody, but she had refused. Two weeks ago, she'd received a letter from his lawyer stating the petition had been dropped, but Michael was still requesting monthly visitation at his family estate with his daughter.

He'd called repeatedly, but since she hadn't decided yet if she was going to grant his latest request, and didn't want to be pressured into a decision, she hadn't taken any of his calls. She'd claimed she hadn't seen Michael since his return to Christmas, and her alibi confirmed her whereabouts for the night of his murder.

Another dead end.

Lisa finally came in for her shift around twelve-thirty and settled down in his office for an afternoon of reading through the Dayton files. She took the jacket and shoes from his desk and stuffed them in her bag. He was able to breathe a bit easier after that. He checked his watch. Would Miranda even remember last night's conversation when he'd told her to come by to talk about letting her help go through the files?

Did he want her to remember? Having her here would probably be too much of a distraction. Hell, the stupid coat she'd worn had been. The woman in the flesh would be a doorstop to any progress he hoped to make today.

As Lisa began pulling files from the large box, his phone rang. "If that's your new girlfriend," Lisa said, "tell her she scuffed up my heels."

"Ambrose."

It was his sergeant, Jim Franks.

"Hey, Chief. Um . . . You might be wantin' to come on down to the mill."

He sighed. He hadn't had a chance to go through those files yet, and he was itching to do so. "I'm in the middle of something, Sergeant. Try Lieutenant Bowen—"

"Well, sir . . . I, um . . ."

The man sounded ill and tired but Tucker was in no mood to baby anyone today. "Spit it out, Franks."

"There's another body, sir." The faint sound of heaving followed those words on the other end of the line, and Tucker felt his own stomach churn.

He grabbed his hat off the door hook, his feet like lead as Franks filled him in. "Looks like the other one. Think I saw a Bible but it's pretty dark in there and I didn't want to linger . . . you know, contaminate anything?"

The churning was becoming a typhoon. Tucker left Lisa alone with the files and stormed out of the station. "You did good, Jim. I'll be there as soon as I can. Go 'head and start roping off the area. I'll get the details when I get there."

"All right, boss, but you should know . . . I don't think this is a fresh one. It smells something fierce in there. And . . . looks like a kid. Might be the one you've been searching for."

"Jesus." Tucker hung up and froze in the middle of the parking lot. *Ricky.*

Already, he was picturing Ricky Schneider dressed like Michael Levi and ripped to shreds by a sadistic madman. He'd moved here so he wouldn't be faced with homicides as often as he was in Chicago, and yet in less than a week, he was about to deal with his second body.

Please, God, don't let it be Ricky.

But would it really be any better if it was some nameless stranger?

No. But he couldn't stomach the thought of it being the kid. Such a shitty life shouldn't end in such a shitty death.

The cruiser had a layer of snow covering the roof and hood, but someone had dug the tires out since he'd parked it there that morning. He tossed his hat on the passenger seat and took a deep breath before heading toward the old mill and granary Jim had called from, forgoing the lights and sirens in hopes of keeping the town in the dark just a little bit longer. The Christmas Grain and Grist Mill was still functional and a tourist haven. Not exactly a secluded place to put a body.

He hadn't seen a damned thing yet, and he was already willing to bet the body had been placed there as recently as today. Relocated from wherever he'd been stashed this whole time. Likely, the killer wasn't pleased that this one hadn't been found yet and had moved to remedy that. There was no way a tourist wouldn't have stumbled upon it at the granary by now, otherwise.

He pulled off the road and followed the curved, paved drive to the front of the granary, where Jim's partner, Darren, was waiting. Tucker rolled down his window. Before he could say anything, Darren said, "Franks's around back. Mr. Mackey found the body in one of the roped-off outbuildings."

Tucker nodded. "Call Doc and make sure she finds her way back." He started to pull away and stopped. "And if anyone asks, we're checking up on a break-in."

When Darren nodded, Tucker followed the narrow road, pulling up beside the other squad car. Jim leaned against the trunk while the owner, Floyd Mackey, paced. They both greeted him with looks of relief.

Floyd rushed to his side. "Chief, thank God you're here. I don't know how that kid got here, but I want him gone before my wife or sisters come out here to find out what's taking me so long to get back to the shop."

Tucker pulled out a pair of latex gloves and put them on. "Just a couple questions and you can head on back before they get suspicious. Might want to take them into town so they don't see the coroner arrive."

"I'll give her directions to the rear entrance," Jim said, joining them. "Probably better that no one sees the meat wagon pulling through the front and asks questions."

"All right," Tucker said. "Fill me in."

"I have his statement, Chief," Jim said, pulling out his notebook.

Floyd nodded. "Told Jim everything."

Preferring to hear it firsthand, Tucker motioned Floyd to continue.

"My wife sent me to get the decorations stored in there." He pointed to the building behind him. "This is just for storage now since it's so far from the main buildings and getting tourists out here was a pain. Anyhoo, the minute I walked in I knew something was wrong. The smell, ya know? Figured it was just a dead animal but when I went behind the old wheel . . . well, that's when I saw him."

"Did you recognize him?"

Floyd paled and swallowed loudly. "I didn't get that close. Knew there wasn't much I could do for him so I came back out here and called Jim."

"Why didn't you call the station?"

Floyd shrugged. "He always makes his rounds about this time of day. Knew he'd be close by."

"Do you keep the building locked?"

"There's an old padlock on it, but we never bother locking it. Haven't even been in here in weeks."

Tucker headed to the trunk of his cruiser. "You head on back to your family. We'll get this taken care of and get out of here as quickly as we can."

Floyd nodded and shot off on a mud-encrusted four-wheeler.

Tucker waited until he disappeared, then grabbed his duffel from the trunk, took out his camera, and tossed the bag over his shoulder, motioning for Jim to follow.

Inside the little building, cracks in the ceiling and walls let in muted light. Tucker walked the perimeter. He was procrastinating. He couldn't help it. No part of him whatsoever wanted to lay eyes on the body and confirm that it was Ricky.

Two sets of muddy, almost imperceptible footprints came in and retreated practically on top of one another. Another set started through the middle of the room before they disappeared. Those probably belonged to Floyd. They were too messy to belong to anyone calculating.

He placed markers and a measuring ruler by each of the impressions and snapped a photo before moving on.

The old granary was one room, with the remains of a grinding wheel in the center. Boxes and crates were neatly stacked on the shelves lining the walls. Nothing looked disturbed or out of place. In fact, if it wasn't for the smell of decomp, Tucker wouldn't suspect anything out of the ordinary.

Behind him, Jim ducked inside, notebook in hand. "I took notes, sir. Of what we found when we got here."

"Go ahead."

The sergeant cleared his throat. "At exactly four-fifty-three, Sergeant Goiter and I entered the building. Upon seeing the body, we immediately exited and I secured the scene and called you." Jim stopped reading long enough to point to the corner behind the wheel. "He's over there."

"Did anyone touch him?"

"No, sir." Jim tucked his notebook back into his pocket. "If it's all the same to you, Chief, I'd rather wait over here. I've never seen anything like that before and really don't want to see it again."

Images of Michael Levi's body flashed through Tucker's mind. He couldn't say he blamed Jim at all. "You did good. Why don't you wait outside for Doc while I photograph the victim?"

He snapped photos, his flash lighting up the granary as Jim all but ran from the building. The guy wouldn't be sleeping through the night for weeks. Sadly, Tucker had become all too used to such things long ago.

Satisfied that he'd documented the entrance, he moved behind the stone wheel. Stretched out on the cold ground, dressed in a dark suit, no shoes, belt, or tie, lay Ricky Schneider.

A Bible and large crucifix rested on his stomach, his hands folded over them. A burn, much like the one on

Michael Levi's forehead, was visible despite the condition of the body. There was no blood pool beneath him or blood spatter on the old wheel or shelves behind him.

As Tucker had guessed, the body had been staged here. The blood they'd found behind the library was Ricky's, and there was no more denying that he'd likely died there. So close to where Tucker had been patrolling. So where had his body been all this time?

The click of a camera from the entrance pulled Tucker's attention away from the body. Doc stood in the entryway recording the scene as she did her walkthrough. She made her way through the building to stop beside him, documenting her path. "You're keeping me busy these days, Tuck."

"Yeah," he muttered. "Tell me about it."

Kneeling beside the body, she scribbled on her clipboard before taking more photographs. Seemingly satisfied that she'd detailed all her findings, she lifted her recorder to her lips. "The deep discoloration of the body indicates he's been dead for some time."

Tucker knew she wasn't talking to him and remained silent. Carefully, she eased the blood-encrusted collar of the white shirt away from his neck. "Garroted. Like Levi. Almost decapitated. There's no tearing or sawing. The ligature marks near the neck were made prior to the cut at the throat. Could be a sign of hesitation." She looked at Tucker. "Grab the items on his lap for me, please. You can bag them now."

Tucker quickly grabbed the Bible and crucifix and placed the items into large evidence bags, then labeled and signed each. She rolled the body toward her, checking the pockets for a wallet or any other personal items. The skin at his wrist made a sucking sound as it slipped toward his elbow,

"The condition of the body makes it hard to identify defensive wounds or other traumas, but autopsy should help with that. Hmm."

"What?" Tucker asked, not caring if he'd interrupted her recording.

"There's almost no evidence of insect activity. Even with the cold temperatures I would expect to see more bugs or signs of scavengers. There are too many cracks in these walls for this place to be that secure from nature."

"Even bugs?"

"If the body was covered in snow before it was placed here and kept off the ground, insects wouldn't necessarily be an issue." She shut off the recorder and motioned over the two assistants who'd entered with a gurney.

Tucker walked outside, contemplating Sam's deduction. There had been heavy snowfall over the last few weeks. If Ricky's body had originally been staged someplace else, staged to be found as Levi and the Dayton victims had, the snow might have screwed up their killer's plans, forcing him to dig Ricky out of the snow and put him here, instead. There was every chance that whoever did this didn't know the shed wasn't in constant use. The rest of the granary was constantly trafficked.

He leaned against the wall and waved Jim over. "You do a walk of the grounds?"

"Yes, sir." Jim wiped his hands on his pants. "I didn't notice any footprints or tire tracks or anything else, for that matter."

"Not surprising with all the snow we had last night." At least this time they had footprints in the building. "The back way in, the way you brought in the doc, is that common knowledge?"

Jim nodded. "That's where delivery trucks come and go. The main gate's too small for them to pass through.

I asked Floyd. Last delivery was two days ago, though."

Sam stepped out of the building and made her way to Tucker. "Hi, Jim. Can you give us a minute?" When Goiter stepped off to talk to the attendants, she said, "As I'm sure you've already guessed, I'd say that's your missing teen."

"Cause of death?"

"Technically, undetermined right now. Off the record? The garroting obviously would have done it. But autopsy will let me know whether that was done postmortem or not." She sagged against the building next to Tucker. "That wound . . . it's the same as Michael Levi's, Tucker. You ready to tell me what we're dealing with here? This a serial?"

Tucker blew on his hands then shoved them in his pockets. He took a couple of beats, then told her everything he knew. He hadn't wanted to taint her findings with Miranda's suspicions. But now there was a second body. A fucking kid. He couldn't pretend they weren't dealing with a serial killer any longer, even if the textbook three killings hadn't yet happened. If Tucker didn't find the son of a bitch, it would only be a matter of time.

Sam's pale face had little to do with the cold. Like him, she had probably thought taking a position in a town like Christmas would mean she wouldn't have to deal with shit like this. He was sorry to be the one to lay it on her.

She raked her messy blond hair and sighed. "I'm going to get him back to the morgue and do the prelim before sending him to Knoxville. I'll let you know what I find. And without saying too much, I'll let them know it's even more crucial that they move us up on their priority list."

"Thanks, Doc."

She smiled up at him, and he saw her struggle to hold it together. "Things like this aren't supposed to happen here."

"No. They're not."

She gave his arm a light squeeze, then climbed into the coroner's van while the assistants rolled Ricky's bagged body into the back on a gurney. When the van disappeared from sight, Tucker made his way to Jim, who was sneaking a cigarette behind the outbuilding.

"On your way out, make sure you let Floyd know to lock up the back entrance if possible, and absolutely no one enters this area until I give the all-clear."

"Sure thing, Chief."

Tucker climbed into his cruiser. He'd be willing to bet this staging was meant to mimic a confirmation, the next in the order of sacraments, but if anyone could tell him for sure whether it was a crazy notion that the Rosary Killer would strike a kid, it was Miranda.

Blasting the heat, he let the engine idle while he flipped through his phone for previous calls and located her number. He waited for her to answer, wondering if she even would. When her throaty voice greeted him two rings later, he was more than a little surprised.

"Where're you at? Do you have time to meet me?"

He could hear music in the background being turned down.

"Tucker?"

"Yeah, sorry, it's me."

"Everything okay? I haven't heard from you since—"

"Yeah, sorry about that, too. I'd like to swing by your place if you have time."

"I don't have anywhere else to be."

Tucker lifted his free hand in front of the vents and let his fingers thaw. He'd have time to shower and get the stench of Ricky's death off him. "Eight-thirty? I can bring food."

She laughed, and for a moment, the sound eased the tension in his shoulders and loosened the knots in his gut. "You don't have to feed me every time you want to see me."

"I like feeding you."

"And getting me drunk."

"I'll bring burgers. No wine."

"Like I said, you don't have to feed me. But hold the mayo on mine."

She hung up.

As he stuffed the phone into the console, he found himself smiling, but quickly sobered as his gaze connected to the building where Ricky's young body had just been bagged and tagged. An enormous burden of guilt made him sick to his stomach all over again. But he hadn't called Miranda so she could share a meal with him. He had a very valid reason for wanting to see her. She had been living and breathing this case for months and now that he had another body on his hands, he had to seriously consider the fact that she might have insight they'd overlooked.

He definitely needed insight. And probably a fresh set of eyes. He grabbed his phone again, dialing a number he'd had memorized for years.

"What the fuck, Tuck. Been a while." No matter how long it had been, his old partner, Finn Donovan, always greeted him the same way. "Man, I thought you were dead or something. How the hell have you been?"

Tucker adjusted the volume on the speakerphone

and put the cruiser into drive. "Decent. Or at least I was. That's why I'm calling. You got any vacation days saved up?"

"In fifteen years here, you think they've given me even one of my owed days willingly? Of course I have days. What's up?"

Tucker provided a brief rundown of his two scenes and gave the detective a minute to let it all sink in.

"But you think it's just a copycat?" Finn asked.

Tucker could picture him rubbing his jaw, sitting on the edge of the desk like he did whenever he was trying to piece facts together.

"I'm not stupid enough to call it anything yet," Tucker admitted. "Or willing to risk lives because I left some stones unturned."

"You got an extra bed?"

Tucker smiled. Finn didn't do hotels. Some people couldn't piss in public bathrooms, Finn Donovan couldn't sleep in other people's cum stains. His words, not Tucker's.

"I'll even buy new sheets to go on it."

"I can be there in a day or two. Will let you know when the lieutenant gives me leave."

Tucker thanked him and hung up feeling immensely better. He'd worked enough murders with Finn to know his chances of finding his killer had just improved tenfold. Finn and Tucker had held the record for most cases closed successfully in their run as partners in the Chicago PD.

Things were starting to look up.

Chapter 26

TUCKER JUGGLED THE bag of burgers and fries in one hand and hip bumped the car door closed. The tray of sodas slipped from his arm, and he barely caught the drinks before they smashed on the gravel path.

He knocked on Miranda's door and could hear the television playing. Lamplight peeked from between the drapes, then she opened the door and beckoned him inside. "Hey."

"Hey yourself."

She tightened the belt on her robe and padded in a pair of socks to the kitchen. "Coffee?"

He held up the tray. "I brought drinks. Maybe after?"

She diverted from the path to the coffeepot and took a seat at the table. "Okay, then. Let's eat while you tell me why you wanted to see me."

If he told her now, she'd probably lose her appetite. "Eat first."

He opened the bags and passed her a burger. They ate in silence, an awkward tension hanging between them. He swallowed, looking for the right thing to say to ease the obvious embarrassment she was feeling about last night.

"Miran—"

"Tuck—" She laughed. "You first."

He smiled around the straw of his soda. "It's been a long day, but I should have made sure you were okay about—"

"It was just a kiss. Not a big deal. Let's drop it, okay? I want to work with you on this and I don't want things to get awkward between us."

Just a kiss. Right.

He nodded and returned his attention to his fries. Not awkward, his ass.

"So? What happened today?"

She'd pretty much finished her food. No more reason to delay. "You said confirmation was one of the sacraments."

"That's right. It's usually high-school-age kids. I think it depends on the parish, but typically eighth graders."

"What would he be dressed in? Anything special?"

"Did something else happen, Tucker?"

"Yeah. I . . . we found that kid we were looking for. I'm pretty sure he was the first victim here in Christmas."

She sat in silence for a moment, and he thought she might cry. Instead, she surprised him by squaring her shoulders and taking a deep breath. "And you think it was confirmation."

"Possibly."

"It would make sense. They're usually around fourteen, fifteen years old when they're confirmed."

Which explained why the killer had strayed from his MO with a teen rather than an adult this time. He must like the power that came from killing a grown man, because any of his victims could have been younger, easier prey. And while he could have chosen an adult to use in his confirmation scene, a young boy would make a much louder, sadder statement.

"And you have no idea why the Dayton PD thought these were re-creations of sacraments in the first place? I still don't see anything that leads me to believe it's anything more than a religious-set murder."

She shook her head. "You haven't found anything in the files, yet?"

"I've barely had time to open them. Lisa has been combing through them, but she hasn't said anything."

Miranda placed a hand on her belly and sighed. "I'm telling you, it's the Rosary Killer. It's confirmation. He'd choose someone he could cleanse, force him into a confirmation of his own making."

"I didn't find a rosary, but that doesn't mean there wasn't one. It was partially hidden on the other victim." He scrubbed his eyes. "This is not how I wanted to find Ricky Schneider."

"I'm so sorry. I just wish . . . Maybe if I hadn't waited . . . Excuse me." She clamped her hand over her mouth and ran from the room.

He wanted to go after her, make sure she was all right, but was certain his witnessing her weakness would be worse than any comfort he could offer. Moving to the kitchen, he started a pot of coffee and returned to the table to clean up the remnants of dinner. When the coffee finished brewing and Miranda still hadn't returned, he ventured down the hall and called out for her. He found her sitting on the bathroom floor, her head cradled against her raised knees. She didn't even look at him when he knelt beside her.

"It's so wrong. That boy never should have died. If I could've made the Dayton police listen to me—"

He dropped to the floor beside her and pulled her against his chest. "You can't think like that. There was no way for you to know what he was going to do. You're not a cop, Miranda. There was nothing you could've done."

He held her, rocking her softly until her tears stopped and her breath normalized. Pushing himself up the wall, he carried her into the bedroom, jerked the covers back, and settled her in the middle of the bed. This was the second night in a row he found himself tucking her in.

"Tucker . . ."

There was no way he was leaving her. Not like this. It was his fault for telling her about Ricky's murder. He didn't know if his being here would keep the nightmares at bay. If not, at least she wouldn't have to wake up and deal with them alone.

"Go to sleep." He clicked the lamp off, then collapsed in the chair in the corner. He could sense her desperation to protest as she realized his intention to hunker down and babysit her. She tried to muffle her sobs against the pillow but they echoed through the room, murdering his conscience.

He didn't fall asleep until the soft sounds of Miranda's snoring became his lullaby. When the sun was safely up again, he made sure she was still tucked in, and headed home for a shower.

Chapter 27

Saturday

MIRANDA WOKE SLOWLY to find Tucker's chair empty. She lay in bed, wondering what time he'd left. How long had she cried before finally falling asleep?

That poor kid. Was there anything she could have done differently to prevent his death?

Nauseous, she stumbled to the bathroom. Twenty minutes later, the long shower had refreshed her, but by no means had it erased the guilt from her heart or the queasiness of her stomach.

Chucking her soiled clothes into a plastic laundry bag, she pulled on fresh jeans and a turtleneck, then grabbed her dirty parka and purse. She had to talk to Tucker, make sure he knew she was strong enough to help. If he considered last night's reaction a testament to her grit, he might not tell her anything else.

She crammed her wallet and a pair of spare gloves back into her purse, then tossed her car keys and phone inside, too, and seeing the cruiser gone, headed off Tucker's property toward town. It took two trips around the Town Square to find the little bakery tucked along a side street, where she purchased two coffees and cheese Danishes before continuing on to the police station.

Lisa greeted her from the front desk.

"Is Tucker around?"

"He's on a call. I'll let him know you're here."

Miranda set the Danishes and coffees on the counter. "I have food . . . if you're hungry?"

Lisa helped herself to a Danish. "I know who you are, you know. I should be mad as hell at you. I don't like being made a fool of."

Miranda frowned. "It was never my intention—"

"Whatever. What's done is done. Just know that secrets don't make you look so good, all right?"

Miranda opened her mouth to respond, but the bell over the door chimed, silencing her attempt at an explanation. A woman with pale yellow hair and a scowl marched to the counter.

"Helen," Lisa said, folding her arms over her breasts.

"Where's the chief?"

"Busy. Want me to tell him you stopped by?"

"I heard there's a second body. I can't keep holding on to this information. It's jeopardizing my ethics as a reporter."

"Ethics? Since when do you have those?" Lisa shuffled some papers and leaned back in her chair. "I'll let Chief Ambrose know you want a statement as soon as he's ready to release the news. Not before then. We know you've been paid to keep your mouth shut, and judging by that handbag you're carrying, I doubt you have any of that money left to pay back, so keep your pen still, got it?"

"The people of Christmas deserve to know—"

"The people of Christmas deserve a holiday that's not filled with panic that's going to drive out the tourists. When we know something for sure, trust me, you'll be free to write about it."

"Are tourists more important than people's safety? Breaking the story could save lives."

"More like give you more bylines when you freelance it out to the surrounding counties." Lisa crossed her arms, her glare not wavering under the other woman's intense anger. "When we feel that keeping quiet is jeopardizing our citizens, you'll get the green light. Not before."

"Just because Ethel Levi has the power to keep her son's death quiet doesn't mean this other family would. It was a *kid*, for God's sake, Lisa. You think you're going to keep those parents as quiet as our mayor has been? Whether it comes from me or not, news is going to leak. You'd better start preparing this office for a panic because that's what you're about to get."

"Go home, Helen." Tucker's voice was audible before he appeared from the hallway. He cast Miranda an acknowledging glance, then returned his stare to the woman. "Nothing goes in the *Chronicle* yet. I need a few more facts and then I'll give you a release. That *kid's* parents haven't even been notified yet, so zip it. Got it? We get a legit ID on him before anything's released."

He motioned Miranda back. She gathered her belongings and followed him into his office.

"Didn't think I'd see you this early," he said, shutting the door. "How're you feeling?"

"Peachy." She handed him his cup of coffee but kept the remaining Danish for herself. She popped the top off her cup, happy to see it had retained a bit of its warmth.

She clenched her fist in her lap.

"I'm sorry I upset you last night," he said.

"I'm a big girl, Tuck." She glanced at the box in the corner. "How long till you're done going through the Dayton files?"

"I haven't even had a chance to really start yet. I have a friend coming in this afternoon to help. Things will speed up with us both looking things over. Don't worry. I still plan on letting you help."

She frowned. "That's not what I was concerned about."

"What then?"

"Because. Today's Saturday. That means there's only one day left before Anatole will strike again. We have to work faster, Tucker."

FINN DONOVAN ROLLED into Christmas, Tennessee, via airport shuttle bus, wearing jeans, a thick wool coat, and a scowl the size of Texas. Tucker greeted him with a handshake and helped him get his duffel bag out of the van while Finn stepped back, lit a cigarette, and glowered at the half dozen other passengers he'd obviously hated spending the hour ride with.

"That one smelled like Ben-Gay and her husband nearly killed us all with his farts," he said, thrusting his cigarette toward an older couple making their way inside the hotel. Since the Marriott was close to the department, it had been easier to have Finn meet him here at the shuttle drop-off than at the airport. Tucker hadn't been able to sacrifice the hour drive.

After Miranda had left his office that morning, Andy had called in with a positive ID from Stan and Tanya Schneider, and Tucker had spent the next few hours trying to make them understand that going to the press right now would be bad for the town, and more important, could hinder his efforts to find their son's killer.

"Hasn't been so long that I've forgotten you know how to let one go with the best of them, man," Tucker muttered.

"Least I'm nice enough not to do it in close quarters with no open windows. Smell my coat! Smells like fucking sulfur and old people." He shuddered. "Next time, pick me up at the airport or work your damned case without me."

"You wouldn't have come if you didn't miss working with me, so quit bitching." Tucker slung the duffel over his shoulder and waited for Finn to finish his smoke and toss the butt in the nearby ashtray before leading the way inside the police station.

As they strode into the heated reception area, Lisa glanced up, the phone tucked between her ear and shoulder. "Yes, ma'am, I understand it's an emergency that your cat can't get out of the tree, but you still need to call the fire department." She covered the phone with her hand and smiled. "You must be Finn. It's really nice to meet you."

Finn winked. "We haven't officially met yet. Maybe you'll let me buy you a drink later and we can correct that?"

"Sure, and she can bring her two kids along so you can get to know them, too." Tucker walked back to his office, trusting Finn to follow. The man had one hell of a reputation when it came to police work and an even bigger one with the ladies. The last thing he needed was for Lisa to get hurt by yet another emotionally unavailable cop. Andy Bowen had done enough damage in that department as it was.

The office door closed with a firm thud. "Didn't mean to step on your toes there." Finn perched on the edge of the desk. "Got a thing for her?"

"No." Tucker flicked the lid off the Rosary Killer box and pulled out the folder with his notes. "She's got a lot on her plate and doesn't need a side of Donovan heartbreak to fill it even more."

"You wound me." Finn grinned and took the file. He sat and scanned the pages, flipping through them much too fast to be reading more than the highlights. That was how Finn worked. Catch the gist of the situation, hear the details and questions that came with it, then go back and read everything word for word to make up his own mind as objectively as he could. It was one of the things Tucker liked best about him—that he had no agenda other than putting bad guys behind the bars and pretty girls between the sheets.

Finn tossed the folder on the desk. "I take it you called to make sure this Bobby Harley guy is still where he's supposed to be?"

"Yeah, he's present and accounted for. No visitors and only one letter received once a week. No outgoing mail at all."

"Did you talk to that detective in Dayton? Find out if anyone might have been overly interested in the case?"

Just Miranda, but he wasn't offering up that information yet. He shook his head. "Let's suppose we're *not* dealing with a copycat here. What if an innocent man is sitting in prison and the real killer is picking up where he left off, here in my town?"

"That's a big jump. You have anything to back it up?"

"Just my gut."

And Finn knew as well as Tucker that a cop's gut was the most valuable weapon he possessed.

Tucker ran through Miranda's version of the Dayton killings, making certain to leave her name out of it. He wanted Finn's infamous objectivity, and the minute he learned that Miranda was Bobby's sister, that objectivity was going to be sorely tested.

"And you think it's a priest? That's a mighty big accusation to cast without proof. The church has been under a lot of fire lately, and something like this . . . you just better make damned sure you're right before you tell anyone else this theory."

"I know. And I'm still not sure I believe it. It's just . . . a theory."

Miranda's theory. One he was believing more every day.

"The Rosary Killer struck every Sunday for three weeks in Dayton," Finn said. "If you're right, he's done two more here, and you have two more coming." Finn sat up straight and hooked the box with his foot, dragging it to his side. "In the meantime, we go through every piece of this and find a connection between your two dead guys, your priest, and anyone else we can tie together."

"Go for it. I'll get Lisa to help you. I have something I need to do first."

Finn raised a dark brow. "You call me down here for help, then leave me to do it alone? What the hell could be more important than getting the facts in this box?"

Tucker opened the door. "Getting the facts from the source. I'm going to see Bobby Harley."

Chapter 28

WELCOME TO DAYTON

TUCKER EYED THE city sign, his back aching from sitting for so long. He should have come here days ago, but hadn't. Why? Maybe because he hadn't known exactly what questions to ask until now. Shit, that was a lie. He still didn't know everything he wanted to say or ask.

Guess he'd figure it out when he got there.

He turned onto Germantown Street and into the Dayton Correctional Institution. He used his badge to get past the twenty-four-hour reservation rule, thanked security, handed over his weapon, then waited in the small meeting room where he'd be allowed to speak to Bobby Harley face-to-face.

When Bobby was escorted in, the guards placed him on the opposite side of the table, cuffed him there, and left to stand guard outside the door.

"Didn't know what you preferred but help yourself," Tucker said, pushing the can of Coke he'd stopped for on his way in across the table.

Bobby popped the top and took a sip. "Should I know what this is about?"

Tucker studied him for a moment, noted the similarities and differences between Miranda and her brother. His hair was blond, and Tucker knew from Lisa's snooping that Miranda was a redhead under all that black dye. But their eyes were the same. As was their demeanor, the same posture and fidgeting habits like drumming their fingers on the table and the inability to sit still.

As Bobby shifted, then shifted again, Tucker smiled. Definitely Miranda's brother. "My name is Tucker Ambrose. I'm Chief of Police in a town called Christmas, Tennessee. Ever hear of it?"

The look that flashed in Bobby's eyes was one of suspicion. So distrust for the law was another shared trait.

"No. Should I?"

"Your sister—"

"Miranda?" His dark eyes widened, the suspicion disappearing beneath a new sheen of worry. "She okay?"

"She's fine. She came to me . . . she's working her ass off to get you out of here. Do you realize that, Bobby?"

He squeezed his eyes shut, the worry not leaving his face. He couldn't be much younger than Miranda, but his clean-shaven face looked barely out of college. "I told her to leave it the hell alone. What is she doing?"

"Tell you what. If you answer a few questions for me, I'll tell you whatever you want to know about your sister. Deal?"

Bobby didn't answer for a long moment. He took another deep sip of his Coke, rubbed his wrists beneath the cuffs, and finally nodded. "What do you want to know?"

"Tell me about Peter Anatole."

Bobby cussed. "I told her . . . damn it. I told her to leave that trail alone."

Intrigued, Tucker leaned in. "You don't agree with her suspicions about Anatole?"

"I agree that I was set up. I know that I'm innocent. I also know that she needs to keep her nose out of it. If anything happened to her . . ."

"Why would you think something would happen to her unless you suspect him, too?"

Bobby leaned forward, his gaze unflinchingly holding Tucker's. "Listen. I don't want to believe her theories. A man doesn't offer a hand to lift you out of hell only to ensure you spend the rest of your life there, does he?"

Unless Father Anatole had extended that hand to pull Bobby in close enough to make him a prime suspect for crimes he knew were about to be committed.

"He was my friend," Bobby continued. "But if she is right . . . then she's risking her life by poking a hornet's nest. It's not worth it. *I'm* not worth it."

"Your sister doesn't agree with that sentiment. She's a pain in my ass, but she's fighting for you."

Bobby squeezed his eyes shut. "Tell her to stop. Maybe she'll listen to you."

Yeah. If Tucker had learned anything about Miranda, it was that she didn't like the word *no*. He was pretty sure she'd feel the same way about the word *stop*.

"If there's a chance he's guilty, that he set you up . . . wouldn't you want her to bring that to light?"

"Not if it puts her at risk. I owe everything I have . . . *had* . . . to her. I won't let her get hurt for me. I know her. If she finds out Anatole is innocent, she'll keep poking until she finds out who the real Rosary Killer is and she'll get herself killed. I can handle spending the rest of my life in here. But only because I know she's safe out there."

Bobby rubbed his wrist again where the cuff attached him to the table. "Not to mention she'll be destroying another life if she's wrong. I don't want Anatole to go through the hell I'm going through if he doesn't deserve it. He's had a hard enough life as it is."

Tucker's ears pricked with curiosity. "What do you mean?"

Quicker than Tucker could blink, the wall around Bobby Harley erected again. He sat rigid, watching, tapping his fingers on the table. "He didn't join the seminary because he wanted to. His father made him. And when he got a girl pregnant, he was almost unable to—"

"Pregnant?"

Bobby nodded. "It's not my business, or yours. But yeah, Anatole had a kid in high school. They gave him up for adoption and Anatole's been guilt-ridden by that his whole life."

He thought of the medallion Miranda had found at Walt's. It still hadn't come back from forensics in Knoxville, but the word *orphanage* had been unmistakable. That had to mean something, didn't it?

"Do you know what orphanage he sent the kid to?"

Bobby shook his head. "Somewhere here in Dayton is all I know. He used to volunteer there a lot, just so he could see the kid. Don't think he ever stopped making sure his son was taken care of. I'm surprised he moved, to be honest. I didn't think he'd ever move that far away from his kid, even though the kid has to be what, thirty-five? Forty now?"

Tucker stood and thanked Bobby, his brain reeling. If what Bobby said was true, why *had* Anatole moved so far away? Maybe he'd intended to move back to Dayton once he'd completed his rituals?

"Is there anything you want me to tell Miranda?" He remembered Miranda telling him that Bobby wouldn't see her and hadn't written.

"Just . . . I love her, but I don't want her coming here. Don't want her seeing me like this, you know?"

Bobby was trying to preserve whatever positive image Miranda still held of him. "Yeah, I get it. Anything else?"

"I don't have much left, but if you can tell me where to find her, I can have my attorney wire her some funds." He closed his eyes and shook his head, a sad smile on his face. "You know she quit her job when I was sentenced? Stupid. I couldn't talk her out of it. She's living off her savings now, so yet again, she's giving everything she has to me."

"She wouldn't be doing it if she didn't think you were worth it. Don't prove her wrong. If you think of anything that will help her finish this faster, tell her."

"That's all I have." He looked genuinely sad about that, and Tucker believed him.

The whole way home, Tucker couldn't shake Bobby's words.

He's had a hard enough life as it is.

He'd already run a background check on Anatole, but it was time for Tucker to dig a little deeper.

Chapter 29

Sunday

TUCKER HUNG UP his phone and stared at the spot on his desk where it lay.

"I take it by your face that wasn't good news." Finn looked up from the Dayton box and reached for his cup of coffee.

"Nothing I thought would pan out anyway. Bowen hasn't been able to locate a single teen who'll admit to being at the make-out point at Walt's the night Levi was killed." Tucker ran his hands through his hair and gave a light tug at the roots.

"So no witnesses."

"Nope." Just like every other door he'd turned to in this case, it was getting shut in his face.

"Maybe you'll get lucky and hear news about that medallion today, then. Something's gotta turn up. I have to admit, it's a bit suspicious that Anatole gave a kid up for adoption and an orphanage medallion was found at one of your scenes."

Did Miranda know that Anatole had given a son away?

No, she couldn't have. It was a major flaw in Anatole's past. Something to make him far less pious. If she knew, she would have told him just to make him see Anatole as a man with a past just like everyone else.

Tucker had gotten back into town too late last night to stop by Miranda's and tell her about his visit with her brother, but he'd spent the morning filling Finn in on his conversation with Bobby, and it seemed, finally, that Finn was beginning to see past the copycat theory long enough to look harder at Anatole, too. His objectivity was back. That was one good thing in Tucker's favor at least. Shit and objectivity were going to hit the fan when Finn found out Miranda was Bobby's sister, however. Nothing Tucker could do about that right now.

Lisa stuck her head in the door. "Got a minute?"

He beckoned her inside. She pulled a rolled-up newspaper from behind her back and handed it to him. "Thought you might want to see this. Think it's the reason our phones have been ringing off the hook all morning. I had to call Shannon in to help man them."

She handed him the *Chronicle*, gave him a minute to scan before she started talking again. "How pissed is she going to be?"

Don't shoot the messenger.

"Pissed," he grumbled. "Thanks, Lisa. I'll take care of it."

"What is it?" Finn scooted his chair closer to Tucker's desk so he could read. "I don't get it. What's the big deal?"

Before Tucker could answer, the door opened again and Miranda strode inside. He dropped the paper they'd been reading and tried to kick it under his desk without her seeing.

"Hey," she said, smiling. "Lisa said I could come on back. Hope that's okay."

Finn twisted in his chair to greet her and his smile faltered. "Jesus. It's like Sandra Bullock and that chick from *Lost* had a hot-ass lesbian fling, defied biology, and somehow created *you*." Finn looked at Tucker. "I call dibs."

Tucker sighed. "Finn, meet Miranda. Miranda, this is my old partner from Chicago, Detective Finn Donovan."

Tucker moved a chair closer to his side of the desk and motioned for her to sit. Before Finn could retrieve the half-hidden newspaper, she grabbed it.

"Some reason you don't want me to see this?"

Tucker reached for the paper but she stepped out of reach and opened it before he could snatch it away. There, on the front page, was Tucker's missing teen.

Ricky Schneider. The latest victim of the Rosary Killer. Of course, it didn't say that. It merely said the boy had been found dead at Christmas Grain and Grist Mill. There was no mention of Michael Levi, no mention of a serial killer. But near the end of the article were the printed words he hadn't wanted her to see.

He waited for her to finish the article, the front office phones ringing off the hook in the background. Now he knew why. The town wanted assurance that they were doing all they could to find Ricky's killer, that their own children were still safe in Christmas.

Miranda's hands shook slightly, and he knew she'd reached the end. She began reading out loud, " 'Sources confirm that a nurse with Ohio plates is assisting on the case, though the reasons for this are unclear. Is it a statement on the fate of our town that we're now relying on medical professionals to solve Christmas's crimes? Perhaps it's time to start rethinking our staffing choices. What do you think, Christmas? Please send all editorial letters to Helen Stillman."

She tossed the paper on the edge of the desk and glared at him. "Did you tell her that?"

Tucker took the *Chronicle* and threw it in the trash can. "Of course I didn't. That's just how Helen works. She's not happy unless she's stirring up trouble."

"Trouble? She mentioned me and Ohio in the same sentence, Tucker. That's more than trouble for me. If he reads this . . ."

"I'm assuming you mean Father Anatole?" Finn asked. "Someone fill me in here. What's the big deal?"

Tucker scowled. "I'll explain later."

He was going to be doing a lot of explaining later. Somehow, he still had to figure out how to tell Miranda he'd visited Bobby yesterday.

He caught Miranda staring at him. "What?"

"He's here to help?"

"In any way you might need me, ma'am," Finn said, grinning like an ass again.

Miranda didn't appear the least bit fazed by his charm. "Okay. Forget the article for a minute. Nothing I can do about that, and I'm pretty sure you'd take issue with me strangling that Helen woman."

"Yes, yes I would."

"So, where are you at with all this?" she asked, gesturing to the files spread out around the office. "It's Sunday. Please tell me you have something."

"Finn and I have been bouncing ideas around and I have eyes on Anatole all day. I'm doing my job, Miranda."

"Don't snap at the pretty lady, Tuck. Didn't your mama ever teach you—"

Miranda jerked her head toward Finn. "That crap really work for you?"

Finn held up his hands in mock surrender and Tucker silently gloated. "My bad." He raised an eyebrow at Tucker.

Miranda swore. "It's"—she checked her watch— "almost noon. We don't have a lot of time here."

She was damned prickly today. The article probably hadn't helped. But Tucker didn't mind since it seemed the prickliness was mostly aimed toward Finn.

"We've been discussing possible victims. Trying to narrow down who we might need to keep watch on," he said. "We still have anointing the sick and holy orders."

"I'm thinking we should find a list of citizens who might have terminal illnesses." Finn leaned back in his seat, away from Miranda.

Miranda shook her head. "He wouldn't kill someone just for being sick. He'd have to see it as a sin to cleanse. A sickness they could have controlled maybe."

Finn plucked the cigarette he kept behind his ear. "Some people think smokers are asking for their cancers. An obese person with diabetes? A prostitute with gonorrhea? Shit like that?"

"It's possible, but with the exception of the prostitute, none of that sounds overly sinful to me, unless he sees it as gluttony maybe," Miranda said.

Tucker's cell phone chirped. He gave them an apologetic smile before answering. "Ambrose."

"Chief, it's Sam Murray."

Tuck held up a finger and left the office so he could listen without distraction. He'd been waiting for this call for days, but having a deputy coroner call on a Sunday usually wasn't good news. For him, he hoped that wasn't the case. "Hey Doc. Tell me you're back in Christmas."

"If you're free in about two hours I will be."

"My office?"

"Make it mine. I have Michael Levi's autopsy report."

SAMANTHA MURRAY'S OFFICE was warm and stuffy, which did nothing to help slow the sweat collecting under Tucker's collar. The pictures spread out on her desk were no more horrific than any other autopsy he'd been witness to, but somehow, these were making his hands clammy. If Miranda was right, another murder just like this one could happen again in a matter of hours.

"There are half a dozen cuts across his legs and arms," Sam said. "They're deep, but missed the major vessels so he bled out slowly. Until he was garroted, anyway."

Tucker popped an antacid.

"His jaw was pretty much shattered and his spine was broken in two places," she continued. "His neck was nearly severed and clumps of hair were pulled out at the roots." She pointed to a bald spot near Michael's scalp above the left ear.

"Nothing under his nails? Maybe his knuckles if he put up a fight?"

"Only dirt under the nails. No evidence of anything biological left on the body belonging to your killer." She pulled out another picture and handed it to him. This one showed a man's bare abdomen, pre-autopsy, his ribs punctured with gouges the size of baby fists.

"Knife wounds?"

She nodded. "Could be. It's an odd knife though. Kind of curved, you see?" She pointed to the photo at three sloppily placed, almost crescent shaped wounds between Michael's ribs. "Doubt you're dealing with a surgeon or anyone skilled with knives because there's no finesse here."

He pointed to a section of thin scratches below Michael's navel. "What're those?"

She passed him a magnifying glass. "See for yourself."

He bent over the photo and held up the glass. Tiny scratches, barely an inch long, made out the numbers 196 518 across Michael's lower belly.

"Jesus." He thought of Anatole and his stomach clenched. A priest washing away a victim's final sins? Casting judgment before God could? "What the hell do those mean?"

"No idea. But, Tucker?"

"Yeah?"

"The other body you had me pick up—the teen—I don't have his reports yet, but I can tell you, he has the same thing scratched on his stomach. Different numbers, but same placement." She flipped through a notebook she'd pulled out of her purse. "816 135."

Silence hung between them for a long moment. "Nothing?" she asked.

"No."

He had no clue what those numbers meant. He needed to see if the Dayton victims had anything similar on their bodies. Maybe there was something in those files that explained it. If not, maybe Miranda knew.

He grabbed his hat. "Get me something soon."

It wasn't a request.

TUCKER SPED FROM Doc's office on the opposite side of town back to the station. How was it he had more questions than answers again?

He turned onto Main Street and pulled over in a pharmacy lot. His whole body was cold, and it had nothing to do with the weather. One of the reasons he'd left Chicago was that it had become more and more difficult to separate his own memories from the cases he'd faced. Now, he found his brain continually returning to his youth and the smiling face that would never smile at him again.

Ricky's face in that granary was haunting him, and now that he'd seen Levi's autopsy photos, he was imagining Ricky on that same cold slab, waiting to be sliced open yet again. The brutality in that kid's life was never-ending.

Olivia. Ricky. Something in him ached, and before he could put thought to his actions, he pulled his phone from his pocket.

"Hello?" His sister's voice was painfully familiar, and yet completely foreign on the other end of the line.

"Gloria? It's Tuck."

There was a long silence. Some breathing. Then . . . "Tucker? Is that really you? Turn down the television! I'm on the phone!"

He smiled, picturing her folding laundry while his niece and nephew watched Nickelodeon. Did the twins even remember him? He hadn't seen them since they were in diapers. They had to be at least six now. Maybe seven.

"Yeah, it's me. How is everyone?"

"All right. Tommy, no. Not now. I'll get you some milk in a minute. How are you?"

He was having trouble figuring out when she was talking to him and when she wasn't, and it took a second to realize the question had been directed at him. "I'm . . . good. Homesick maybe. How're the twins?"

"Up to no good. Listen, no one's been able to reach you. Is this your new number?"

He sighed. "Yeah. Keep it."

"So are you done staying away? Are you coming up for the gala?"

The gala. Christ. Was that why he'd had the itch to call? He'd forgotten all about the annual fund-raiser. "I can't. There's this case—"

"There's always a case," Gloria grumbled. "She was your sister, too, Tuck. This charity keeps her alive."

Every memory kept her alive. He didn't need to put on a tux and pass around a plate for victims' advocacy to make it any more so. It had been a mistake to call.

"Do me a favor, tell Mom and Dad I said hi, but don't give them this number, all right? I'll . . . try to visit when all this is settled, but for now—"

"Same old Tuck. Living your life without any remorse over leaving the rest of us behind. You should be an uncle. A brother. Hell, a son . . . whether they deserve one or not. They're not perfect, Tucker. But neither are we."

No, they weren't. His parents had tried to be the best parents they could be, but for their family, that had meant passing the kids off to nannies and speaking to their children only when they wanted it to be known they were disappointments. Which was always.

"Soon, Glor. Not yet."

Another silence deadened the line, and just when he thought she'd hung up, she said, "Dad's sick, you know."

Tucker clutched the phone tighter. "What do you mean?"

"Heart issues. He might have to have surgery. Come home, Tucker. Please. I can't do all this alone."

Guilt sickened him. He'd been able to escape the life he hadn't wanted, but he'd left his baby sister behind to hold down the fort, alone.

"I really do have a case here. But give me a few weeks, a month . . ."

"Right. Good-bye, Tuck."

This time, the silence was deafening.

Chapter 30

"I KNOW YOU reminded me this morning and I forgot. I'm sorry." His cell phone pressed against his cold ear, Josh Longwood rushed from the late night pharmacy, the prescription for his daughter in one hand, the candy his son needed for school in the other. He couldn't believe he'd forgotten the medicine of all things. He'd never hear the end of the nagging now. Kissing ass was his only option. "Yes, I got the stuff for Jack's party, too."

He listened to his wife's panicked voice on the other end of the line and tried to calm her down. "Her inhaler will help. I'll be home in a few minutes."

He closed his eyes and lifted the phone from his ear to give himself some relief from her berating. When she took a breath, he said, "I know and I said I was sorry. My meeting ran late and . . ." He sighed. "Yes, I'll hurry. Love you, too."

Swamped with guilt, he disconnected and fumbled to get his keys out of his pocket. He had no one to blame for the mess his life had become but himself. He'd forgotten about his children, for cripes' sake. Again. He was a shit of a father.

He leaned against the driver's seat and shut his eyes. He couldn't keep living like this. This double life. This lie. It was killing him, and even worse, it was hurting the people he loved most. His wife. His children. But if they ever found out . . .

He couldn't stand the thought of it. Not for the first time, he told himself to end it. But other than the hour every night he spent tucking his kids in, the only happiness he had came from the life they knew nothing about.

No matter how desperately he wanted to be a good husband and father, he couldn't stay away from his lover. He'd finally accepted that. He couldn't tell Sara that he wanted a divorce, and he couldn't tell David that he was married with two children.

So many lies. Sometimes, even he couldn't remember what was truth and what was fiction. Last week he'd told Sara he was working late. He was supposed to have met David for dinner. Instead, he'd found himself at his office, wondering why the hell he was there.

His phone rang again. Certain it was Sara with another rant, he nearly shut off his phone. It was David. The usual gut-wrenching longing made his finger tremble as he hit the accept-call button.

"Hey babe," David said. "Bed's already cold. You sure you can't come stay the night?"

Josh sighed. He'd stayed the night with David only three times in their relationship. It was becoming harder and harder to find excuses to leave when, in truth, all he wanted to do was stay.

"I wish." Josh put the phone on speaker, looked at the image of David staring back at him from the caller

ID. How much would he give to wake up in David's arms? Have breakfast? Spend the day walking the park or riding the Ferris wheel without worrying about what others might think of him?

His throat gave a painful squeeze. "You know I wish," he said again.

As far as David was concerned, Josh could never stay because he lived with an un-understanding, sickly mother who required his help at all hours of the evening. Too frail to live alone.

Another sick lie. Josh's mother had been dead for a decade.

He looked away from the phone. Stared out the window as he listened to David turn on the charm. *A can of whipped cream*, David says. *Kisses, everywhere*, he says.

A tear tickled the tip of Josh's nose and he brushed it away, feeling like a pathetic ass.

A shadowy figure joined his in the glass. A man was hunched over from the cold, quaking as he rocked back and forth, huddled beneath his hooded, dingy coat.

"David, I have to go. I'll call you back in a bit." Without waiting for a response, Josh tossed the phone onto the passenger seat and bolted from the car. "Hey man. Off the ca—"

The man whirled, and in an instant, something metal struck Josh in the face, knocking him to the pavement. His head slammed against concrete, and he fought to keep his eyes open, struggled to raise an arm against the second attack coming toward his throbbing skull. He rolled in time for the lead pipe to hit the asphalt and scrambled for the keys he'd dropped in his haste to get out of the car. They were a sorry excuse for a weapon, but they were the only thing within grabbing distance.

The world spun, and the need to vomit seized him as blood ran down his forehead, over his left eye. He reached again for the keys, ready and willing to stab the son of a bitch in the eye, but as his fingers brushed the cool metal, a rag was stuffed into his mouth and his arms were jerked and bound behind his back. Something thick fell over his head, cloaking him in darkness as arms wrapped around his stomach like steel bands.

He kicked out, trying to catch the bastard behind the knees, but he couldn't see. Disoriented, he kicked the wheel of his car instead. Most of his movements uncontrolled and manic, he managed to contact something with his fist, pummeling whatever it was to the bone. He heard a grunt, felt the weight of his attacker on him for an instant. He gagged, vomit rushing up his throat, choking him behind the cloth filling his mouth.

A blow struck his temple. The fight temporarily knocked out of him, he fell limp and his body was lifted as easily as if he weighed no more than a ten-year-old girl. His attacker smelled of sweat and Irish Spring, and Josh caught a whiff of onion through the cloth covering his face as he was tossed into a vehicle. As he tumbled inside, his head smashed something hard. The soft bounce of tires beneath his weight induced a stronger wave of nausea. He vomited again, swallowing it back down to keep from choking to death.

Stay calm. Jesus, just stay calm.

There was a loud bang, then silence cloaked him along with a sheen of sweat. A trunk. He was in a fucking trunk. As the vehicle began to move, Josh fought not to panic, desperate to remain focused on the turns to figure out where he was being taken. A left. A right. A long, endless stretch with no swerves at all. Then, a rutted road.

His head bounced, his body thrown about in the compact space. His nose smashed against the side of the car and warm, sticky blood dripped onto his lips beneath the gag. It had already been difficult to breathe. Now, with his nose clogged, tiny little gasps were barely giving him any air at all.

He thought of Sara, of her pain-filled face as she told their children that Daddy was dead. Fuck that. He was not ready to die. Not like this, damn it. Never like this!

The car stopped, throwing him against the rear of the trunk. His fingers grappled behind his back, searching for anything to throw at the bastard or stab at him or . . . Jesus, *anything*.

There was nothing. No more time to gather his bearings or form a real plan. No more time to think of his children and pray that they forgave him for forgetting them tonight. The trunk opened. Hands gripped his arms and lifted him upward. Jesus. He weighed a solid two hundred pounds, yet he was being lifted like a fucking woman. His stomach scraped against metal and he grunted as he was dropped to the ground and dragged over unforgiving concrete.

Where was he? How much time had passed? When would Sara report him missing?

Jesus. JesusJesusJesus.

The covering was snatched off his head and a chunk of his hair with it. Josh blinked. His surroundings slowly came into view as his vision cleared, but it was too dark to make out any life-saving details.

He heard a soft scratch, then caught a whiff of sulfur. A tiny flame sparked to life a few feet away, but the soft glow didn't offer enough light to see anything that might help him. Just shadows. He watched candles flicker as their wicks caught fire.

The man kept his head down. There was no way to see who he was, but Josh did recognize *something*. The stained glass windows. Even dirt-encrusted and green from months of neglect, he knew he was in the old, abandoned First Baptist Church near the edge of town. Away from anyone and anything that might help him.

"Repent." The voice vibrated near his right ear, bathing Josh's neck in sticky, warm breath as the gag slipped away from his mouth.

He spat, desperate to rid himself of the coppery and acidic tastes trickling down his throat. He tried to twist, tried to glimpse the maniac holding him hostage. A knee to his back held him securely to the ground, making his attempts to move futile.

He tried to speak, but found a shaky voice buried beneath a fear he'd never known in his entire life. "What do you want?"

"Repent," the man repeated, his voice so soft Josh could barely hear him. "Repent and this can all end right now."

Josh fought against his bindings. What felt like wire bit into his wrists. His shoulders burned from the strain, and his whole body felt as though it had been pulled behind a pickup.

"R-repent what?"

But he knew. Even without the words spoken, Josh knew what this was about.

Someone had found out his secret. Someone was finally going to make him pay.

The weight lifted from Josh's body and he seized his chance. He clambered to his knees, but his off-balance attempt to charge was waylaid. He slammed into a marble table instead. No, not a table. An altar. *Jesus.*

Hands gripped his ankles and jerked his feet from

beneath him. Josh's forehead connected with the unforgiving marble before slamming onto the floor. His nose gushed blood again and a steady drip from the gash on his head ran into his eye, blurring his vision. Strong hands clasped his leg just below the knee. White-hot pain cut into Josh's thigh. Warmth pooled beneath him, instantly chilled by the cold in the vacant building.

"Please," he said, the mere effort of speaking like razor blades in his throat. "I haven't seen you. I don't know who you are. Let me go. Jesus. Let me go."

"To the family you don't deserve? Or to the lover with whom you sin?"

Fire engulfed his left leg until it finally went numb. The man moved so quickly that Josh couldn't pinpoint him in the candle-lit chapel. A slash cut through his coat and sweater. More pain. More blood. He bit his lip to keep from crying out.

"Repent."

Josh tried to move his leg but it wouldn't cooperate. "Okay. Okay. T-tell me what you want me to say. I'll do whatever you want. Just stop."

He fisted Josh's hair, jerking him to his feet. The slashes made it impossible for his legs to support his weight. The hold on his hair released. His forehead smacked against the altar again. More blood spilled into his eyes. A long, curved object swung into view, and he fixated on it, his imagination spiraling out of control with ways such a weapon would cause him pain.

He was going to die; there was nothing he could do but pray it was as swift and painless as possible.

"Do you love your children, Joshua Longwood?"

Tears spilled down his cheeks at the mention of his children. Fuck. Fuck fuck fuck. Images of Jack and Audrey, their smiling faces and love-filled, innocent eyes, squeezed his chest. They were good children. They were the only thing in his life he'd done right.

"What do you know about my goddamned children?"

The man yanked on Josh's hair and hot breath tickled his throat again. "You dare use His name in vain? You blaspheme in my presence?" A fist smashed against Josh's neck, sending him back to his belly.

He knew that voice. How did he know that voice? His brain reeled. "Who are you?"

"If a man lies with a male as he lies with a woman, both have committed an abomination. They shall surely be put to death. Their blood shall be upon them."

Spots floated before his eyes, and he rested his head against the altar.

How had he come to this? How was it that he'd been running errands and was now tied up, the victim of a madman's self-directed horror flick. Somehow, he knew Josh's secrets. Secrets Sara and David had never figured out.

The pain or the cold or the blood loss—possibly all three—made him shake. He had to concentrate to control his chattering teeth so his words could be understood. "I'll tell them the truth and end the affair. Is that what you want? I'll do it, I swear."

"The truth would only hurt those you left behind. I'm not so cruel or heartless as that. I am generous. I am benevolent. You will tell my God this when He judges you."

As realization settled in his bleeding gut, a primal roar ripped from Josh's throat, muffled by a cloth falling once again over his head, secured at the neck with an unforgiving cinch. He clawed at the gloved hands squeezing off his airway. This time, the darkness brought no fear. It offered comfort that he clung to as thoughts receded, his own name all but forgotten.

But just as he'd found the precipice of peace, the choking ceased and chills set fire to his oozing wounds. He was being stripped, his body bared. He lay still, listening, waiting.

Just hurry home. I love you.

Sara's last words to him kept his burning eyes open. He had to make it home. Beg forgiveness. Tell Sara the truth. Be who he'd been born to be and stop living in shame.

A glint of silver flashed in the candlelight just seconds before it pressed to his neck.

"No!"

Cold steel sliced through his side. Slid into him like he was made of bread rather than sun-toughened flesh. His lungs burned. Air whistled through his ribs with each struggling breath.

"Without you, everyone you've lied to will have a better life. Lying with a man, it is a sickness. A sickness of the mind, deviate and filthy. I anoint you as the sick should be anointed! The Holy Father anoints you! "

And with those words, the man yanked Josh's neck backward, snapping his spine like it was nothing more than a twig. Josh's body went numb again. The pain, mercifully, gone.

He'd nearly found the bliss of unconsciousness when he was flipped onto his back. He couldn't see through the darkness to identify his attacker, couldn't raise a fist in self-preservation, or even work his lips to spit in the son of a bitch's face. He could only lie there, waiting. Praying. Wishing he hadn't forgotten Audrey's prescription or Jack's candy. Would that be the last memory his children had of him? That Sara had of him?

The smell of leather clogged his nostrils and a gloved hand pried open his mouth. A bottle hovered over his face, just above his lips. Clamping his mouth shut, he tried to twist his head, tried to prevent what was about to happen—but his neck wouldn't obey.

The man grabbed Josh's chin, pried his lips apart. Josh clenched his teeth so tightly, several of his fillings cracked. The bastard pinched Josh's nose. He fought against opening his mouth. His body betrayed him. His mouth fell open, and he pulled in a huge gulp of icy air. Before he could release the scream ringing in his head, thick liquid filled his mouth, spilled up into his nose and one eye.

"Is anyone among you sick? Let him call for the elders of the church, and let them pray over him, anointing him with oil in the name of the Lord."

He wailed against the acid he knew was eating away at his guts though he couldn't feel it, and melting the flesh from his face—a pain he was all too aware of. Keeping his uninjured eye focused on the candles beside his head, he prayed for death. As a blade sliced through his chest, Josh Longwood swore he saw the hand of God reaching toward him as the devil pierced his heart.

Chapter 31

THE MINUTE SHE returned to her cottage that night, Miranda checked the microwave clock in the kitchenette, visible from the doorway. As she feared, the bright digits read the same time as her watch: 12:17 a.m. Whatever was going to happen, had already happened. The killer wouldn't allow Monday to come before he'd performed his rite.

Having spent the evening trying to keep an eye on Anatole, her back ached and her rear end was numb. She'd parked her Range Rover across from the church, her laptop securely on her lap, one eye on the door, the other on her screen. She'd seen him leave his house around eight, and had somehow managed to lose him in town around eight-thirty when he'd headed into Town Square. She'd given up her search fifteen minutes ago, frustrated and pissed off that he'd given her the slip. She could only hope Tucker's officers had been better at stakeouts than she was.

She tossed her purse and keys on the table. They promptly slid onto the floor. She left them there.

She was so exhausted she could've slept on her feet where she stood. A shower didn't help. Neither did fresh pajamas or the hot tea she choked down while she collapsed on the sofa and mindlessly watched the late news on television.

When the news ended, she turned off the television, tossing the remote on the floor, her mind still tumbling over the events that had likely occurred tonight. Whose fate had landed on the wrong slot of the roulette wheel tonight?

Questions piled up in her brain until they spilled down her throat and settled like pebbles in her belly. She turned off the lamp and dragged the afghan from the ottoman and buried herself beneath it, her eyes open in the pitch-black room. There was no ticking of the grandfather clock to distract her, as in the apartment she'd rented in Dayton. Even the Christmas carols playing over town speakers had finally quieted for the night.

Frustrated, she put the throw pillow over her face and smothered a scream beneath it before throwing it across the room. It hit the curtain by the front door, letting in a bit of light before landing on the sill, holding the crack in the fabric open a couple inches. Her gaze strayed to the door. A tiny stream of light poured in through a crack. In her exhaustion, she hadn't closed it properly.

With a groan, she crawled off the sofa and inched behind the recliner to retrieve the pillow and fix the drapes. Before she could extract herself to lock the door, a sound held her frozen. She jerked her head toward the door, certain she'd heard the handle move. Her breath hitched in her throat and stayed there until it burned.

She stood, watching. The handle moved slowly upward. Then down. She could rush the door, try to slam it shut before it opened . . . but she was stuck between the window and the recliner. Could she move that fast?

The door cracked. She ducked behind the chair, her breath trapped in her throat. A figure stepped inside, draped in shadow. It crossed to the hall, then moved toward the bedroom. Miranda inched toward the door, ready to bolt, but the shadow turned. She carefully placed the pillow over her hunched body, praying he wouldn't turn on any lights. Her gaze landed on her purse and keys, still lying where they'd fallen. Watching the shadow, she inched her arm out and clasped the keys in her fist so tightly, they couldn't make noise.

The sounds of the intruder came closer. A pair of black shoes faced the table, only inches away.

She clamped her hand over her mouth to keep her cry silent. She watched her purse rise from the floor by the chair. Heard the jangle of her belongings inside. A door closed outside, and laughter from her neighboring cottages created an eerie symphony through the partially opened door. Her curtains moved, casting more light into the room. It did her no good.

Without sticking her head out, she couldn't see beyond the intruder's knees. He stood at the window for several seconds—just inches from her. The curtains clanked against their hooks, then darkness again.

Jesus, her heart was pounding so loudly, he was going to hear it. She focused on those shoes, the only thing she could see clearly enough to tell Tucker. Boots. Wet from snow. Black and worn. They could belong to anyone. She didn't hold out hope that the pants would offer any more details. From what she could see, they were also black, loose-fitting, nondescript.

The shadow disappeared, but she could hear movement toward the tiny closet by the front door, still blocking her escape. The closet opened and something heavy dropped to the floor. Something was being unzipped. Her bag?

She seized her phone, dialed Tucker's number, kept the speaker on so he could hear and the volume down so her intruder couldn't. If Tucker was home, he could be here in seconds. If he wasn't . . .

He answered. She thanked God.

"There's someone here," she whispered, certain he wouldn't understand her muffled words.

The shadow whirled in her direction. Had she given herself away? She eased her hand around to the front of the chair and gently placed the phone there, praying Tucker would hear if something happened.

He stopped by the window again. Miranda held her breath. Waited to be found. When the shadow moved again toward the hall, she bolted from her hiding spot. Her hand barely brushed the doorknob to freedom when strong arms grabbed her around the waist and threw her to the floor.

Her skull hit hardwood, jarring her teeth and her spine. She screamed, desperate to make enough noise now that Tucker would hear.

The figure strode to the chair, and she tried to scramble to her feet but was too dazed to do more than slide onto her belly. The intruder snatched up her phone and pressed it to his ear. She had no idea what he heard on the other end, but he powered it off, slipped it into his pocket, and bent over Miranda.

As he reached out to grab her again, she closed her fist around the nearest thing she could find. The floor lamp. It was heavy and awkward but she rolled over, swinging with all her might, sending him sprawling. Something slid across the floor toward the kitchen, and Miranda pulled herself to her knees, hell-bent on reaching the door before he could regain his footing.

She wasn't fast enough. He fisted her hair, threw her as though she was made of air. Her back smacked into the kitchen table, her cheek coming down hard on the seat of a chair. Lights burst behind her eyes, but she willed herself to remain conscious. She hadn't hit him hard enough to do damage the first time, but this time, by God, she would. She grabbed the coffee carafe, raised it over her head, and charged him. Glass shattered around his shoulders. He staggered. Swayed, but lurched for her again.

Ignoring the pain screaming through her body, she dashed for the door and headed for the party outside her neighbor's cottage, casting only the briefest of glances behind her to see that Tucker's truck and cruiser weren't there.

The laughter stopped as she approached the group of five smoking on the porch. Someone grabbed her arm, the muffled words "Are you okay?" barely audible beneath the blood rushing in her ears.

"Ph-phone," she panted.

Someone handed her a cell phone. She held it uselessly, realizing she didn't know Tucker's number without her contacts list. She dialed 911 and collapsed onto the stairs, trying to regain her breath. From here, she could see her cottage was dark and lifeless. Where had he gone?

A thick, smoke-tainted jacket was placed around her shoulders. As Shannon's voice answered on the other end, Miranda's thoughts grew cloudy. The phone fell from her hand and consciousness slipped from her grip.

IF TUCKER HAD been near his cruiser when Miranda's call had come in, he would have had lights blazing and sirens blaring as he raced down the streets of Christmas. As it was, his cruiser was still parked at the station and he could only be thankful that the streets were quiet enough to allow him to maneuver his Raptor at full speed, taking no notice of red lights or stop signs or any other rules of traffic.

The two beers he'd had with Finn at the bar churned in his stomach as he pulled into his drive to open the gate. He didn't even bother to cut the engine or pull up in front of his house. He just ran . . . straight to Miranda's cottage.

He'd just made it to her open door, his heart in his throat, when he saw Miranda stumbling across the property from her neighbor's. She was wearing a long shirt and an oversized jacket he'd never seen before.

He jogged toward her and she fell against him, sobbing. He lifted her, carried her back to his place and set her on his sofa, cranking the heat before she was fully settled. "I need you to tell me what happened, Miranda. Can you do that?"

"H-he . . . my cottage. He was th-there."

"Who? Who was there?" He chafed her arms to help warm her. A bruise was forming on her cheek, but he couldn't see any other marks right off. "Did he hurt you? Miranda?" He forced a calm into his voice he didn't feel. "Did he touch you?"

She took a deep breath. "He just . . . came in. Wouldn't let me run. I tried, but he's strong. He was l-looking for something. I don't know wh-what. He t-took my phone and I—I think I hurt him."

"Where are you hurt?"

She shook her head. "I'm fine. Sore but not—nothing serious. He might still be in there, Tucker. I n-never saw him leave."

"Let me look at you."

"I said I'm fine." She jerked her chin from his grip. Large, brown, watery eyes blinked up at him, and all he wanted to do was make her fear disappear.

He tucked her against his chest and placed a soft kiss on the crown of her head. She threw her arms around his neck and shook with sobs. Her skin was ice-cold, the strange jacket and the heater a sorry substitute for the feeling of security.

He rocked her, rubbing her hair in a pathetic attempt to offer comfort, but inside, his body was alive with adrenaline. If fear had a smell, she was coated in it. He wanted to push her aside and hunt down whoever was responsible for putting her in this state.

He gave her another light kiss. "Do you think you can walk up there with me? See if anything other than your phone is missing?"

"H-he checked my bags. I heard him. But I don't think he took anything else. I think I took him by surprise. Please. Just make sure he's gone."

"Lock the door and stay by it. If you get scared, come outside and call for me, got it?"

He couldn't tell if she nodded in understanding or if she was just shaking really hard.

"Tucker?"

"Yeah?"

"Why would he take my phone?"

To find out who the hell she was, more than likely. All of her personal information would be there. He didn't think she'd appreciate hearing that, however, so he simply said, "I promise, I won't be long."

"Be careful," she said, rubbing her cheek. "Really strong."

He closed the door and waited until he heard it lock

before making a quick trip around the exterior of her place. No one was hanging around outside. No one sped off in any cars from the property.

Satisfied that Miranda was safe where she was for the time being, he made his way inside her cottage. He wanted to dust for prints, even though he'd be willing to bet the guy was wearing gloves. He'd ask Miranda about that when he was done since he didn't have any of his gear with him anyway. Just one piece that mattered most right now. His gun. With it held at the ready, he covered the place inch by inch. Every crevice and corner until he was certain he was alone.

There was no one there.

As he made his way back to the kitchen, his chest squeezed painfully as he saw the broken coffeepot, the overturned chairs. She could have died tonight. He hadn't been there to protect her. He grabbed his phone from his pocket and angrily punched the number to the station, ordering an officer to the property to do a more thorough search so he could take Miranda's statement and make sure she was all right.

As he bent to stand a fallen chair back up at the table, something in the corner caught his eye. He flipped on the kitchen light and saw, half hidden beneath another chair, a pocket-sized Bible.

Adrenaline pumped through him and he scavenged the kitchen for any baggies he might be able to use. The only thing she had was an empty grocery bag. It would have to do.

He slipped the Bible inside, holding it protectively with his plastic-coated fingers as he flipped the pages. It could belong to anyone, but from his quick scan, he could see several passages marked with glaring red circles.

He closed it, covered it fully in the bag, and headed

back to his house to check on Miranda. Not wanting to scare her, he used his key to let himself in, calling out for her so she'd know it was him immediately.

She was sitting on the window seat, her gaze fixated on the door.

"Whoever it was is long gone."

"Good." She'd managed to pull herself together a bit in his absence, but while her voice no longer shook, fear still dulled her eyes and skin.

He had nothing to say that might make her feel better.

"You're staying here."

"Okay," she whispered. In her lap, she wrung her hands together, and he could see the tremble of her fingers as they interlaced. She let out a breath that fogged the window.

He squeezed her hand. She didn't let him go, clung to him even while looking away. Outside, he saw Bowen's cruiser pull up and gave her hand another squeeze. "Let me talk to Bowen. I'll be right back, all right?"

She gave a halfhearted smile. "I'm fine, Tucker. Just scared. Go. Do your job."

By the time he finished telling Andy what he wanted done, Miranda's color had returned to her cheeks. She'd found a blanket and had nestled beneath it, but she hadn't moved from her spot by the window. When he sat beside her, she surprised him with a low giggle that turned into outright laughter.

"You okay?"

She nodded, struggling to compose herself.

"What's so funny? You could have . . ."

"Died tonight. I know." More laughter. "I just can't help thinking . . . Bobby is so going to owe me."

As he pulled her against his chest, her laughter turned to heartbreaking sobs.

Chapter 32

Early Monday morning

ONCE TUCKER GOT Miranda settled in his guest room, he padded his way back to the kitchen and found Finn sitting at the bar, coffee already in hand. He hadn't even heard Finn come in. Now more than ever, he needed to be on guard.

"When did you get back?"

"Long enough ago to make coffee. Have a cup. Look like you could use it."

He splashed water on his face from the kitchen sink and contemplated refusing the coffee, knowing it would prevent him from sleeping. But who was he kidding? He wouldn't be sleeping anyway.

He took the cup. "Thanks. I pulled your sheets off the bed so you could use them on the couch. Gave her some flannel ones since she can't stop shaking."

He filled Finn in on the night's events, pushing the bagged Bible toward him on the counter. "I'll be checking that for prints first thing in the morning. I want to look it over as soon as possible."

"She going to be all right?"

Tucker nodded.

"Think it was someone who figured out she was the nurse with Ohio plates?"

"*Someone.* Yeah. I do. I think we're going to have to bring Anatole in. How do you think the judge will react when I ask for a warrant for a priest with no substantial proof that he's my guy?"

Finn chuckled. "Pretty sure that one won't see the light of day. You can at least bring him in for questioning, though. Find out where he was tonight."

"Already had Bowen put out an APB." He still couldn't believe his Sergeant hadn't had a visual on the priest since he'd returned home around ten Sunday night and hadn't bothered to let Tucker know. Goiter had seen Anatole enter his house, seen it go dark, and assumed the man was inside sleeping. Until Tucker had sent him to check, anyway. And he still hadn't heard a word about the priest being picked up. Maybe he was off somewhere licking his wounds. If he showed up with so much as a cut on his cheek from Miranda's attempt to ward him off, Tucker was going after that warrant, proof or no.

Goddamned reporters. If someone was copying the Rosary Murders, or even if it really was the actual killer, placing Miranda in Dayton had just put her life in danger. He wanted to wring Helen Stillman's neck.

"You ready to give me the whole story on her yet? What the hell is a nurse doing snooping around a murder investigation?"

Tucker scowled. "I just want you to focus on the facts.

Help me figure out who's behind all this. The Miranda details . . . will have to wait."

"I'm starting to feel like you don't trust me or something."

"Not the case. I swear. Just for now, leave that bone alone, okay?"

Finn sighed and dumped the dregs of his coffee in the sink. "All right then. Think that's my cue to turn in for the night. On the damned couch."

Tucker smiled. "Sorry 'bout that."

"Uh-huh. Don't ever let it be said I'm not a gentleman." Finn dropped over the side of the couch onto his temporary bed, disappearing from sight, and Tucker pushed to his feet. He could barely keep his eyes open. The coffee hadn't done anything but speed up his pulse. He headed down the hall and collapsed onto his bed, shut his eyes, and tried not to think about the woman occupying the room down the hall.

He woke a few hours later with a headache the size of Wrigley Field and stumbled to the bathroom. He unbuttoned his jeans, tore off his shirt, and turned the shower on full blast.

"Morning."

He whirled around to find Miranda in the doorway. She wore black circles beneath her eyes, highlighting the lovely bruise forming on her cheekbone, her wrinkled pajama shirt, and little else. Her hair was tousled, her bare legs shifting back and forth, leading him to guess she needed the bathroom.

"Yeah," he said. "How'd you sleep?"

Her gaze lingered on his belly for a long, uncomfortable moment before she seemed to register what he'd asked.

"I didn't. Not really. Thanks for letting me crash here."

He nodded and stepped around her. "I'll let you use the bathroom before I get in."

She thanked him and shut the door, and by the time it opened again, the bathroom had filled with steam from his shower. "Thanks. I can make coffee while you shower. Do you—do you have a pair of sweats or something I could borrow until I get my things?"

His gaze drifted down to her long, smooth legs. A pity to cover them. "Yeah. Help yourself. There's a pile of clean clothes I haven't put away yet in the laundry room."

She slid past him and disappeared, and Tucker locked himself in the sanctuary of his bathroom.

MIRANDA TIED THE drawstring on the black sweatpants as tightly as she could. Luckily, Tucker was slim, and the elastic wasn't *too* baggy, but he was taller than she by a good foot or more, and every step she took got caught up in the extra fabric dragging beneath her feet.

She rolled them up, but they wouldn't stay, so she slipped her way back to the kitchen to begin her hunt for coffee. Being as quiet as possible to keep from waking Finn on the couch, she found the bag of grounds, played with the coffeepot until she was pretty sure she'd figured it out, grateful that the residual fear she'd woken to was mostly gone.

The muffled sounds of the shower shut off and she poured two cups before taking a seat at the small round breakfast table. She inhaled the rich aroma and let her mind wander. It didn't take a second before her thoughts turned to Tucker.

It had disturbed her to find him half dressed this morning. Mostly, she was disturbed because she'd noticed. He had a swimmer's body. Strong, broad shoulders. Well-sculpted abs that V'd nicely between his hips to disappear beneath denim.

She sighed. In the light of morning, recalling the terror that had paralyzed her wasn't as easy. It was almost as though it had all been nothing more than a nightmare.

But it hadn't been. It had been very real. Her back, ribs, and face were a testament to that.

She shuddered.

Tucker strolled through the kitchen and smiled a greeting at her. The jeans and bare chest had been replaced with his uniform—a far safer choice for her sanity.

Not that he didn't look great in the khakis, too. Miranda sipped her coffee, studying him as he placed strips of bacon on a skillet. He was one of those rare men who looked good no matter what he wore. He was comfortable in his skin, not caring what people thought because he wasn't out to impress them. Another rarity in her book.

She sat in silence while he worked, watching the fluid movements of his body as he cracked eggs into a skillet and flipped the bacon. A few minutes later, he set a plate of bacon, eggs, and toast in front of her.

"I found something at your place," he said, sitting beside her. "Something he might have dropped."

Her sore muscles forgotten, she leaned toward him. "What?"

He pulled a plastic bag from beneath the table and set it in front of her. "Don't touch it. I want it dusted for prints first. But thought you should know."

She gently pried the tied ends of the bag apart and

peered inside. It was a small, leather-bound Bible. The spark of hope engulfing her nearly made her want to cry. Finally, something tangible.

"There are passages circled inside. I want to go over them to see if any pertain to our murders."

"You'll let me help?"

He studied her, then took the bag, retied it, and placed it back at his feet. "We'll see. First, tell me everything that happened last night, okay?"

"I already told you everything."

He placed butter and jam between their plates before taking the chair across from her. "Start from the beginning. Everything you can remember. Now that you've had time to think, you might remember something useful."

Miranda nibbled a piece of bacon and filled him in on everything she'd done from the minute she'd returned to her cottage. " . . . and no, I never got a look at him. It was too dark."

"Where did you come back from so late? Could you have been followed?"

She swallowed. Time to come clean. "Maybe. I was trying to keep an eye on Anatole."

Before he could interrupt with a burst of angry chastising, she held up her hand to silence him. "I wasn't stupid about it. Until he disappeared in Town Square, I just sat in my car and—"

"The one with the Ohio plates? Perfect."

She frowned, wishing that didn't make her feel like an idiot. Maybe she *had* been followed. How else would Anatole know where she was staying? She'd been so careful about concealing her plates, and last night, she'd just been plain stupid.

"I wasn't trying to break your rules, Tucker. But I had to know where he was."

"But you lost him?"

"I waited till Mass ended. He went home after that, then back to town. No idea where he went from there." She wasn't quite ready to confess about her spy cameras. They hadn't been useful anyway.

"What time was that?"

"About eight-thirty."

"I told you I had men watching him."

She nibbled on her toast. "Yeah, then where did they say he went?"

Tucker frowned. "No one's seen him since Mass. No one knows where he was."

So she wasn't the only inept surveillance member. "I do," she whispered. "He was killing someone, and then he was in my cottage."

He slathered his toast in grape jelly and took a huge bite, brushing crumbs off his chest. "I put out an APB on Anatole after the break-in last night. We'll find him."

Miranda grabbed a triangle of toast, trying to figure out how to ask him the question burning her brain. "Was there . . . last night . . . anyone missing? Found?"

"No news. I've had patrols running all night with orders to report anything suspicious." He refilled their cups.

Her breakfast soured in her stomach. She'd have given anything for her roll of antacids. She rubbed her belly. "He kills every Sunday. A few extra patrols aren't going to make him change his ways. It took you over a week to find Ricky—"

"I'm doing all I can, Miranda."

Miranda studied her coffee to keep from looking at him. It wasn't that she didn't believe he was doing everything within his power. It was just that she was beginning to think his power wasn't all that powerful.

"I need to tell you something else, Miranda. You're not going to like it, but keep in mind, I'm doing my job here. Which is what you want, right?"

She nodded, a sense of foreboding churning the acid in her belly. "Okay."

"I went to see Bobby Saturday."

She dropped her bacon. "What?"

He lowered his voice and peered over her shoulder at the couch. "Finn still doesn't know you're his sister so keep it down. I need him to remain objective."

"What could talking to Bobby possibly accomplish?" She wasn't sure she was mad as much as she was upset that he'd seen her brother and she hadn't. She wanted to ask how he looked, how he seemed. Was he all right? Did he look healthy?

"Maybe something important," Tucker said. "Did you know Anatole gave a kid up for adoption before he became a priest?"

She felt her jaw drop. "What? No! Bobby told you that?"

"Yeah. That medallion you found . . . we're trying to see where it came from. If it came from the same place Anatole left his son, we might have something."

Her brain boggled. Anatole had a son. Holy shit. More fucked-up DNA out there to screw with the world.

Finn began to stir from the couch and Tucker gave her a silencing look that declared the conversation was over. She was sure Finn probably already knew about the visit, but agreed that it was probably best that he not find out she was Bobby's sister.

Lowering her voice, she asked, "Did he say anything about me? Ask about me? Anything?"

Still whispering, Tucker smiled. "He wants you to stop risking your neck for him. He's worried about you."

For some reason, that made her feel better. Not that Bobby was worrying . . . but that he did still care about her.

"Feel up to getting your things?"

She nodded, grateful for the opportunity to get her own clothes. A bra, her antacids. No phone though. God, the bastard had her phone. She considered calling to cancel her service, but it wouldn't do any good. He'd still be able to access her information. She'd never gotten around to setting up a pass code for it.

"You don't mind me staying again?"

She knew it was silly to want to stay another night at Tucker's. Her cottage was so close, he could be there in seconds if she needed him. But he hadn't been home last night. He had a job to do and she couldn't have him babysitting her. At least here, she'd feel safer when she was alone.

"Not at all. Been a while since I had so many people here. It's kind of nice." He offered her a heavy wool coat and she slid it on, smiling at him.

"I'm sure you're rarely lonely, Chief Ambrose. I'm willing to bet women are more than willing to keep you warm at night."

He chuckled. "You're the first woman I've had here in months."

She found that hard to believe. She wiggled her bare feet in his direction. "Shoes?"

He grabbed a pair of rain boots sitting by the door and helped her put them on. When he stood again, he was so close she could smell the coffee on his breath. Her cheeks flushed.

"Thank you."

He nodded. "Anything else?"

"Think I'm good." Other than her nightshirt, she was

fully wrapped in eau de Ambrose. Totally department-store worthy. She sighed. The bottle would probably be khaki.

"I have a lot to do today," he said, opening the door and waiting for her to pass through. "I'll make sure you have a key, but I probably won't be home till seven or eight. Will you be all right alone?"

"Yeah. I'll manage." She hated feeling like a charity case. She was going to have to think of some way to repay him.

He led her back to her place and made her wait while he opened the door and took a look around. When he returned, he ushered her inside, helped her fill a bag with some personal items, then took her back to his house. In his doorway, he stopped her from going inside by taking her by the elbow and making her face him.

His dark eyes simmered with something she could feel between her thighs as his gaze bored into her face.

"What?"

He ran a hand over his face, and when he dropped it again, he looked . . . defeated. "You should know . . . before you agree to stay here longer . . . I want you, Miranda. Make no mistake about it. I'm not sure how long I can remain a gentleman about that."

Her belly gave a little quiver and her body warmed. "I . . . This case is important to me. I don't think—"

"Yeah, I know." He opened the door. "Just thought you should know where I stand."

He stepped through first, leaving her standing alone on his porch, her entire body tingling with a heat that made her numb to the cold around her. She'd known he was attracted to her. Their chemistry was undeniable. She'd felt it from the moment he'd taken a seat in her booth at Peggy Jo's.

But he *wanted* her. She'd had relationships. Had dated her fair share of men over the years. But never in her thirty-three years had she had a man tell her so blatantly that he desired her.

Miranda entered Tucker's house and stumbled to the kitchen, retaking her seat at the table. She could hear him talking to Finn but couldn't bring herself to look at him. She needed to figure out how she felt about all this. She liked Tucker. Had been attracted to him from the get-go. But that didn't change the fact that, once Tucker gathered the evidence he needed to put the right man behind bars, she'd return home to the life she'd put on hold.

Knowing that, it was wrong of her to even contemplate where this thing between her and Tucker might lead . . . even if, at that moment, it was all she could think about.

Chapter 33

TUCKER CHOSE THE department's break room as his work space that afternoon, his body unable to take another long day sitting in his worn-out office chair. They were still waiting for his guys to finish the dusting process on the Bible, but there was something useful they could do in the meantime.

Finn plopped onto the couch and sprawled out while Tucker carefully slid the Dayton autopsy photos from their file. He placed them side by side with Michael Levi's, then pulled the numbers he'd copied from the picture of Michael Levi's abdomen and what Doc Murray had given him from Ricky's preliminary report.

196 518.

816 135.

Tucker pointed to the photo of the first Dayton victim. The baptism re-creation. The body on the morgue table had yet to be touched by the coroner's blade, his white, fleshy belly almost blue. Tucker held it up, squinted. "You see anything there?"

Finn took the picture from him, held it up to the light. "Where?"

"The abdomen. Anything that looks like the scratches on our vics?"

"Yeah, can't make them out though. Got a magnifying glass anywhere?"

"Yeah, Watson. In the evidence closet."

Finn disappeared and Tucker pulled out the victim of the confession rite. Again, he could see scratches, but they were indecipherable. When Finn returned with the glass from the evidence locker, Tucker took it and held it over the photo.

417 2813.

He remembered something he'd seen in the files and cursed. He knelt on the floor and pulled a manila envelope from the bottom of the Dayton box.

"Yes," he said.

"What is it?"

"Finally a reason the Dayton PD thought all of these murders were re-creations of the sacraments." Tucker held up a sheet of paper separated into columns of numbers, names, and three other sets of boxes labeled Rites, Sins, and Verses.

He double-checked the number he'd written down for the confession victim. Under the Rites box on the Dayton paper, the numbers 417 had been written. Same as what he'd seen on the photograph of the man's body. Under sins: 2813.

"You think they're verses?" Finn asked.

"They all have them. Maybe the killer is carving not only the rites he's creating on his victims, but also why they were chosen to die," he said, showing Finn. "If we know Michael Levi was used to recreate the rite of marriage, then those numbers, 518, have to be his sin."

Finn sat on the edge of Tucker's desk. "Which we can already guess. Divorce. Abandoning his child. His family already told you that and you met with the mistress."

"Yeah, and I sent two of my men to talk to the wife. She wasn't able to tell us anything new," Tucker said. "Now I can figure out why Ricky Schneider was targeted."

It wouldn't do much to figure out who was responsible for Ricky's murder, but maybe it would tell Tucker how the victims were chosen in the first place.

"135." He stood and stuck his head out the door to call out to Lisa. "That Bible ready yet?"

"Darren's finishing up now!"

"Tell him he has five minutes before I take it back."

He heard Lisa chuckle as he shut the door. When Darren knocked on the conference room door a few minutes later, he looked out of sorts. "Sorry, sir," he said, handing over the Bible, still in its evidence bag. "Tried to hurry."

"You did good."

He shut the door in Darren's face and tossed the bag onto the table. "Start looking at all the first chapters in that Bible."

"Too early in the damned week to be Bible studying," Finn grumbled, snapping on a pair of latex gloves.

Tucker put a pair on, too, and bent over Finn's shoulder to look. Every book of the Bible had a chapter one, verse three, which was what he was pretty sure those numbers meant. And there were seventy-three books in the Catholic Bible. If he had to look through every chapter one of all seventy-three books . . . It was going to be a long-ass day, even if the passages were marked. It wasn't like they stood out, begging to be noticed.

"Let me look," he said, taking the Bible back and thumbing through the pages.

He flipped through the historical, the sapiential, and the prophetic books of the Old Testament, looking for any marks or dog-eared pages. He couldn't even find the one circled passage he'd seen when he'd first found the thing. The pages were so thin, each flip nearly earned him a rip, and while he didn't relish the idea of damaging evidence, he also needed to speed this process along.

"This blows." Finn reached for the file of autopsy photos and leaned back in his chair while Tucker kept flipping. "Give me something interesting to do. Let me go talk to this priest of yours and scare the truth out of him. That sounds fun."

"Yeah, you do that. I have men searching for him still. Nothing on the APB."

Finn set the file down, stood and stretched. He fiddled with the misplaced ceiling tiles. "Your *men* aren't exactly crack detectives. Bet I could find him."

Tucker rolled his eyes. Finn had always been like this. Too much pent-up energy, and he got restless. He needed to find a basketball court, or a willing woman. Otherwise, he was going to drive Tucker crazy.

"Go take a smoke break."

Instead, Finn straddled the opposite chair backward and plucked the cigarette from behind his ear, rolling it between his fingers as he pulled the file toward him again.

"Cutting back," he muttered. "Maybe I'll go flirt with one of your dispatchers."

"Shannon's in *school*, and I already told you, Lisa's off limits. Go find a tourist to play wi— Here it is!" A circled passage finally fell into view. Chapter thirteen, verse five. " 'That prophet or dream interpreter must be executed because he encouraged you to turn away from the Lord your God who brought you out of Egypt, who redeemed you from the house of slavery; they tried to lead you away from the path the Lord your God commanded you to take. Remove such evil from your community!'"

"Okay, so we know the kid was killed because what? He was a rebel against God? That's some— Hey." Finn held up the folder he'd been perusing. "This is a confidential folder. Those carvings weren't leaked to the press."

Tucker sat back, a bit of his adrenaline ebbing. "Shit."

That meant the chances of this being a copycat had just all but disappeared.

MIRANDA PULLED INTO a space in front of a small grocery in Town Square and killed the engine. She probably shouldn't be driving the Range Rover anymore, but what did it matter, really? Anatole already knew who she was now that he had her phone, and he sure as hell knew where she was temporarily calling home. Her back had been too sore to make the walk, and the bruise under her eye had turned a gnarly purple. She didn't exactly relish the thought of being stared at as she made her way through town.

Leaning against the seat, she closed her eyes. Her head ached, her belly was queasy, and her emotional state wasn't much better. She was so confused, with thoughts of Bobby, Anatole, and Tucker's proclamation of desire . . . she was finding it hard to focus on any one of those problems at a time.

She checked her watch. Almost six hours had passed since Tucker had left for work that morning. God, she really wanted to find out if any news had come in about another victim. Not that she was praying for anyone else to die. But she was sure there was another body somewhere, and the sooner they found it, the sooner they might catch a break in stopping Anatole. Surely someone would have reported a missing husband or father or son by now?

She frowned. It had been less than a day since the killing would have happened. Too soon, maybe, for anyone to believe the worst had happened to someone they loved.

A tap on the driver's window nearly caused her to jump out of her skin. She gasped and found Lisa peering at her through the glass.

Opening the door, Miranda tried to find a smile.

"Everything okay?"

Miranda climbed out. "Sure."

Lisa frowned, studying the bruises on Miranda's face, but instead of asking about it, hooked her arm through Miranda's elbow and led the way inside the store. She grabbed a small basket and handed one to Miranda. "Want company?"

"I just needed to pick up some antacids—"

"Come on. Consider it bonding time."

Unsure what to say to that, she followed Lisa down each aisle.

"I know how you feel about nosy people, but I overheard Tuck and Finn talking about the break-in last night. Looks like you took a nasty hit. You okay?"

Touched by the concern in Lisa's eyes, she smiled. "I'm fine, thanks."

Lisa placed a finger to Miranda's chin, forcing her to tilt her head. "Don't look fine to me."

"Looks worse than it is, but not by much."

"Listen, I know you don't know me from Adam, and

Lord knows you seem to have more secrets than a dog
has fleas . . . but if you need a friend while you're in
town, my offer still stands."

Miranda swallowed. "Thanks, Lisa. That . . . means
a lot."

She meant that with every fiber of her being. Her old
friends, and the few of Bobby's friends she'd been able
to contact, had treated her like an outcast when Bobby
was arrested. It was one of the reasons she'd wanted as
few people as possible to know she was Bobby's sister.

They moved to the pasta aisle and Lisa dropped a jar
of sauce on top of her sanitary napkins. "So who else
other than Tucker and me knows who you really are?"

Anatole.

Not that she was going to say that much out loud.
Miranda alternated between looking at items she didn't
need on the shelves and listening to snippets of the news
from the small television by the register, and trying to
figure out how to ask Lisa if anyone had been reported
missing . . . or worse.

"No one that I know of. He hasn't told Finn yet.
Wants to keep him objective."

"Woo hoo. I have a feeling that man's going to flip his
lid when he finds out. He's going to have some choice
words to say for Tucker getting involved with you."

"We're not involved." Spotting a bottle of Rolaids,
Miranda snatched it and threw it in her basket. "And
I hope not. I've been enough of a headache for Tucker
without causing friction between him and his friend."

Lisa smiled. "Maybe he'll handle it well. You never
know. You have to learn to have faith in people. I can
understand that it's not easy for you, but not everyone
is a jerk. Not all the time, anyway."

Miranda grabbed a package of chocolate cookies

from the end cap, mentally counted the money in her bank account, and followed Lisa down the next aisle as she tried to think of how to broach the topic on her mind.

"I haven't talked to Tucker since this morning and—"

"He's been at the office all day with Finn. You try there?"

She shook her head. She'd wanted to give him a little space, and herself as well, after his declaration that morning. Stopping by his work hadn't seemed wise, and since she didn't have her phone . . .

"He won't take calls when he's real focused workin' unless it's a nine-one-one call."

"And you haven't sent one of those today?"

"Since I've been at the office, I wouldn't need to." Lisa raised her eyebrows. "You wanna know if anyone's been reported missing?"

"Or . . . found."

"Not even a missing pet. And we usually get a couple of those a day. Patrols have been checking in hourly since yesterday. So far no one has found anything suspicious."

Miranda scowled.

"Still no sign of your priest, either."

Her scowl deepened. "Tucker told me about the APB."

"Maybe he left town."

Miranda didn't know if that would be a blessing or a curse. If he left, the people of Christmas were safe . . . but that meant some other town could be next on the victim list, and she wouldn't be there to prevent it.

Not that she was doing a bang-up job of that here.

"You don't look too pleased that no one else is dead."

"Of course I am. It's just . . . it's not right. Why would he change his MO now?"

Lisa looked around to make sure they weren't being overheard. "Who knows, honey. All I know is that if he's really gone, I say good riddance."

"I can't wish all this on anyone, or anyplace." She looked at her watch, pretended the time the little hands showed mattered. She wanted to get back to her cameras, see if she could catch Anatole at his place and alert Tucker to his whereabouts. "Wow. It's nearly six. It was nice seeing you again, Lisa, but . . . I should go."

Lisa scrunched her forehead as though looking at Miranda the way she might stare at a difficult puzzle. "You don't have many friends, do you, Miranda?"

"Sorry. I'm not trying to be rude, but . . . I should really go. Enjoy the rest of your day."

The entire time she stood at the register waiting to pay for her items, until she finally made it back out into the cold, she could feel Lisa watching her. She knew she'd been rude, leaving Lisa to finish shopping alone, but she hadn't asked for the company in the first place.

Still, maybe Lisa had a point. If Miranda kept expecting people in this town to give her answers and be on her side, maybe she should make more of an effort to at least be pleasant and give them a chance to see she was actually a nice person under all the paranoia.

She'd start with Tucker. He'd come to her rescue and he was giving her a place to stay. She owed him something. Some kindness.

The kindness she *wanted* to show him was probably a bad idea, so she waited until Lisa left the store and went back inside. She'd still have time to check her tapes before Tucker got home. Plenty of time to cook him a meal afterward. It had been nearly a year since she'd cooked for anyone other than herself, and a rush of excitement stayed with her as she picked out tomatoes and peppers and three steaks that cost more than she could really afford. She could replace her shoes for all this . . .

But no. She'd cook Tucker a gratitude dinner, instead. Finn would be there, too, which made her frown as she picked out a bottle of wine and tossed baking potatoes into the basket.

It was probably a good thing. Wine. Good food. Yeah, it was definitely a good thing to have Finn chaperone dinner tonight, or she might do something stupid like seduce Tucker and make things far more complicated than they already were just so she could forget the hell her life was swiftly becoming.

Chapter 34

TUCKER CUT THE engine and leaned his head against his seat, too tired to even push open the door and walk into his house. A house that wasn't exactly his at the moment with Finn and Miranda underfoot. At least Finn was doing Tucker a favor. Miranda, on the other hand, was going to suck all the comfort out of his damned house. She was going to permeate every square inch of parquet floor and crown molding in the place with her smell and essence.

With a groan, he pushed open the door and all but crawled out into the snow. He'd spent the last three hours alone in his office, waiting on word about Anatole and combing every single orphanage in Ohio that he could find, hoping he'd be quicker with an answer than the labs were proving to be.

He hadn't been. Everywhere he looked, it felt as though he was staring at another goddamned closed door. It was frustrating as hell.

He left his hat on the passenger seat, but leaned in to grab a few of the Dayton files he thought Miranda might want to look at. Coroner reports, depositions. Nothing that would put her feet too much deeper into the case, and yet would give her something to occupy her time and keep her out of trouble.

He took the porch steps slowly and tested the door. It was unlocked, and the minute it cracked open, he was assaulted by an aroma so delicious, his stomach cramped. It wasn't a fresh smell, more like something that had been cooked hours ago, and since it was so late, that was likely the case. Still, he turned for the kitchen in hopes of scrounging leftovers when he found Miranda and Finn watching him from the kitchen table.

"You're late." Miranda stood, opened the oven, and pulled out a plate of roasted vegetables, steak, and a baked potato. "I tried to keep it warm, but I'm pretty sure it dried out two hours ago."

She set the plate at the empty setting between her and Finn, then sat back down, returning her attention to the detective. Tucker had obviously interrupted a conversation, because they fell back into it as though he wasn't there. He didn't like the way Finn refilled her wine without asking. He didn't like that neither seemed to care that he was quiet, and he sure as hell didn't like that they were laughing at jokes that were obviously private.

"Not hungry?"

He looked up from his potato to find Miranda watching him, chin on her hand, elbow on the table, her eyes slightly glazed from wine.

He cleared his throat. "Yeah. I—yeah. Looks great, thanks."

She lowered her hand and laid it on his thigh. "It's a sorry thank-you for all you've done, but it's all I've got."

The weight of her hand disappeared, leaving a circle

of warmth in its place and sending a rush of blood to his crotch. His attention fixated on the dark red liquid staining her mouth. He downed half his beer to keep from leaning over and kissing the wine from her lips.

He pressed the cold bottle against his forehead. It was late and he was too tired and too hungry and too . . . Miranda's scent wafted in his direction. Horny. Yep. He was too fucking horny.

"You okay?" Miranda asked.

"I'm fine." He hadn't meant to snap, but everything in his body was too tense to do anything else right now.

She didn't look at all fazed by his tone. Instead, she lightly touched his arm. "I can get you some aspirin. My treat. I bought out the pharmacy today. Let me go get it."

"I'm fine really—"

Miranda ignored him and disappeared down the hall; the scent of her went with her. It didn't matter. It was probably going to linger in his blood for the rest of the night.

Finn strode across the kitchen and set his wineglass in the sink.

"Get some sleep. Your mood is worse than the smell of cow shit that blew in tonight."

"We didn't all get a nice dinner cooked for us. Enjoy it?"

Finn grinned. "Ah, now I get your mood. Hell yeah, I enjoyed it. But she made it for you. Not me." Finn clasped Tucker's shoulder and gave it a brotherly squeeze. "Try to be a little nicer to—"

"Found them." Miranda reappeared, shaking a large bottle of Bayer in her hands.

Finn kissed Miranda's cheek. "Thanks again for dinner and the company. I thoroughly enjoyed both."

To Tucker he said, "I'm going to step out back for a smoke, then call it a night."

"Take the guest room tonight. Miranda can crash in my room and I'll slum it on the couch."

Of course, Finn didn't argue. He wasn't one to sacrifice lightly where comfort was concerned.

When the back door shut, Tucker took the bottle of aspirin from Miranda, filled a glass with water, and swallowed a couple tablets. When he turned around, she was sitting on the couch sipping her wine and watching him.

"Thanks for saving me dinner."

"Sorry we didn't wait on you. It was getting late and I couldn't let the food go to waste. Finn said you wouldn't mind if it was reheated."

He didn't. In Chicago, he'd worked cases that didn't give a shit about time clocks. He'd learned a long time ago to eat whatever was available without complaining about *when* it was available.

He took another sip of beer. "You two seemed to hit it off."

Miranda tucked her feet under her bottom and swirled the red wine in its glass. "I like him. He's nice."

"Yeah. Nice." He grabbed the wine in one hand, his plate in the other, and carried them into the sitting area, carefully choosing a spot on the sofa that wasn't too close—which wasn't nearly far enough for his peace of mind. He wasn't sure Timbuktu would have been far enough to accomplish that.

She took the bottle from him, topped off her glass, and sipped while he adjusted the plate on his lap. Even his damned bones were tired. He leaned his head back and closed his eyes, rubbing circles at his temples. He could sleep for a week, but even cold and dried out, he was too hungry not to eat first.

"How's the cheek?" he asked, cutting into his steak.

She brought two fingers up to her face and gently pushed on the flesh there. "Tender. Didn't swell too bad at least."

"That's good." He took a bite and moaned. He couldn't remember the last time someone had cooked for him and hadn't presented him with a bill afterward.

"Anything new today?"

He stopped chewing to look at her.

She held up her free hand. "I'm not asking for details. Just trying to make polite conversation."

He took a deep swallow of wine straight from the bottle. "You know, there are those days that being a cop . . . it's not what I thought I was signing up for. I'm not sure I've sat and read anything for as long as I did today. Might need bifocals now."

She leaned her head back, watching him, her eyelids droopy and her features soft. "Thanks again for letting me stay here. I didn't feel safe being alone tonight. Tomorrow, maybe."

"But you feel safe staying here?"

"Yeah, I do."

"Even after what I told you?"

She blushed, the pink adding a deeper hue of purple to her cheek. "Yes."

That rendered him speechless for a minute. He'd never been so blunt about his feelings before, but with Miranda, he didn't trust himself not to act on his desire. She had a habit of bringing out the protective caveman in him without even knowing it. Turned out his caveman half was also sex-starved for her.

"Glad to have you, then." They'd lifted plenty of prints from her cottage, but because renters came and went, there were too many to be useful. And Miranda had said the guy had been wearing gloves. Still, processing-wise, she was free to return to her place whenever she wanted. Courage-wise, he wasn't so sure she was ready. Which meant she'd likely be sleeping here tomorrow, too.

Her sleepy smile did nothing to ease the doubts he had about his ability to keep his hands off her if she stayed here too long. Who was he kidding? Even if she left right now, he doubted he'd have the good sense not to track her down. He'd been intimate with women who hadn't moved into his brain and his blood the way she had with a simple smile and a shared table.

"You're quiet tonight," she said. "Everything okay?"

He set his plate on the coffee table. It wasn't an intelligent question. Of course everything wasn't okay. He had a killer in his town and didn't feel any closer to stopping him.

"The weather," he lied. "This kind of cold can seep into your bones and make you do stupid things."

He heard the back door open and close. Heard Finn's footsteps disappear down the hall. He should've called out. The way his gaze kept falling to her mouth . . . yeah, a chaperone was probably a good idea.

"What kind of stupid things?"

He rose, moving slowly toward her. He could tell by the way she looked at him that she knew exactly what sort of *stupid things* he was talking about. She looked scared, and a hell of a lot intrigued. It was the intrigued part that made him lean closer.

Careful to keep his weight off her, he propped his hands on either side of her head, holding her captive between his arms. "Showing you would be a hell of a lot more fun."

She looked at him, her eyes sleepy, but not dulled from the wine. "Showing will move us into dangerous territory."

"Sweetheart, we've been there for a long time." He dipped his head and dragged his lower lip lightly over hers.

Her arms drifted up to circle his neck as she opened up to him. He slipped his tongue inside her mouth, moaning against the silky feel of her tongue. The heat of her mouth made him instantly hard, and he pressed himself against her thigh, letting her know how deeply into this he was so she could stop it now if that was her intention, before they went too far.

Her body responded to his like they'd danced this dance a hundred times already, and his thoughts became indecipherable as the need to bury himself inside her turned his blood to liquid fire.

"Miranda," he sighed against her mouth.

She pulled back, clasping his face in both of her tiny, warm hands, and looked him in the eye. "Me too."

His gaze trailed over her chin, down her throat, and settled on the buttons of her sweater and the promises that lay beneath them. He moved slowly, the way a man moves when touching a skittish colt, afraid she'd make him stop and yet giving her every opportunity to. Bracing himself on one arm, he used his other to carry his fingers over the buttons, toying with them, searching her gaze for permission.

She bit her lip and smiled. Tucker didn't need anything else. The buttons were opened within seconds, her pale, flat belly appearing below a soft pink bra that cupped the most delicious-looking flesh he'd ever seen.

Creamy white mounds of cleavage beckoned him, and he went willingly, spreading his hand over first one, then the other.

They filled his palm perfectly, and as he leaned back down to kiss her again, he slid his hand inside the fabric and pushed it away, freeing her breasts and finding her nipple. She moaned against his mouth and his dick strained against his pants.

Something feathery-soft brushed the tip of him and his entire body jolted as though he'd just been plugged into an active socket. Then she was stroking him through his uniform, fondling him, killing him slowly and sweetly. When her fingers brushed his belly and tugged his shirt from his pants, he adjusted to help her, desperate for her to feel his skin the way he was feeling hers.

He nearly died when she unbuttoned him and slipped her hand inside.

He adjusted again, giving her room to play. "If we don't stop, you're going to wake up in my b—"

She rose up and kissed him again, burying his warning with frantic strokes of her tongue. She was tugging at his pants, as desperate to get them off his body, it seemed, as he was. He was so lost in the sound of her breaths and moans that he thought the shrill ringing was coming from inside his own head.

It wasn't. The vibration of the phone in his pocket broke the spell. He rested his forehead against hers.

"Do you have to answer that?"

The ringing stopped. Hoping to recapture the moment, he bent his head and took her exposed nipple into his mouth, brushing his lips and teeth against the tender nub while her fingers began playing once again to strip off his pants. He rose to help her, but the phone interrupted again. This time, it let out three rapid, high-pitched beeps, alerting him to a waiting text message.

He claimed her lips with a hard kiss. "Hold that thought," he mumbled, digging his phone out of his back pocket. He looked at the screen. The 911 message cooled his desire. Zipping his pants, he moved off the couch and away from Miranda. He took several deep breaths. Distance helped. The taste of her still clung to his skin, but the fire in his blood and fog in his brain dissipated.

Once again in control of himself, he called Andy back.

"It's Tucker. What's the emergency?"

"Sorry to bother you so late, Tuck, but you're going to want to join me out by the old First Baptist Church."

He glanced at Miranda. She sat on the edge of the sofa, her hands trembling as she refastened the buttons on her sweater. Her questioning gaze watched him. He turned his back to keep her from seeing his unfiltered reaction to Andy's phone call. "What happened?"

"We found another body."

Chapter 35

MIRANDA PACED TUCKER'S small bedroom, her nails chewed to the quick. Finn was gone. Tucker was gone. She was alone with nothing but her fear and her morbid hope that whatever had happened would finally point the finger at Anatole and stop him once and for all.

Tucker hadn't told her much, but then, his phone call had been too brief to give him any significant information, either. But he *had* told her that another body had been found.

Could be natural causes.

She didn't believe that.

She wrapped her arms around herself and climbed into Tucker's bed. The smell of him offered her a bit of comfort as she wrapped herself in his sheets and smothered her face in his pillow. They'd come close to something real tonight. She tried to process how she felt about that. Closing her eyes, she tried to conjure his face, but before she could latch on to it, the image morphed into what he might be seeing at that moment.

She shivered, rolled to the right side of the bed, and peered out the parted curtains. From her position on her side, she could see the moon beaming down on her Range Rover. She'd never put it back in the garage. Hadn't seen the point. She wanted to go, to see for herself. But where? She had no idea where they'd found the body, and even if she did, she was finally beginning to trust Tucker and she wanted the same in return. If she did anything stupid now, all that momentum would be lost and he'd push her out of the loop even further.

It was after midnight. They'd been gone only an hour. More than likely, the sun would return before Finn and Tucker did.

No way would she be able to sleep.

Climbing back out of bed, she padded her cold, bare feet to the bag she'd finished packing that evening before dinner. Buried beneath her sweaters, she reached her fingers around her icy, metal laptop case and pulled it out. She settled herself back on the bed with it and waited for the video app to load.

So far, no one had called in Anatole's APB. Her viewing of footage last night hadn't shown her anything useful, but maybe she could try again to catch him on film, give them some direction to look . . .

It wasn't much, but for the moment, it was all she could do. She plugged the laptop in . . . It was going to be a long night.

TUCKER CHECKED HIS watch again. What was taking Doc so long?

Finn shoved his hands in his pockets, the hood of his

coat pulled low over his head. "She better hurry. It's fucking cold."

"She'll be here," Tucker said, not pulling his attention off the rutted path leading from the road to the old church. The building had stood on this ground since Christmas was founded. Even when the new church had been built several miles away, the townspeople had elected not to demolish the First Baptist Church. Not that it was being maintained, either. Tucker had never seen it in its heyday. All he knew was that in the dead of night, the wooden structure with green lead glass windows made it the perfect setup for one creepy-ass haunted house.

God, his head hurt. They already had half the property taped off and Tucker had done all he could do until Sam collected what she needed and they could all go home. That they had a serial killer in their small town was making him nauseous. As was the fact that they still hadn't been able to locate Anatole. Officers had been to the priest's house and office, but there was nothing to indicate where he might have gone.

Maybe Finn was right. These cops weren't cut out for a case like this. It was fully possible that they'd missed something he or Finn would have known to be important.

He squeezed his eyes shut against the images of the scene inside that wouldn't leave him alone. It had to be connected to the others. The religious undertones were unmistakable. The man had been kneeling at the altar, a Bible and rosary positioned at his knees. All he needed now was for Doc to confirm that there were numbers carved into the man's abdomen.

Finn paced a rut in the snow, lit a cigarette, and blew

the smoke in Tucker's direction. Tucker swatted it away, checked his watch again. Doc had been called before Tucker had even left his house. Where the hell was she?

Finn pushed his hood off and resumed pacing, the red glow of his cigarette tip dangling from his fingers like a devilish firefly. "Fuck this. I'm cold. I'll be in the cruis—"

Headlights broke through the trees and bounced down the road toward them. "Thank you, Jesus."

A few moments later, the coroner's van pulled up beside them and idled. Sam hopped out, looked Finn over from head to toe, then directed her attention to Tucker. "Sorry. Just got back from Knoxville when I got your call. Caught me in the shower." She jutted her chin toward the church. "Is it ready for me?"

"Anything new from Knoxville?"

"Nope, but Shannon called, said you didn't answer your radio, but would want to know the crime lab got a lead on that medallion. St. Jerome's Orphanage for Boys. Just outside Dayton. She said it's the closest match they could find to that emblem."

The pleasure that the smallest break in this case was giving him warmed Tucker from the inside out. He quickly retrieved his notebook to write the name down before he forgot it.

"I'll fill you in more about Knoxville . . . after this. I need to focus." Sam returned her attention to Finn. "And who might you be?"

Tucker introduced them and led the way to the church. Whatever sparks were exploding between them was none of his business. Sam could handle herself with Finn. He wasn't so sure Finn would be able to handle himself with Sam, however.

His sigh escaped with a puff of white. It wasn't much warmer inside the church, but at least they were out of the snow. "I wouldn't touch anything more than necessary. Whole place is a scene and it hasn't been properly contained yet."

"Right-o."

As Tucker fished out his flashlight, he heard the distinctive snap of Sam's gloves in the dark. He trained the beam on the path to the altar. "Watch your step here. We already photographed the footprints, but I'd rather they not be disturbed just yet."

The floor was covered in dust and debris, which had been a boon. That meant footprints were pretty visible, and at least this time, there was no snow to wash them away.

From the doorway, Tucker listened to the sounds of Finn's camera. Sam took her own pictures as she walked, the click-click-click sounding like a pathetic BB gun in the otherwise quiet chapel. She turned back to look at the doorway and traded her camera for her own penlight, which she dug out of her pocket.

She aimed the small light at the doorway, up the left side, across the top, down the right.

"Already checked," Tucker grumbled. "No blood. No noticeable prints."

Shrugging, Sam turned back toward the altar. "Never know. If there was an escape attempt . . ."

When she reached her final destination, she studied the altar, pulled her camera off her neck again.

"The blood is on the altar, but also around it and under it," Tucker said.

Finn stepped beside him. "It was on the floor, too, nowhere near the body."

As Sam made notes and took more photos of the

scene Tucker had already captured, he moved to the far side of the body.

"You ready for me to collect these?" Tucker asked, gesturing to the floor beside her where three white candles had been placed on either side of the altar. "There's a cup, silver dish, and some oil on the right corner over there." Usually, he remained silent and let Doc do her job. This time, however, he wanted to assist, get the body on its way to the morgue, and return to giving the old church a thorough check.

She peered around the corner to where he'd shone his beam. "That's a chalice, not a cup." She took a picture. "Go 'head and collect them."

Tucker handed his light to Finn, adjusted his gloves, and pulled out the stack of baggies from his uniform jacket. He removed all the rulers he'd placed around the objects, and then carefully slipped the *chalice*, dish, and oil into the bags.

He signed off on them and passed them to Finn, trading them for the two flashlights.

Finn stuffed them into his duffel. "Which sacrament was next? First Communion, maybe?"

Tucker thought of the oil he'd just bagged. "There are only two left. Anointing the sick and holy orders. That was probably anointing oil."

"Autopsy should tell us if he had any diseases or whatever. Here, you can bag these, too." Sam handed him the Bible that had been placed at the victim's feet, and the crucifix that had lain against his stomach.

Tucker took them, bagged them, signed and passed those to Finn as well. "I feel like your damned caddy."

Tucker ignored him. "Can you check his abdomen here? I really am sick of waiting on reports."

He held his beam steady as Sam carefully pried the

fabric away from the victim's chest, lifted the oversized shirt, and revealed tiny, bloody scratches just below the man's navel.

Another Scripture. Tucker took a close-up shot of it.

"I'm going to call Detective Langley, let him know what's going on here," Tucker said. "There are things on these bodies that weren't leaked to the press. This has to be enough to make the people of Dayton reopen the case."

Chapter 36

TUCKER SCANNED THE photos he'd taken on his camera's display while Sam instructed her assistants on how she wanted the body bagged.

"What are you doing?" Finn asked, hoisting his duffel higher up on his shoulder, his gaze finally leaving Sam's ass long enough to notice Tucker.

"Trying to figure out if these photos are too gruesome to show Miranda."

Finn didn't respond, but Tucker could feel him watching him. "What?"

Brushing his hands off on his jeans, Finn made his way around the altar to stand at Tucker's side. "Look, man. I respect your instincts and I'm trying real hard here not to question you on this, but I don't understand how you expect her to see something we can't. We're trained to look for this shit."

Tucker leaned against one of the pews. He'd been waiting for the right time to tell Finn who Miranda was. He had no choice but to come clean now. "The reason I asked you here wasn't just because I needed a set of fresh eyes to review the Dayton files."

Finn's brow creased, but he remained silent, his intense gaze watching Tucker.

"I needed your objectivity. So I've . . . kept some things from you that might have tainted it."

The crease in between Finn's brows deepened. "Like what?"

Tucker sighed. "Miranda isn't just a nurse from the same town as Anatole. She followed him here because she has a personal stake in this."

"Relative of a Dayton victim?"

"No. Worse. The guy convicted of the murders. She's Bobby Harley's sister."

Tucker tensed, readying himself for the outburst that was sure to follow this confession. Finn's face turned purple and in the moonlight, his glare became almost sinister.

"Have you lost your damned mind? That woman shouldn't be involved in this case even indirectly, and sure as hell shouldn't be connected to you in any way."

He shouldn't have put his friend in the middle of all this, but he trusted Finn. Finn knew he wasn't some dumb-ass rookie making a novice mistake. He needed to process what Tucker had told him, and Tucker would give him the quiet to do so.

"We have got to cover your ass. It's going to be real easy to pin all this on her. Not the murders, maybe, but the desperation of freeing her brother making her point fingers at a goddamned priest. This is not going to be pretty when it hits the papers."

"We have a bit before that will—"

"If you're right about this, people are going to start asking a lot of questions. They're going to say you didn't do your job and that she's manipulating you. Eventually it's going to bring the state police down on your ass and lock you out of this investigation completely."

Tucker didn't bother to respond. There was no point. Finn was on a rant and there'd be no stopping him until he'd finished, anyway.

"If you fuck this up, the state will take over and there will be an investigation. Best case, you lose your job. Worst case, your reputation. We're going to have to pull some quick shit to keep them out of it. Damn it. I seriously can't believe you did something so stupid."

Tucker had prepared himself to turn over the case and face whatever shit flew down the pike when there was no other option. Calling in the authorities was sometimes part of the job. But Finn was right. It was a *shitty* part of the job. One he wasn't willing to volunteer for so easily.

"So what do you suggest I do?"

Tucker followed Finn outside and watched as he lit a cigarette. Finn puffed quietly, the red tip glowing in the darkness. He began to pace, mumbling under his breath and occasionally shooting Tucker with a glare.

"If you have to call the state boys in, make sure you tell them that she came to you with her suspicions when the first murder occurred. Make sure they know that you called me in to help with the investigation and to keep tabs on her to assure that she isn't involved in any of this."

Tucker shook his head. "You're not taking the heat for me."

"Don't be a martyr, asshole. You can help your woman more if you're still active on the case than if they throw your ass off of it."

"She's not my woman . . ."

"I hope that part's a lie. It's bad enough that you did something so stupid. I just pray your reasons are worth it. Catch a ride back with the coroner. I'm taking your cruiser. I need to think about this shit you've dragged me into." He tossed his bag at Tucker's feet. "Chain of command can't be broken. All evidence collected is in here. Sign off on it."

"Finn, my intentions—"

"We'll worry about your intentions later. Right now, I need to see if we can toss some dirt into that hole you've dug for yourself."

AT THE SOUND of a car's engine stopping outside, Miranda was out of the bed and peering out the window. She spotted the squad car, watched long enough to see Finn exit the vehicle, then greeted him in the living room. She'd hoped it would be Tucker, but Finn might share a few of the details.

She heard him stamp his feet but it still took a good five minutes before he let himself inside. He spotted her right away. "Didn't expect that you'd still be up." He hung up his coat and moved to the kitchen. "Going to make some coffee. Join me."

It wasn't a request, and she didn't like the way he glared at her. "What's wrong? Where's Tucker?"

"Still at the crime scene."

He stood at the counter until the coffee finished, poured two cups, then took his to the table. Crime scene photos were still spread across Tucker's small kitchen table. Miranda stayed as far away from them as possible, choosing a stool at the bar instead.

"Finn? What's wrong? You look . . ."

"Pissed? Yeah, color me that, Miranda *Harley*."

Her heart sank. She knew Tucker would tell Finn the

truth eventually, but she'd really hoped it wouldn't have been until after the case was solved. Looked like Lisa had guessed Finn's reaction. He was pissed.

"I hope you understand why we didn't tell you."

"What I understand is that a shit ton of trouble could fall on Tuck's head because he's trying to help you out."

"Trouble?" Who the hell did this guy think he was? "He's closer than anyone has been to catching a killer!"

"That's not the way the state boys are going to see it. They're going to see a woman hell-bent on saving her brother. A woman who has stalked a priest in Ohio, and was so obsessed that she followed him here. They're going to haul you in for questioning, and Tuck, too. After twenty-four hours, they'll probably let you both go. You'll get to go on with your life. Tuck, however, will most likely lose his job, be brought up on charges for allowing you anywhere near these crimes, and then have to take a job in security because his reputation will be shot and another force won't give him the time of day."

She clenched her fists around her coffee mug, contemplated chucking it at Finn's head. "Tucker hasn't done anything wrong."

Except let her review evidence with him and not arrest her when she'd gotten caught trying to break into the church. He didn't know about the cameras she'd set up in Anatole's home and office, but after what Finn said, she didn't expect anyone to take her word for that.

"There's protocol that has to be followed here."

"I know that." Tucker had told her that numerous times.

Finn drank deeply from his cup. "Did you consider the possibility that the priest looks guilty because you *want* him to be guilty? Are you okay with sending another innocent man to jail to free your brother? That he'd want someone else to go through what he's gone through?"

"Big difference. Anatole isn't innocent!"

"Maybe. Maybe not. It's my job to figure that out."

"I thought that's what juries were for? Besides, it's not your job. It's Tucker's."

The kitchen grew quiet while they stared each other down. She liked Finn. Or at least she'd thought she did. Now he was coming across as a pompous ass, not much different from the chauvinistic cops in Ohio.

"Tucker brought me here because I'm damned good at my job, and even better at it when I'm partnered with him. He wants to help you, and all you're doing is fucking up his career. Do you even see that? Do you even care? Can you even get your head out of your ass long enough to see that you're going to cost a good man his job and his reputation because you're too damned selfish to just stay the hell out of his way and let him do his job?"

His words couldn't have cut deeper if they'd been slathered onto the pointy end of a kitchen knife and driven into her heart. "I'm not—"

"You *are*." He sagged in his chair, the look of burning anger in his eyes fizzling out. "Look, I'm not trying to be an asshole. But Tucker is like a brother to me, and I don't like seeing him put in this position. If you care about him at all, and I think you do, you'll deal with me on matters of this case and leave him out of it."

She *did* care about Tucker. A lot more than she was willing to admit right now. And she certainly didn't want to be the reason he lost his job. She chewed her lip, her whole body suddenly exhausted with worry as she slipped off the bar stool and walked wordlessly toward

Tucker's bedroom. The whole way, she could feel Finn watching her, and didn't feel safe to fall apart until the bedroom door was closed behind her.

She wanted to hate Finn. To call him every ugly name she could think of, right to his face. But she couldn't. Because he was right.

Falling onto the bed, she buried her face in a pillow and tried to cry. She couldn't. Nothing would come because there was nothing left in her. She'd given every bit of herself to this case, and now she was bone dry.

Chapter 37

TUCKER SPED DOWN the quiet streets littered with festi-val trash that would be cleaned before sunrise, vendor booths lining the walkways a blur as he maneuvered the cruiser down Main Street. The green and red lights wrapped around every signpost and fence were giving him a migraine, the irony of their cheerful brightness pissing him off with every wreath-covered street sign he passed. Soon, he was going to have to put out a state-wide APB for a man of the cloth. Nothing about that made him feel any better.

But he didn't see where he had a choice. He'd gone by the priest's home where Goiter was positioned. There hadn't been any activity inside the house. His next stop had been the church. The deacons were seated in the vestibule, their Bibles clutched in their hands. When they weren't answering questions about the father, they were praying that he'd be found safely. In short, they hadn't told Tucker anything helpful at all. The priest had been at Sunday Mass, professed that he wasn't feel-ing well, and had gone home. Their phone calls and visits hadn't reached the priest and when even his car hadn't been seen, they were worried that perhaps they should start contacting local hospitals.

Tucker already had Shannon working on that, but told them that wouldn't be a bad idea—after extracting a promise that if any of them found the good father, or spoke with him, they would call Tucker immediately.

It was nearly dawn and since there was nothing else he could do tonight, he went home. All the lights were off at his place, and when he pushed open the front door, there was no one to greet him. He'd half expected Miranda to be waiting up with questions he had no answers to, and, disappointed, he tossed his hat on the coatrack and gritted his teeth against the thought of another night on his own sofa.

Outside his bedroom, he could hear the muted sound of the television. Knocking softly, but not waiting for an answer, he opened the door. Miranda's gaze shot to him, but his dropped to the laptop sitting on the nightstand. It only took a second for his brain to register what he was seeing—the tree-lined driveway and the Christmas squad car sitting there were a dead giveaway.

Pushing the door closed, his gaze sought out Miranda's. "How the hell did you get a live feed on Anatole's house?"

She reached across the bed and closed the lid on the computer. "Tucker, I can explain."

Somehow he doubted that. "Start talking."

Her fingers worried the hem of her pajama top. "When I arrived in town, I knew I couldn't watch the priest all the time, something I really needed to do if I was going to find something that would prove Bobby is innocent."

"What did you expect to find? Him carrying a dead

body into his own home? Or into the church? Even if he had done that, the evidence would have been obtained illegally and wouldn't be admissible in court. He'd walk."

"I really didn't think—"

"That's the problem, Miranda. You don't think. You've nearly screwed up my crime scenes, inserted yourself in my investigation, now I find out you have a camera on Anatole. If I didn't know better, I'd swear you were working with that son of a bitch to make sure he was never convicted."

The color drained from her face. "You can't believe that."

No, he didn't, but that didn't stop him from wanting to shake some sense into her. But he knew if he touched her, he'd lose himself in the desperation filling her big brown eyes. He slammed the door, grabbed his coat, and headed back outside.

TUCKER DIDN'T KNOW how long he'd walked his property, but when he returned to the house, he was completely frozen. He leaned against the door, huddled over in near agony as the heat brought life back to his extremities. The walk had helped him clear his head, think rationally, and cool his anger.

He'd been outraged when he'd seen that feed. She should have come clean, told him the truth. Hell, it might have helped him pinpoint Anatole's location by now.

He didn't believe that any more than he believed she was working with Anatole. Miranda knew there was an APB out for the priest. If she'd seen him, she would've told Tucker.

Pushing off the door, he moved down the hall to his room before remembering it wasn't really his anymore.

He turned for the bathroom. A hot shower was required if he was going to get any sleep at all. The sound of water running stopped him. If Finn was killing all the hot water, he was going to kick his ass.

But when the door opened, it wasn't Finn who stared back at him. It was Miranda, standing in front of him with a startled expression, her hair wet, dripping down her shoulders and arms and a body that was bare except for the brown towel wrapped around her.

"Hi." The word escaped her in a whisper and for the life of him, he could do nothing more than repeat it back to her. "Hi."

They stood there for a long moment, an unexpected game of chicken in his hallway. Who'd move first? Who'd be smart and get out of harm's way before it was too late?

"Tucker, I'm so sorr—"

He grabbed her by the waist, pulling her into him before he'd even rationalized his intention. She was soft, moldable, unresisting. She fit against him perfectly, and as the towel fell from her body onto the hall carpet, he slowly backed her into the bathroom and shut the door.

"Tuck—"

He buried her trembling voice beneath a kiss that pinned her to the wall. She was naked, and as badly as he wanted to look, he was terrified to. The minute he gave in to that need, he was a goner. Until then, she could still say no without thoroughly destroying him.

Her arms snaked around his neck and he lifted her by the waist, forcing her to wrap her legs around his hips. Hungrily, he devoured her mouth, her neck, her shoulders, groaning as her nails dug into his back. He needed to be as naked as she was, but he couldn't bring himself to separate from her. This was no gentle make-out session, and the need in her kisses matched his own as he reached for the drawer beneath the sink and retrieved a small foil square.

She tugged at his shirt, pulled it over his head, leaving his bare chest pressed to hers. Her nipples brushed him and he finally dared to look down and catch a glimpse of the pink buds. And below that, the faint shadow of her heat pushed against his unbuckled belt.

As he worked to unzip himself, balancing her between his hips and the wall, his finger brushed the slick folds between her thighs and he froze, devastated by the sweet feel of her. She whimpered, and then her hands were on his zipper, frantically working to finish what he hadn't been able to accomplish as he popped open the button.

He wanted to take off the pants, but Miranda wasn't having it. The moment he popped free, she had the condom, opened it, and slid it over the length of him. He was struggling to register all she was doing, but thinking would have to come later.

She was riding him, burying him so deeply inside her before he could prepare that he lost control. He buried his face in her neck and stayed as still as possible, gripping her hips so tightly, he knew he was bruising her. But he had to stop her from wiggling. Had to keep her as still as he could or else risk ending this before it could really begin.

"Stop," he breathed, the scent of soap and shampoo wafting off her damp skin and momentarily clearing his head. "Miranda, stop."

She didn't obey. She moved again, forcing him more deeply inside her. From this position, he couldn't control her movement without risking dropping her. He turned with her in his arms, attached to him, coating him, and set her backside on the bathroom counter. She leaned back, her head against the mirror, and watched him.

No, not *him*. *Them*. Her gaze fastened on the very place where they were joined and as he followed it, and saw himself inside her, he lost his mind. He braced his hands above her head and gritted his teeth as she began to move again. He let her. If *he* moved, he was done for.

"Miranda, I can't last if you—"

"Shut up and kiss me." She arched toward him, wrapped herself around him again, and licked his mouth until, finally, he gave in and opened for her. He was able to lose himself in the feel of her mouth enough to chance moving, taking control. He thrust inside her, slowly, testing her ability to hold all of him. As her tongue slid along his, he reached between them and found the center of her need and rubbed, gently, slowly bringing her to the same realm of madness she'd already driven him to.

When she began to buck against his hand, he knew she was close. Their kisses became disconnected, as though she had to keep pulling away to catch a full breath. Each time she pulled away, inhaled, he looked down, watched their bodies move together for an insane moment, and then she was kissing him again. Over and over they danced that way, until she moaned into his mouth and her body went rigid against him. Slick wetness coated his finger, slid down her thighs to coat his. Her orgasm snapped the last thread of his control. He came with the force of a volcano, wincing against the pain of it, the ecstasy of it. The magic of it.

"Miranda," he whispered, his body pulsing, his arm no longer strong enough to hold him against the mirror on its own. He pulled the other from between her legs,

braced himself on the counter, but couldn't bring himself to withdraw from her. He'd known Miranda for
only a few weeks, but he felt as though he'd wanted to
make love to her his whole life.

Make love? He hadn't done that. He'd taken her in
his bathroom, for God's sake. Had used her. Fucked
her. Guilt forced him to slide out of her, made it difficult to look her in the eye as he cleaned himself up.
When he finally got the nerve to do so, he expected to
see confusion, maybe a disconnection in her gaze. She
was smiling.

"Thank you," she said, shimmying backward so she
could sit upright.

Thank you? How was he supposed to react to that?

"I'm sorry, Miranda. It wasn't my intention—"

"Don't." She reached for the small hand towel hanging on the wall and covered her breasts with it. "Please
don't apologize. That was . . . exactly what it needed
to be."

She leaned forward, buried her face in his chest, and
gave it a light kiss.

He wrapped his arms around her, slid his fingers in
her hair, and held her to him. Leaning down, he kissed
the crown of her head and said, "Thank you, too."

She looked up at him, her eyes still near-black from
passion, her lips puffy and red from his kisses. "Are
you—are you still mad at me?"

He swallowed. "Yes."

"Can I sleep in your bed tonight? With you? Can I try
to make you *un*mad?"

"I'm counting on it." He helped her down, gave her a
fresh towel to wrap around herself, and leaned over the
tub and turned on the shower. He stepped inside and
held out his hand. "Come here."

He took her hand and pulled her forward.

Gingerly, she stepped over the rim of the tub and into his arms. He spent the next five minutes gently washing her body and allowing her to wash his. There was no way to keep from getting hard again, but it was too soon. He had to process all this first. Had to give her time to do the same. As she slid her soapy hand over his cock and around his balls, he drew blood from his lip as he bit down against the impulse to take her again. Hell no. Next time—and there *would be* a next time—he was going to make love to her in a bed, as she deserved.

"Dry off," he said, kissing her nose. "I still need a real shower. Help yourself to my closet if you need something fresh to sleep in."

"And if I choose to sleep in nothing?" She kissed his chin before pushing back the curtain and letting the cold air in.

"Then there won't be much sleeping going on."

"I can live with that." She smiled over her shoulder at him, wrapped the towel around herself again, and disappeared, the soft click of the door closing behind her an unspoken promise of the night still to come.

Chapter 38

Tuesday afternoon

MIRANDA CAME AWAKE slowly and stretched. Her muscles pulled with the sweet ache of a long night spent in Tucker's arms. She'd lost track of the number of times he'd filled her so completely that she couldn't tell where she ended and he began. Hiding the smile spreading across her face would be impossible. Instead of trying, she rolled over and reached for him.

She touched nothing but a cold pillow.

Opening her eyes, she scanned the small bedroom. The only thing keeping her company were a few dust mites floating in the little beam of sunlight filtering in through the gap in the curtains. She rolled over onto her belly and hugged his pillow. When she'd stepped out of the bathroom this morning and found him standing in the hallway, any words she might have found would have been pointless and foolish. He'd kissed her, and their fight about her cameras had dissolved into the most passionate night of her life.

And she'd thanked him.

A bubble of laughter worked up her throat. She might be embarrassed about that if he hadn't thanked her in return. They'd needed each other. Tucker hadn't said as much, but the way he'd pulled her against his chest and held her until she'd fallen asleep had been proof enough.

Hadn't it?

She didn't know where they were going from here, but they certainly couldn't go back.

Climbing out of bed, she grabbed a shirt from his closet and a pair of pajama pants from her suitcase on the floor. Running a brush through her hair, she detoured by the bathroom to brush her teeth before venturing toward the kitchen.

"Yeah, thanks. I'd appreciate that list as soon as possible . . . yes, that's the fax number for my office. Someone should be there all day to receive it . . ."

Miranda stopped in the large archway. Her skin warmed just watching him pace the small kitchen as he talked on his cell phone. As if sensing her, he stopped pacing and slowly turned. Their gazes locked briefly. The stress lines had returned around his eyes but his gaze trailed over her and a smile graced his lips before he returned his attention to the call.

Miranda cast a glance at Finn, who was scarfing down a plate of eggs. Every ounce of stress her night with Tucker had washed away returned. Tripled. She sighed and joined Finn at the table, nursing a steaming cup of coffee as she tried not to stare at the crime scene photos spread out in front of him.

Instead, she chose to pin Finn with a glare. He was the easiest target for all her frustration, and he'd earned it. He'd crossed the line last night. What pissed her off the most was that he'd been right. She *hadn't* given much thought to what Tuck might be facing by helping her. That he was going out on a limb for her, possibly putting his career on the line, hadn't occurred to her. But Finn didn't have to be an ass when he pointed it out to her.

Finn stabbed his egg with his fork. "You have to sanitize the bathroom. I can't brush my teeth or even shower knowing what you two did in there."

Miranda blinked. "Excuse me?"

"You heard me."

"That's none of your business!"

Finn grinned. "If you don't want it to be my business, maybe lower the decibels of your moans next time you two go at it."

Heat steamed her cheeks. "You really are an ass, aren't you? I'm beginning to see why you're not married."

He wiggled his bare ring finger. "Thank you, Jesus."

Tucker joined them at the table, slid his hand onto Miranda's thigh. "That was St. Jerome's. They're going to send a list of kids in their care around the time Anatole might have given his son up. Hopefully, we'll find some records that point to Anatole and we can use that medallion as proof to put him behind bars."

Finn cleared his throat. "Maybe you want to go shower or something, Miranda."

Confused by the odd change of subject, Miranda broke her gaze from Tucker's. "What?"

"Tuck and I need to talk work, and we agreed, remember? You're not going to compromise this case anymore."

When Tucker made no move to disagree, she sighed and strode from the room. It was more important to catch Anatole than to keep her in the loop. And Finn was right. She didn't want to cause Tucker any more problems.

But once she'd grabbed her clothes and returned to the hall to head to the shower, she stopped and listened. She couldn't help it. This case was in her blood, and if they didn't know she was listening, they couldn't get in trouble for it.

"The call before that? The doc?" Finn was saying. "She give you anything useful?"

"Same as before. She hasn't had time to do more than a prelim, so all she could tell me was that he was dressed in clothes that didn't fit properly, and a chemical of some kind caused the burns we saw on his face. The man's nasal cavity and esophagus are completely eaten away. Her guess is acid, but I can't quote her on that until the lab results come back with the autopsy."

Miranda covered her mouth. That poor man . . .

"She did an X-ray and saw trauma to his heart but she's not able to determine the extent of the damage or what exactly caused it until she gets the body to the coroner in Knoxville. Same song as last time—she's going with the body and will let me know when the autopsy report comes in."

"That's one sadistic fuck. And a smart one at that. Usually at this point they've accelerated and started making mistakes. This guy's freaky calm. Leaves no trace of himself at the scene. Doesn't rush his schedule."

"Makes me wonder if we'll catch him before he moves on again."

"Still nothing on the APB?"

"No. He might have already gone . . ."

She couldn't listen anymore. She ducked into the bathroom and quietly closed the door, leaning against it. There had to be a way to stop Anatole before he concluded the rites. He had to have made mistakes. No one was that good. Were they?

And she had to admit, she was more than a little freaked out that they couldn't find him. Was he going to finish the rites somewhere else? Now that he knew who she was, she didn't like not knowing where he was. He was like the bogeyman, and at any moment, he could pop out of anywhere and . . .

She didn't want to finish that thought.

After taking a quick shower, Miranda dried off, wishing she could wash away the anxiety that had settled in every pore covering her body. She stepped out of the bathroom to find Tucker standing there. Memories of last night heated her blood. Tucker took her hand.

"I have to head to the office. Can we talk for a minute?"

She followed him, and when the bedroom door closed behind them, he pulled her into his arms and kissed her hard. "I've wanted to do that since you walked into the kitchen."

Cradling his face, she kissed him tenderly. "And I've wanted to do that since I woke up, but you were gone."

"Phone started ringing early this morning. You looked so peaceful I didn't want to wake you up."

Miranda watched him change into his uniform. When he sat on the bed to pull on his boots, she sat next to him. "Any word on who the victim is?" She grimaced at her inability to keep out of it, but before she could take back the question, he answered.

"No missing person reported yet. I've got Lisa calling the surrounding areas to see if anyone matches our guy."

The ease in which he talked about the case made her stomach cramp. Before last night, he'd been very careful with the details about the case he'd shared with her or in front of her. He was getting more comfortable with her, and she didn't want that to be a reason he lost his job.

"Okay, out with it."

She frowned at him. "With what?"

"Whatever is going on in that head of yours."

Hoping to avoid answering, Miranda rose onto her knees. She brushed her lips over his jaw, loving the prickle of his stubble inside the sensitive inner pad of her lip. "Don't worry about me. Really."

He scowled. "Don't change the subject."

"It's nothing, Tuck." She ran her finger over his brow. "You have enough to worry about without adding me to the list."

He kissed her one last time before climbing off the bed. "I'm only letting you off the hook because I have to get to work. I'll call you if I have anything I can share, and tonight we'll talk. Okay?"

Miranda nodded and watched him leave, hating that she missed him already.

IT WAS JUST past two in the afternoon and the fates had been kind enough to provide an ID for their latest victim. At noon, a woman by the name of Sara Longwood had called in, worried that her husband, Josh, hadn't yet come home. Even though it wasn't unusual for him to disappear at times, she had "this feeling," and had called.

An hour later, a man by the name of David Barnes had come into the department when he'd received a call that his name had been found on the title of a car that had been towed from a local pharmacy. A car he'd bought for his lover, one Mr. Josh Longwood. One look at the photo David Barnes had provided was all it had taken for Tucker to recognize their latest victim. A quick look at the pictures he took of the victim's abdomen provided him with the numbers to search for in the Bible.

If a man has sexual intercourse with a man as he would with a woman, the two of them have done something detestable. They must be executed; their blood is on their own heads. Anointing the sick. The man had been killed because he was gay. Anatole had seen that as a sickness to be cleansed?

Disgusting.

The most pressing matter on Tucker's agenda was finding Anatole. Since no one in the department had had any luck with that so far, Tucker was pulling out the big guns. Thirty minutes ago, he'd hung up with the town judge with the promise of a warrant to search both Anatole's home and St. Catherine's, on the pretense of making sure the priest was all right.

That would save him from making an accusation for at least one more day, and would give Tucker the opportunity to search every inch of both places for the evidence that would finally lock the bastard up.

The fax machine whirred to life behind him and he jumped. In his excitement over getting his warrant approved, he'd forgotten about St. Jerome's. He checked his watch. It would be at least another half hour before the warrant was ready. He sat down to read the blurry list of names and called Lisa in to help.

Handing her half the stack of paper, he said, "Any Peters or Anatoles in the parent list, highlight."

She scowled, flipping through the pages before settling in to read. "Tucker, hate to tell you this but the parental side is blank."

He swore. Of course they were. A lot of these kids

were dropped off anonymously. He didn't exactly see Anatole signing his name on the dotted line, especially if he'd already had seminary in his sights.

All the excitement he'd had over nailing Anatole to the medallion washed away.

Was he ever going to catch a break? "Damn it."

Lisa jumped at his outburst, and he apologized, gathering the papers back from her. As he prepared to toss them into his files, a name on one of the lists caught his eye. He checked the date at the top: 1974. It fit.

"Fuck me," he said, dropping back into his chair.

"What?" Lisa stood and peered over his shoulder. He pointed to the name listed under abandoned children from that year.

Simon Capistrano.

What was the possibility that Anatole had dropped off a son in the same orphanage, around the same year that Simon had been sent there, and now they were both in his town? And that same damned orphanage held the emblem they'd found at the crime scene?

"Oh my God," Lisa said. "Do you think—"

"I don't know but I'm going to find out. Where did Simon move here from?"

"I can call the church. Ask them to pull up their employee records and find a previous address."

Tucker stood, his body on fire. "Do that. That name isn't so common that I can believe this is a coincidence. I'm going to get my warrant. If Simon is Anatole's son . . . I might be asking for a second one."

Lisa's eyes widened. "You think he's a suspect?"

Tucker didn't answer. Too many thoughts were rolling around his head. The child was far more likely to carry the medallion of the home he'd grown up in than

the parent. Their killer was cleansing people of sins. If
Simon blamed his parents for giving him up, and possibly knew the very man who'd given him up was a priest
. . . yeah, Tucker could see that fucking with his head.
Maybe he was trying to be like his ol' dad. Cleansing
the world of sin.

Jesus.

Chapter 39

ON HIS WAY out of the station, Tucker told Lisa, "Let me know immediately if anyone calls in about Anatole. I don't care if they claim they saw him in Timbuktu, I want to know. And have Simon picked up. I want him brought in for questioning before I get back."

"You got it." Lisa stood and surprised him by throwing her arms around his neck.

"What's that for?"

"Just be careful. And watch Andy's back, too. If you do run into Anatole, and he is the one doing this . . . I've seen some of those photos, Tuck. He's dangerous."

"Yeah?" Tucker smiled, appreciating her affections. "Well so am I, darlin'. I'll check in when we're done at the house and moving on to the church."

"I'll be here."

By the time he walked to City Hall, the warrant for the search on Anatole's work and home was ready. He called Andy, instructed him to pull in as many officers as they could spare and meet him at Anatole's house within the half hour, then called Finn and told him to head that way.

Twenty minutes later, warrant in hand, he found Finn leaning against the hood of the squad car. "You got it?"

Tucker waved the document. "Yeah, I got it."

"Then why are you dragging your ass? Let's go."

"That medallion has me thinking. Anatole wouldn't have something like that. The kid who was raised there would."

Finn rubbed his chin. "Last night you had a hard-on to arrest this guy. Now you think he's being framed, too?"

"I don't know what I think anymore."

"Well, we have the warrant, we might as well serve it." Finn opened the squad car door. "If we don't find anything, then you get to tell the judge you made a little mistake in judgment and get another one."

Tucker climbed behind the wheel. Oh yeah, that advice made him feel a lot better.

They hightailed it to Anatole's secluded house. Three squad cars were already parked in the drive. Tucker pulled to the side of the road, got out, and checked the mailbox. The stack was thick. More than a couple days' worth—among which was a catalogue of religious trinkets. Tucker thumbed through that as he walked up the drive to join his men. Nothing in the catalogue resembled the rosaries found on the victims, but the Bibles did. Of course, they also looked like Bibles found at any bookstore, too. Just in case, he'd hold on to it, have Anatole's prior purchases from the company looked up.

As Tucker approached, Andy gathered the other three men around the front stoop and waited for instructions.

"I want everyone wearing gloves at all times. I want photos of everything and a thorough search of every square inch of this place." Tucker pointed at one of the officers who'd just joined the force this past summer. "Franks, I want you and Braydon to search the woods on the property. We only have a warrant for this place, so make sure you stay on property lines—about ten feet into the trees in all directions. Andy, take Sergeant Goiter with you around the perimeter of the house, check the carport out back, trash cans and the like. Smith, you can join me and Finn inside. I want you to bag any computers, phones, and electronics. Let's get them into tech for a search back at the department. We do this quick. St. Catherine's is going to take a while and I want to hit it before it gets dark."

The men scattered to do as they were told, and together, Tucker and Smith headed up the porch, while Finn headed around to the back door. Tucker knocked. Called out a warning that he was coming in, even though he knew he'd get no response. He twisted the knob, and finding it locked, nodded to Smith, who broke open the front door, and they entered.

It took less than thirty minutes to clear the living room and kitchen. Both rooms were so sparse, there hadn't been much to look through. He'd lifted the sofa cushions, checked under and behind all the furniture while Finn took pictures and walked the kitchen. The refrigerator contained only sandwich meat and condiments—the oven, microwave, and cabinets all bare. Not even a box of crackers or a can of coffee.

Tucker made his way down the hall, poking his head in the home office where Smith was unplugging a desktop, and left him to it. He'd give it a once-over when the kid was done. He gave the tidy room a quick glance. Should he even be here at all? His gut was telling him that he'd gotten the warrant for the wrong house. Everything about this screamed at him that they were searching for the wrong man.

He'd face that possibility once he finished serving this

warrant. As he walked into the bathroom, he pulled out his cell and called Lisa.

"Any word from the employment records?"

"Not yet. But they promised to call back within the hour."

"Good. In the meantime, get someone from the nearest crime scene unit you can find down here. Doc doesn't have everything we need, so it's going to be an out-of-town favor. I want a luminal check and a professional dusting, just in case. This place is way too clean."

"It will take a while for anyone to get there," Lisa said, the sound of her clicking keyboard in the background.

"I don't care. I'll keep one of my men here until they're done. I want them at the church, too. This has to be done right."

He hung up and stared at the empty bathroom sink. If blood had been washed down the drain or the tub, they'd find it when the scene team got here.

The sink cabinet contained a few rolls of toilet paper and a small stack of hand towels. On the counter, there was a toothbrush, a razor, and a can of shaving cream.

He checked the medicine cabinet. Deodorant.

No weapons, no little dots of red anywhere. Not that he'd expected to find any, really. The notion that Anatole would kill in his own home was far-fetched. But there was always the chance he'd cleaned up here. *If* he was their murderer.

The sparsely decorated bedroom held very little of interest, either. The nightstand held only a Bible and a notebook of future sermons and Scriptures—none of which had anything to do with the numbers found on his victims. Finn joined him, and as Tucker checked the closet, Finn used his flashlight to search under the bed.

Tucker took the camera from him and snapped photos from every possible angle before returning to the small office. The desk, now bare of its computer, gave no clues to Anatole's whereabouts or pointed to any victims.

"I got nothing," Finn said, passing the evidence bags to Smith. "We'll have better luck at St. Catherine's."

"We'd better."

When they exited the house, his officers had finished their assignments and were waiting for further instructions.

"Smith, you're going to stay here. I have a crime scene pro coming in. Make sure you document anything they find. Andy, make sure all the evidence collected is tagged correctly and locked in your trunk. I don't want a broken chain of evidence to bite us on the ass."

"Already taken care of."

"Then let's get to the church."

He waited for them to clear out, headed to the points Miranda had told him about and removed her cameras, slipping them into his pocket before anyone could notice.

MIRANDA ROLLED THE kinks out of her neck and opened her laptop screen again for the third time that morning. She knew Tucker was supposed to search Anatole's house this morning, and had to see what was going on. She hated that she was being excluded again, but understood the reasons. That didn't mean she couldn't watch from afar.

Or maybe not. She smacked the back of the computer but the staticky image remained. Nothing. She hit the button that showed the church. Still working. Tucker must have already taken down her cameras at Anatole's house.

Damn it.

The church office was empty, just as it had been the last few days. The wonky camera view showed just the slightest edge of Anatole's chair, and the window.

Nothing new.

She rewound the recording to when she'd last viewed the church the previous night. She didn't know why she even bothered. She hadn't seen a single person enter Anatole's office in days.

But, as was her habit, she settled against the pillows and started the recording. She watched the room slowly lighten as the sun began to rise. Saw the priest's desk and chair come into view. Mostly, all the camera captured was the gently falling snow outside the window. She fast-forwarded a little, then jumped when something moved past the office window. She hit rewind. Watched in slow motion.

Leaning closer to the screen, she squinted, trying to decipher the grainy image.

It took rewinding three more times before she could piece together what she was seeing.

Every cell in Miranda's body began to tingle. How could she have been so wrong? Anatole was innocent? And . . . She swore.

Holy orders. The last sacrament. Of course it would be a priest chosen as the final victim. Who else would fill that requirement?

She reached for her phone to call Tucker, forgetting it had been stolen. Cursing, she shoved her feet into her shoes, grabbed her parka, and flew out of Tucker's house, laptop tucked securely under her arm.

Simon. The groundskeeper.

All this time, she'd been so very wrong.

Chapter 40

AFTER CLEARING ST. Catherine's of the few people inside, Tucker and Finn ushered the deacons outside to wait on the sidewalk until their search was complete. They didn't look at all pleased, and had wasted a good ten minutes of Tucker's time reading the search warrant word for word, protesting when they found out Tucker intended to search Anatole's office when the man wasn't around to give permission. Nor were they pleased when Tucker reminded them that the warrant was all the permission he needed.

By the time they finished with Anatole's office, it was completely ransacked. Sergeant Goiter and Sergeant Franks were sitting on the floor in the corner, combing through every Bible and notebook for any references made to the Catholic rites or the Scriptures found on the victims, and Tucker, Finn, and Andy made good use of a box of trash bags, loading them up with Anatole's work computer and files to comb through later.

There was nothing worth claiming as evidence in the chapel or confessionals. Still, he wanted the luminal team here. He couldn't imagine Anatole killing anyone in the church where he worked, but if Anatole wasn't their killer . . . if Simon had anything to do with this, there was no telling what they might find.

As for dusting, what was the point? Of course Anatole's prints would be here. Simon's as well.

Along with a million others.

His cell rang. It was Lisa.

"Tell me you have something or I'm going to make them pull those damned employee records up right now anyway," he said in greeting.

"No need. I think you guys showing up scared them into complying. I called them back when I didn't hear from them, told them you were on your way, and voilà, I have answers." She paused, and for a moment, he was afraid he'd lost the connection. "He was from Dayton, Tuck. I think you found the owner of that medallion."

Motherfucker. "When was he hired?"

"About three weeks ago . . . November twenty-sixth, according to his file."

Tucker did the math. Bobby Harley had been convicted on August twenty-seventh. A little *more* than three months ago. If Simon had waited until Bobby had been found guilty, moved here before beginning again, that would have put Ricky's murder at just the right time . . .

"He been brought in yet?"

"Can't find him. The deacon I talked to said someone from our office had already been by looking for Simon, but they haven't seen him since last night."

Tucker's headache turned into a full-blown migraine. "Put out an APB on him, too. Then call the judge. I'm going to need another warrant."

"I'll let you know when it's approved."

"Thanks, Lisa."

Grumbling, he hung up and walked back outside with Finn and Andy, eager to get a look at Simon's home base, the gardening shed. As they walked, he filled both men in on what Lisa had told him.

"So we really have been looking for the wrong guy this whole time," Finn said.

"It's a possibility."

"Fucker was right under our noses," Andy grumbled, stopping short once they reached the front steps. "Freaking great."

Tucker followed his gaze to find half the town standing across the street, watching them.

They'd suddenly become the town's festivities for the day. He spotted Helen Stillman snapping pictures from the iron gates and stomped over to her. "Goddamn it, Helen—"

"Free country, Chief. How 'bout you tell me what's going on so I don't have to create something to go with my photos here?"

Anger knotted Tucker's guts. "How 'bout *you* go to—"

"Hey Tuck? You might want to see this!"

Tucker glanced over his shoulder to see Finn waving at him from the toolshed. He looked back at Helen and said through gritted teeth, "Take one step on this property while we're doing our job, and I'll toss your ass in jail. Got it?"

She grinned like the bitch she was. "'Course, Chief."

Still cursing under his breath, Tucker made his way toward Finn. "What is it?"

Finn led him behind the garden shed. A pair of hedge clippers lay in the snow. Next to a cane. He knew that cane. It was Father Anatole's.

He stepped closer and saw that what he'd thought

was rust on the blades was actually dried blood. Finn swung his arm toward the exterior wall of the shed, leading Tucker's gaze to a distorted red handprint splattered down two panels of weathered wood.

Trying not to damage any evidence the snow hadn't already destroyed, he carefully picked up the clippers, intent on having them dusted and tested at the lab.

"Wait." Finn knelt across from him, snapping a couple of photos. "What do we have here?"

He slipped his fingers beneath the blade, showing Tucker a large, ragged strip of black fabric stuck to the blood, and quickly snapped a picture.

The blood. The cane that Anatole was never without. The black cloth—a piece of Anatole's frock? They might have just found their next victim . . . and it looked from all sides like it might have been Anatole.

He really had been chasing the wrong fucking dragon.

Finn slipped the clippers into an evidence bag, signing and sealing it.

Tucker knelt in the thin layer of snow. "That's Anatole's cane. I'll know as soon as we can get this blood tested whether it's his or someone else's, and I'm fairly certain I can get those details quickly. The church ran a blood drive in late November, and as far as I know, they all participated. Even Anatole, I hope."

And Simon. He had to find out more about that man.

"So this Simon guy came here and took Anatole as your final victim?" Finn thought about that for a moment.

Tucker pressed his palms into his eyes, praying the pain in his head would go the hell away. "Holy orders. Makes sense to off a priest. If Anatole is Simon's dad, and he knows it . . .

"Then he's made an ass out of you for chasing Anatole these last couple weeks."

"Long as I catch the right guy in the end, I can live with that."

Finn raised a brow. "It's only Tuesday. Why take the victim so early? It's a long time till Sunday."

Tucker took samples from the wall and ordered a bigger bag to be brought over to secure Anatole's cane. Who the hell knew why the last victim would be taken off schedule? Maybe Simon wanted to stick it to his old pop and just couldn't wait anymore.

Finn touched a gloved finger tentatively to the sticky blood while Tucker signed his name across the red seals on the evidence bags and passed them to Andy to do the same.

"Get these over to the doc," he instructed Andy. "I want to know whose blood this is, and she needs to move this up to priority one."

Finn stepped away from the scene and lit a cigarette. He kicked the large green Dumpster that sat about two feet behind the shed. "Why isn't anyone searching back here?"

Goiter quickly answered Finn's summons and climbed into the Dumpster. Trusting Finn to keep a handle on the situation, Tucker pulled out his phone, punching in Miranda's number. He needed to let her know what he'd uncovered. When she found out she'd been blaming an innocent man . . .

"Uh, Chief?" He spun, the faint sound of a phone ringing pulling his attention to the trash. Goiter was standing with his head poked out of the Dumpster. "The trash can is ringing."

Tucker hung up, stalked toward the large green bins, and dialed again. The trash rang again, the faint, muffled melody of "I Shot the Sheriff" singing out from below a black plastic bag.

What the hell? He glanced at his phone's display, double-checking that he hadn't dialed the wrong number. He hadn't. Shit, he'd forgotten Miranda's phone had been stolen.

"Look who's here," Finn said, jutting his chin toward the fence.

As though summoned by his confusion, Miranda ducked between the deacons and jogged toward him, ignoring the invisible line the rest of the crowd—even Helen Stillman—had the decency not to cross. As he watched her run, he dialed her number again. The ringing once again came from the Dumpster.

Shit. "Find the source of that song!"

"Tucker, I have to show you some—"

He held up a finger, silencing her. "Recognize anything?"

He hit redial again, saw her face crumple as she recognized the ring tone.

"Got it!" Goiter yelled, leaping out of the bin and thrusting a dirty white iPhone at Tucker.

Tucker carefully took it with his thumb and forefinger and dangled it in front of Miranda. "Yours?"

She reached for it but he pulled it back. Her face paled. "Yeah. Mine."

" 'I Shot the Sherriff,' huh?" he asked, trying to clamp down on the overwhelming anger, frustration, and fear that was making his body hum.

She shrugged, her wide eyes still focused on the phone hanging from his fingers. "It fit."

"Get in my cruiser and wait for me. I don't want you alone again until I say. Understand?"

"Yes, but—"

"No buts!"

"Tucker, shut up and listen to me. I have to show you

something. I think I saw what happened to Anatole. You won't believe this, but I don't think he's our killer. I've been wrong—"

"It's Simon," he muttered.

"Yes and . . . you know?"

"Yeah, I know. Show me what you have."

She stood where she was, staring at him as though trying to figure him out, then opened the laptop she'd had tucked under her arm and punched a few keys until camera images flickered onto the monitor.

"I know you said no more video, but look . . . I saved the file. Just let me . . . there. Watch!"

Tucker tilted the screen, trying to clear up the image. He watched the recording, shaking his head. "Play it again."

Miranda clicked the buttons, restarting the grainy video. Finn joined him. Together, they hunched over the computer. As he watched, the garden shed door slowly opened and Simon stumbled out. He nearly toppled over and fell against the side of the wooden building. The long, bloody garden shears dangled loosely from his grasp before falling to the snow where Finn had found them.

As Tucker was about to look away, another man stumbled from the shed. His hand gripped his side. What looked like blood seeped from between his fingers. He gripped the door, sliding along until he stood just outside the shed's entrance.

"Turn it up," Finn said, leaning closer to the screen.

"There's no sound."

"Damn it," Tucker mumbled, his gaze riveted to the images. "I really would like to know what he's saying."

Simon lunged at the priest. They struggled and the cane fell from the priest's grasp.

Then . . . both men disappeared from the screen.

Chapter 41

EVERYTHING THEY'D COLLECTED from Anatole's home and St. Catherine's had been brought to the evidence room. Andy stood by the tech guy going over the computer, locating files, as they had been since noon. No one had expected finding connections to their case would be easy, but hell, someone had been going through this information, nonstop since it had been collected. So far, they hadn't found a single piece of evidence associated with any of the murdered men.

On top of that, when patrol had arrived at Simon's house, they'd found it up in flames. It had taken the rest of last night for the fire department to finish putting it out. There'd been no sign of anyone inside, but Tucker wasn't surprised by that. What better way to hide evidence than to burn it to the ground?

Tucker grabbed his hat and coat and darted out the door. Maybe Finn was having better luck getting answers from the doc. Instead of calling, he made the short trip over to the coroner's office.

"Tell me you were able to prove paternity from that blood," he said by way of greeting as he entered the lab.

Sam stepped away from the microscope—and from Finn—her cheeks flushed and her lips swollen. "I was going to check for results one more time before closing up shop, sorry. I got . . . distracted." She smiled shyly at Finn. Tucker had never seen the woman have a shy moment in all the time he'd known her. He didn't much care for it.

So much for her being able to handle herself with Finn.

"I'll bet," he grumbled.

"I can do it now." Obviously flustered, she hustled to the other side of the lab.

Tucker raised an eyebrow when she was out of earshot. "Is this really the time for you to be chasing your next conquest?"

"You got time for *your* girl?"

"*My* girl isn't getting distracted from getting my test results back because you're stuck to her face."

"Touché." Finn grinned, sat on the swivel stool beside the microscope, and spun it like a six-year-old child. "Gotta get my kicks somewhere though, and Doc . . . tastes like honeysuckle."

Tucker groaned and left Finn to join Sam at the computer. She looked up at him from over her glasses, her cheeks still pink. "Both donors are in the system from the blood drive we held in November."

"Yeah?"

"So I compared their blood to see if they shared any markers."

Adrenaline sent a little vibration through his veins. "And?"

"Um . . ." Sam typed quietly, her face scrunched in concentration. "Sec."

Tucker checked his watch. He was starving, and he wanted to check on Miranda since he hadn't talked to her since breakfast. He'd picked up a temporary, disposable phone for her to use until her iPhone could come out of evidence, and he'd left her in Lisa's care. None of that stopped him from worrying.

"Oh, come on," Sam groaned, cursing her slow connection. She shook the mouse to make sure it hadn't locked up, then hit the side of the machine. "Finally." She paused and looked up at Tucker. "Peter Anatole shares markers with Simon."

"So the priest is Simon's father?"

"All this test tells me is that they're definitely related. Father, uncle, or brother."

"You can't narrow it down any more than that?"

"I'm running DNA from the priest's house. If there's anything left of Simon's, bring it to me and I'll compare the sample, but that takes longer. Right now, this is all you have. Take it or wait *weeks* for more results."

"We'll take it." Finn kissed her cheek and took the printout of her findings. "And I'll let you know if I need a rain check on dinner."

Sam glared but her grin ruined the effect she was going for. "Call me."

"You're going to call her, right?" Tucker asked as they left the building.

"If she's off-limits, too, your warning's come a bit late. Who knows, you might get lucky and I'll take this one with me."

That made Tucker laugh. Never-Play-It-Again Finn wasn't about to settle down with a one-night stand. Or a steady, for that matter. It wasn't his style.

Hell, it wasn't exactly Tucker's, either. At least it hadn't been. But the thought of Miranda leaving when this case was over was eating a hole in his stomach.

TUCKER ARRIVED HOME with Finn to find a note on the counter from Miranda. She was at Lisa's having dinner, and he should either pick her up or call when it was safe to return to his place so he could take over his shift of babysitting.

He could hear the sarcasm in the ink-stained Post-it memo.

"What are you doing?" he asked, watching Finn pull scattered file papers from the table, stacking them.

"Putting this shit away. I'm sick of looking at it."

"Leave it. I want to go over it ag—"

"We have our guy, Tuck. Now we just have to find him. Nothing here is going to make that happen."

"What else am I going to do? I have an hour before I'm back on the streets searching. I have three counties looking for these guys and no one's coming up with anything. There has to be something in these damned files that will tell me where they are."

Finn stopped shuffling and sat down. "You're assuming Anatole is even still alive. He could have been killed this morning and Simon is probably already long gone. New look maybe, new name. Who the hell knows? If the job is finished, why stick around? He already burned down his own fucking house. Pretty sure that tells us he's done here."

That thought soured Tucker's stomach. "Just leave the papers alone."

He called Miranda, made sure she and Lisa were all right. He hated her being out there when they had no idea where Simon was. There was a good chance he'd want to make sure she was silenced before he left town. After all, Simon couldn't know he'd just been discovered as a murderer by anyone else.

Hearing her voice on the other end of the line made him feel a little better, however. Knowing Finn was sticking close to home tonight helped, too. He promised to pick her up soon and hung up. "I'm going to take a shower, then go pick up Miranda. Help yourself to whatever's not green in the fridge."

As he walked from the room, he could feel Finn's middle finger aiming at his back.

LISA'S EX HAD her kids for the night, so instead of coffee, she poured two glasses of wine and slid one across the Formica countertop to Miranda. "Make yourself at home. I'm going to change." She maneuvered her small body around the counter and headed down the narrow hall off the living room, calling back over her shoulder, "Pick a movie to keep us entertained while we wait for Tuck to get here."

Miranda knelt before the small entertainment stand and scanned the DVDs lined up on the shelf. She bypassed the horror, suspense, and murder mysteries, which left very little to choose from, but she wasn't exactly in what's-around-the-corner type of mood. "How 'bout *The Proposal*?"

Lisa didn't answer. Miranda ventured back to the kitchen. She'd seen a bag of popcorn by the coffeemaker. Movie, popcorn, and wine. Not the best of combinations, but at least it would give her something to do while she waited for Lisa to return from the bedroom.

She tossed the bag in the microwave and hit the button, watching the bag swell as the kernels popped.

As she grabbed a bowl from a dish drainer, a faint thump stopped Miranda cold.

"Lisa?" Going down the little hallway, she called out again. "Lisa, are you okay?"

A shuffling noise came from inside the bedroom. Miranda froze, her skin turning clammy. She reached for the knob. The door swung in. Lisa lay crumpled on the floor. Her blond hair tinted red with blood.

She sprinted across the room, falling to her knees. "Lisa?" She brushed the hair from the woman's face, thankful to see the slight rise and fall of her chest.

She pressed her fingers to Lisa's pulse, glancing over her shoulder, her heart racing. She couldn't see anyone. The room was fully lit but—

The door swung closed and a figure stepped from behind it, snatching Miranda by the hair before she could make it to her feet. A rag, covered in a potent, vile stench, covered her mouth. Breath warmed her ear as the figure leaned even closer, yanking her body into his chest.

"You should have minded your own business and kept your nose out of mine."

Then, the room went black and Miranda's body fell limp.

Chapter 42

TUCKER WAS JUST pulling out of his drive when Finn ran out of the house and jumped in the passenger seat. "Yeah, I checked your fridge. *Nothing* in there is dinner worthy. You can buy me a burger on our way back."

Rolling his eyes, Tucker continued pulling onto the main road. His cell rang. It was Lisa. He answered on speakerphone so he could talk and drive.

"Hey Lis, tell Miranda I'm heading that wa—"

"T-Tucker?"

Lisa's shaky voice raised every hair on his neck and arms. His blood ran cold. He looked to Finn, who was staring at the phone. "What is it?"

"Miranda . . . she's gone. I—I'm in my car, but I'm not sure where I am, exactly—"

Tucker slammed on the brakes, swerving to the shoulder of Main Street.

"What the hell do you mean Miranda's gone? What happened?" His chest squeezed painfully as he tried to catch his breath.

Tucker put the cruiser back into drive, waiting for Lisa to tell him which way to go, her voice difficult to hear over the pounding of blood in his ears.

"I was changing . . . we went back to my house like you said. Someone must have followed us, Tuck. S-something hit me. I blacked out. I didn't see wh-what happened, but when I came to I saw him putting Miranda in a car. Looked like the gardener's truck. I f-followed, but I'm afraid to use my headlights."

"Look around you, Lis. What do you see? I need to know how to find you."

"Wait! There's a street sign . . . I'm on Manger Road, about three miles from my house. I— My head hurts, Tuck. I'm having problems concentrating, I'm sorry!"

"It's okay, Lisa. Stay on the line, all right? I'm on my way."

MIRANDA MOANED, HER head throbbing and her throat on fire as she slowly pried open her eyes. Where was she? The room smelled musty, and other than a ray of moonlight penetrating one single slat in the shutters, she couldn't see a thing.

"Hello?" She strained to hear anything other than her own heartbeat, and brought a hand to her head. Whatever he'd knocked her out with had sucked all the moisture from her brain and had left her with one hell of a headache.

She tried to move to her knees and found herself immobile. Something tugged at her waist and as she felt for the source, a new wave of panic nearly drowned her. Rope. She was tied to something, something that wouldn't budge as she tried to move forward.

She felt behind her, found a large pipe bolted to the

wall, the rope around her waist figure-eighting around the pipe as well. But he'd left her hands free. Why? Surely she could untie—

"Try if you like, but unless your fingers have teeth to gnaw through it, you're not going anywhere." Someone knelt beside her, fiddled with the rope, gave it a hard yank. "I know my knots, Ms. Harley. Tell me, how is your brother?"

Miranda strained to see in the darkness. She wanted to scream, to fight, to claw the bastard's eyes out. She swallowed to coat her throat.

The figure moved away. Miranda strained against the ropes, searching for the knots holding her against the pipe. Pain shot down her arm as she twisted her wrist. The knot was right there . . .

A deep, pain-filled moan came from across the room. Her blood chilled. There was someone else in the corner. She couldn't make out anything more than a shrouded shape moving in the shadows.

"I bow to you, Father, and seek your guidance. I am your willing servant, here to do your glorious work. Help me, Father. Help me to understand what I am to do."

The chanted prayer pulled Miranda's attention from whoever had moaned. She twisted her neck, her bones popping loudly in the otherwise silent room. A flame flickered to life and fell upon two candles near the window. Finally, she could see, at least a bit. Near the candles, a man knelt before an altar. The wood, warped with age, caused the candles to lean precariously.

"Why am I here? You could let me go. I haven't seen your face—"

"Shut! Up!" He turned, the candle flames glowing eerily behind him. "Don't you think I've heard that before? Do you think it will make a difference coming from you?"

His body was backlit by the glow, casting his face in deeper shadow. But as he struck another match, a bright orange light gave her a full view. The blood in her veins ran cold as she realized who she was looking at.

She'd been right all along. It was Anatole.

Chapter 43

"YOU'RE NO BETTER than the pathetic, wretched sinners. And now look. You're making me commit murder!
Lower myself to sin against my God and take a life,
your life, without the cause of a justifiable sin that God
will condone. No. No. I cannot. Father, tell me what
to do!"

Anatole's last words were bellowed, his face tilted
toward the ceiling. An uncontrollable tremor consumed
Miranda. He wasn't just a killer. He was fucking insane.
Ranting to himself, to God?

Incoherent sentences poured from his mouth as he
paced before the little homemade altar. She was in a
house, she could see that now. An old, closed-up little
cottage of some kind. Trapped with a madman and a
. . . Another moan sounded from far across the room.

Anatole disappeared into the shadows again and
after a lot of shuffling and panting, returned, hauling
another figure behind him. He wasn't limping. It was
a pathetic detail to notice at a time like this, but the

sight of him, strong and capable, refueled her anger and controlled her trembling. The asshole had been faking it all these years.

"You framed my brother," she whispered. "He loved you and you set him up."

Anatole turned on her, his face ugly and contorted in the candlelight. "You mean the man who tried to take my place? Who my son looked up to like a father? The greedy, money-loving brother? That's who you refer to?"

He bent once again and lifted the other figure over his shoulder, stood, and placed him, with unexpected gentleness, on the altar.

Miranda worked the knot furiously, her skin raw and chafed.

"Like Abraham was tested by God, so have I been." Anatole's voice cracked, and she realized, startled, that he was crying. "I don't know what to do, Father!"

Was that his son on the altar? She strained to see, but couldn't. "Anatole, you're confused and I can help—"

"My sin has been pride all these years. My own greed to keep my position in the church. I couldn't tell them, could I? That my teenage sins had created a child I couldn't keep? That I signed away my rights to him so I could join the church?

"I tried to make it right! I watched over him, took care of him in my own way, all these years. But who did he turn to? Your brother!" Anatole shot across the room and delivered a swift kick to Miranda's ribs. Her head slammed into the pipe behind her, the ringing in her ears nearly as intense as the pain in her side.

Anatole returned to his pacing and odd rambling. "I give him to you, Father, if that is your wish. Please, tell me what to do."

The burning in her sides made it difficult to breathe. She fought against the ropes, trying desperately to find the knot again.

"You, my son. All this has been for you. I waited . . . worked diligently to make certain I could find you a post here, with me. Prayed you loved me enough to join me again, and merciful God, you did. I had to wait. Had to have you here with me before I could finish God's work. All of this, for you. My sin and my greatest love." Anatole brushed the dark hair from the face of the man on the altar and cupped his chin. "Your sins will be cleansed. Your induction and blessing into the holy orders will purify your soul. You will be able to sit at the right hand of God for all eternity."

The last rite. Miranda swallowed back bile.

Anatole shifted; the candlelight flickered across the pale face of his son.

Simon.

TUCKER PULLED ONTO Manger Road. His tires slipped on the black ice, nearly sending them into the ditch. He couldn't get Lisa's panicked voice out of his head. He had to find her. Find Miranda. They had to be all right.

"You need to slow down," Finn grumbled. "We're not going to be any help to them if you kill us."

"Try Lisa's cell again," Tucker snapped, slowing slightly to take the next turn. The call had dropped and even though they'd tried half a dozen times, they'd been unable to reach her since.

They crested a bend and his headlights illuminated a black Toyota, the nose wrapped around a large pine. Tucker slammed on the brakes, cursing when the squad car fishtailed across the road. He managed to regain control before heading into a cluster of trees, and threw the car into park.

"Lisa!" He ripped open the driver's door. There was blood on the nylon detonated airbag and on the door. But no sign of his dispatcher.

"Over here," Finn called.

Tucker followed the glow of the flashlight. "She's okay?"

"Injured," Finn pointed to the set of blood-dotted tracks in the snow. The gait was off, as if she'd been dragging one leg.

"Where the hell is she?" Tucker snatched his cell phone out of Finn's hand and dialed Lisa's number again.

"Tuck?"

He could barely hear her. "Where are you, Lisa? How badly are you hurt?"

" . . .'Kay . . . slid out of control . . . damned tree."

Tucker gripped the phone tighter. "Where are you?"

"Followed on foot. Small cottage, end of the road." He heard more shuffling, then she added, "I can see her through the window but no way to reach her without being seen."

"Stay out of sight, Lis. I'm coming."

Chapter 44

Simon was Anatole's son.

Miranda's head swam with this new tidbit of information as she watched the priest strip Simon of his pants. She could see now that Simon's hands looked to be bound behind his back, and as he turned his head, his gaze caught hers, frightened and wide and as confused-looking as she felt.

"Peter, I don't . . . understand," he pleaded as Anatole lifted one of his legs and pulled his pants from it.

"Shh, my son. Don't you see? I've completed every rite to ensure my sins . . . your illegitimacy . . . could be righted. It's all going to be okay now."

"You're a fucking murderer!" Miranda bellowed, terror reaching into the furthest reaches of her soul to bring that scream forth.

Anatole spun on her. "Murderer? I do God's work. Killing you will be the only murder on my hands. The rest were condoned, no, *commanded* by God. I can only pray He'll forgive me for moving forward early to ensure it is complete. You forced my hand, following me to Christmas. My son should have the privilege of his sacrifice falling on Sunday—*God's* day—like the others, but because of *you* he won't!"

"Yo-you're my friend!" Simon screamed, trying to turn on his side. But whatever bindings Anatole had placed on him kept him still.

"No. I am famil— Yes . . . yes, that is it!" Anatole reached heavenward as though he'd plucked an answer from the sky, and Miranda caught a glimpse of a ripped section of his frock, crusted with blood. He was wounded. "If I don't kill her . . ." He began his rambling again. "Then there is no sin on my soul when I join you. I'll be as pure as you'll be. You'll kill her. I can cleanse you once it's over. Make certain her death doesn't stain your soul. Don't you see?"

He really was fucking insane. Miranda could barely keep up, her head spinning, throbbing. The knot at her back slipped. Just a little more . . .

She was trying to piece it all together. Had it been guilt that had driven Anatole to murder? Did he really believe that by killing people for their sins and recreating the holy sacraments he was doing God's work?

The knot slipped. The pressure around her chest eased. Miranda nearly gasped in relief but bit her lip to keep quiet. The less attention she drew to herself, the better. If she could just catch Anatole off guard . . .

TUCKER DREW HIS weapon and cut the cruiser's engine halfway down the road leading to the cottage. As quietly as possible, he and Finn crept toward the window that flickered with light—candles?—and saw a figure hunched beside a heating unit beneath the shutters.

Lisa.

She heard them, her little body crawling on all fours

in their direction until she crumpled at his feet. He knelt beside her, checking for injuries. "I've got an ambulance on the way, Lisa. I need to get them out. Finn will stay with you."

"Just go, I'm fine. Miranda's fine. For now. But someone else is with them—"

"Must have Anatole," Tucker said.

"Anatole," she said. "It's him. He has her."

Tucker frowned, his gaze fixated on that damned window. "Anatole?"

"Yeah, he has her, Tucker. Go get her."

Then the other person inside must be Simon. Shit.

"I got her," Finn said. "Just go."

He hated seeing Lisa like this, but not knowing what Miranda was going through inside, he ducked low and ran, stopping only when he reached the windowsill and could see inside.

ANATOLE UNTIED SIMON and pulled him into a sitting position. It was obvious the man was weak, possibly drugged, by the way he swayed on the altar. Anatole pulled something dark from his pocket and held it toward Simon.

A gun.

The bile returned to Miranda's throat. She gagged it back down when Anatole took a long, curved knife from the floor of the altar and handed it to Simon.

"Now don't be foolish, my son," he said, aiming the gun at Simon's head. "Finish her quickly and we can be done with it. Go. Now."

Simon stared at her, his hand shaking beneath the weight of his weapon. "I—I can't. Peter, please."

"I am your father and you will address me with respect!" Anatole roared, jabbing Simon's temple with the barrel of the gun. Then he calmed—a calm so eerie that Miranda broke into a cold sweat. "It's not so hard really. The first cut, I admit, I wasn't sure I was strong enough to have been chosen. But God will grant you the strength you need. She is nothing more than butter for the rolls upon which you shall feast with Our God in Heaven, my son."

Simon started toward her, a million apologies in his eyes. She couldn't tell if he meant to save his own life or hers, but either way, he seemed to know the same fact she did. They were both going to die here tonight if one of them couldn't figure a way out.

TUCKER COULD BARELY see past the two candles about six feet from the window. Whatever Lisa had been able to see, he wasn't as lucky. The position of the moon had shifted behind the trees, the little bit of light they'd had all but gone now.

He thought he'd heard something just below him, but at this angle, he couldn't see what. It was too damned dark inside, but it wasn't like he could just shine his flashlight through the dirt-crusted window.

It was killing him—the not knowing. What if she was already dead?

No. No way was he letting any of this happen. He crouched lower, duck-walking toward the rear of the building in search of a door.

"I CAN'T DO this!" Simon's voice had developed a new strength, and his glazed eyes became a bit more focused. Whatever he'd been drugged with was apparently wearing off.

"No," she whispered. "You can't. And you don't have to." She glared at Anatole before returning her gaze to the sickle-shaped blade. "You're a sick son of a bitch, Anatole. You think God wants this? That He wants you to force your son to murder? God is watching you. God is *judging* you!"

"Yes," Anatole said, the pistol shaking only the slightest bit. "And He is proud."

"J-just shoot me," Simon said, the knife falling to the floor at his feet. He dropped to his knees, hung his head as though he expected to die execution style.

Miranda sobbed, terrified of what might happen next. If Anatole would just put the gun down, she would be willing to take her chances . . .

Anatole fired a shot and Simon screamed.

Chapter 45

THE SOUND OF gunfire pressed Tucker low into the snow, his hands over his head as he listened, waiting, his heart beating so fast, he was getting dizzy.

Miranda.

A deep scream followed the sound, but Tucker couldn't tell who it might belong to. He had to find a way in

He'd been foolish not to expect a gun. Just because the victims hadn't died from a gunshot wound didn't mean Anatole hadn't had a gun on him in case things got sticky. Christmas wasn't exactly a Kevlar town, but it wasn't his life Tucker was worried about.

He found the back door locked. If he broke it down, there'd be no hiding his approach. There had to be another window, something. He checked the far side of the building and was further discouraged. The only window on that side was boarded up.

He'd instructed the ambulance to come in quietly, to save their lights for their trip off the property, and to park as far away as possible. Now he was probably going to have to blow his own cover in order to get his ass inside to save Miranda and Simon.

MIRANDA'S EARS RANG and the cloud of gunpowder filling the room burned her eyes. Her watery gaze shot to Simon. He lay before her, his hands gripping his foot. Blood spilled between his fingers.

"You're going to be all right," she whispered, praying it would be true. She shifted her gaze. Anatole was pacing again. Rambling as he looked at the ceiling.

Something brushed her ankle and she nearly screamed. Simon held out the long silver blade. She gripped it in her shaking hand, and waited until Anatole turned his back to her. When Anatole dropped to his knees and raised his hands in prayer, Miranda lunged.

The knife cut deeply into his arm. Anatole howled in pain; the gun fell to the floor. She grabbed it, holding it awkwardly in her left hand. Before she could form a plan, Anatole grabbed her leg, pulling her off balance. She crashed to the floor, the wind knocked out of her, both weapons falling from her grasp.

"Grant eternal rest unto her, O Lord, and let perpetual light shine. May her soul, through the mercy of God, rest in peace. Amen." He straddled her, his hands closing around her neck. "Forgive me, Father, for I have sinned . . ."

Miranda spread out her hands in search of either the gun or the knife. If she died tonight, she would do her damnedest to take him with her.

Her fingers touched cold steel, but she couldn't grasp the gun. Spots danced before her eyes. Her lungs screamed for air. Blackness shrouded her. Her fingers locked around the barrel. With the last of her strength, she swung. The butt of the gun slammed against Anatole's temple. He collapsed against her.

Miranda struggled to free herself from his weight. Blood oozed from the gash on his temple. His breath was shallow, but he wasn't moving.

Pushing to all fours, she crawled to Simon. "We have to run. Can you stand?"

"Yeah, I'll . . . He pushed himself up to his feet, hobbling on his one good foot, the other bloody and shattered. "Just go. I'll slow you down."

He wasn't wrong. But she couldn't just leave him behind. If he wasn't fast enough, Anatole could wake and finish what he'd started. She should kill Anatole. Shoot him where he lay. He'd caused so much pain. So much death.

She thought of Bobby, raised the gun.

Then lowered it again. She wasn't a killer. She couldn't . . .

Rushing to the bag by the altar, she dumped the contents on the floor. Folding the white, silky robe, she wrapped it around Simon's foot, then used the sash to hold it tightly in place.

"You're going to be okay," she whispered, brushing his damp hair from his eyes.

"So sorry. I—I didn't. I couldn't . . . I stabbed him . . . when he took me. He came for me at my shed and I . . . I stabbed him. God, I wish I'd killed him!"

She glanced at the door. "We're going to be okay."

Simon gave a tentative test of his foot, but it was no good. "Jesus, just go."

Anatole stirred, and as he started to push himself to his knees, Miranda pointed the gun at him and all doubts of her capability to kill dissolved in a rush of rage.

She fired.

Click.

Her blood ran cold. The gun was out of ammo. She looked fervently around for the knife, but could see very little on the floor in the darkness.

"Listen to me," she whispered to Simon. "If I run, he'll chase me. Stay in the corner. He'll have no choice. Understand?"

"What if he catches—"

"Just stay hidden until he runs after me. Then go as quickly as you can to the road, or the trees . . . wherever you can hide . . . and stay there. Don't let him find you. I'll be back for you. Understand?"

Anatole was moving again. He gripped his head, his murderous gaze locked on her.

She looked at Simon. "I'm not leaving. I swear I'll be back with help. Just go when he follows me."

When he nodded, Miranda took a deep breath.

Then, she ran.

TUCKER MADE IT back to the front of the house, determined to burst in regardless of what it cost him. He had to get to Miranda. He hadn't heard anything since the gunshot and there was no telling . . .

As he approached the front door, it burst open and Miranda came flying out, running like the devil was at her heels. He opened his mouth to call out to her, but another figure stumbled out behind her.

Miranda shot past Tucker without even noticing him. He chased after her, biting down on his tongue to keep from hollering out her name. If she didn't realize he was there, neither did Anatole. Tucker wanted to keep it that way.

He took the path to the right of her, desperate to get

in front of her where he could make her see him without Anatole being the wiser. When she stumbled into the clearing ahead, he holstered his weapon, grabbed her around the waist, and pulled her tightly to his chest, covering her mouth and silencing her scream. "Shh, I got you."

When she sagged against him, he removed her hand. She spun in his arms. "Tucker, it's Anatole," she whispered.

"I know. I know, babe."

Anatole broke into the clearing and Miranda screamed.

Tucker shoved her behind him and slid his gun from its holster. "Peter Anatole, you're under arrest. Put the gun on the ground and place your hands behind your head." He flipped the safety off. "There's no need for anyone else to get hurt."

"You tried to kill me," Anatole snarled, his gaze looking through Tucker to Miranda. He jerked the slide, ejecting a bullet and reloading the chamber. "If you do evil, be afraid, because I am the minister of God, a revenger to *execute* wrath upon those that do evil."

"Well then." Tucker raised the gun. "May God have mercy on your soul."

He pulled the trigger.

Chapter 46

THE AMBULANCE LIGHTS whirled in a blur of red and white. Miranda huddled under the blanket the paramedics had provided and watched as they carted Anatole's bagged body into the back of one of the vans. A man was dead. She should feel something. But she was simply glad to be alive.

Other than her bruised and battered body, the only real harm done had been to her psyche and her heart. She'd been right all along. No one had believed her, and had even gone as far as to make her doubt herself.

Simon lay in this ambulance with her, and sitting on the tailgate was Lisa, her forehead being bandaged while Simon's foot was being examined. He glanced at her from his gurney.

"So many people hurt. Because of me."

"No, Simon—"

"We're taking him to Knoxville," a paramedic said. "He's going to need surgery."

Lisa and Miranda were helped out of the ambulance,

and they stood shoulder to shoulder until the lights disappeared.

Lisa gripped her hand, and there were no words to express how grateful Miranda was that she'd actually made a friend here in Christmas. Lisa had dragged her wounded body behind Miranda, had followed a madman to a secluded place to help her. She would never forget that, not if she lived a whole other lifetime.

"How're ya holding up?" Lisa asked, tentatively touching the bandage wrapped around her leg. The dashboard had sliced it up pretty bad, and her head had looked like a slab of beef before the paramedics had bandaged it.

"I'm—I'll be okay." She pointed toward the second ambulance. "I think they're getting tired of waiting on you."

Lisa sighed. "They're taking me to Sevierville on Tuck's orders. Have him bring you by when he's finished here?"

"I'll do that." On impulse, she gave Lisa a tight hug. "Thank you. For everything. I don't know how—"

Lisa returned the hug. "We're friends. That's what friends do."

Miranda watched the ambulance drive away before searching for Tucker again. There were so many people that she couldn't find him in the chaos. She hadn't seen him since he'd carried her to the ambulance.

She sat on the hood of the nearest squad car and cradled her head in her hands. This place was going to forever hold bad memories for her, but the thought of leaving him now, after all this . . . What if it was only just beginning to get good between them? What if this was supposed to be the start of something amazing?

Did location really matter? She'd told him she was leaving as soon as the Rosary Killer was stopped. But did she have anything calling her back to California?

She was still trembling when a pair of boots filled her vision. Lifting her head, she smiled at Finn while looking over his shoulder to see if Tucker was close by. She still didn't see him.

"You okay?" he asked, surprising her with a hug. She let him hold her, took comfort in his strong arms though they weren't the arms she wanted around her.

"I'm fine. Where's Tuck? I need to see him."

"On the phone with Detective Langley in Dayton. He wanted him to know what was going on right away so they could get started on getting your brother out as soon as possible."

Was it really going to be so simple? She pictured Bobby's face when he found out the news. She sobbed against Finn's chest, felt him release her, then hold her again. But this time, his arms felt right. She looked up and found Tucker smiling down at her, his fingers gently rubbing the small of her back.

"Tell me again that you're okay?"

"I'm fine." She pulled his head down and kissed him. His warm lips chased away the last of her fear. "Guess there's something to be said about running like a little girl."

His arms tightened almost painfully around her waist. "Nothing wrong with running unless you're running from something good."

She smiled and played with a button on his uniform. "It's just . . . I've dedicated the last year of my life to this. To proving Bobby's innocence. What am I supposed to do with myself now?"

"I have a couple of ideas."

"I bet you do." He bent and kissed her again, this time so feathery soft it tickled. "For now, can you just get me out of here?"

Tucker released her and slid his hand into hers, guiding her away from the cruiser she was sitting on to his.

"I just don't get it," Tucker said. "How was killing Simon going to erase Anatole's sin of having a kid?"

"I think Anatole was trying to cleanse his son of his illegitimacy by inducting him into the church, completing the rite—holy orders. I guess his sick mind thought that would free them both from sin. He was rambling about Abraham. I think he saw himself that way. Sacrifice your own son to prove how much you love God. But I think he had to perform *all* of the rites to feel as though Simon's death completed some sick ritual. He brought Simon here. Made sure he had a job. I'm guessing with Bobby locked up, Anatole was all Simon had, so he came. That was all Anatole was waiting on before starting the killings again."

"You probably saved Simon's life by running."

Miranda shook her head. "No. He saved mine. The only reason I was able to get away was because Simon hadn't been able to follow orders and kill me. Not even to save his own life."

"Guess I owe Simon more than just my gratitude." Tucker buried his face in her hair, then reached around her to pop open the passenger door. "I thought I lost you tonight."

Miranda didn't care how many people were close by or who might overhear. She smiled at him. "Why don't you take me back to your place and show me how great it is to be alive?"

Epilogue

MIRANDA STOOD ON the steps outside the Dayton courthouse. It had been a long six weeks, but finally, Bobby's release date had arrived. She'd been in the courtroom when Tucker, Finn, and Detective Langley had presented the case to the judge. Had openly cried when the judge ruled that Bobby was free to go.

Cameras flashed. Reporters shouted questions. And Bobby stood just outside the door beside his attorney. A huge smile spread onto his face as he took his first breath of air as a free man.

"Mr. Harley just wants to thank the courts, Chief Tucker Ambrose, and Detectives Finn Donavan and Ben Langley for working so diligently to get to the truth," the lawyer declared, ushering Bobby slowly down the steps, pausing every now and again to answer another question being shouted from the crowd.

"A full statement will be released shortly," he said. "Right now, Mr. Harley just wants to put this behind him. He and his family would appreciate it if you'd give them a little time, and a lot of privacy."

Not able to wait another minute, Miranda sprinted up the steps. She could hear cameras clicking, but for once, she didn't give two shits about appearing in the press or what they might say about her and her brother. She launched herself at Bobby. He caught her around the waist and squeezed the breath out of her.

"I can't decide if I should spend the rest of my life thanking you for what you did or be so pissed off that we never speak again."

"I knew you were innocent. I had to do something."

Bobby set her on her feet. "You could have been killed."

"I got lucky. I found someone who believed me."

Tucker strolled up beside her and snaked his hand around her waist. "Take your time, babe. Have dinner, enjoy your brother, help him get settled. I'll be by with the moving van in the morning."

Bobby stuck out his hand. Tucker shook it. "You sure, Chief? You're practically family now. "

Miranda smiled. "Hey, I haven't moved in yet. There's always a chance he'll do something stupid before tomorrow and I'll just take the moving van back to California instead of to Tennessee."

"Like hell you will," Tucker said. "Doc Sam is expecting you to start Monday."

And Miranda couldn't wait. It wasn't exactly what she'd thought of when she'd gotten her nursing degree—helping a small-town coroner, dealing with death and dead bodies. But after what she'd lived through, she'd taken Sam Murray's assistant position within twenty-four hours of it being offered. She'd gotten into this profession to help people, even if they were dead.

"So you guys are heading back to Tennessee in the morning?" Bobby asked.

Miranda shook her head. "Finn's driving the moving van back for us. We have a detour to make."

"You didn't mention a detour."

She cleared her throat. "I get to meet his family."

Bobby laughed.

"Stop it. I'm looking forward to it. His dad just got out of the hospital and—"

"And I've already apologized in advance for the experience," Tucker said. "My family can be a little much. But it's time to put the past to rest."

She smiled up at him. "Yes. It is."

"Oh, almost forgot," Tucker said. "Mind if I steal her for one sec?"

Bobby nodded, shook Tucker's hand again, and followed the lawyer to the waiting car at the curb. Curious, Miranda followed Tucker to his truck and waited while he dug something out of the cab.

"A gift."

She smiled, her heart full. Falling completely in love with Tucker over the last few weeks had been the most amazing thing she'd ever done. And to think she never would have met him if it hadn't been for Father Anatole.

"What is it?"

"Well, for starters . . ." He pulled a black Stetson out of the bag and put it on, flashing her a grin. "You said—"

"I know what I said! I love it!" She laughed, her body purring at the sight of him dressed precisely the way she'd asked him on their first real date so many weeks ago. "I think it will look even better when it's all you're wearing."

"Well, I'd say the same about these, but I'm not so sure." He pulled out another box and held it out to her.

She lifted the lid and choked on another bubble of

laughter. Inside the box lay a pristine, brand spanking new pair of Converse.

She looked up at him, curled her hands around his neck. "I love you, Tucker."

"I love you, too, Miranda."

They kissed again, and the explosion of lights and camera clicks began anew. Miranda ignored them, lost in the man nibbling her bottom lip. Let them take their pictures. Let the whole world know that Miranda Harley, pariah and outcast, finally had a family again.

Next month, don't miss these exciting new love stories only from Avon Books

Vampire in Paradise by Sandra Hill

It's been centuries since the Norseman Sigurd Sigurdsson was turned into a Vangel—a Viking Vampire Angel—as punishment for his sin of envy, but he's still getting the hang of having fangs. Then Sigurd is sent to Florida's Grand Keys Island as a resident physician . . . where he encounters a sinfully beautiful woman. Could this too-hot-to-resist Viking doctor be an angel or is he just a vampire bent on breaking Marisa's heart?

The Duke's Guide to Correct Behavior by Megan Frampton

When Miss Lily Russell crosses the threshold of the Duke of Rutherford's stylish townhouse, she knows she has come face to face with sensual danger. His behavior is scandalous, his reputation rightly earned, and his pursuit of her nearly irresistible. Lily has aroused his most wicked fantasies—and, shockingly, his desire to change his wanton ways. He's determined to become worthy of her, so he asks for her help in correcting his behavior. But Lily has a secret that could change everything . . .

REL 1114